PlanetB2

PlanetB2

HUMAN WAR AGAINST NATURE

M C Raj

PARTRIDGE
A Penguin Random House Company

To order additional copies of this book, contact
Partridge India
000 800 10062 62
www.partridgepublishing.com/india
orders.india@partridgepublishing.com

Contents

Dedicated to . . .

Preetam, my friend for eternity . . . .

CHAPTER ONE

"Oh bloody shit! What a total disaster! We spent a few billions on this project. Never thought it would end in a fiasco" Rustler, the American President was fuming and frothing. He puffed away an awesome cloud of smoke from his pipe. His mouth was like a chimney of German Nuclear installations that emitted billowing smoke like a set of clouds. They also travelled all the way to the sky and began to laugh at humans who created them. Clouds that gather in the sky to poke at the cosmic order and create gaping holes in the ozone layer! He coughed heavily even as the heavy smoke departed his mouth with gay abandon. Rustler had developed this habit of puffing his smoke away in small circles and used to enjoy his skills at that. Under his feet was the debris of billions of dollars that had gathered from the latest failure.

"Never mind the billions of dollars, Sir. Our American pride has been wholesomely punctured by this debacle. We have many roadmaps. Some roadblocks are bound to come up as we make our moves. This is a small inconvenience in our grandiose plans to overcome the universe. Let us try to brush it aside and move forward." Plumbel the Director General of the Space Research Organization in the US blurted out words without sewing them together even as he and the President were gulping a few pegs of the finest whisky. The spirit found its way to the inner membranes of both much easier than water would.

Knitting at such moments was always difficult for both of them.

"Brush it aside? What do you mean, Plumbel? I wanted to have this news announced before the next elections so that our party would win with a thumping majority. You scientists have spoiled the party. I have a big dream for America. You know it well. I want America to be the only country that can dictate economic and political development for the entire world. This is my pet project and you are so cool about its failure." Rustler was becoming angry.

"But this has become a stale story about our country by now Mr. President. The entire world knows this about us. Let us focus on the new mission that we have set for ourselves. In order to achieve this we shall have to spend billions of dollars without grumbling. We need to sell only some more arms from our arsenal in order to make up the loss." Plumbel tried to make some sense already in the beginning. He had a failure to account for and now he did not want the President to go haywire.

"Are you speaking about another mission? I cannot but admire your capacity for hoping against hope. We have not even analyzed as to why the present one was a failed mission. And here you are speaking of another venture. Is this American baseball game that when we lose once we develop the hope that there is yet another chance the next time?" Rustler still sounded harsh in the way he spoke.

"As a space scientist, I cannot look at our attempts from the prism of success and failure. We shall be doomed if I do that. For you it is a failure because you reckon it from the prism of political gains. For me it is just one of the steps we take to finally reach the goal we have set for ourselves. You had better acknowledge that you are a politician and that I am a scientist. There exists a world of difference between the way we scan realities." Plumbel tried to put himself in a pedestal above the President.

"Okay, I accept your position. But first let me have a full analysis of what happened from the time you started this space mission and till the time it met with a grand failure." The sarcasm in the voice of the President did not escape the attention of Plumbel.

"Do you have the time for an analysis straightaway?" Plumbel enquired as a matter of fact.

"No, no, nothing doing! I don't want to listen just to one person's opinion on such an important mission, especially as it has failed miserably. Much preparation has gone into this monumental project and it has come to a complete waste. I want the entire secret team of the space mission that I specially set up for the project PlanetB2. Call all the top guys to our Cubicle11 for an initial evaluation of the failed mission." The President was livid.

"I think you have taken this mission too personally. Please calm down a bit. It is in the best interest of humanity that we have taken up this mission and all of us in the team are as much worried as you are about the setback that the mission has suffered. But be calm till we meet in our secret place Cubicle11." Plumbel tried to play down the negative impact of the failed mission in the psyche of the President.

"I am perplexed that you take this failure so light. Do you realize the disgrace of the loss that we have suffered? Fortunately, the entire world does not know about this mission. If only it had known, by now our party would have bitten dust. Anyway let us face the music in the meeting. Every effort that we Americans make must result in success. I do not believe your crap that your failure is just one step of the entire mission. I want success at any cost and I can sacrifice anything, even half of the world to achieve this success for America." Rustler slowly began to reveal certain unknown corners of his personality that made him the American President.

The President was as touchy as ever. He sat with a frosty face as soon as he entered Cubicle11. He had made it a strict point to hold all meetings related to PlanetB2 only in Cubicle11. There was no deviation or any excuse. This was his life mission that PlanetB2 must succeed. He was madly fond of this project and had to take extra caution not to blurt out even a word about it to anyone else in the world. A mystery of secret shrouded the entire project. Secret was integrated into the design of the project and Rustler was stickler to this mysteriously cloak-and-dagger project.

Cubicle11 was an underground construction. Anyone who entered there could get out only to remain within the buildings that housed him/ her also underground. No one knew the external world once they committed themselves to spend the rest of their lives for the Kabbalistic mission of the President of the US. The secret space mission was codenamed as PlanetB2. No one knew why it was codenamed thus except the President himself. He did not reveal it even to Plumbel. The underground construction was surrounded heavily by space stations and those who worked in space stations did not know that they were standing on a virtual landmine. Those who were recruited for PlanetB2 did not know they were being trained for a very special mission. They went through rigorous exercises that all space stations imparted. There were special classes and exercises for them. They did not know in the first place that they were recruited for a special mission. Plumbel himself carefully watched them all the time. All their intellectual acumen came into systematic scrutiny. Their entire psychological disposition was meticulously tracked. Their relationship with girls and boys of their age and men and women of different age groups went through diligent observation and analysis. Their likes and dislikes were tabulated in computer and were matched with the requirements for astronauts of an extraordinary order. There were hosts of computer analysts in Cubicle11 and the future astronauts would not have any inkling about the personalities they were dealing with. They only knew the data that were provided to them and the screen of their computer.

Rustler and Plumbel had handpicked the Awesome5 from among the scientists and were entrusted with task of designing and operating Bigbelly1. This was the name that Rustler gave to the historic spacecraft. Both of them also had set up a ground force that strategized both technically and operationally the success of the space mission to PlanetB2. Both the teams were not allowed to interact with each other. Awesome5 even did not know the existence of the ground force. Rustler and Plumbel would strategize with them and take all necessary information to Awesome5. They did it together sometimes. Often Plumbel would not even know that Rustler had his own meetings with Awesome5.

Each one of Awesome5 was called to the private chamber of the President and was asked if he was ready to give his life for America with blind faith in the goodness of Rustler. When they pledged their unflinching loyalty to the Nation and its President they were driven straight into Cubicle11. Rustler had clearly instructed the Chief of the American Intelligence Agency not to track anything of what happened in his private chamber. He made double sure that the AIA obliged by asking Plumbel to double check that no one in AIA double-crossed the President.

"My countrymen! You must be wondering why you have been brought into Cubicle11 as soon as you agreed that you are ready to lay down your life for your country and its President. A country is ruled by its President and I am glad you have opted for both. I have studied you for a long time now and have become sure that you have no other inclination in life than serving your country and that you are ready to forego even your sexual life for the sake of fulfilling your duty. As you are aware I am a bachelor. That is something that I have chosen to be. It is because I do not want to trust anyone in my life with the plans I have for this nation. For me this country takes precedence over everything else in life . . ."

". . . From now on you will be known as the Awesome5. It is the codename for the five of you who are members of the core group that would execute our historic project PlanetB2. You will come to know in due course of time what PlanetB2 is. It will be revealed to you progressively. What is important for you now is that you have complete faith in the country and in the President. You must believe that your President can and will lead your country to a glorious destiny. This kismet will be unmatched by any other country at any point in history. The success of PlanetB2 will determine the future course not only of America by also of the entire world. As you know well, we Americans are the ones who have the power to determine the fate of the world. Planet B2 will be our ultimate message to all other people of the world that their prosperity will depend much on their acceptance of American wisdom. Our nation is the harbinger of hope for progress of the entire world because we ensure individuality and freedom of the people of the world. The safety of the rest of the world will much depend on accepting this unique position of the United States of America . . ."

". . . The Awesome5 has a special responsibility to fulfill in the best interest of America and the rest of the world. We have a greater responsibility to the rest of the world than to America. But the safety of the rest of the world will much revolve around the prosperity of America . . ."

". . . You are a select and elite group of scientists. You have to work day and night in order to make our mission to PlanetB2 come true. Plumbel will explain to you what we mean by PlanetB2 and its special significance in the history of humankind. It will be your responsibility as the best scientists America has ever produced to present to me a blueprint towards the achievement of the mission to PlanetB2. You are a group of no-nonsense scientists. We have done our homework well to select the five of you after secretly observing you for a long time during your training in the space center here. Now you are a world of your own. You will be provided with everything you want in this Cubicle11. Remember that all these are done to you to safeguard the freedom of America and peace of the entire world. Any questions or doubts that you have about PlanetB2 will have to be addressed to Plumbel and not among you. All sharing among yourselves should take place through the computers that we have provided to you. Remember that your computers are connected only among you and will not be accessible at all to anyone else in the world. But your data sharing will be known among all of you and Plumbel will keenly watch what you are sharing among yourselves."

Even as he was speaking, the President disappeared from their sight and the best scientists in the world wondered how this could happen. They could not explain to themselves the phenomenon of disappearance of Rustler at the most unexpected time. Their self-image nosedived into non-existence.

Plumbel took over from where the President had left. "PlanetB2 is a mega project, nay it is not a project, and it is a life mission of the US that will take the world into a new orbit. We have discovered that there is another planet in the universe. There are living beings in the planet. We have noticed heavy movements of some bodies in PlanetB2. This discovery itself is a major victory for the US in the history of the world."

"But what the heck is the meaning of PlanetB2?" This was the question in the minds of all scientists. No one dared to give words to what was running in their mind. They had pledged their mind to America. For them America was no more a country. It was the essence of life that guided them in their thought and emotions. They had very little of emotions and their entire bodies were enveloped by unending thoughts. Cubicle11 had produced endless thoughts specifically for the minds of Awesome5.

Pretending not to hear their inner thoughts Plumbel continued his monologue. "America and the American President are interested in capturing this PlanetB2 so that people on earth may move to that planet. We shall settle Americans in PlanetB2 so that they may have absolute freedom and unlimited prosperity. It will be our victory over nature. With our planned capture of PlanetB2 we shall prove to the entire world and for all histories to come that Americans are the masters of the Universe and no power on earth can subdue the American spirit. We Americans, the Masters of the Universe!"

Even as Plumbel yelled at the top of his voice one of the scientists clapped her hands with legitimate pride. She was shocked that none of her compatriots joined hands with her. She looked around and put her head down. Plumbel forced her to raise her head as he shouted at her that she was not expected to show any sort of emotions at achievements. Awesome5 was expected to be completely rational about everything that they were dealing with and not become emotional at all at any point of their achievements. The woman scientist understood her folly and said sorry that only she could hear. Plumbel knew the movements of her lips.

"It is your mission in life to put in all your intelligence, expertise and genius to design a spacecraft that will carry the five of you to PlanetB2. America has had many secret plans in the interest of the rest of the world. But you must realize that this is the topmost secret of America. Only the five of you, the President of America and myself know this grand plan. The spacecraft that you will design for this special mission will be known as Bigbelly1."

'Do you understand your unique position in making world history?" Plumbel now asked in a thundering voice.

"Yes, Sir" All the five of them shouted in unison so loud that the entire United States of America could have heard it directly. But Cubicle11 was constructed in such a way that no noise of any volume could go out of it. Plumbel was happy that Awesome5 had imbibed the spirit of America with their awesome approval of his secret plans.

"The five of you will design together the entire Bigbelly1 that will be able to travel 600,000 miles into space and return to earth with all the data that you will collect in PlanetB2. Prepare all communication materials and fit them into your craft. Fit the spacecraft with attack machines and laser bombs just in case you are attacked when you land. Prepare a blueprint and let me know what parts of the craft you can manufacture by yourself and what should be produced outside in the space station. We shall only produce these parts in bits and pieces in different workshops so that no one will have inkling on what we have planned. I shall take care of this aspect." Awesome5 was watching the mouth of Plumbel with a characteristic awe. Unmindful of their admiration for his genius he continued his foray into their inner world.

"In order to have better coordination among yourselves in your mission the President has appointed Mr. Burns, Peter Burns as your Team Leader. You will listen to all his instructions carefully and obey his orders as much as you will obey the orders of the President of America. Burns is not his real name. None of you will ever know his real name. Likewise each of you will have a pseudonym. You will know each other only by your pseudonym. We have not given your real names to anyone including Awesome5. With four men and one woman in your team, I am sure you will succeed. I am sorry, America will succeed."

Having satisfied himself of instructing his wards adequately Plumbel retired to his nest that no one knew of.

Burns called his team together as soon as Plumbel left them. He did not try to motivate them. His job was to give orders and assign work to members of his team. Since project PlanetB2 was shrouded and clouded in mysterious secrecy it was imperative that different parts of the vessel they prepared with technological precision was visited by him personally to make sure that they were in 100% flawless condition to be sent for assembling together. He was very proud of this team and his own leadership. They finished their job on time.

It was an awesome job by many standards. Awesome5 took just two years to complete the project. They were very proud of their neat job done with precision of a super human artist. The outer body of Bigbelly1 was secured for the long journey and for movement into empty space. The climatic conditions that it would have to negotiate were taken into due consideration too. There was an inner layer of the body that was separated from the outer body by an impenetrable vacuum so that the 'skin' of the craft, if one may call it so, became very thick beyond the comprehension of ordinary scientists. It was light in weight all the same. Burns made thorough researches on exactly at what position temperature would go down below 300 degrees and also on the distance at which temperature was so hot that water would boil instantly. Bigbelly1 had to adjust to this fast changing fluctuation in climatic conditions in the outer space.

The interior of the spacecraft had everything friendly that they needed for survival for a long time and four layers of support for all machinery. If any of the machines failed for one or other reason they did not have to worry much as there were four standbys for every machine. The belly of the spacecraft had adequate space for all of them to move around and to have meetings. There were exquisite specially prepared skin creams and other medicines to take care of all the needs of all astronauts. Even the slightest exposure could cause skin cancer in them. They discovered special equipment to hear each other even if they had to only whisper to one another. They knew well that they should not speak loud so that they did not have to expend the energy level in their body.

Bigbelly1 was fitted with many propelling devices for the bombs it contained. If the spacecraft happened to be attacked by beings in PlanetB2 then Awesome5 would not hesitate to fire on all cylinders at the beings. None of those outlets were visible from outside. The vessel would open the outlets as soon as it felt the command of the computers. Awesome5 was totally happy about the completion of its work on record time.

Plumbel came again and gave them a pat on their back for the excellent work they did. He inspected the round shaped vessel all around. They allowed him also to inspect the interiors but asked him not to touch anything. He had to walk with his hands down like a robot. Most of his mates in the Ministry were by then used to walking like robots even in normal places. They were so obedient to the horrible power display of the President that no one wanted to be mistaken of being too big for his bitches. It became a habit. 'Quite un-American' many among Americans thought. The American President – a super vessel, a carrier of millions of assumptions!

When Rustler went to Cubicle11 to inspect the Bigbelly1 it had been proudly mounted in order to be taken to the space station for its formal launch. The spacecraft needed explicit approval of the President of the US to make its first move into space. He started from the inside first and got out to see its outer appearance and strength. The Awesome5 could make out that he was proud of their work. Just as they were waiting for his pronouncement of approval he gave them the shock of their lives.

"Thus you will betray the confidence that I had reposed in you. I appreciate your technological genius. But I deeply mourn your strategic faux pas." The tough nut started hitting them on their temple. Their legitimate pride began to deflate itself slowly under the mighty pronouncements of the President.

'What went wrong?' The Awesome5 thought unanimously in their individual minds. They stood still with their stony faces without looking at Rustler. He had come to rustle them up. He did not wait for any of them to say anything. It was not in his design of governance that his subjects should say anything to the ruler.

'We have done everything with such care and precision. What went wrong in your opinion? Are you bigger scientist than we are?' Rustler could easily read what went on in the minds of Awesome5.

'What sort of President is he? We expected the President to have some decorum and good manners. He is such a weird guy who does not know even the fundamentals of a space mission. We have given our life for this project. Does he understand our difficulties? He is slighting all our efforts with such casual imperiousness.' Rustler could not read this chain of thought in the minds of Awesome5. It was too fast for him to follow.

Rustler mellowed down a bit and Awesome5 could see the sudden change on his face. He could even try to smile with much difficulty. He did not succeed however. But he started with a placid voice. "I sincerely appreciate all your efforts. You have manufactured this magnificent edifice of a spacecraft in record time. I know the level of sacrifice that you have made to bring this dream of mine into a reality. You are already well on your way to create a new history of America."

The Awesome5 began now to mellow out. They regretted their mad rush to a seat of judgment that did not legitimately belong to them. Two of them expanded their lips a bit without trying to put too much of a control over their smile. Rustler noticed both of them and quickly reversed his spongy position. He became quite cockeyed all of a sudden too soon. He became pork faced in no time. He opened his big mouth. "I do not consider your mistake as just a slip. It is the most serious blooper that can blow all my dreams into thin air. I would have condemned you to sure death had this not been the first attempt we are making to land on PlanetB2. All of you now please come around the spacecraft you have made and I shall show you the biggest blunder of your life."

Awesome5 walked behind him with downcast eyes. Rustler made them stand in a row. He stood in front of them and began to lambast them mercilessly. Plumbel refused to look at their eyes all this while. He knew his President more than anyone else in the whole of the US. He knew that the President of America could be the most weird man on earth and he had to be accepted so. Otherwise with one stroke of his fingers he could order the entire world to be destroyed in no time with the stockpile of nuclear, biological and chemical weapons that his country had stored. He kept his wisdom to himself.

Rustler ordered all members of Awesome5 to take a good look at Bigbelly1 that they created to their heart's content. They did as he told them to do. Their hearts were throbbing fast wondering if it would be the last look they had at their creation.

Even as they were wondering what was in store for them Rustler asked them if they were able to see their spacecraft clearly. They said yes in unison.

He then went to each of them and handed over a set of dark glasses. He asked Plumbel to put off all the lights in Cubicle11. He ordered the Awesome5 to wear the set of glasses he gave. "Can you see anything now?" he shouted. "Yes sir" They too shouted more loudly in unison. Then he gave them a second set of dark glasses and indicated to Plumbel to switch on all the lights. The entire area became as bright as day. "Wear your glasses now and try to see". He shouted at them. "No Sir. We cannot see a thing." They shouted obediently.

"Yes, that is the difference between you and me. Plumbel and I have told you repeatedly that this is the most secret mission that we are launching in human history. Yet, you have made a vessel that can be seen with naked eyes in the open and with special glasses in total darkness including night. You know that with the first set of glasses I gave you could see the spacecraft that you created in utter darkness. How can you make it secret if the entire world can see your spacecraft when it blasts off into the sky, be it day or night? Your spacecraft can be seen with naked eyes during day and with special glasses at night. But the second set of glasses that I gave proved to you that the vessel couldn't be seen either with naked eye or with special glasses if we apply the special type of chemical that we have used in those glasses. It is not that you don't know the technology. It is your carelessness that deserves condemnation. We cannot have such slovenliness in this mission.

You have to be 100% perfect in all your intentions and actions and all these have to be focused just on one goal and only one goal. The goal for you and me is the accomplishment of landing Bigbelly1 on PlanetB2. There cannot be even a speck of compromise on this."

Rustler had a second visit to Cubicle11 and asked Awesome5 "What did you do to the spacecraft that you created with so much of hard work?"

Awesome5 laughed openmouthed at least to please the President. Now the spacecraft was totally invisible even to the President of the US. He had however, taken those special glasses with him and had a good view of the vehicle that would spell the future pride of America.

Bigbelly1 almost reached PlanetB2. Just at a time when the secret ground force was monitoring every second of the movement of the spacecraft it disappeared from their computers in no time. Flash of a second! That was all required for the huge spacecraft to vanish into a vast space of emptiness. The ground force tried its best for several hours to trace the entity and bring it back to life. It was a nightmare for Rustler. The plans and execution came as a dream and it vanished as an empty dream as fast as any dream could do.

Rustler would not accept defeat of any kind. It was not in his vocabulary in any language. He believed that his entire body was constructed from his mother's womb to succeed. Any talk of defeat would arouse all cells in his body as an army that was in total rebellion. He would sweat and talk endlessly whenever he was faced with apparent defeat. 'I am the total embodiment of success' he would swank to Plumbel every now and then. The dilemma now! Defeat was staring at him. It was ready to burst out into loud laughter on his face.

"Leave alone the billions! We have lost a very invaluable team of scientists. Who will now carry forward the mission? I am sure you are not going to stop this effort. You are not the one to leave any mission half done." Plumbel tried to assuage his bloated ego while simultaneously reminding him of the enormous loss to US pride. Loss to exchequer could be easily made up with plunder from oil rich nations and sale of weapons. But who could repair the damage to the human caliber of Awesome5?

"Do you think I am a fool just to depend on one set of human beings? You should always know that machines could fail your vision and calculations any time. They are machines after all. They have no sense of success and failure. Human beings can be worse. You can never predict the trajectory of human mind. They are much worse than machines. I do not trust both at any time of my life. I am the President of the most powerful nation in the world. I cannot afford to repose my faith and trust on anything other than my own self. Only those who can be part of my grandiose designs for the future of the US and of the world can rise to the position that you have risen, Plumbel." Rustler was puffing up his words just as corns of maize in a frying pan. Though they did not taste well in the eardrums of Plumbel he smiled all the same in order to please his master and to save his skin as well.

"But how do we carry on our mission without those well trained and committed scientists, the Awesome5?" Plumbel had already become pregnant with this question in his mind and it was swelling to the point of breaking out. It was an apt moment for delivery.

"You think I am a fool, Plumbel? Such a big mission cannot be taken lightly. Awesome6 is ready to take over from where Awesome5 left. The only difference this time will be that the group of scientists to carry this mission forward to unquestionable success will consist of six members. The sixth member of Awesome6 is a mystery till now." Rustler said unmindful of the ruminations within the mind of Plumbel. He cared a damn about the feelings of Plumbel. Arrogance and insensitivity are conjoint twin brothers in the massive world of Rustler's.

"Who is the mystery man, the sixth member of Awesome6?" Plumbel asked the question more to get out his frustration than to really know the true identity of the person.

"You are going to train them, Plumbel. You are my most trusted man for the mission on hand. You will meet the person when Awesome6 is entrusted to your custody for training. You will meet the person yourself. Be patient for some more days. But this time the team of scientists has to work harder. They must explore all possibilities of machines going wrong at any time and plug all possible loopholes. They must be trained to imagine of all parts of machines going wrong in umpteen numbers of ways and invent appropriate mechanisms so that nothing will go wrong in the next mission. You should fail the machines on purpose and check if the scientists are capable of repairing them within a fraction of a second. It will be your special responsibility to spend more time personally with Awesome6 and monitor all their assembling of Bigbelly3. We avoid number 2 here so that our scientists do not get confused with PlanetB2." The mission seemed to be as big as the talk of Rustler.

"Yes, Mr. President! I am ready for the job once again. You can be sure that I shall accomplish my task to the best of my ability and we shall overcome all hurdles the next time. Let us call Awesome6 in two days and I shall begin to work on them." Plumbel wanted to prove that he meant serious business.

CHAPTER TWO

"Mr. President, we are almost at the threshold of great success. In a few seconds from now Bigbelly3 will land in PlanetB2. We are keeping a track of its movement and it is visible in our computers. America is only a few moments away from making history." Plumbel was excited beyond expression.

Rustler, the American President was making all mental preparations to announce the history that he made to the American people. Billowing smoke from his pipe were making perfect circle of illusions in front of him. He knew that his people would consume anything that he announced. 'Naïve consumers of the third order' he had often remarked to his close associates about his people. He knew that American pride would envelop them and could even submerge them over all other needs of life. Progress of the rest of the world mattered very little to him and to his people. But this was not the time for self-castigation and flagellation of his people. He buried everything else about his people. It was time for euphoria, collective euphoria of unprecedented achievement. 'In god we believe' he mumbled to himself like all faithful Americans.

The next call to the President was a drooping of bitter honey. Bigbelly3 landed successfully in PlanetB2. However, on landing it melted into an unseen entity and disappeared from sight.

Scientists on ground were unable to make out what really happened to the spacecraft. However, there was still a big sign of hope for the haughty President of the United States of America. Scientists were still able to show to him the mangled remains of the robotic outer cover. One member of Awesome6 survived. What happened to all other 5 was presumed to be the same as the fate of Awesome5. But there was an improvement from the previous landing attempt. There could still be one survivor. Or was the sixth one already dead?

Rustler called for an evening meeting with Plumbel. It was their habit. He was a full-grown bachelor. He had no time and inclination to women. Success had got into his head irrevocably. That he became the President of the US surviving all odds and heavy battle against his opponents was itself a Brobdingnagian triumph. Being in compulsive pursuit of victories he needed a lot of help from others. He did not have the capacity to trust others as his rise to the top was wrought with heavy odds against human beings. The deficit level of his trust was much worse than the quality of support he could draw from people around him. Trust had to emanate from him. Support had to come from others. Power and position could easily draw power but not trust. He sought more and more power and finally achieved the aggrandizement of power by becoming the first man of the US.

Being the President of America was only the beginning of his search for endless power and fame. While the US made use of the world for its advancement he made use of the US for his personal advancement. Both of them had a very pleasant evening with exchange of their regret over the second failure. But they also were gloated together in their pride that not everything was lost. There was still a lot of room for legitimate pride and hope for future success. Plumbel knew his President well and therefore, he had blocked the regular flow of information to him after the news that the second mission of Bigbelly3 was a failure though not a complete washout.

In the cool of the evening with a few pegs of whisky Plumbel gathered necessary strength to inform the President of the exact situation of Bigbelly3. The truth of the mission was that Bigbelly3 failed to reach PlanetB2 in the last few minutes. However, the spacesuit of the sixth member of Awesome6 was still communicating signals from PlanetB2. Though signals were quite weak it was still a major achievement for future designs of space communications. It was evident that the person inside the spacesuit was still alive but quite immobile. Nothing much could be said about the astronaut's survival till there was some movement from the body.

The signals did not reveal anything significantly different from what the secret forces of astronauts had already discovered. It was now confirmed that there was movement of some unknown bodies in PlanetB2. But the big mystery was how they lived. Nothing much could be said for sure till the sixth astronaut of Bigbelly3 began to move around in the planet.

Anxiety and anticipation made Rustler quite restless. He had no control over his words in such situations. Fortunately for him it was one of his closest colleagues who was with him sharing a glass of drink. He could afford to let his tongue a bit lose. He began to speak up.

"I am not sure who is the one person among Awesome6 that still has a hope of surviving in that bloody outlandish planet. I must tell you now that besides five scientists I decided to add a sixth one to the group, a very special woman. I took the biggest risk in this new mission of ours by recruiting a Native American woman as an astronaut. She manifested astounding knowledge and aptitude. I liked her at the first interview, as she appeared to be a genius. She not only loved America but also loved everything related to the cosmos. She was explicitly excited about becoming an American astronaut and was determined to achieve the impossible. I liked her ambition. That is why I chose her and gave her to you for training." Plumbel was rustled mildly by what Rustler told him. He did not go into the ethnic background of Carolina, the lone woman astronaut in Awesome6. He was anxious to know more about her. His mobile vibrated in his pocket.

"Just a second. I shall be right back in a minute." Rustler excused himself from Plumbel as soon as his mobile vibrated. The ring of smoke was in hot pursuit of him. "Ha, that is a million ton good news for us Plumbel. The news is that the one astronaut who survived in PlanetB2 has started moving. It is the Native American girl whom I recruited who has survived the cataclysm. She has got out of her spacesuit and is moving around. Since she did not eat anything for three full days, she is quite weak and tired. We need to see how she will survive in that god forsaken planet." Rustler mixed his elation with a proportional doze of pessimism.

Plumbel was equally pessimistic. He was already preoccupied as to why even at his position Rustler was keeping many secrets. He was the guy who ranked next to the President and shared many of the secrets of Rustler and yet on this one thing Rustler refused to believe even his own shadow. He was wondering if he should call the Ground Force that monitored Bigbelly3 for a total evaluation. His concern was not the evaluation per se. He was worried if Rustler would welcome the suggestion if he proposed it.

As if he read Plumbel's mind Rustler asked him to call the Ground Force immediately for an overall assessment of what went right and wrong with the mission and also plan for the next mission.

"We already had an evaluation when our first mission failed. Do you want to have one more? In the best interest of the secrecy we maintain do you want to risk one more evaluation?" Plumbel tried to be much concerned. He wanted to assure himself that he was the unquestionable number two in the US.

"What are you saying? Do you not see the difference? Our first evaluation with Ground Force at the first failure of Bigbelly1 did not throw up much information on our strategy. Our scientists were simply aghast at the failure and were unable to identify any substantial reason for the failure. They got stuck. I made a difference in Awesome6. It is an apparent failure that we are unable to locate Bigbelly3. But we have made huge progress in the second mission. We still have one person moving around in PlanetB2. We need to strategize appropriately and monitor the movements of Carolina, the survivor. We have clear evidence that the survivor is our only woman astronaut in Awesome6. However, nothing much could be said about her potential to survive for long until she removes her spacesuit. Call the Ground Force immediately to my secret chamber in the space station." Rustler was loud and clear. Plumbel could not mistake his President this time.

"Gentlemen, the President and I are very pleased with the way you have made marginal progress with your work in the present mission. The President is of the opinion that though the mission has failed overall, we are happy that we were able to land a person of our mission on the surface of PlanetB2. Now we like to draw all your assessment on the present half aborted mission." Plumbel looked at the President with legitimate pride. His face betrayed a search for approval.

Rustler bent over to him and whispered in his ears. "Your arrogance knows no bounds Plumbel. I, and only I have the right to start this meeting. You have borrowed my ideas and have created an impression that you are in command of this mission to PlanetB2. Just know your place and behave." Plumbel smiled in order not to show his embarrassment to the scientists of Ground Force.

"Yes, Plumbel always believes that there is no success and no failure. There are only different steps towards reaching our goal. It is a good way of thinking. A night is a night whether it is black or colorful. But I do not agree with this bullshit as far as this mission to PlanetB2 is concerned. I want only colorful nights and I do not believe in black nights. I want every step of ours to be a success and we need to build success upon success in order to reach our final goal of occupying PlanetB2. Therefore, I see our present mission through Bibgbelly3 as a clear failure. There is just an indication that we can still succeed with one more attempt and that is the reason I have called you here. You have indicated that we may succeed with another attempt. It is US pride that will be at stake if you do not succeed with the next attempt. I shall not compromise with any more failures. We should succeed in our next mission. You, all of you have to work harder, identify new strategic focal points and the end result should be a success for the US. I want to announce to the US that we have landed in PlanetB2 when we succeed. Till then this entire operation will remain a top secret of the President of America. You will have no way of communicating with the external world from Cubicle11. Now you may let me know what you plan to do for the future." Rustler did not mince any word in his communication. This was one of the reasons why he succeeded. He was clear and articulate and made himself look and sound trustworthy.

Rustler looked at Plumbel who did not want to be embarrassed once again and therefore, refused to look into the eyes of the President. Rustler cared his foot for anybody's attitudes. He continued his interaction in style. "Yes, all of you must speak out one by one your perception on future strategies for the success of our next mission to PlanetB2.

The leader of Ground Force picked up the courage to speak first. "Mr. President, we have just now received unclear images of the moving astronaut. Our computers have confirmed that it is the image of a woman. Therefore, we can conclude fairly easy that the lone woman astronaut is the one who has survived. She is still alive and is moving about."

In order to keep the President entertained another scientist spoke up. It was partly also because he did not know what else to say to the President. "We do not know how long she would survive as there is not enough food for her. We are not sure if there is something in PlanetB2 that she can eat."

"That is very interesting" Plumbel stepped in. He did not want to lag behind.

"Sir, it may be good that we have more women astronauts in our next mission." Another scientist pulled up his collar thinking that he asserted something futuristic. He put his head down seeing a sarcastic smile on the face of Rustler. It was this scientist who used to joke among his mates that the President of the US was a rubble-rouser, true to his name.

Rustler turned to Plumbel and whispered in his ears. "We do have such idiotic and naïve scientists who have unshakable confidence in women. Remove the fellow from the group of scientists."

Plumbel advised him not to do any such Don Quixotic misadventure such as removing any scientist from the group. They could reveal many secrets of the mission and America would come to know that there was a secret mission for which billions of their tax money were spent without their tacit approval. Both Rustler and Plumbel had previously agreed that if they wanted to remove any scientist from the group it was much wiser to physically eliminate such scientist than to send them out of the space station. They would be entrusted to the care of CIA and the rest was a routine business.

"Mr. President, we must take note of this point. The space vehicles involved in both previous missions have vanished from our computers and we do not know yet what has happened to them. We must find out what really happened to them before we launch again construction of the next vessel. Added to this is the fact that there is a lone survivor in PlanetB2 who is a woman. This is an important dimension for future research. There may or may not be any significance in the fact that the survivor happens to be a woman. But we cannot afford to dismiss the fact lightly that the survivor among six astronauts is the only woman. If there is any inference that we need to draw we should do so." The youngest scientist in the group spoke clearly and assertively. Rustler liked his style of giving life to words that manifested his thinking. Here was a rare occasion when Rustler was mildly proud of one of his wards.

The leader of the group intervened once again without asking for permission. "Mr. President, we have just now received communication that the space suit of our lone survivor has melted and disappeared from the surface of PlanetB2. This is a clear indication that there is something in PlanetB2 that melts the metals that we sent from here. The obvious inference is that our previous space vessel must have melted as they landed in the surface of PlanetB2. We should strategize further based on these assumptions for which we have some evidence." He said it with utmost seriousness.

"Yes, there seems to be some substance in what you say. Pursue the veracity of your assumptions and present me the evidences that should have no blemishes at all. It also means that you scientists must redesign the metal that goes into making the body of the next Bigbelly." Rustler's veiled appreciations had serious warning in the air for all scientists.

The lone Indian scientist in the group by now felt much left out. He wanted to make himself relevant and knowledgeable. "Sir, according to the science of Vastu the body of our space vessel spells disaster. We should change the shape of our vessel from its present circular one to a four edged or an eight-edged vessel. It should also be sharp in front, which signifies the northern corner. It is harmless if it is flat at the bottom, which is the southern corner. We are moving into space and the science of space is very important to follow. Vastu is the science of space."

"Bullshit! Absolute bullshit from the land of cows! Concentrate on the science that is the source of this mission and do not try to unnecessarily insert any cow science into our endeavor. I know you are a very intelligent scientist but you must know that this is the US." Rustler dismissed his suggestion with a scorn that was characteristic of American derision of many things Indian.

"Arrogance! Absolute American arrogance!" The Indian scientist could not gather necessary courage to stand up and say it loud. He buried it successfully in the realm of his mind. He was an expert in mind science as well and an adept swallower of his own words.

Rustler ended the meeting abruptly in an apparent angry mood and left the place with Plumbel closely following him.

The group of scientists enjoyed much more freedom than Awesome5 and 6. They were more in the open though they were constantly aware that CIA knew every movement of theirs. It was like a shadow personality. Every decision in their lives, every move they made bore the indirect stamp of CIA's eyes. Their psyche was conditioned so much that even when CIA had other business they would behave exactly in the way CIA expected them to behave. That evening they gathered together for a party to celebrate the marginal success they had in making one person land on PlanetB2.

Exactly at the same time Rustler and Plumbel met together in Rustler's private room to have their usual drinks. One group did not know that the other also was gulping down a few pegs of whisky. As usual Rustler began to open up slowly in proportion to the level of whisky. As its level rose up he used to sink. However, he never allowed himself to be drowned in it. He was too alert a guy to let anything in the world either down him or drown him. It was as if Plumbel was waiting for the President to loosen himself up.

"I am still ruminating over the fact that the lone survivor of our mission is a woman whom I had selected for Bigbelly3. I am happy that she survived though I am unsure if she would continue to survive." The doors were now screeching.

Plumbel desisted from provoking him with any question. He knew only too well that the moment anyone asked any question Rustler would become hyper alert and would begin to close up. He bade his time for the flow of information from the mouth of his President. "Yes Mr. President! I too found her to be genius of a woman. All our scientists in Awesome6 were genius in their own right. But Carolina was exceptional. She was intellectually sharp, balanced in assessing everything, humble to learn any new lesson that came on her way and determined to do what she had decided to do. Her determination did not have any paraphernalia of arrogance, an awesome genius." Plumbel provoked the President without asking a question.

"I was not much impressed with her the first time she came for the interview. However, she fared well enough to be short listed for the second interview in which she began to shine better than others. In the third and final interview she made a helpless victim of her genius. I liked her enormous potential and commitment. I knew that she was the type of person we needed for such an important mission. I hope she will not die in that unknown PlanetB2. If only she can survive for some more months we shall send Bigbelly4 and bring her back. She will be our treasure trove." Plumbel found Rustler unusually open bordering on a bit of what he could describe as emotional realm. He now began to be happy for Rustler. He remembered having read somewhere that a man without emotions can not only destroy himself but also destroy the entire world if he had a chance.

"I also found her to be a fascinating woman. Being the only woman in Awesome6 she did draw the attention of everyone else. But it was not because she was a woman. She outdid the other scientists often in her strategic and technical perspectives. I did not know her much more than that as a person." Plumbel added the last sentence on purpose knowing fully well that he was stuffing the President with a rare falsehood. He did this so that he did not have to ask Rustler a question.

"Oh, you did not find out her antecedents?" Rustler asked in mock surprise. He was happy inside that Plumbel did not go too far with his wards. With this acquired confidence he began to let the cat out of the bag. He made sure that the cats were harmless to him when he let them out.

"You will be almost shocked to know the President of America had the courage to select a woman from the First Nations for this very important mission. Their resentment about American history makes them very susceptible. They are vulnerable when it comes to gaining the trust of Americans. She was very happy that she won the confidence of the American President. She almost jumped in the air when I told her that she was selected for a very important mission and what it would imply in her personal, family and social life. She was ready for anything in order to be a creative part of the history that I wanted to create." Rustler talked like a man possessed with unlimited love. The proclivity of an ageing bachelor to praise a woman was evident in him. Plumbel laughed within and pitied Rustler who would not even trust any woman to have sex with her. He was gripped with so much fear of possible commitment to women with whom he would have sex that he shunned sex with worthy women. All women were sexy in his bachelor eyes. Depravity, what is thy name? But only some became sex-worthy in his consideration. He would close the doors as quickly as his desires came lest he became vulnerable to women. He preferred self-sex to reposing his trust in any man or woman.

Plumbel waited for the President to come out more and more of the fortress that he had constructed around himself and was pretending to be strong inside the fortress. Plumbel knew what a weak person was hiding inside those walls only to falsely convince himself that he was very safe inside. However, he loved his President despite all his hidden weaknesses.

"It is very necessary to study her background. That will help us to understand better if her survival has anything to do with the construct of her personality or it is a mere accidental survival. We should study her life history already from her birth. Even her background a little before her birth would help us a lot to construct her personality. Her growth in her own surrounding needs to be carefully researched. Her choice of her friends and colleagues will also be important for us to fabricate her personality trait. Once we have this we can put all the data into processing and let us see what we get. But am wondering who will do such thorough job on our behalf." Plumbel could see that Rustler was gulping a few pegs faster than he usually did.

"How can we entrust this very important task to anyone else? The shroud of secrecy that we have weaved around our project may begin to tear into pieces if we make even the slightest mistake. Therefore, I shall go myself. I shall take a holiday for a month and accomplish the job." When Plumbel said this Rustler was more than happy. He knew that there was no one else in the entire US who can be as loyal to him as Plumbel was. He patted himself at his own back for having discovered a person such as Plumbel. He was very proud of himself like the giant spider that weaves beautiful cobwebs to entice its victim only to later suck all life out of it. Rustler was double happy that he had a very willing victim in Plumbel.

"Done" is all what Rustler said and the chapter was closed.

CHAPTER THREE

Carolina got up slowly and began to walk around PlanetB2. She had no consciousness of her self. She did not realize that she was surrounded by beings of the planet in which she was a total stranger. They felt a new tremor in their being as soon as Carolina fell into the planet and surrounded her in order to wake her up. She saw them but could not communicate to them, as they looked completely strange and different from her. There was a very pleasant feeling in her body about being surrounded by such strange beings. She smiled in that atmosphere of total welcome. They smiled back to her. They moved with her wherever she went. She could feel strongly in her body that they were full of love and appreciation for her. Her body began to speak a new language. She was able to perceive what her body wanted to communicate to her. But she did not understand anything of what they wanted to communicate to her. As she kept moving with them she could see many such groups of people moving about all over the place. Some from different groups left their groups and joined her group.

She had no consciousness of herself as an earthly being. She thought but was not aware of her thoughts at her conscious level. She felt but lost track of her feelings at the rational level. Indeed rationality seemed to have deserted her. She was moving about with the other beings without being conscious that she was with a set of new beings that she had not encountered before in her life. It was a new world the characteristics of which she could not bring together to her consciousness. All that she could understand and feel was that she was and they were.

One being among them kept moving close to her. It would not walk away from her. A few others kept close to her. She had a feeling of inexplicable happiness filling her. It was like bliss, full body bliss. There was not any place in her body that was not experiencing this bliss. Her body was gripped with a bliss that was inexplicable to her. It was her first time. She had earlier experience of orgasm while masturbating all alone. But this was full body orgasm. Her entire body was quivering with orgasmic bliss. She had become a new being that existed always in bliss. The being was bliss. Carolina, the being in eternal bliss!

"It took about 100 days in human measurement to bring you back to your human consciousness. We filled your body with all the energy waves that emanate from our bodies and slowly our energy waves began to enter the cells in your body. Then the miracle began to happen. It is because of your shamanic background that it was possible for us to fill your body with our energy waves." The being spoke a language that Carolina could understand.

"Who am I? What is this place? Who are you people? What is your name? I experience such bliss amidst you but I do not know you all yet. Please tell me more about me." Carolina said that same things that are usually said in all novels. The difference was that she did not even know that she had read many novels when she was on earth.

"My name is Thayamma. All of us here are known as Thayammas. You will soon come to know more about yourself. We do not have to tell you much about you. But know that you have come here from the Earth. It is a small planet in the cosmos. Your name was Carolina when you were on earth." Thayamma gave the same answers that are usually said in fictions. She knew that she was only a fiction for earthly beings.

"What is earth? How does it look like? Why am I different from you?" Carolina asked. She was like a little child flooding her mother with a volley of questions.

"We shall soon show you the earth. Just as you are walking here you also walked on earth when you were there. But not all beings living there experience bliss as you do here. All of us here live in bliss. You are different from us because you are still living with the body that you had on earth. Soon your body will change and will become like ours." Thayamma was patience personified.

"Did you also come from the earth as I did? How did you change your body? Why did you change your body? Should I not have the same body here? Why did I come here?" Her questions showered like rain in a planet that did not need any rain. Carolina was beginning to pollute PlanetB2 with her intermittent questions.

"We did not come from the earth. However, we have our origin from earthly beings. Just as you have a body all earthly beings have different bodies. Unlike us human beings can have feelings and thinking. There are billions of them living on earth. Their thinking and feelings come out of their bodies and begin to move into space of the cosmos as waves. When these waves emitted from bodies of earthly beings merge together through a process known as entropy small little beings come into being. They keep floating in the cosmos." Thayamma began her explanation of space science.

"But you are not small little beings. You have bodies that are much bigger than I have . . ." Thayamma knew that Carolina still had her human proclivities and wanted to shape her to become a being of PlanetB2.

"The small little beings made out of waves further merge among themselves and become bigger beings like us." Thayamma was like a teacher in the kindergarten schools of the earth.

"I have come here with this body. How did you come to this planet? How did I come here?"

"Well, you did not come here. You were sent here by some other earthly beings. Actually six of you came here in a big vehicle with weapons created by earthly beings. Only you survived here. All others are dead along with their machines." Carolina did not recognize a word of what Thayamma said.

"What means to die? Why did the others who came with me die? Why did they send me here from earth?" The little child Carolina again!

"I shall explain to you now everything one by one. Soon when you lose this body of yours and become like one of us you will not need any explanation. You will understand everything instantly." This was Thayamma

"How long will I take to have bodies like yours?" Carolina again.

"You will understand it if you understand how we gain this body. I told you about small little beings. They merge further and become as big as we are. Since you did not come here through such merger you have a different body and you will continue to have the same body till you become like us."

"What should I do then to become like you all?" Question after question!

"You do not have to do anything just as we did not do anything to become what we are. Unlike you are we were never human beings. We are the amalgamation of all types of waves in the cosmos. Such amalgamation is what I earlier communicated to you as entropy. It is the merger of waves that created us. It is the entropy that created us. This merger of waves is not just one time event. We keep on merging with cosmic waves till finally we become wavial beings. Ours is not a body like the human or animal body. Ours is a form. It takes time; a lot of time in human measurement to take this form and become wavial beings, as we are. The faster the entropy the sooner we get this form. We are the cumulative essence of many cosmic waves. We are cosmic beings. You are not produced out of any entropy. You have the body of an earthly being. But your body has been trained to receive waves from the cosmos in your cells. Your body is full of cells that have the capacity to receive and send out waves. Since you have such a body soon you will lose this body and become like us. Your body was filled with life giving energy waves just as we have. This is why you are different from other earthly beings and it the reason for your presence here with your human body. However, you will not need the body of earthly beings to become like us. Your present body will disappear as you begin to receive more and more positive and life giving waves from us. You have already started receiving such waves from us and that is why you are living in this body without eating anything."

"What is eating?"

"You will understand many things as soon as you begin to interact with us and with the waves from the body of earthly beings. Your body is well tuned to receive life giving energy waves from all cosmic beings including those in other planets who live in harmony with the cosmos. The more cosmic waves you receive in your body cells the more you will begin to lose your present body and will begin to assume a body like ours. Your coming here is a blessing of all your ancestors." She was able to receive the communication of Thayamma with bliss unlimited.

"How did I come here? Why did I come here? Who sent me here?" Self-consciousness slowly began to take grip of Carolina in a totally different way.

"There are some earthly beings who want to overpower the rhythm of the cosmos. They are very curious to explore all that exists in the cosmos. They believe that with their human power they can master the cosmos. They think that nothing in the cosmos can do any harm to them. Very silly beings! They do not understand that all of them would die in a short period of time. With their proclivity for dominance over cosmos they are hurrying up their own destruction. Not all human beings are the same. There are many earthly beings that live in harmony with the cosmos. They do not have much access to what is called technology and science. They just live their lives. They flow with the rhythm of the cosmos. You were one such being." Thayamma was filling the body of Carolina with her thought waves and feeling waves. She was in full bliss, a full body orgasm.

"Oh, that is why you brought me here! Where was I in the world?" She kept the communicative interaction going.

"We did not bring you here. It was not yet time for you to come here all by yourself. But your country, the people who rule over your country wanted to reach to the skies. You see there the moon. That is your grandmother. They sent their space ship to the moon with some human beings in it. You see there in the yonder another of your ancestor. It is Mars. Now the same rulers are sending human beings to live there. They know that we are living

43

here. Therefore, they also want to send human beings to live here. They made two attempts to land here. They designed a vessel specially to land in this planet. They have named it as PlanetB2. They filled the space ship with weapons of destruction. That is why the first ship without human beings just disappeared into nothingness. In the second ship they put five human beings and also a lot of weapons. This Planet cannot have anything that indulges in destruction. The energy waves emanating from the body of all of us living in this planet will automatically subsume anything that comes here with negative energy. We are created through entropy, I told you. We are the cumulative essence of all life giving and positive energy waves. When we live together in this cosmos nothing that contains negative energy can enter here." There was no need of any interruption in Thayamma's communicative interaction. However, Carolina still had the limitation of her body and could not enjoy bliss, as did Thayamma in all its intensity as full body orgasm.

"But then, how did I survive? It was the same people who sent me here along with others from that country. Why was I not destroyed?"

"You were not destroyed because your body was different from all those who came from earth. Your body was full of life giving positive energy and the cells in your body are even now open to receive such life giving energy in the cosmos. It is not your conscious choice. But from the way you grew up in your family and community you developed the aptitude to receive either positive or negative waves that fill the cosmos. You actually lived often in fully body orgasm when you were on earth. The energy level in your body was able to dispel all the negativity that filled the space ship in which you came. They had named it Bigbelly3." Thayamma was fluent in her communicative interaction. The others around her were silent till then. But now they began to communicate with Carolina with certain intensity that was not the same as that of Thayamma's.

"How was I different from all others? If I were different why did the rulers in that country choose me?"

"Stay in silence for sometime and travel deep within you. The answer to all your questions lies within you Carolina. You will begin to communicate soon with all of us just as we communicate with one another. The intensity of your bliss, of your full body orgasm will be the same as we experience. Look at your body. It is beginning to disappear slowly. This is the glory of this planet. When you begin to drink the fullness of energy from the cosmos you will not need your body. You will become waves just as we have become. Many other cosmic waves will begin to enter your cells and you will enter into a process of entropy. Entropy is the emptying of your old cells in the body, of your old waves with which you communicated and assuming new cells and even new body and beginning to communicate with new waves that emanate from your new body. In that intensity of entropy you will become a form. We are all forms of waves. We are not bodies in the way you have body. Very soon you will become a form just as we are." Another of the being in PlanetB2 joined in the education spree.

Carolina became totally silent. She was in the midst of the beings of PlanetB2. But she was in such cosmic intensity that she once again lived the blissful way that she enjoyed for a short while on earth. She did not realize the slow disappearance of her human body. "Yes, my ancestor was a buffalo. It was from him that I drew immense energy and life when I lived on earth." Just as she said this a few of the beings in the planet moved towards her and surrounded Carolina.

"These are the ones who have assumed this form from waves that emanated from the aspirations of your ancestors. All their waves for the well being of indigenous peoples went through entropy also with waves from other ancestors, trees and humans and came to this form. As soon as your body send out emotional waves that were related to buffalo as your ancestors they are here with you." Thayamma explained their presence to Carolina.

"My mother was a shaman and brought me up in shamanic tradition. We worshipped buffalo as our ancestor. But we also saw the destruction of millions of our ancestors and began to lose our strength. Our bodies became weak and it was easy for the Americans to subjugate my elders in the community. We became deprived in many ways, especially of the right to live our lives the way we wanted. We had to scurry around for land. We were a people who worshiped earth as mother. But we were deprived of land. Our strength dwindled further." Carolina began to relive her energy that filled her body when she was on earth.

Thayamma was now experiencing Carolina in her level of bliss. So were a few more beings in PlanetB2. Carolina did not have to speak so many words any more. All her thoughts spread into the Planet as waves and all those who lived in the Planet were able to receive the new form of wave that surrounded them. All of a sudden all of them began to experience a new gush of waves in their form. They knew that Carolina was angry about something.

"My ancestry was from Indigenous Peoples, the Native Americans. We considered ourselves as children of Mother Earth, known as Pachamama. Mother Earth is a living being in the universe that concentrates energy and life, while giving shelter and life to all without asking anything in return. She is the past, present and future. This is our relationship with Mother Earth. We have lived in coexistence with her for thousands of years, with our wisdom and cosmic spirituality linked to nature . . . ."

In this intensity of communication with the cosmic beings of PlanetB2, Carolina became a ball of fire all of a sudden. She became very angry and began to dance in her new form. Her human body was completely gone. In her heat wave she traversed PlanetB2 several times in no time. With her were thousands of other cosmic beings in the planet that burned with the same anger and they took the flight with Carolina around PlanetB2. It looked as if there were flashes of lightning all over the planet. Any human being on earth would have mistaken it as if thousands of satellites were encircling PlanetB2. She began to affect the form of the beings in the Planet with her waves of anger. There was a reason for their angry communicative interaction.

"The aggression towards Mother Earth and the repeated assaults and violations against our soil, air, forests, rivers, lakes, biodiversity, animals, plants and the cosmos are assaults against us. Before, we used to ask for permission for everything. Now some human beings have made Mother Earth to ask them for permission. We are sure that Pachamama protects us. But many humans on the earth have come to be convinced that they have to protect Mother Earth. This violation of the integrity of Mother Earth will not be tolerated." In her dance of anger Carolina encircled all the beings of PlanetB2 with her new energy. She began to communicate through cosmic waves without any movement of her body.

"It was not at all a mistake that you joined the space mission of the American government. Much before you ever thought of it waves from our bodies reached your body and we began to attract you towards us. It was this attraction of waves and the receptivity in your human body that worked in your subconscious and made you seek a job in the space mission" Thayamma's waves reached the new body of Carolina without any time gap.

"Yes, I can also see some contradictions in the world. While I was acting through the 'impulses' of my body and that gave me immense pleasure, my companions joined the space mission with clear calculations of the profit they would make out of the mission. For them the profit was more attractive. They were part of the rationality of absolute dominance of humans over cosmos. Their body cells were filled with waves of dominance and they enjoyed it at their subconscious. They desired achievement and they were ready to do anything for it." She was now an eternal source of waves that emanated from her new body.

"Yes, this is the problem with humans who live on earth. They allow their bodies to be open always to thought waves and feeling waves of dominance. Everyone has the desire to dominate over all the others. The entire world is filled with such dominant waves and it is only natural that many whose bodies are more open to such waves join the dominant world. You must have come across those religions that teach that salvation is in knowledge. Their type of knowledge is the knowledge of the head. For us the cosmic beings on this planet knowledge is in the entire body." Thayamma's body began to emit a mix of thought and feeling waves.

"Yes, when I was on earth even I believed in my conscious that the American President was the most courageous person on earth. If I had continued there, even my body cells would become tuned to his waves because I admired him a lot. A lot of people on earth believe that he is the ultimate authority on everything that matters in the world. Since their bodies are full of dominant waves they are unable to see or perceive that it is harmful to a lot of other human beings, animals, plants and all other living beings." Carolina still emitted residual waves of her understanding.

"Actually we do not receive such dominant waves in this planet. Our forms refuse to allow any dominant waves to enter our wavial bodies. We do not have a set of knowledge as you had when you were on earth. Now that you have assumed our form through entropy even you will not know what the US President is planning for the future invasion of our planet. All that we feel in our form is that no negative and dominant waves can even reach our planet. We are just forms that exist filled with life giving energy waves. We do not like interference in the way of any other beings in other planets. We just live by ourselves. That is the reason why we remain in eternal bliss. We are just being. Our becoming takes place by the enormous level of energy we share with other forms in this planet. We did not plan to destroy the spacecraft sent by the US. It was simply that our energy level does not allow any influx of negative waves into our planet. Machines that carry such waves or produced out of such designs will not have any entry into our planet." It looked that Thayamma was giving a lecture. But actually it was the floating of waves within her form that gave this perception to Carolina. It was knowledge transfer. Carolina was not totally new to such transfer of body knowledge. She was used to such transfer in her community of indigenous peoples who depended on their entire body for knowledge and not on their brains. This resonance once again brought full body orgasm in her.

"Did you know that our spaceship was coming here? Did you know that I was one among them? Why did you not spare my companions? Is there a problem if human beings come and live here?" Carolina was still oscillating between her past and present existence. Residual effects of her human body's very recent disappearance!

"Our knowledge is not like the one that human beings have. We have no science and no non-science. We have no rationality and emotionality as human beings have. We have no thinking and no feeling. We have no plans for the future. We are just there. We are just beings. Our actions are just love. In love there is no classification. It just exists. It is human brain that classifies love into many categories. We only know eternal bliss in love and nothing else. We did not spare you. We did not destroy your companions. The difference was in you and your companions. We are essentially life giving and non-destructive. Those with bodies that are capable of receiving negative waves cannot enter here. Only those who are capable of receiving positive energy from cosmos can enter here. No one can come here by mere force. The spaceship in which you came had no chance of entering here. I have told you why you survived here." Both of them said this together and enjoyed unlimited body bliss.

"Do we all move to other planets? Do we have any mission to change the universe and human beings as cosmic beings?"

"We only live in space, the cosmic space. We have assembled here mainly because this is the space that is most hospitable to us. In this planet the space is fully conducive to receive life giving positive energy waves. We do move to other planets. Just as similar waves are attracted to each other and enter into an entropy process we too are attracted to life giving waves wherever they exist. If there is a person in other planets who has only positive waves in her body those of us who are made of similar waves start moving towards them. Our movement begins to enhance their level of blissful existence already in other planets. Unfortunately, the earth with all her human beings is filled with negative energy and therefore, only very rarely are we attracted to earth. However, some of us do interact with human beings on earth before coming here. As we are in the process of entropy it is possible that some of the human beings who live in intense harmony with nature attract the merging cosmic waves towards them because of their ability to receive positive waves from the cosmos in intensity. This is often interpreted by earthly beings either as devils and or as messengers from god. As such waves enter the bodies of human beings even without their conscious acceptance they are said to be possessed by departed people."

"Ahh, that is very interesting." By then quite a few cosmic beings in PlanetB2 were attracted to the communicative interaction between the two and there was a big group around Carolina.

"This is how most ancestors of indigenous peoples received communication from their dead ancestors. They were able to hear the words of their dead ancestors and talk to them. They were able to feel the communication of ancestors at a very emotive level." Another cosmic being started interacting with the body cells of Carolina.

"But then there are those who act with bad spirit on the earth, I mean, not bad will, but with what they call evil spirits. They mesmerize people with many tricks of casting out devil." Carolina's old habits still found their residual presence

"We do not know what it is. We have nothing to do with such evil spirits. It is possible that just as we are the cumulative consequence of entropy of positive and life giving energy there could be such entropy of negative waves in the cosmos. It is simply that we have no reference to such entropy. We live by ourselves without any deterministic reference to anything else in the cosmos." Another cosmic being made her communicative interaction at that stage.

"Your father, for example went away from your home for a few days when you wanted to go to New York and study. This was something very new in his life and in the life of your community. He slept on the face of Mother Earth with his body fully touching the earth. He deeply desired to know if you were making the right choice in your life. You had imbibed the Shamanic culture and spirit. But then you wanted to become great in life and were ready to face any consequence in order to achieve what you wanted. Usually he gets a word, a feeling deep inside his body that Mother Earth approved or disapproved of decisions. But in your case he did not feel anything in his body, neither positive nor negative. He came back home and your mother was highly disappointed. You father knew that she had more capacity for communicative interaction with cosmic beings. He suggested that your mother should do what he did. You mother got a word of approval from Mother Earth on the very first night that she slept. It was her body bliss, a sort of orgasm that runs through every cell of her body with her body totally touching the earth." Carolina was just seeing stars in the empty space receiving this communication in her body. She did not recognize who her father and mother were. There was no human identity to the communication that she received from other cosmic beings.

Just then there was a big tremor among the cosmic beings. This was quite unusual among them. They had such mild tremor when the first space mission of the Americans tried to land on PlanetB2. But then it did not last long as Bigbelly1 vanished from PlanetB2 in the same speed with which it came. The tremor was much more severe when Carolina landed on PlanetB2. All cosmic beings knew that some alien being had landed on the Planet. But they lived as if nothing happened. It was only when the metal spacesuit around the body of Carolina dematerialized that the little disturbance the planet had vanished. With the body of Carolina being exposed to the cosmic beings in the planet they felt attracted towards her and started an intense communicative interaction.

Once again the tremor in PlanetB2 was more severe and vehement than the previous one. Carolina could feel a little bit of that tremor in her new cosmic body.

CHAPTER FOUR

Plumbel thanked all the members of the community of Carolina and left them. He was not completely satisfied with the research he had done on her. He went around to neighboring places, to other tribes. Not many were willing to talk to him. He also saw quite a few houses of white people in the area and many modern houses were being constructed. Some had already moved into their houses. There were many houses that were yet to be completed. Such new houses dwarfed the traditional huts of indigenous peoples. The newly constructed houses were far off from each other unlike the way they were being constructed in cities. They were characteristically different from the close-knit houses of indigenous people. Each of those modern houses seemed to be worlds of their own. Plumbel was wondering why Americans were distancing themselves from one another in such strange places. He ventured into one of the occupied houses and found a family sitting over a table and chatting aimlessly. In the midst of them were a few bottles of wine and cans of beer. When Plumbel introduced himself as a researcher the head of the house welcomed him with open arms.

"Come in please. I was a professor in Bard College in New York. Now I am retired and am relaxing with my family. Please meet my wife Elena. She was a teacher in Manhattan school. So we are all researchers in a way." By the time James finished his welcome speech his wife rushed to meet the new guy who had gone that far to meet them.

'What research are you doing at this age? Yah, but you are still very young compared to us. I think you have not yet forgotten the lessons you learned in the American military. You keep yourself fit and trim." Elena joined in the conversation and quickly began to take the leadership.

"What do you like to drink? Water, beer, wine or do you like to have some military stuff. We have them here stacked in our rack." James extended his hospitality a bit; it was rarely that someone went to meet them in that distant place.

"I shall have some beer please. I am doing a research on the animal life in this area. I am a natural lover of nature. I want to recommend to the government of the US to protect animals in this region so that they do not become extinct in the course of time. The US government should already take protective measures." Plumbel stage-managed his play perfectly. He was taught that game in his training to speak to people exactly the opposite of truth so that he did not give even the remotest clue to his true mission in a particular place. Only he knew in his depths that neither the love for nature nor telling the truth was natural to him.

His eyes were constantly focused on the landscape of the place. Each house of White Americans was almost at the center of a forest so to say. Many had told him earlier: 'You Americans do not cut your own trees. You go to South

America to cut their trees for your needs. The only legitimization that you give is that even the Japanese do that. But it is quite a lame excuse.' It looked very real when his eyes traversed the entire stretch of land. He could see many wild animals roaming around the houses. Deer and bear were the most common. Occasionally he could also hear the howling of foxes. His mind was fixed on the sight he had as he walked along towards the house of the professor. There was a big river that passed through the entire area and the chirping and cooing of the birds filled the ears of any casual traveler in the area. The place was filled with natural wealth and now all these belonged to the Americans who were Europeans earlier.

James came in with a big tray filled with glasses and bottles. He also brought some small cookies to entertain his guest. "Yes, it seems this place was full of bison before we came here. In order to occupy the place and put down resistance from the uncivilized Natives, we Americans had to just shoot them down in millions. We thrived on the leather market with their skin." He was talking and walking. The professor was always in excitement

"It is cruel to kill so many animals only because we had a good market for leather. It provided the much-needed livelihood for the Natives. You are speaking in millions. It immediately takes me to the scenes in Germany where Hitler massacred millions of Jews only because it suited him. Don't you think so?" Plumbel tried to provoke the old couple.

"But Native Americans are barbarians. They did not welcome our coming here. Look how much we have developed America within the short period we are here. They should join us in developing America. It is to their advantage. But uncivilized as they are, they never understand the importance of modernizing our society. We come from an era of enlightenment and we know better what is good for others and for the entire world." It was James the professor who taught some fundamentals of American ways to Plumbel. Even in his glorious days in Bard he never cared to see what type of students were in front of him. He strongly believed that his mission was to teach such 'truths' in order to indoctrinate his students to make them think and act in ways that suited the American system. They paid him.

"They are not Christians. A lot of them refused to believe in Jesus Christ. They are all animists who worship the devil. They call them ancestors. These ancestors have animal figures. You are a Christian. We know that Jesus is the only way, the truth and the life. Who can do any good to them? They have no future unless they believe in Jesus Christ. See how we are developing those who have converted to Christianity? Instead of listening to our priests they continued to listen to . . . er, what is it James? The name of their priests?" Elena gave a strong assertion of her Christian faith. Nay, it was an assertion of her American faith. She skipped the issue of Hitler quite conveniently. Plumbel did not pursue it, as it did not fit into his 'research' designs.

"Hmmmm! I think it is Shamans. Yes that is how they call their priests. Even women become their priests. But what is our problem? Pagans can do anything they want. They are doomed to eternal fire unless they convert themselves." The Professor solemnized the initial discussion. He turned to Plumbel. "Yes, young man. Tell me what you want from us? Why have you come to us in your research? If there is something that we can do in the best interest of America we shall be more than happy to do that for you."

Plumbel was taken aback as he had not prepared himself for this question. But he was a master artist who could hoodwink the worst crook in the world. Very spontaneously he said that he was there to ask them a few questions about the Natives of the region.

"Oh, we do not mix with them at all. They are very low in their origin and in their habits. They can never measure up to our standards . . ."

Plumbel could not help remembering what he had read in the book 'Black Skin, White Masks'. It was about the Europeans and Malagasy among many other things. The passage that he had read flashed across his memory lane sitting in front of the professors.

"Here again we encounter the same apprehension. It is of course obvious that the Malagasy can perfectly well tolerate the fact of not being a white man. A Malagasy is a Malagasy; or, rather, no, not he is a Malagasy but, rather, in an absolute sense he "lives" his Malagasyhood. If he is a Malagasy, it is because the white man has come, and if at a certain stage he has been led to ask himself whether he is indeed a man, it is because his reality as a man has been challenged. In other words, I begin to suffer from not being a white man to the degree that the white man imposes discrimination on me, makes me a colonized native, robs me of all worth, all individuality, tells me that I am a parasite on the world, that I must bring myself as quickly as possible into step with the white world, "that I am a brute beast, that my people and I are like a walking dung-heap that disgustingly fertilizes sweet sugar cane and silky cotton, that I have no use in the world."

The mindset of the professor couple was a grim reminder of the darker side of humanity. Plumbel had never liked the way America overpowered the Native Americans nor did he subscribe to the way Blacks and Native Americans were treated in his time. He was a naïve human being at heart and a genius of a thinking being in his head. He could not argue with Rustler with what went on in his heart. Rustler would organize immediate decapitation of anyone who picked up the courage to deviate from his path. His path meant the way he thought and panned. He would of course do it without showing any remorse. Plumbel kept his wisdom to himself. However, he gave a free vent to all his hidden anger at America whenever he was alone in prayer or in meditation. He could not argue with the professor couple, as he was afraid that he might in the bargain betray his true identity.

In sheer helplessness Plumbel got up to leave saying that he would then go to other Americans living in the area. It was worth walking. But before leaving he mumbled to himself that he wanted to meet some Natives in order to get vital information about any girl who studied in any University. The professors heard him mumble and the words reached their ears.

"Yes, we know that two of the brightest girls in this area went to New York to study. We do not know what happened to one of them. We have never seen her for years now. But we see the other girl occasionally walking around in the nearby forest. Her parents and community live near the lake about a kilometer from here. But soon our white people will take over the lake to make it a tourist center for Americans." They said this as Plumbel was almost at the door. He did not show any excitement at the vital clue he got. He thanked the couple and left their house as if nothing happened between him and them. "Be careful as you walk. There are bears in this region. They can be dangerous sometimes." They sent him away with a serious warning.

A despondent Plumbel walked all alone for a kilometer. The birds, deer and foxes found an apt companion in him. They screeched and flew in all direction communicating the arrival of a strange and eminent figure in their region. By now they were quite used to the intrusion of Americans in their native country. They had intruded into their spaces and claimed the forests as their own. But Plumbel seemed to be someone special to them. He did not understand a simple note of what they communicated among themselves. There was that lonely gigantic bison that passed a strange look at him. It was quite hostile in the eyes of Plumbel. The man who represented the massacre of millions of them had come all-alone. It was the bison's time. He was itching to take revenge on the aggressor. He looked around for his companions to tell them that their time had arrived at last. But there was none that he could see. He took a few steps and stood in the way of Plumbel. His hand went automatically into his pants pocket. Both were ready for the kill. They stood still gazing at each other for sometime. As if violence did not pay in the long run the bison scratched the ground four times with his front leg and withdrew himself backward. Plumbel took his hands out from his pocket in great relief. Plumbel regretted that he was ready to take recourse to a weapon of killing when faced with an animal that had no weapon even to defend himself. Strange are thy ways, oh human. He heaved a big sigh of relief and walked further.

He sighted the cluster of indigenous huts at a distance. His steps became longer and faster. He was anxious without anybody's permission. "Can I meet the Chieftain of your community?" Stereotyped questions. There was no stereotyped answer this time.

"What is the matter? Why do you want to meet the Chieftain?" The animosity was more than evident in the tone of the questions. 'We have no business in common with our killers.' The tone seemed to say. Plumbel exercised extreme patience.

"I am not one of those hostile persons who walk around in this place man. I have come here to do some study on the plants and animals. There seem to be quite a lot of birds and animals here in the wood. Your place is naturally very rich. I have a desire to develop many areas of the US in the same way you have developed. I want to meet your Chieftain and get some ideas about native agriculture technology that you have used."

'Harmless fellow!' the man thought. Spontaneous outgoing to help the needy! "Come with me. I shall take you to the Chieftain. What is your name? Where do you come from?" He extended his hand in friendship and Plumbel reciprocated.

"I am Plumbel from New York. I am a researcher by profession." Plumbel repeated his lies to perfection.

"I am Allan, the Chieftain of this community here." He stunned Plumbel. Here was a man with teeth painted in red and not so well arranged in a row. Plumbel returned the compliment also by showing his row of teeth, white and well arranged in a row. Both of them laughed aloud at each other's folly of suspecting each other without a valid reason.

Plumbel's research paid rich dividends. It was the place he wanted to visit. Carolina was not the only indigenous girl who went to New York in pursuit of American studies. There was a friend of Carolina's who also went with her to pursue her higher studies. Marissa was one year junior to Carolina and was still in New York. Just as Carolina's Mother was a Shaman, Marissa's father was also a Shaman. Plumbel met him and found out about all the antecedents of Marissa. She was also fond of her native shamanic tradition. Unlike her friend Carolina she refused to be converted to Christianity. She was much stronger in pursuit of her indigenous traditions and spiritual path. She was much pained by the tragedy that struck her people after the arrival of Europeans in their otherwise calm and peaceful country. She wanted to study well and had a great desire to come back and help her people by educating them. She wanted to unite her people and make them become worthy of the new developments that were taking place in their life situation. She used to argue with her elders that they should fight against the onslaught of Europeans. However, they had to do the battle by equating themselves to Europeans in all the fields. She was in a mad mission of challenging the future of her people with her past.

Plumbel went back to put the CIA on task to capture Marissa. Only some people were captured forcefully. Marissa was persuaded gently to meet Plumbel without even knowing that her enticers were from CIA. It was an attractive meeting full of promises of a bright future. There was no advertisement for job and no application. There was no shortlisting.

Rustler was very angry when Plumbel told him that he went personally to the Native region of the United States of America in order to recruit Marissa for the next mission to PlanetB2. He lived in constant threat of everyone around him. The threat came from inside. He thought that all his threats were outside of him. He could not trust even his most trustworthy colleague. Nay, indeed he did not have any colleague. He only had subjects. No, subject is a gross misnomer. He only had objects.

Plumbel knew the nature of the most powerful man in the world. He knew that Rustler had the power either to make or to destroy the world at his whims and fancies. But he also knew that Rustler's power was his weakness. The power of the President of the US made him one of the weakest persons in the world. Plumbel empathized with Rustler often and he also sympathized with his President occasionally. It was this empathy that kept him together with Rustler.

"How can you go and recruit a Native American girl on your own without even discussing the matter with me? You know well that on this one mission I want you to discuss every letter with me. This is our most ambitious project and only both of us know how much we work towards its success through our darkroom strategies. At least now tell me why you did this. I like to know the reason." Rustler would have just dismissed from service anyone else who behaved the way Plumbel behaved. It was not a strategy that he employed to preserve his services. It was simply his helplessness that compelled him to pretend to Plumbel as a friend. If it were anybody else Rustler would have pumped him off through his CIA agents by then.

"Yes, I should have discussed the matter with you before I ventured out to the Native American land. However, I wanted to first study the issue and only then have I come to speak to you about the need for recruiting this girl, Marissa. My reasons are very simple. You know well that the only woman who has survived in PlanetB2 is from the Native American community. Our first mission failed without the world noticing it. Though we know that Carolina lives in PlanetB2 our communication with her has stopped suddenly. It will be important for the success of our project to send once again in our next mission another Native American girl and see if she would be the only one to survive. If she survives then we can draw our conclusions that survival in PlanetB2 will have something to do with what is common with both of them. This commonality between both of them will have to be researched thoroughly in order to ultimately succeed in our mission to PlanetB2."

"Yes, your idea sounds brilliant. I agree with your logic and allow you to continue to do things in the lines that you have pursued till now. Yes, keep in mind that you need to inform me of your every decision and step related to this project. It is simply not a project. It is my dream for America. It is my dream for the world. America should lead the way for a prosperous world. This is my promise that we will succeed." Rustler became emotional whenever he spoke to Plumbel of the greatness that he wanted to achieve for America. He sprinkled his love for America with adequate pegs of whisky. When the ratio of intake of whisky was high it was difficult to tell whether he loved America more than himself or him more than America. But whisky did have a say in his pronouncements. Rustler rustled more with more whisky.

Plumbel was happy that he obtained the much-needed approval for his plans even if it was blended well with whisky. "Bring the girl to me. I also want to talk to her before she goes for your regular interview." Rustler did not want to leave anything to chance. He wanted to be in personal command over everything that took place vis-à-vis PlanetB2.

"I have not yet talked to the girl. The CIA has brought her to a secluded place and is talking to her. When they bring her back with a basket-full of information both of us can speak to her together. Only after that let us introduce the processes for her commitment to our project." Plumbel wanted to put Rustler in comfort, as he did not have any hidden agenda. He simply loved Rustler, as they were close friends from college days and Rustler singled him out to be his close confidante. Between friends many idiosyncrasies were easily ignored. Plumbel also enjoyed the special informal status he was given as the person next to the President in American policy making. But Plumbel and Rustler carefully avoided getting Plumbel entangled in the murky affairs of American politics only to safeguard the success of PlanetB2.

The informal interview of Marissa was a preaching by Rustler on the need for being a true American in spirit and commitment to the cause of greatest America that would overpower the Universe in the best interest of America. Plumbel did not speak a word to Marissa. Nor was there any chance for her to speak. It was a big mystery for her about the man sitting in total silence only listening to the preaching of Rustler, the President of the United States of America. Rustler also informed her that Plumbel would give her all details of her actual job and future mission. He also insisted on the need to keep everything in secret about her work. Both Rustler and Plumbel understood that they had to inject indoctrination to her on a regular slow motion style lest she rebelled and decided to leave. It was a tradition in America. The newly recruited soldiers in the army were first indoctrinated thoroughly to believe that America was the top priority for American soldiers and that they should do everything that they did on order blindly.

At the end of the conversation Rustler sprang a surprise to his two listeners. He apologized for all that had happened to 'her' people in the hands of the invading Europeans. Hearing this Marissa put her head down and ruminated over all that happened to her people in a flash of a second. There was a strong rebellion in her body and she became hot and red all over. But she had learned from her father already in early childhood the art of beautifully blending her emotions with her rationality without allowing anyone of them to take control over the other. She came back to her normal self much before Rustler and Plumbel noticed changes in her body. Plumbel thought that it was unnecessary on the part of Rustler to have added this note of apology, as it was evident from his tone of speech that Rustler did not let his heart out but only his words apologized. He was more focused on this strategically pretentious side of Rustler and failed to notice that Marissa's body rejected all sorts of pretensions instantaneously. Appeasing the victim, a stereotyped strategy of the ruling class!

❧❀❧   ❧❀❧   ❧❀❧

Plumbel led Marissa gently out of the door and took full charge of her. That was a bit automatic without any formal introduction. The CIA personnel who took Marissa to Rustler had by then disappeared with only a paper trail. They had been untypically nice to her, as they had a heavy load of instructions from Plumbel to handle the girl with care. He introduced himself to Marissa as the one who would be fully in charge of her and her work. He made it clear that from then on there was not a big distinction between her self and her work. He had by then mastered a few delicate ways of handling indigenous people. He read a lot about their psyche, the Black people's psyche and also the European ways. He put things across to Marissa in a very spiritual way and she began to look up to him as a father figure though he had not graduated as a shaman yet. The freight that enveloped her while in the secret place of CIA now gave way to the slow emergence of confidence in Plumbel. However, it was not organic like that of the evolution of larva from egg, cocoon from larva and the development of fully-grown butterfly from cocoon. The artificiality of confidence building was evident. Marissa had to go a long way to transform her confidence into trust. She felt all her body cells being liberated from an unknown shackle as soon as she left the meeting room of Rustler.

Plumbel was not in a hurry to mold Marissa into anything according to his design. He knew that he had to take her time and his time to shape her. He did not want to threaten Marissa with many serious things to come except communicating to her that she should be prepared well to fare successfully in the interview. He also revealed to her that she would be on a mission to another planet if she succeeded in her interview. Marissa liked the idea of going to another planet, as did her friend Carolina.

"Which planet will you be sending me to? Is it the moon?" It was a full moon day. Marissa could have glimpses of the moon through thin clouds that draped the moon. She always thought that she was ugly and tried to hide her face with thick clouds. Now that Marissa was looking at her intently she started playing hide and seek with her through the clouds. Marissa always thought that her grandmother moon was a scintillatingly beautiful woman and always liked her. The glow on the face of moon increased multifold. Marissa wanted to touch her grandma one day and sleep on her lap.

"No, not to the moon. As you know, the moon has become our neighbor. We are still looking for ways of settling human beings on moon. However, our scientists have not yet succeeded. They are still groping in the dark. Look today is full moon and the world is supposed to have bright light. But in our country we are still in the grip of darkness, as the clouds hide the true glory of moon to our naked eyes. Dark clouds hover over our sky and let the moon hide herself from us completely even on a day like this." Plumbel's blabbering reminded Marissa of how her father used to lament to her about the injustice done to her grandmother, the moon by the way the world was treating her.

"Then are you going to send me to Mars?" Marissa tried to pull his legs even in that serious moment. Plumbel perceived it as her eagerness to touch another planet at the earliest possible time. He could not get any joke right at any time. His association with Rustler from his college days made him to look at only the serious side of anything and any situation. Neither he would enjoy a joke nor he would allow anyone to enjoy a joke by converting it into a serious discussion.

"Oh child, we have already landed several times in Mars and are organizing space voyages for tourists. There are millions of people all over the world who have applied to go to Mars. Why would I want to send you to a planet about which we already know? I want to send you to a planet that we have not yet landed. Our scientists are working on it. We have discovered a planet with life and someone must go and explore all that lives in that planet. You have been handpicked by me for this mission." Plumbel narrated to her all that transpired from his research to her selection as the star of the mission to PlanetB2. He started preparing this star slowly for the most important mission. He was deeply aware that it was a do or die mission for Rustler his friend.

Marissa wanted to raise the next logical question that spontaneously sprang from her heart. But then she saw that they had arrived at a grand looking house with bright light inside and dimly lit outside. The huge Chevrolet landed smoothly in front of the house with its four tyres rolling out a red carpet for her and coming to a halt to make her alight from the belly of the car. On both sides of the road leading to his house there were many trees making the place look like a mini forest. The deer that were lying down and ruminating over their hard work during the day got up when the light of the car flashed on to their eyes. They were quite used to light flashing on them but they did not like it focused on to their eyes. That day was special. They stood up and saluted the new guest in their premises. The way they got up and saluted her looked as if they had done a rehearsal of what they should do when their esteemed guest arrived.

Plumbel was used to their presence as much as they were used to the untimely arrival of people in their vicinity. But he was dumbfounded at what followed. Deer on both sides started moving towards the car. It was very unusual. He stood still even as the deer started moving towards the car. He had never seen them doing that. "They are wild deer. They live in this forest. Be careful. They have seen people but not so near. He thought the deer moved closer menacingly with their wild horns. He pulled out the gun from inside his dress revealing a weakness for the first time to Marissa. She stood still with a large smile on her face. The deer reciprocated her gesture and went near her body. She understood what they were up to. She stretched out her hand and caressed them gently on their head. They were meek and not wild as Plumbel made a picture of them. One after another they came to Marissa and took a share of caressing from her. Marissa caressed at least six of them and they were waiting there still surrounding her with love and affection. She began to speak to them while keeping her hand on one of them. Plumbel had only studies about shamanism. But now he saw it in operation.

"Now go back friends. Go and sleep. We shall meet tomorrow. I shall be here for a few days and we shall have a lot of time to meet one another." But they would not move an inch. Marissa moved into the house along with Plumbel turning backward and glancing at all the deer that still kept looking at her. She waved her hand to all of them when she entered the house and Plumbel shut the door. "Lovely beings. I love these animals." Marissa mumbled loud enough for her words to pierce the ears of Plumbel. He got a point for the future.

"So you love animals. They seem to love you more." Plumbel started the conversation with Marissa while handing over a glass of red wine to her. Both of them had gone into their rooms, had a wash, changed their clothes and sat for a drink. Just before Marissa went to her room, Plumbel enquired if she preferred white wine or red. "Very nice" Marissa said aloud as she took the first sip of wine. He looked at her face and made sure it was genuine. For the first time Marissa saw a glimpse of what looked like a smile on his face. "At last" she thought to herself about the man who began to matter a little in her life. His smile was like the 'Kurinchi' flower that blossoms once in twelve years only in Kodaikanal of South India.

"Yes, animals and plants have been a very important part of my life. It is not I alone. Almost all members of my community grew up with animals and plants as part of the family, part of the community. We have been part of the universe in which they live. It is they who accept us as part of their family. We have never tried to establish our superiority over them. The land, the forests, the rivers, the oceans, the mountains, everything on this universe belongs to them. We own none of them. In our community we consider that we belong to land and all that lives in it." Marissa let out much more information than Plumbel asked for. His container began to be filled to the brim.

"I could see how you relate to animals. I am sorry. Actually I saw how they relate to you. It is wonderful. I wish I were so close to all living beings. But I have been trained to look at everything in life from a dominant male point of view. I belong to a culture that believes that we are here to master over everything in nature. I like the way you and the deer communicated to one another. Let us go out and relive that experience." He held the hands of Marissa and led her out of the house. The deer were still standing there without going for their usual chewing over. They had positioned themselves all around the house so that whoever spotted Marissa first would communicate her location to others and they would rush to have one last look at her. They were totally surprised by seeing Marissa and her friend. They assembled together from their strategic positions that were rendered irrelevant now by both of them coming out of the house. She put out her hands and invited them. They moved towards her. Plumbel put out his hands too. They hesitated a lot before one of them took the lead to touch his hand. He caressed. The others did not seem to be interested in him. After much trial and tribulation two more deer moved closer to him and accepted his caress.

Marissa was very happy and put her hand up in sheer excitement. Plumbel enjoyed every moment of her excitement. He put his hand around her shoulders and she liked it. As they looked up with Marissa's extended arms they realized that the dark clouds had already given way to grandmother moon. They seemed to have anticipated the great expectation of Marissa and took a flight to unknown world. Grandmother moon was inundated with a galaxy of stars plunging her in a glittering ocean in the sky. With her hunchback grandma moon gave a big smile to Marissa with her wide opened mouth. It looked as if she was ever ready to devour all human beings who landed on her lap if they did not behave well. Marissa rotated her body three times in sheer excitement of seeing her grandma's big smile and remained with her arms spread out wide thinking that the ocean above would shower its blessings on her.

"See how all my ancestors are joyfully glittering at the sight of our grandma." She said sipping her wine. Plumbel took a sip from his glass without having a clue of what Marissa was talking about.

"Ancestors? What is this girl talking about? Is she a mad girl? Did I make a right choice? She seems to be quite abnormal." Plumbel gave a serious thought about the totally unexpected behavior of Marissa in his house.

"You did not make a mistake, Mr. Plumbel. Do not worry about me. I shall fulfill all your expectations." Marissa gave loud voice to her words. This is the assurance that Plumbel needed. He was at ease. The words clouded his face filled with stupefaction.

"Did you read my thoughts Marissa? Do you have any supernatural power to read peoples' mind?" Plumbel struggled hard to make out if he was surprised or shocked at the way she took his breath away by reading his thoughts without any spelling mistake.

"It is not any supernatural power. I do not know, to be frank, what power it is. I simply knew in my body what you thought. I heard it in my ears. This is what my father used to do. He could understand what other people thought before they said it in words. He had shamanic power."

"Oh, shamanic power. Yes I know what it is. I have heard about it from your community people. You people are greatly blessed. You live in close connection with all living beings. Tell me one thing. Can you read also the mind of animals? Do they think or are they guided only by their instincts?'

"Mr. Plumbel, you are a scientist of the first order. I am a budding scientist. We have a world of difference between us. All I can say is that the question should be different. We should ask if the animals can understand our thoughts and if we can hear our own thoughts adequately. But tell me when did you meet my people? I never knew this. Did you also meet my parents?" Marissa was a bundle of mixed excitement that slowly turned into butterflies in her stomach.

"Yes, my understanding of you people, the Native Americans went through a radical transformation after I met your father. He does not know that I am a space scientist. He only knows me as a researcher. That was my little ploy to make your people speak to me from their depths. I could understand that your father was not convinced of my self-introduction as a researcher. I spoke to your father in general that I would take you in the government service in space stations. He agreed very skeptically. I wondered why there was that big skepticism on his face at such big good news. Now I know why. Perhaps your father read my mind and knew that I was lying about my research." Plumbel was also excited with a free flow of wine and beer.

"Don't underestimate my father. He probably knows everything about your plans. But he may not have said anything to you about it in order not to hurt you. We are also generally hesitant to show off our capacities and knowledge to unknown visitors." Hearing this from Marissa Plumbel's anxiety began to take the shape of jitters in his raw nerves. He gave a lame excuse to go inside the house only to come back a little later after wiping all traces of sweat from his forehead and face. He hardly imagined that Marissa knew his sweat much before it started smelling.

"Hey there, be careful with that bear. It is a dangerous animal. It has bitten a few people in the vicinity. What are you doing with that wretched creature?" Plumbel was quite disturbed at the way Marissa was feeding that black bear with honey taken from the kitchen. He got up much later than she did and did not have the foggiest idea of what she was doing. She went out to have her talk with deer. But they had gone for grazing. In came a bear. He was moving about freely searching for some food. Marissa went for her early morning discussion with nature. She touched all the trees and could see that they started giggling and dancing at her unexpected touch. Everyone in the world treated them as 'non-beings'. At last they were happy that they found one of their sisters who treated them for what they were worth. Amidst the trees was the bear that began to walk with her. She put her hands out for him and he reciprocated the same. They shook hands in the western style. Marissa shook his hands more than what a normal westerner would do. The bear liked it much and he ran two wild rounds in that place in total excitement. When he came back she hugged him and kissed him. That was when Plumbel came into the picture. He was a bundle of nerves with total surprise and shock. He ran for his gun. As he picked up his gun he realized that both actually loved each other and there was no threat to anyone of them. However, as a routine security measure he tucked his gun inside his trousers. The look on the face of the bear almost asked him to fuck the gun.

Marissa turned towards him slowly and said: "He is my brother. How will he ever harm me? My people worship him as one of our ancestors. He can only wish everything good for me and not harm me at all. Come here Mr. Plumbel. I shall introduce you to my brother. Come near. Do not fear. He is a good fellow." Plumbel moved near her slowly totally perplexed as to what was going on in his place. She asked him to touch the bear's silky fur. But he desisted. Then he informed her that he knew a Native American five kilometers from there who lived among such bears and wolves. Every day morning he used to feed them. He refused to meet any human beings. People could only see him from a distance and not go near him at all. They were afraid on the one hand and surmised on the other hand that he would chase them away. Then Marissa reminded him that being one with animals and trees was not any weird behavior among her people. It was just normal for them. Plumbel was convinced now that his picture of Marissa as a weird person was wrong. He began to develop the thought that perhaps he was weird to be associating himself only with human beings and robots.

Plumbel had spread out a sumptuous breakfast. It was his habit to have a good breakfast. He knew that he would have to skip lunch often in the thick of diplomatic and scientific action in the space station. Dinner often was more ceremonial than enjoyable. Life was hectic once he got into it. He warned Marissa about what could happen that day. He had a plan to take her into the space station to give her a first hand knowledge of different things that were taking place in that unique place in the world. She was excited to hear of that plan. He began to realize a strange feeling within him. He began to like Marissa immensely. Was it love of a man to a woman? She was young enough to be his daughter. Was it that immense concern that he had for her future? Why should he? Was it his desire to fulfill all the ambitions of Rustler who wanted to overcome the cosmos? He just dismissed the questions and began to be free with her. She took it well as her body did not feel any repulsion to him. She listened more to her body than she listened to Rustler and Plumbel.

CHAPTER FIVE

"Rustler has said that you need not go through the regular interview and selection process to become part of the American space mission. I have convinced him that you are a very suitable person to join the team that will take out the next mission to PlanetB2. It is our most decisive mission." Plumbel put himself up in a pedestal convincing Marissa of her special position in his heart and designs of work. She liked it much.

"Oh thank you Mr. Plumbel. I feel very privileged. So, what do I do next?" Marissa was quite casually formal in her reply. She was more focused on the amazing inside of the space station. People there were moving around fast no one talking to another. Everyone wore a serious looking face and a smile was hard to come for the passers by. They did not even bother to know who was crossing them. There was a frightening silence in that place where hundreds of scientists and computer personnel worked. All communications were digital. Marissa was awestruck at that mechanical communication. But that seemed to work in that place. Indeed anything that seemed to work there was mechanical.

"Our next space mission to PlanetB2 will start in a few months and you have to peak for it fully at the ripe time. In a few days you will go into a special world that will prepare you to be fully fit for the mission. Once you go in there you cannot communicate with anyone outside that small little place. It will be a totally self-sufficient place. Till then you will stay with me." Plumbel now began to reveal more and more of what was in store for Marissa.

"Why do you say that I cannot communicate with anyone outside that small place? Does no one know about what we shall be doing there? Why such secrecy?" Marissa began to be equal to him.

"Well, you will know everything when you go inside. For the time being please be sure that no harm will come to you. I am much interested in you. I shall not allow any harm to come to you from anyone. This is a promise. When I am with you I have that special inexplicable feeling of comfort. This is something totally new to me. You seem to have become part of my world." He began to open up at a very personal level in the most unsuitable place.

"Why do you think I have been following you without much argumentation? It is because I also have total trust in your goodness. The waves that come to me from you communicate an essential goodness about you. I have accepted you as my father. Therefore, let us enjoy that freedom." Plumbel was a bit overwhelmed when he heard this from the mouth of Marissa. He grabbed her with both his hands and kissed her on both the cheeks. She returned the compliment in true American style that she picked up in New York.

"Why is it that you have waived the formal interview for me. I know your level of confidence in me. But I do not think it can be adequate excuse to skip such an important formality in this mission. I am just curious to know what makes you waive the procedures in my case. Will not the President find fault with you about this preferential treatment that you have meted out to me?" Marissa now began to dig deep into the plots.

"The President is fully aware of this decision. Indeed he is the one who took this decision to waive all procedures in your case. It is simply because this space mission to PlanetB2 is his personal plan and insatiable ambition. The President feels that not all the selectors will be able to vibe with his ambition fully as almost all of them do not know his secret plans. I am the only one to whom he confides on this special mission. We have chosen you precisely because you are from the Native American community. It is also because you are the daughter of a shaman. I have done some researches on the effect of shamanism in human beings and understand that you are a perfect fit for this mission. However, there will be other companions of yours who will not be shamans. All of them will be from the topmost scientific family of the US. You will be known as Awesome7. The space shuttle that you will travel in will be known as Bigbelly4. All of you are expected to keep absolute secret of whatever you do. This is a supreme order from the President of the US." Plumbel gave her a summary of the speech he or Rustler would give to Awesome7 at the beginning of their mission.

Marissa had other concerns. "Plumbel, from the time I came to your house I have a strange communication in my body from my cousin Carolina whom you took into your service for space missions. She seems to be communicating something to me but I do not know what exactly it is. I only have an unknown communication from her. It chills my body. Is she also in that secret place where you are going to put me in for the next mission?" She almost threw a cluster bomb on the head of Plumbel. He held his head together with both his hands lest it shattered to too many pieces.

Of all the things that took place between them this was the most unexpected question from his daughter. In the beginning he fumbled in his reply. Marissa could immediately perceive his perplexity and knew there was some shrouding of certain truth about Carolina. She tried to put him at ease by apologizing for asking that question and asking him not to speak about it if it were still a secretly kept truth. But Plumbel recovered like the basketball player who gets up as soon as he falls. Otherwise his team would lose another basket perhaps. It was a quick reflex and not a conscious decision. The more a player is blessed with quick reflexes the better is his game. Rustler had such political quick reflexes, quicker than all of the people living in America. Plumbel had his share of quick reflexes in the field of science.

"I must tell you the true truth about your cousin Carolina. For us she was just another very important astronaut in the Awesome6. This was how the previous team was known that went to PlanetB2. Your cousin did not return to the earth after the shuttle landed in PlanetB2." . . . .

"What? Did America already land in PlanetB2 as you call it? Why does the world not know of it? None of us know about this great success of America. Did Carolina perish in the space mission? What happened to her?" Marissa pleaded with him.

"On the contrary. She is the only one who has survived in the mission. All other astronauts of Awesome6 have perished. Despite all our mechanical excellence we do not know where the shuttle and the inmates perished leaving only Carolina in PlanetB2. We used to receive feeble communications from her as long as her space suit remained with her. But soon she got out of it and the suit just disappeared. We do not know what has happened to her after that. But we are sure she lives there as we could see her moving about for a few more months even after her suit disappeared. Now we can only see the beings moving about in that planet and are unable to make out who among them is Carolina." Plumbel sounded quite serious and sad when he narrated this to Marissa. There was a lingering fear in him that he spilled the beans in front of her too early. 'Will she take her steps back?' was what was constantly transpiring in his muddled head.

There was a long silence, a very long one. A few drops of tears from the eyes of Marissa finally broke it. She felt the physical loss of her cousin deeply. Plumbel went near her and put his hands around her shoulders as a mark of his outreach to console her. "Both the President and I did not expect Awesom6 to fail. That is why the President did not prepare a team in advance to take up the next mission to PlanetB2. When Awesome5 failed he had already prepared Awesome6 even without informing me. But now we are scrambling all over the place for people who will dare to take up this mission. That Carolina manages to live in PlanetB2 raised the suspicion in me that it must be because of her shamanic body. That is why I took up a visit to your people even without discussing with Rustler. After meeting you I am feeling awesomely sure that your love for animals and plants, your ability to communicate to beings in a totally different way may have something to do with the beings in PlanetB2. The success of this mission depends entirely on you. I have reposed my full faith in you and shall do everything possible to make you succeed. Your success will be my success and my success will be your success. Ultimately it will be the success of America." His loyalty to Rustler and America was unquestionable. It was a huge change that he began to like someone for the first time in his life on his own.

It was like a biological bomb and a nuclear bomb dropped together on the people of America. The entire citizenry of America and of the world woke up to the news of America's mission to PlanetB2. Rustler had made a formal announcement of the news that he had kept close to his chest for a long time. Even Plumbel never expected such a bombshell. He felt like being in Hiroshima and Nagasaki immediately after the nuclear blast. Rustler announced it with an arrogance that was normally associated with him. He acknowledged that the mission to PlanetB2 was a temporary failure because of human and mechanical issues that could be rectified in the future missions. The enormity of the voyage to the planet demanded careful planning and even a small miscalculation could misfire the entire mission. He also acknowledged that the billions of dollars spend on the mission was taken out of the American treasury without appropriate procedures. It was done mainly because he did not want to reveal the finer and technical details of the mission to public knowledge. Any discussion in the Senate on the budgetary demand would make an untimely exposure of the mission to international forces. He asserted that Americans would not be cowed down by such failures and promised the nation that the next mission to PlanetB2 would become a roaring success.

It did not take much time for Rustler to realize the ineluctability of compulsive politics in America. In normal times his charisma would work wonderfully. But when elections drew near he knew that the Republicans would take out all the skeletons from his cupboard and expose him to the public. Then his charisma would begin to wane. He knew the compulsions of American democracy. Yet he did not want to discuss the matter with anyone including his confidante Plumbel.

The biggest compulsion however and the vulnerability of the President of America was the budget. He had already spent thousands of billions of dollars towards the failed project. If he had to spend more money without formal approval of the American Senate he would be exposed. He also needed a reason to transfer the failure to another body in American politics. Finally if he failed he should not be blamed. He would take only success and had to pass on the failures. If his plans backfired he could always put the blame on the Senate and American space scientists.

Revelation of the mission to PlanetB2 had to be timed well. He had to fabricate adequate reasons for the people of America to celebrate and not mourn over the failure of their President. Therefore, he found that the revelation of the lone survivor in the Planet was the most opportune moment to let the cat out of the bag. Such timely revelation would boost his political image among the naïve American voters and nullify the attempts of critical rivals. Plumbel had a serious puncture in his heart that his friend for whom he was throwing in the wind all his personal aspirations did not care to discuss such an important strategy in US history with him. He tried to plug the hole and it was hard doing it. Marissa felt quite helpless in such top level politicking in the US.

Newspapers all over the US wrote all sorts of stories fabricated out of their wildest imagination that had very little to do with truth. They said everything bordered on some truths about the all-important mission but failed to touch the core. The American public dismissed their critical surmises as the usual business of American media. However, they too liked the gossip that newspapers and TV channels churned out everyday. Hollywood was already at serious work to explore the possibility of making a movie out of the failure of the mission to PlanetB2.

The discovery of PlanetB2 fascinated the people of the US. They pushed aside the failure of the mission with the strong hope that Rustler dared to do things and that he would dare to succeed. With such euphoria surrounding their American psyche they were ready to put the impropriety of not going through legal processes down their feet and crush it. That psyche lent a lot of support to the charisma of the President. He might have done something wrong. But no one wanted to question his love for America and its people. They wanted to make sure that he understood their unstinted love for him and insoluble hope in him.

Sales of alcohol and food reached dizzy heights in pubs and departmental stores in the US and UK. There was marginal increase of the same all over Europe. People started celebrating everywhere. Not many even bothered about the fact that two of the previous missions had failed and that there was no guarantee about the success of the next mission. They were getting ready to pay a hike in their taxes only in order to take pride in the fact that they belonged to a nation that achieved what was impossible for many other countries. The US Senate met together and gave Rustler a special recognition for his achievements in space technology. The Nobel Prize for science and technology was awarded to Rustler for his singular success in space missions. The Nobel Prize Committee hardly took five minutes to deliberate the pros and cons, merits and demerits of the awardee only because he was the President of the US. Many in the Republican Party admired Rustler's capacity to turn an apparent failure into a story of success in his favor. The Senate approved all future projects related to PlanetB2 in terms of both finances and decision-making. The latter was what Rustler needed.

The international media eulogized the great courage of the American people to have paid so much of tax as to make any such mission affordable. They highlighted the discovery of PlanetB2 as a mark of history. They also appreciated the technological superiority of the US in tracing movement of strange beings in the planet. They had no words to explain the discovery of movement of these strange beings in a strange planet. Above all they were mesmerized by the fact the America succeeded in landing one of its women astronauts on PlanetB2. According to them it was then only a question of time for America to hoist its flag in the planet. Taxpayers in America went crazy and ran amuck in the streets of New York, Los Angeles, Washington DC, and Detroit etc. They imagined that they would soon become masters of the universe. What was seen as an unachievable illusion now was at their reach.

There were also the serious left wing intellectuals in the media who were terribly critical of the capitalist march of America towards the destruction of the world. There was no dearth of prophets of doom who reaped a rich harvest in the disasters of the world. They analyzed threadbare the deteriorating situation of the working class in American industries and the increase in the levels of poverty and homelessness within the richest nation in the world. They exposed the weaknesses of American ruling class in sucking the blood of the common people through an exorbitant tax regime.

The poor were unable to afford to live in the US. One of the most ironic cartoons presented a huge spacecraft called Bigbelly and a homeless poor American hanging with a thin thread on its tail. The cartoon said clearly "Proud to be American".

The Prime Minister of India was the first one to call up Rustler on his hotline and congratulate him. Rustler invited him to the US and the PM of India accepted the invitation without any hesitation. It looked as if he was always at the beck and call of the US President. But the PM of India legitimized it by saying that it was the unflinching love of the people of India to the President of the US. So did the PM of Pakistan. Later he was disappointed that the PM of India outwitted him. Rustler also understood that Pakistan became increasingly sluggish in its relationship with US. But then he welcomed this lethargy of Pakistan, as India was a better bet for American trade. He had many other Islamic nations to support him blindly and hardly needed Pakistan as a strategic partner any more. The European Union was quick enough to call for a meeting of the European Parliament and pass a resolution appreciating the great effort of Rustler. The German Chancellor headed the European Union at that time. Britain refused to join the efforts of the European Union. Instead it brought together Canada, Australia and New Zealand and many other suzerainties of Britain from Africa, Asia and Latin America and passed another resolution in appreciation of Rustler. Russia, China, Vietnam and surprisingly the Scandinavian countries decided to keep their wisdom to themselves. They neither appreciated nor condemned the efforts of Rustler. India's close neighbor, the only Hindu nation in the world refused to be dragged into this affair. Rustler called up the Secretary of State and asked her to keep a close watch on countries and observe the aftermath of his revelation to the world. CIA was put on extra alert so that no international spies could even dream of reaching the space station of the US.

"Will I be perched high above in the sky like one of those stars?" Marissa talked to herself in the hearing of Plumbel.

"Of course you will be passing through many of them to reach PlanetB2. This planet that we try to occupy is also a big star. It must be one of your big ancestors waiting for you. I wish that day came sooner than we expected. Please keep sending me messages when you reach PlanetB2. I cannot think of losing communication with you. Being with you and communicating with you fills me with a new type of energy." Plumbel did not have a clue to the emotions that sprang from his body so spontaneously. He was unable to contain his love for the little girl in front of him. However, it was the constellation of stars that kept winking their eyes at Marissa after listening to the innocent love moorings of Plumbel.

"I shall be the most privileged person to pass through the galaxy of my ancestors there. Oh, may be my cousin Carolina has already done that. I shall be the second one to live amidst my ancestors." The emotions that were bottled up began to ooze out of Marissa slowly.

Plumbel was completely bamboozled at the type of personality that was walking along with him in the woods around his house that evening in a relaxed mood after a heavy day of work and discussions. It was a different world. When she got out Marissa seemed to enter a world of her own, a world to which he did not have even a clue. He could never open this world. She had the key and she held the right to enter her world. "We call them stars. You call them ancestors. What kind of a person are you Marissa? You seem to see everything differently from what the rest of the world sees. Are you weird or are we weird? What you say is Greek to me often."

"It is not that any of us is weird. It is simply that we have different belief systems. We are sure that all our ancestors are perched in the cosmos as stars and other celestial bodies. We keep communicating with them and they do the same with us. It is not that you are incapable of that. It is simply because you grew up in a different cultural and religious milieu that cells in your body are not open to receive such ancestral waves. You are more tuned to believing in a bodiless supreme being called god. For us it is a weird thing. I would ask how could anyone without a body receive waves from the cosmos? We would laugh at the way you worship an idea that you have created. But can anyone shake your faith in god? We are just different." Marissa proved to be much deeper in her perception of the world than he presumed her to be.

"Yes. I am more inclined to agree with you. Do you realize that it is because I find a value in your value system that I chose you for this impossible mission? But look at this Rustler. He does not trust any human being and he takes refuge in his trust in god. It seems to be a self-serving faith. I hate his ways. I like his ambition as the President of the US. But it is very difficult for me to accept the way he treats his most trusted friend as shit. Look at the way we Europeans have butchered you people, million of peoples of the First Nations. Look at the way we have enslaved the Black people. Look at the way we are starving millions of poor in the world. How can our faith in god be legitimate?" Plumbel started pouring out his frustration in front of the girl who was his apprentice.

"Yes, I can see that you are very different from your friend. Your upbringing must be very different from his. There may be many cluster of cells in your body that open up for cosmic waves. This may be one of the reasons why you had a natural inclination to think that the survival of Carolina in PlanetB2 might be because she belongs to the indigenous community. You are a blessing to America. But you will be despised by 'Americans' for trying to save America in the way you believe they should be saved. This is not going to be easy for you. It will be still a big struggle for you. There will be an internal conflict between the values that you have imbibed from your upbringing and the values that may enter your body cells and work in your subconscious." Marissa now started to become the teacher of Plumbel.

"Marissa, Marissa, where are you?" With a torch in his hand Plumbel was beside himself in search of Marissa in the woods. His heart was throbbing hundred times faster than it normally should. At night he had taken a little more peach schnapps than necessary. His tummy had its own dance of joy in a pool of the exuberant visitor. He got up to take some digestive. Seeing the doors of Marissa's room wide open he took a peep. Her bed was empty. He knocked at the door of the rest room. There was no response. He became panicky and opened the bathroom in a hurry. She was not there. He gave a few mild shouts within the house. All the rooms in his house were giving out a wild look at him. Armed with his weapons he dared to venture into the woods in search of his beloved. It was not yet a Bollywood love story, the girl hiding herself among trees and her lover in frantic search of her. Finally she runs from tree to tree and he embraces the trunk of the tree in an apparent effort to catch her body. Plumbel belonged to the Hollywood culture. He measured his steps one by one to see if he could at least see a piece of her corpse left over by wild animals that could have pulled her body out of her room.

For the first time in his life he became panicky. He did not understand this dimension of his personality. Why was he in so much love with this little girl? She was not old enough to be his girlfriend. He checked his heart. In any case one of his hands was on his chest, on the side that his heart was supposed to be. It was still throbbing for her. He tried to identify something carnal in his love for her. There was nothing of that kind. He pinched himself to make sure that he was not infatuated with her. He simply loved her without knowing in his conscious why he loved her. It was different. He knew it. Only for sometime! As the intensity grew he lost the desire to know anything of it. He just wanted to live in that state of bliss. It was like having a full body orgasm always whenever he realized that she lived deep inside him. He had an irresistible urge to share this with Marissa the next day. He had decided to do that. It was then that she disappeared from his home.

He had fixed his powerful torch on his forehead in order to search for her. It was pitch dark over there. Deer stood still at the brightness of the light. They did not know how to react to such powerful light that pierced their eyes. They were unperturbed by his anxiety and were ruminating the gains of the day as they usually did. Loud and dark howling of foxes at distant places welcomed him wherever he went in search of Marissa. All beings in that forest knew that there was an unwelcome movement in their world. They alerted all their friends. Only the bats and owls seemed to be dancing in the dark. They fumbled to find their way at the splash of light on their path. Nocturnal animals! The beings that defiled the logic of man who could not have normal life without light! It was a knee jerk reaction that came without his deciding to react that way. His hands went as if by a fast reflex to hide the brightness of the light on his forehead. A big bat had struck his forehead as if to remind him that the torch did not belong to that world. It fell on the earth for a while and flew away as a nocturnal Indian bride who fled from her newly wed bridegroom. She would only go near him if he put off the light and pulled her to himself. She waited for it. But not the bat! Plumbel had no clue where it flew away.

Not being nocturnal Plumbel scrambled around with the help of the big torch on his forehead. He wanted to shout aloud to Marissa but he was frightened of awakening ferocious animals around. He was still thinking of the bat and planted his legs firmly in a quagmire tilting his balance. Fortunately for him it was not deep. However, he slipped and fell backward and got up as fast as he fell. It was against his prestige and position to slip and fall. Even before he regained his balance his hands went automatically to his ass in order to wipe off the wet mud that stuck to his pants. He regained his balance with much difficulty keeping his legs firmly in the depth of the quagmire. Very instinctively he looked around to see if anyone watched him falling down. Only when he looked up he realized that it was still dark and that no normal human being would venture out at that part of the night in an area surrounded by all sorts of animals.

That instinct was very productive. At a distance in the banks of the big pool of water he found a human being sitting silently without any movement of the body. He rubbed his eyes to see if he was seeing an illusion with his naked eyes. That spontaneous feeling deep inside his body became familiar. All anxiety and fear were gone. He began to experience that full body orgasm that was inseparably associated with his experience of his beloved Marissa. He knew that it could not be anyone but Marissa. She did not show any body motion to have noticed his presence. She seemed to be deeply absorbed in her own world of interiority. No light and sound could disturb her serenity. Her feminine beauty did have its stirring effect on his manly desires. Her long hair shining at the flash of the torchlight made her face radiant as an angel. He could only see the pictures of angels when he was young and went to church holding the fingers of his mother. Now he saw one for real. Gone were the illusions of angels from his memory. Her young breasts protruding straight through her transparent nightdress invited his gaze to both of them. They vied with each other to grab his attention. Her nipples on both breasts seemed to be ready to pierce his carnal flesh and make deep inroads into his heart. The curve in her hip mesmerized him. He had never seen woman so beautiful in her hips. Marissa was a special production from nature. She had not worn anything to cover her legs inside her nightie even in that cold wind that was rushing to have a taste of her entire body. She seemed to be enjoying their caressing all over her body and hardly realized that they had provoked her nipples to stand erect. Her young breasts had not yet learned to be humble and bow down to any man. Her beautiful and shapely legs were like some of the wax statues taken out fresh from London Museum. It was like a flash of a moment. Plumbel put his one hand gently down to put at rest his cock that was ready to assert his presence violently to him. It obeyed.

"Hey Marissa, what is happening to you? Why are you here at this part of the night in such lonely place?" He shouted in her ears.

She was still motionless. The gentle breeze that was caressing her body soothingly was now getting excited and started playing truant with her dress. It slowly lifted the fringes of her dress and began to have a stealthy peep at her beautiful pussy. She had not worn her panties for the night and Plumbel could see her nakedness with his naked eyes. She was stunningly beautiful. His cock had already gone to sleep in the utter darkness of the night. He was shocked that he had no sexual feeling to her whatsoever and was wondering if he had become impotent all of a sudden. His cock used to be the first one to notice such things even before he could spread his eagle looks on the exposed portions of women's bodies. He gathered her dress and covered her waxy legs. They lent a lot of supportive side effects to her clean-shaven and comely pussy that was largely unused. She did not know that the breeze had played with her body and that Plumbel had prevented the breeze. He was not jealous of the breeze. But his traditional morality blinded his eyes to the openness she had to nature.

Seeing her completely motionless Plumbel took her hands gently in his. She raised her eyes towards him and smiled. The serenity in her eyes captivated him instantly. He looked at her even as she was looking into his eyes. He could not bear it and the darkness turned out to be his biggest rescuer. He sat near her with the comfort that she was still alive and was not yet devoured by some wild beast. The breeze rescinded feeling shy to paly with Marissa in the presence of a man. He understood that Marissa was deeply engrossed in something that looked like mysticism to him and did not want to disturb her further. It was enough for him that she was alive.

It took a neat 30 minutes for Marissa to come back to herself. When she opened her eyes on her own she realized that she was sitting with Plumbel. "Hey Plumbel, when did you come here?" she asked. He understood that she had not realized his shaking her body when she was in her trance.

"Just wake up Marissa. I should be asking you that question and I already asked you once loudly. When you came here is not the issue any more. Why did you come here in this part of the night all alone? Could you not call me to accompany you?" he asked in return.

She did not reply to him. She kept quiet and got up. She brushed her dress up in order to go with him. He realized that she was not yet fully ready to talk and bade his time. She held his hand firmly. They walked silently to his home. He made some coffee for her. Both of them sipped the aroma as well as the liquid of coffee taking their sweet time to bid good night to each other for the second time that night.

Lazy breakfast! That is how one could describe the breakfast both Plumbel and Marissa had. They were talking and eating, having fruit juice and coffee as and when they wished. Plumbel had decided not to go to the office that day. Marissa was happy that things were that easy. She needed to take her time to live with the full body orgasm that she had throughout the night. This was a different type of orgasm. It had nothing to do with her pussy. The body was much more than boobs and pussy. It was her existence.

"What happened last night Marissa? Why did you leave home in that pitch darkness? What were you doing the entire time all alone there?" Plumbel had a stream of questions welling up within him but he decided to let them out little by little lest they inundated his love Marissa towards suffocation.

"I am not sure if you will be able to understand. However, I shall try to explain to you what happened to me last night. I met Carolina." She said and looked at him. She was keen on watching his reactions in his body. Her looks pierced him and he felt thousand nails were thrust on his raw flesh all at once.

The ultimate bomb was thrown at him. He felt that all the bombs in the armory of the US were made into one huge bomb and was thrown at him. Pupils of both his eyes fled into the corners of his eyelids beyond which they could not run away. His brain said a good bye to him and went into a land of the unknown. All his reflexes ran helter-skelter defying the definition of reflex. Bones in his legs became as cool as ice cream, making him slump into the next available chair.

"Are you chocked Mr. Plumbel? Sometimes such shocks do choke some people. But there is nothing to be shocked. Please get up. I am here, your Marissa." She tried hard to pull him out of the quagmire that he plunged himself into.

He put out his hand to the extended arm of Marissa's and she literally pulled him out. A fragile young girl pulling out the bull that is ready for a fight in Spanish bullfight! He was more confortable now that he was pulled out of the swamp.

"How did she come to meet you? Why did she come without informing us and without even trying to contact us?" Plumbel was seriously disturbed and did not know what to say. His mind and mouth coordination failed him badly. He began to blabber without desiring to control his lips.

"I did not know how she came. All that I know is that I desired to meet her very intensely and there she was. I experienced full body orgasm as soon as she was with me. It was an inexplicable experience. No human words can adequately describe that experience."

"How did she come this far from the farthest PlanetB2? We spent such a lot of money to go there. Do they also have some spaceship as we have?" Plumbel gave expression to his inquisitiveness. That was his primary business. He wanted to extract information from Marissa despite all the love that he had for her. A crocodile hardly sheds it hide. She sat there as a virtual information bank. He wanted to invest his maximum on her. It was still very difficult for him to affirm whom he loved more. Was it Marissa or was it America? He oscillated hopelessly and helplessly between the two.

"Most of the cosmic beings living in PlanetB2 are our ancestors who have become cosmic beings through a process of entropy. They themselves do not have specific identities. However, it is sure that they are largely the thought and feeling waves of our ancestors. In this entropy process their waves merge with similar waves of many good-hearted people who lived through the different epochs of history in this world. When the entropy process intensifies they become cosmic beings reaching ultimately PlanetB2." Marissa shared with him what she understood from the communicative interaction she had with Carolina. Her inner being was filled with unconditional trust on Plumbel. This trust was part of her inner being and her becoming did depend much on the communicative interaction she established with other beings on earth.

Plumbel took careful mental note of all that Marissa said. Some of the things she communicated with him were totally new. He did not want to take notes in front of her lest she became apprehensive and constricted in her communication. Therefore, under the pretext of going for loo he switched on his powerful recording machine. His old habits hardly left him even with his most beloved girl. "But how did Carolina reach the earth. What was the mode of her transport back to the earth?" Plumbel manifested that he could not rise above certain level of understanding the indigenous worldview.

"She does not have a body like ours. She has a different body now, a body that is fabricated naturally out of intensive entropy of cosmic waves. As a positive and beautiful blend of cosmic waves she does not need any vehicle to come to the earth. All that she needs is an intensity of communication with earthly human bodies whose cells begin to open up for that type of communication through waves. If there is complete openness in the cell systems of earthly beings to the waves that emanate from her body, she naturally comes to merge with such bodies. Or if there were such a mystic human being who lives in bliss and his/her waves are able to reach the body of Carolina then she would come to that person. However, because of the limitations of human body that goes through metamorphosis the cosmic waves cannot remain in human body as static waves. Waves are essentially mobile. They live in communicative interaction. If there was not communication and perfect blending with cosmic movement and change they would cease to be cosmic beings in PlanetB2." Marissa became a philosopher of unknown kind to Plumbel. He tried his best to understand her philosophical side. He could not make head or tail out of what she said. He was used to a lifestyle wherein his machines did the job and later he would give it to his scientists for deciphering them. He would be a zero without his machines. Now there was this brilliance sitting in front of him without any machine.

"You have not yet told me how she came to meet you. How did she reach the earth?" Plumbel now became his true self and was trying to fix Marissa to certain focal points of information that he wanted to draw out from her. For him she was still his student by her position.

"You do not understand this. Carolina has become a cosmic being in PlanetB2. Only some beings can actually come to earth for such merger in human body for a short while. She does not need any vehicle to travel. She is the total amalgamation of waves and so when she establishes communicative interaction with a body on earth she is here the next moment. Distance is not a reality in space. There is no distance in space. Distance is a human creation." Once again Marissa was an embodiment of undecipherable philosophical complexities. But Plumbel got what he wanted.

"How did you reach that place at night in pitch darkness? Were you not afraid of the animals? Are you not afraid of darkness? Are you some sort of an abnormal freak? I love you much. But I need to understand you a lot more than I anticipated." Plumbel now began to manifest the other side of his personality. But Marissa was not on a mission to understand him. She was communicating with him even without understanding. She was in a different plane of communicative interaction with him. He had a long way up to be on par with her. He had not even become her student.

"She had come here to our house. She stood beside me and gently stroked me to wake me up. I got up and was dazed to see my cousin beside my bed. I embraced her and she began to lead me out of the house. We walked together." Marissa began to slowly unfold the midnight drama in the house of one who wanted to overcome the cosmos through machines.

"But I did not hear you talking to anyone."

"We did not have to talk to each other in human words. We began to communicate with each other through our body cells. Both of us were in a state of bliss, the full body orgasm. We found this concrete cover a bit uncomfortable in our communicative interaction. We naturally walked out into the woods without making a conscious decision about it." There was no way of stopping the flow of waves from the mouth of Marissa that came out in the form of human words. Plumbel liked it, as that is what he wanted.

"Did you take her out without offering her even a cup of coffee? Did you not offer her anything to eat?" Plumbel was naïve. It was difficult to say whether he was actually naïve or whether he pretended to be naïve.

Marissa laughed loud at such simplicity. "I told you that Carolina has become a cosmic being in PlanetB2. She does not need food like we need with a human body with its multiple needs, desires, avarice, greed and cruelty. She lives by communicative interaction. The cosmic beings, all of them live by their communicative interaction with one another. Their creative energy waves sustain them and they are indestructible."

"And how did she leave you? Will she come again to meet you? Did she leave you before I came? Was she there with you when I came? I would have loved to shake hands with her." Plumbel became once again an insecure bundle of confusions. If it were not for Marissa he would have been easily branded as a jughead.

Marissa liked the beauty of his communicative ways. He had no inhibitions with her. He did not care if he presented himself as a jackass or as the cleverest man on earth. He just was what he was and was very happy with him when he was with her. She became brighter on her face. "When did you come actually? I only know that she went back and when I came back to myself I was with you here in this house." Plumbel stitched the missing links by himself. Marissa did not know that she had walked back with him from the water body to the house. He liked to leave her in that state of forgetfulness. It was good for her not to know everything that happened to her that night. Whatever she remembered was already a churning ocean and Plumbel had to rescue himself from its whirlpool not to be drowned and lost.

CHAPTER SIX

It was a grand party never seen before. Rustler was not in the habit of organizing a party just before the launch of any space mission. But this one was different. He had put his every stake into it. This mission had to succeed. The two previous missions were in absolute surreptitiousness. But now Rustler was in a powerful position of holding the entire nation for ransom if the mission failed. The project PlanetB2 was now out in the open for the entire nation to croak about his uniqueness in history. He had convinced the nation that this mission must succeed in the best interest of the world and in the best interest of the US. All Americans believed sincerely that their President would pull off a neat scoop this time. All the bars and pubs in the US, UK and in many European nations made brisk business with people discussing and analyzing the possibilities and impossibility of Awesome7 landing successfully on PlanetB2. No one was ready to even imagine that America would fail this time after such enormous preparations and spending of many more thousands of billions of dollars. UK contributed its financial part for the success of the mission. Surprisingly European Union desisted from supporting the Project financially while lending its moral support to the success of this 'humanly impossible' mission. Rustler was not happy with the wording of the statement of European Union. He saw it as an attempt to cast a shadow of doubt over his personal capacity to lead America into a new future. He knew for sure that European Union was a small fry to castle him with its empty statement. He was too big for that.

Universities in the US and UK decided to set aside their regular classes for a few days in order to educate the students on the latest science that would make it possible for the US to set its foot in a Planet that had clear possibility of life. Pictures were flashed all across the globe showing movement of some beings in PlanetB2. Special mention was made with euphoria of the existence of Carolina in PlanetB2. Pictures of her staggering and walking on the Planet were flashed all across the globe. Even those Leftist intellectuals and communist countries that are invariably critical of the policies of America now began to faintly believe that America might score a point over Russia.

It became a sort of talk of the town all over the world. Every nook and corner of the world was fabricating a new planet based on the little information that it had on the mega plan of the US to occupy PlanetB2. Many rich people in the world started counting their bank balances to make it adequate in order to ultimately settle down in PlanetB2. Preachers in the Churches preached on the great blessing that god had showered on America to be the first nation to discover planet where human life was possible. Only Americans could do it, as they had the richest blessings of god, asserted the pastors from the pulpit. Shifting their sycophancy from god to Rustler was not a big deal. On any given day Rustler brought much more returns for them than god.

Not to be left behind, Indian politicians and religious gurus instructed temple authorities to make arrangement for special 'pooja' so that the journey to PlanetB2 would go through smoothly. Astrologers in India churned out information after information to prove that they had already predicted long ago that America would one day discover a new planet full of life. They quoted all Hindu scriptures left and right to prove that their ancient rishis had already dwelt in such planets and that America had only discovered something that existed already many eons earlier in the Hindu world. However, they also proved themselves to be faithful acolytes of the United States of America in an effort not to antagonize the American rulers. The non-Resident Indians living in the US poured a lot of money into Indian temples in order to claim later that the mission to PlanetB2 succeeded only because of the homas that were conducted by their Hindu priests in India. They had to be in the good books of their American bosses.

The Christian churches on the other hand pointed out that it was already predetermined that America should lead the world into a new future. They were the chosen race of god. Rustler was the leader of this chosen race. They quoted Isaiah 49 in support of Rustler that he was carved out in the palm of Yahweh and therefore, no one could defeat him in his march forward. The Archbishop of Canterbury and the Pope from Vatican issued circular to their faithful all over the world to pray for the success of the mission of Rustler. They were of the firm faith that no human effort would ultimately succeed without the effect of prayers.

Rustler enjoyed every bit of eulogy heaped on him from all over the world, the media, the common people, the diplomats and the rulers. He was perhaps the only man of his kind who could enjoy what he normally treated as shit. He especially liked what the Christian preachers said about him quoting Isaiah. As if to compliment them he started visiting churches with full media attention. He wanted the entire world to know that it was only the Christian world that could achieve such great scientific magnum operandum. It was not because he was a believer in a Christian god. He was an atheist to the core. But he considered his religion as being different from his personal belief system. He was terribly angry at the silence of the Muslim world and the communist world. No one in the world ever cared for the opinion of the indigenous world. His love for his church was a manifestation of his anger. He could not love anyone in his life except as a strong reaction to something else. He loved himself as a strong reaction to the rest of the world. He gathered all the feathers that fell on the way and fixed them in his hat.

Hindus in New York convinced him that he should visit their famous Shiva temple in order to make his mission a big success. They pointed out that the erect penis of Shiva was pointed in the direction of PlanetB2 and washing Shiva's penis with milk would bring sure success. They reeled out many stories from Hindu mythology to show that Shiva surpassed all planets many millennia earlier. The cactus of Shiva had its flower it the topmost planet in the universe and its roots were in the nether world. Even if he did not worship the penis of Shiva he should spend a few millions for the washing of this erect penis by Hindu women with milk. Millions of women were washing this penis with milk and were caressing it with their bare hands. Shiva had not yet reached orgasm. They interpreted their scriptures to prove that the moment Bigbelly4 landed on PlanetB2 Shiva's penis would ejaculate and he would have his first orgasm. Though Rustler laughed loud in his private chamber hearing what the Hindu gurus placed as necessary prerequisites for the success of the Bigebelly4, he had a tint of suspicion that the mission might fail if he did not listen to them. Therefore, very reluctantly he approved 10 million dollars to the Hindu temple in New York to conduct their regular homa.

Two days before the formal launch of the space mission Bigbelly4, Rustler and Plumbel were together for a drink and dinner to savor the sweetness of the forthcoming success. Both of them had no doubt that they would succeed this time. They had improved the technology manifold. Their recruitment process was much more professional than it used to be. The Awesome7 went through unprecedented rigorous training. Plumbel informed Rustler that all preparations were in place to perfection and nothing would go wrong with the mission this time. He checked with Plumbel if there was enough alternate liquid and a bit of excess solid fuel boosters for any possible delays and casualty. Plumbel confirmed that there was nothing to worry. Everything was set to make the launch a grand success.

Then Rustler proceeded to make enquiries about Awesome7 who were the lifeline of the success that he wanted to taste. He was particularly keen on knowing about the total preparedness of Marissa at all levels. Rustler excused himself to go to the loo. He had no doubts about the honesty of his friend. However, he wanted to extract as much information as possible from Plumbel about Marissa as he had a feeling that Plumbel was getting emotionally attached to the girl who mattered most in the mission to PlanetB2.

"It is a special whisky for both of us Plumbel. It is more than 25 years old. Cheers!" Both of them toasted for grand success of the mission that already filled them with great anticipation. Plumbel went a bit too beyond the formal training Marissa had. He began to explain the private relationship he had with Marissa and made no secret of his love for her as his daughter. He dwelt extensively on his emotive relationship with Marissa and how he prepared her well for the journey in Bigbelly4. Rustler was enjoying the narration of Plumbel to the full. He was laughing his life out and was patting Plumbel for the way he successfully prepared Marissa for the impending mission. Plumbel had no shortage of trust on his friend and so began to speak openly while sipping his third glass of whisky. His mouth was loosened a bit more than necessary. Rustler bade him good night being ever grateful to him for the pearls that he spilled from his mouth. He was particularly happy about Plumbel's information on Carolina's visit to Marissa from PlanetB2 and the uninhibited explanation to him about their communication with each other. He was quite excited when talking about it. Rustler could not contain his surprise and shock when he heard that Carolina had come to visit Marissa. He could not even perceive the type of half-baked exposition of communicative interaction that Plumbel was presenting to him. When Plumbel ultimately returned home he hit the bed straight and slumped on it.

On the eve of the launch of the historic space mission known to the world for the first time Rustler addressed the nation that was telecast direct all over the world. He was always aware that he did not take the nation into confidence when he launched on the greatest mission of his life. He did not care about what the nation thought then. But now he needed much money for the nuclear rocket, the space satellites to keep global communications going, the weather bureau for appropriate predictions of weather to which the machines had to be adapted and also for the Space Committee of the Congress for extensive spending in order to convince the entire world of the propriety of the American space mission. He realized that he could not create an impression that he was slighting the Congress on this very important mission that put the pride of America at stake. He prepared a speech much on the line of John F Kennedy who made an inspiring speech to the Congress on the need for America standing together and spending money in order to succeed in its mission to the moon. He refused to prepare a speech like Nixon's in the event of the failure of the mission to PlanetB2. Though Nixon had prepared a failure speech and kept it ready he did not have to deliver it, as the mission to moon succeeded. Rustler did not even prepare any such speech, as he refused to believe that his mission would fail at all. 'Search for truth and understanding' the main theme of Nixon's prepared speech in the event of failure of moon mission made no sense to Rustler. If astronauts failed there would always be others to take over the job. There was no point in praising the sacrifice of the dead astronauts and inspiring the new ones on the dead body that was a bundle of failure. Rustler stood tall. On top was a towering inferno that kept burning incessantly.

Just before delivering his historic launch speech Rustler introduced all his astronauts to the elite gathering of the Congress. When it came to Marissa Plumbel brightened up manifold. He made it a strict point that when different astronauts presented flowers to members of Awesome7 he would be the one to present flowers to Marissa. Rustler clapped his hands at the presentation of flowers to each member of Awesome7. The entire gathering of Congressmen joined Rustler. When it was the turn of Marissa to receive flowers everyone could hear the loudest clapping coming from Rustler. It was not because he made any special effort to clap for Marissa. It was because many hands among Congressmen got stuck in a quagmire of racism when they heard that she was from the Native Americans. It was unusual to do this for the astronauts. But Rustler waived all conventions only because he saw himself at the center of this historic mission to PlanetB2. Failure would look at him on his face if Marissa were not at the center stage of the present mission to the planet.

Rustler invited his friend Plumbel to say a few words to Congressmen about the preparations that were done to take the mission to the level of launching. He wanted the Congress to know how dedicated his team of astronauts was to have brought the mission to the threshold of success. Being not used to give messages Plumbel took refuge in the technical side of the mission. He was reluctant to reveal many technical details for fear that none in the Congress would understand anything. At the same time he wanted to inform the American public of some of the basics. It was not his habit to reveal anything to anyone about any mission that America took up. He always left information sharing to his friend Rustler.

"Ladies and Gentlemen" Plumbel started in a timid way. Not that he was overawed by the entire Congress that had gathered in style. But he was timid by nature. He was not used to addressing crowds of people. He was a man of maneuvering. "Bigbelly4 is the name of the spacecraft that we are sending to PlanetB2. The President has already introduced the name of the team that is making this historic mission. They are known as Awesome7. The spacecraft has been designed specially for this mission by the astronauts themselves with some assistance from our scientists in the National Space Mission Centre. PlanetB2 is 800,000 miles away from the earth. This is not the farthest planet that we know of. One of the most recent rockets we sent was to Pluto that is 3.5 billion miles away from us. We designed a spacecraft that can travel at the speed of 51,000 mph. Our rocket will take nine years to reach Pluto. But we shall be getting billions of information from the satellite in the meantime. Bigbelly4 has been designed making use of all the information that we have received about space and weather from the space satellite that we sent to Pluto as well as all other known and unknown satellites that we have sent into the orbit. We have also taken into serious account issues such as the atmospheric pressure, structural load and spacecraft propulsion. Bigbelly4 will take on a speed of 75000 mph. This is the highest speed of any spacecraft that we have produced till now. At this speed Awesome7 must be able to reach PlanetB2 within 11 days. Unlike previous space missions we have applied all the three propulsion technologies of Antimatter, fusion and Light Sails in Bibelly4." Plumbel glanced at Rustler with legitimate pride. Rustler winked eyes at him to indicate that enough was enough. He understood that it was time to stop.

How could he stop without mentioning a word about his darling protégé? When he took out the name of Marissa Rustler laughed as if Plumbel did exactly what he expected him to do. He mentioned to the Congress that a lot of extra elbow grease was applied to train a girl from the indigenous Native American community. Rustler intervened at this moment.

"We have specially recruited Marissa in order to proclaim to the world that we consider all people equal and that we owe a special responsibility to our own Native people. We have focused on knowledge, talent and capacity and am happy to announce to you that Marissa has excelled in these three and deserves our very generous appreciation." Congressmen thought that the

President had taken note of their previous indifference and that they were expected to be more generous in their appreciation. They stood up and accorded a standing ovation to Marissa. She bowed to all of them as a gesture of recognizing and appreciating their generosity. Plumbel felt that he was cut short in order that Rustler might steal the show. An imperceptible uneasiness started creeping into his heart about this attitude of his friend's.

The Vice President of the US stood up to say a few words of appreciation to the American President and to the people of the United States for standing up to such enormous challenge in overpowering nature in order to establish the supremacy of human race primary among them being the American Citizens. A few more eminent Congressmen were invited by Rustler to say a few words in appreciation of Awesome7. Rustler and Plumbel appreciated each other in secret about successfully hiding the two previously failed missions to PlanetB2.

Then came the most anticipated moment. It was something very traditional in the history of the US. However, people waited with bated breath and anticipation for the President's address to the nation every time a new President was elected and he gave an inaugural speech. It was also customary that the President addressed the nation on very significant occasions when he had to either inform the Americans or appeal to them on very special issues that afflicted the nation.

All these commotions and excitement in the world created a mild tremor in the bodies of the cosmic beings in PlanetB2. They were not positive waves. All waves that arose from a desire to dominate, to destroy and to hegemonize had its mild flutter in PlanetB2. This tremor was a bit high in velocity as the entire world was looking forward to that moment that would establish man's superiority over nature. Many cosmic beings came together experiencing the sudden onrush of negative waves that penetrated the cosmos and tried to enter their planet. This rustling among them brought them together naturally. In the forefront was the body that was the cumulative essence of the thought and feeling waves of many ancestors, revolutionary philosophers and revolutionaries who desired everything good for humanity such as equality, dignity, justice and prosperity. Some of these ancestors were actually many animals whom people on earth worshiped as their gods. In PlanetB2 there were no humans and no animals. All were cosmic beings by virtue of their total merger with cosmic waves.

One of these cosmic bodies almost enveloped Carolina. Her intensity of full body orgasm intensified multifold. She could see that none of these cosmic bodies had any specific identity though it was possible for her to see that some bodies had much resemblance to some of her ancestors. The one who enveloped her new cosmic body was the same body that received her into PlanetB2. Now she resembled a buffalo. She could easily see it also as bison. It was a presence that brought total bliss to her body. The being started communicating to Carolina many things that she had not been filled with.

"This rustling takes place very rarely among us. When living beings in any of the planets began to disturb the cosmic rhythm with their exorbitant desire for power and dominance and begin to destroy other beings we begin to experience this. As you see our rhythm in this Planet is not disturbed by what happens in other planets. But we do have occasional tremors. Our energy waves are too strong to be affected by such disturbances in other planets. However, we bear a special relationship to earthly beings, as the cosmic bodies we have assumed now are all products of entropy that took place among the thought and feeling waves of earthly beings. The disturbances brought us together in one place through our communicative interaction. We realize in our bodies that the world is in real danger of losing its touch with cosmic waves, movement and change. This could possibly result in an imbalance in the energy level that keeps all cosmic movement and that could spell disaster for the earthly beings . . .

". . . Though most of us lived our lives as normal earthly beings we have become ancestors of many communities of people by wishing everything good for their individual prosperity, community well-being, social balance of life and for prosperity of their children. Our cosmic bodies are result of these unlimited desires for everything good to other beings, to the world and to the cosmos. This was our being. They were essentially a bundle of good concerns, wishes and desires. In desiring good things for others we came into a state of being in bliss, in full body orgasm. Or it can be said the other way round. Because our inner being was very positive and life giving we became a bundle of concerns and good wishes for others . . .

". . . Our body cells being filled with such concerns, it is not part of our being to receive negative waves. When most of us were on earth we were constantly becoming something on the basis of our being. But after intermittent entropy and attaining the fullness of becoming and after reaching this Planet our becoming process in reference to other beings has stopped. However, we were not just static beings incapable of sending out energy waves and receiving positive energies. Even when we lived in other planets and most of us on planet earth we began to experience full body orgasm from time to time. But now it is our state of being. We exist in full body orgasm . . .

". . . The impending disaster to earthly beings did send many signals into our bodies and that triggered intensive communicative interaction with those bodies on earth that were ready to receive our strong waves and resist the onslaught of destruction from dominant forces. Human race is now in conflict. A lot of them are also gathering the courage to stand against hegemony of any kind. In as much as their body cells begin to open up our positive and life giving energy waves their bodies will begin to be filled with life giving energy and that will build a strong resistance to dominance. But unfortunately human bodies have receptivity to both positive and negative waves. It so happens among them that many who have deep desires for dominance fill their bodies with negative waves.

The other beings that are open to communicative interaction with cosmic waves of positive energy will develop necessary resistance. It so happens that the cosmos has an imbalance now. But this will change soon, as we begin to intensify our communicative interaction because of the mild tremors we received in our bodies . . .

". . . The intensity of positive energy waves that we emit in our bodies is an automatic block to any dominant waves entering into our planet. Our waves form a sort of layer beyond which negative energies could not penetrate. They can only touch this layer. If they come in waves and touch the layer we get some tremors in our planet. Since we do not have the possibility of any depletion in life giving energy in this planet, waves of dominance, hegemony, destruction etc. cannot enter our planet. Scientists on earth named it Ozone layer. They have named our planet as PlanetB2. Well, human beings have their own reasons to be funny. This layer has the special characteristic of allowing penetration of positive waves and preventing negative waves. This is done in order to preserve the integrity of the cosmos without which there will not be any cosmos. Such a situation without cosmos is impossible." The ancestor stopped its intensive communicative interaction with Carolina. She looked at herself and found out that she was only another cosmic being and had shed her identity as Carolina completely.

It was the turn of Rustler to deliver his Presidential Address in a solemn manner on the historic eve of the launching of Bigbelly4 into the orbit. He was filled with legitimate pride. Nay, it was much more than that. What everyone around could see on his face was a look of invincibility. His make-up artists had done necessary coloring of his face so that it reflected artificial radiance. That is exactly what the audience of the day wanted, as they did the same when it came to them being in public gaze. There were a few Congressmen to the left side of Rustler as he rose up to speak. They belonged to the Left within the capitalist America.

"My countrymen and Members of the Congress . . .

I am here to announce to you that we as Americans are on the threshold of making one more new history. You are aware that we have behind us successful missions of landing on Moon and Mars. Russia has done this only after we achieved this great feat. I stand before you to inform you that this will be past from tomorrow. Let us not remember our past any more as from tomorrow we as citizens of America and all citizens of the world will be stepping into a new era of space science that will make history irrelevant . . ."

"Taking capitalism to all planets of the universe." One of the Leftist Congressmen remarked. It could be heard only among his comrades. The Left had already become a spent force within the borders of the US. Rustler cared a hoot for them.

". . . Tomorrow will mark the end of history and the beginning of history. That is the special characteristic of us Americans that we always keep discarding our past while simultaneously stepping into a bright future that we create for ourselves. We have been fighting for freedom and have been working tirelessly to establish freedom to all peoples of the world. In order to achieve this freedom we had to even wage war on many nations and kill all those who stood against freedom . . ."

"War for peace is like fucking for virginity". There was a giggle among comrades when they heard it from another of their comrades in subdued voice. The other Congressmen turned to them in disdain though they did not know what was the funny thing that was happening among the Left fellas. But when others started looking at them they tucked their tail between their legs and sat quiet for the rest of the speech.

". . . We feel proud that we belong to an era of freedom though somewhere there is a faint feeling in many of us that billions of innocent lives have been lost in this mission of ours. That is the past that we want to say goodbye to . . .

". . . From tomorrow we shall be entering a new era of freedom. President John F Kennedy gave expression to similar sentiments in his Inaugural Address as the President of the United States of America. I like to quote to you the great words of Kennedy in his Inaugural Address. This is what he said: 'And let every other power know that this Hemisphere intends to remain the master of its own house.' As I said earlier we say goodbye to our past. Today we are standing on the threshold of letting the entire world know that no power on earth can be equal to the indomitable American spirit. We have overpowered the moon. That is history now. We are going to overpower another planet that was not even known to scientists of any other country. We, Americans have discovered it. We have named it as PlanetB2. We shall begin to live in that planet as people can live in this planet. At an appropriate moment in our future history I shall come back to you with facts and figures about how many beings are living in PlanetB2. For strategic reasons our scientists have decided that when Bigbelly4 approaches PlanetB2 visibility of the movement of life in that planet will not be telecast live to the world."

Again he sprinkled his speech with ideas taken from Kennedy. However, he veiled it with his own words. "I have taken the biggest risk of my life by visualizing and undertaking this mission. As the President of the United States of America I am deeply aware of the consequences for the people of America if this mission fails. By believing in democracy and making ourselves transparent we are exposing ourselves to the rest of the world who will be ever ready to ridicule us if we happen to fail. But as Americans we are here to succeed and not to fail. I like to remind you of he famous dictum of Lyndon Johnson in his address to the American people: "We shall overcome." Yes that is the secret of the secret heart of America. We shall overcome come what may."

At this point two Congressmen put up their hands. Though this interruption was not allowed normally, the President stopped his speech with a bit of surprise on his face. There was a smile of disapproval on his face. When others asked them to wait till the President completed his speech, Rustler asked them to allow the Congressmen to speak. They were happy about the President of America.

"The people of America are fully with you Mr. President. We recognize that you have embarked upon this impossible mission and have brought it to such exalted levels of achievement. It is not important that we should see live all the related operations of Project PlanetB2. We are all with you Mr. President. Please go ahead with the strategies that you deem fit. Tomorrow will be the day of history for America." He said that and sat down.

Rustler signaled to the other Congressman to speak up. But he showed his hand to say that his companion had said exactly what he wanted to say. Plumbel smiled to himself giving a side-glance to Rustler who continued his speech with utmost disdain for other Congressmen.

"By undertaking this unachievable voyage to PlanetB2 we are determined to preserve and promote individual liberty of all American citizens and we are ready to pay any price for it. Tomorrow when I press the button to push Bigbelly4 into the orbit you will all be pressing the button of irreversible path of freedom to a new generation. If we succeed in this mission it will be the dawn of a new light to the entire world. In this new light the world will be willing and morally forced to pursue the American path of freedom and peace. Whoever is reluctant to follow the American path is bound to perish in darkness from which he can never hope to recover . . ."

". . . As the President of America I bear an unassailable witness to the world on behalf of all American people. The witness is simple and sure. We Americans will lead the world into the path of prosperity by subduing nature and bringing all forces of nature under our feet. We must all know that when life is lost in any corner of the world it is in the best interest of the future of the world. All people all over the world must be more than willing to lay down their life with utmost trust in the wisdom of America. The world will soon realize that it is the only and the surest path to a bright future. Long live America! Long live the American people! Long live the American spirit!"

The clap and shouting from Congressmen rent the air. It looked as if Congressmen had seen some divine being descending amidst them. But the truth was that Rustler tried to rise above the earth and move into the orbit. It did not matter. They would clap their hands at whatever Rustler said and did. Such was his power. The sound of clapping was almost like the taking off of Bigbelly4. That was more than satisfying to Rustler. That was the type of approval he sought from Congressmen. It was a license to him to go ahead with his ambitious plans. Hardly did they realize that the bigger the volume of their clapping the more money American treasury would be emptied of its stuff.

This was followed by an elaborate dinner organized in honor of Awesome7. After the dinner was over every Congressman made it a point to embrace Rustler and congratulate him for this very daring mission of his. A few of them joined together and shouted: 'Rustler, the indomitable lion of America!' Both Plumbel and Rustler knew they were a bit overdrunk as was usual among Congressmen. After all the hullaballoo they accompanied Awesome7 to their secret place the Cubicle11, which still remained a mysterious place to all Americans except Awesome7. In fact no American knew of the existence of Cubicle11. Both of them advised Awesome7 to have a good night's sleep and be fully prepared physically and mentally for the arduous journey. Before going to rest for the night Awesome7 recollected together the rigorous training they went through and the blind determination in them to design the Bigbelly4. They were wondering what motivated them to be so blindly committed to fulfilling a mission the fate of which they did not know at all. Hope had no boundaries.

Marissa went into total silence as soon as everyone in Awesome7 left to his or her cubicles for sleep. She was much disturbed at the lies that she encountered in that big moment of joy and celebration among Americans. Why did Rustler hide the full truth about Cubilce11 and previous two missions? She knew that only she knew about the previous missions to PlanetB2 that failed. She wondered if she was right in opting to go to PlanetB2 with so much of dishonesty hovering over the mission that she was undertaking. She loved Plumbel but she could not accept the fact that he was also part of a mission that was based on lies. She thought that the people of America were being cheated wholesomely. She was rolling in her bed unable to decide if she should take up the journey the next day. She ruminated over her fate and the fate of her people if she withdrew herself in the last minute. The horror of last minute withdrawal haunted her like thousands of bats rushing to her from nowhere. She thought that the bats were about to devour her. Just at that moment she felt a gentle touch on her shoulder and knew immediately that Carolina was at her side comforting her. She could hear Carolina pleading with her that she should take up the journey next day in order to join her in PlanetB2. Carolina embraced her holding her tight to her chest. Marissa took much comfort in that embrace of love and went to sleep.

After leaving Awesome7 in Cubicle11 Rustler and Plumbel went to the private room of the President. Both of them wanted to spend the entire night together. They knew that they would not get sleep the whole night. The anxiety was too much to bear. Only both of them had experienced the trauma of two failures in the previous missions. In the next ten days anything could happen. They had done everything possible for the success of the mission this time. They were very sure that the mission would succeed this time. Rustler was contemplating suicide if the mission failed. He would not be able to face the scourge of failure once again. He held the hands of Plumbel and wanted a firm assurance from him that the mission would succeed by all means.

Plumbel held Rustler's hands tight. He did not manifest to Rustler the internal conflict he was going through. He was ready to face any ignominy if the mission failed. But he was not ready to lose his Marissa if the mission did not succeed. Rustler could hold Plumbel's hand asking for reassurance. Plumbel could not do the same thing. Both of them had travelled a long way separately now. Ever since Plumbel met Carolina's people and ultimately also met Marissa and her people his personal world began to take a different trajectory far removed from the path designed by Rustler his friend. He began to pity Rustler more and more for his egotistic search of the bloated self. His own path had found new openings after he met the people in the 'desert' of America. They had touched difficult corners of his heart and that transformation in him seemed to be irreversible. He was not ready to let go of the treasure he cherished now in his heart. Rustler became a tiny mustard seed in comparison to what he began to cherish now.

At the same time it was too early for him to let go of his friend either. "Do not take everything negatively Rustler. We shall succeed by all means tomorrow. Everything has been put in place and there is no reason at all to doubt that this mission would fail. Moreover, we also have Marissa who has established contact with Carolina and that should seal our victory this time in our mission. I must confess that Marissa has come into our design of things and she will come back after a successful stay for sometime in PlanetB2. Am also sure that she will safeguard the lives of our astronauts who go with her. Marissa is just an amazing personality. She lives her spirituality in such depths that normal human beings cannot achieve. She is a big asset to our mission to PlanetB2."

Rustler came back to himself through a difficult process. The difficulty was also because of the level of spirit that permeated his body. Both Plumbel and Rustler were quite inundated with alcohol. They could not think of sleep. The next day was very important for both of them. It would be a day either to make them or break them.

Rustler listened to Plumbel in silence and pooh-poohed him within himself. He decided that his friend had become quite weird because of his close association with Marissa and her people. But knowing Plumbel for a long time in his life he did not have much doubt that he would turn normal soon. He was not the mettle designed for the type of spirituality under whose spell he was then. Things would change soon and Plumbel would also change. This was the hope that Rustler had even as he listened to Plumbel with a hard earned marginal smile on his face. He was ready to go ahead with his plans of overpowering the powers of nature with or without any of his friends. He recollected how Plumbel grew up to be such a nice guy right from his boyhood days. It was always Rustler who would be in the forefront of any action and his friend would always paly a strong supportive role to him. At that young age both of them never imagined that one day one of them would be the President of the most powerful nation in the world. But it was not strange to them. Rustler always went after anything that had a semblance of power. Plumbel enjoyed the fringe benefits of power that his friend grabbed through hook or crook.

Plumbel on his part imagined how much his friend had changed over the years. Both of them enjoyed a level of trust that others considered to be unassailable. That he was highly individualistic did not come on the way of their friendship. He liked in a way the high individualism of Rustler. Often it was his individualism that made him a winner in any battle of wits. He had that aggression that had an edge over others who were ambitious like him. Rustler was not only ambitious but was aggressively in pursuit of what he considered as the most important thing at that moment. There were at least five occasions when Plumbel's persuasive power over his friend prevented Rustler from eliminating his school friends. He would go to school with a gun hidden in his trousers in order to take revenge on his rivals. Plumbel had to force him to part with the gun. He would take and hide it. Rustler had no problem with his gun being taken away by his friend. He was happy that he gained the attention that he wanted to but would be angry that he was unable to shoot down his rivals. He genuinely believed that they deserved to be killed and had no right to live only because they opposed his pursuit of power. Plumbel was the only person whom he would at least agree to disagree. He treated all others in school as shit. It was left to Plumbel to take the gun to his home and place it in the right place without his parents' knowledge.

Recollection of their boyhood was not nostalgic in many ways. It was only a grim reminder that the quotient of mutual trust had depleted quite a bit over a period of time. In a way Rustler was even a bit shocked at the turn of events with his trusted friend. Assertion of his individuality in terms of a spiritual identity was totally unacceptable to Rustler. He expected Plumbel to be what he always was and that was non-negotiable for him. He was the supreme commander and Plumbel had to only play second fiddle. On the other hand Plumbel did not venture to assert his individual freedom against the wishes of his friend. He only was in pursuit of something about which there was a new feeling of romance in him. Both of them did not believe in developing any relationship with women. They had discussed it several times and downplayed their proclivity to fall in love. Both of them were quite conscious and afraid that any such relationship of a lasting nature would jeopardize their single minded dedication to the advancement of their ambition for America. Rustler was generally the progenitor of mega ambitious plans. Plumbel trusted in the wisdom and capacity of his friend without thinking much about his intentions. It was immaterial to him whether his friend meant well or not. That he was his friend was enough for Plumbel to fall in line with him. He was not a blind follower of anything or anyone. But when it came to Rustler he always gave top priority to his friendship without ever bothering about why he was doing it. He operated often from his heart and not from his head when it was a matter of Rustler's ambition. His relationship and trust were very close to his heart and he did not allow much rationality to have a role to play.

Such a nature suited the designs of Rustler much. This was what he needed. He operated almost only with his rationality and had very little space in his personality for emotions. His emotive side often seemed to be completely empty. His rational side was unquestionably dominant. All his decisions were taken with clear rational thinking. Over a period of time, being prevented from making use of his gun, Rustler began to take recourse to logic of power acquisition. Drinking from the nectar of power had an ever-flowing effect on the psyche of Rustler. It was not like his gun that gave him a sense of power when he held on to it. He was as highly adept at the use of logic as he was with his gun. He would put down his rivals ruthlessly with the power of his logic and argumentation. When he sensed any sort of logical defeat he would take recourse to abuses in such a way that none of his competitors would be able to stand the filth that stemmed from his mouth. Many of his peers were terribly afraid of entering into any argumentation with Rustler, as they had to invariably bite dust at the end of the argumentation. His teachers admired him for such rational power and logic when it came to meaningful argumentation on issues. They were able to segregate his arrogance from the power of his logic and dismiss his arrogant side. When they were able to do that the personality of Rustler became very attractive to them. Often they told him bluntly on his face that one day he would become a great leader. This was the type of nurturing of ego that Rustler desired.

Reliving of the past helped ease some tensions in both of them. The friction was between two personality traits and not merely between two persons. They had gelled well with their rationality and emotionality. The more each one began to bring these individual traits to full life friction became inevitable. Rustler had just a while ago spoken about discarding history. When it came to him he needed to speak about it in order to be at peace with himself and take pride in his achievements. Much relieved, both of them went to their rooms to get ready for the greatest moment in their history and their lives.

CHAPTER SEVEN

Dawn of a new history! Goodbye to old history. One history of the past! The other history of the future! The end and the beginning meeting at the same moment! That was history in itself. It was one of those rarest moments in the history of humanity where end of history marked the beginning of history. The world waited with bated breath for this moment. Day or night mattered very little. People sacrificed their sleep in order to watch in their TV the launching of Bigbelly4. It was that one moment when the entire world was awake irrespective of what time it was in their place. The entire world blasted the time capsule that encapsulated them with all its limitations. Entire America was pregnant with expectations of an immediate delivery. No one dared a guess. Everyone was sure that America was going to open a new path of liberty and individual freedom in a land of the hitherto unknown. Suddenly the world had become too small for the Americans. Only this part was not new in America. They looked down to see if they were still standing on this earth. Everyone was in a mood to fly as high as possible so that he would be the first one to put his foot on PlanetB2. Each one wanted to do that even before Awesome7 could do that.

Ground Force at the space station was fully busy, unmindful of the commotions in the minds of the people, in the streets of America and in cities and villages all over the world. They had no time for that. They had to concentrate on every nut and bolt to make Bigbelly4 300% fit for the final take off. But all the people all over the world were keenly watching them dutifully performing every small little task in preparation of the great moment in history. Members of the Ground Force talked largely through signs manifesting an extraordinary skill in concentration. That is the way they were trained to do their job. All Americans believed that American interest was the best for them. It was like an addiction to them. Ground force had already completed its job. But it had to make triple sure that everything was okay for the take off.

Awesome7 was working assiduously inside Bigbelly4. An awesome feeling had gripped them from the time they got up to get ready for the great mission. They were the most privileged ones that day. They had been well prepared psychologically not to take on any tension in the final moments. The entire world was waiting for them with bated breath. They were not ordinary human beings. They were highly skilled, professional and hardworking. They did their job with meticulous precision. Everyone knew that there was no time for him or her to take anything light in his or her mission. The final check of all software and their functional preparedness was ensured.

Rustler had been prepared well with many rehearsals for pressing the button exactly at the second when the final count down was completed. He went through the exercises several times with the machines counting from 10 to one and at the count of one he had to just press the button. As he pressed the button Bigbelly4 would emit fire and brimstone and make a big show of its ass power to propel itself into the orbit. On the outer layer Bigbelly4 had been painted grey with American flag ready to flutter as it took off in style.

The question that was in everyone's mind was the same. All thought and asked themselves, 'who will be the first one to land on PlanetB2?'. The captain of Awesome7 was John Stone, a tall and serious looking guy. This was the biggest question from the media as they waited in a big group for news. A larger than life size TV was fixed for them to have a clear view of the blasting off of Bigbelly4. They could take clear pictures from the TV screen. The media manager was present to answer all sorts of questions from media personnel. Rustler had instructed the media manager that he should pretend as if he knew everything about PlanetB2. He should go on bullshitting to the media without creating the impression that there was any mystery about the mission. The media should be fully convinced that the American President was as transparent as a 'see through' glass. The very pretensions should actually camouflage all secrets about the mission. No other super power should be able to make out the technical details of the mission. They should be totally confused with misinformation. The media was the best instrument of misinforming the public, Rustler argued with John Stone. The media manager informed that the first person to set his foot on PlanetB2 would be John Stone and there was big clap as they heard the name. The manager told them with a heavy face that it was not the time to show off their emotions. It was also made clear to them that all the seven in the team would walk around freely on PlanetB2 and interact with the beings there.

"What will be the language of the beings in PlanetB2? How will our astronauts understand their language? Have you already studied their language?" One of the journalists wanted to show off his journalistic acumen.

"We have no clue so far to the type of language and communication they have among themselves. But sign language will be good enough to get a feel of who those beings are. This is going to be only our first trip to PlanetB2. Once our astronauts bring us data on the type of communication that exists of the beings we shall develop a language to communicate with them. It is not at all a difficult proposition for our scientists." The media manager fine-tuned his acumen for interaction.

All offices all over the world had found an easy excuse not to work. Most of them were glued to their computers and TVs. Many applied for leave from office work, stayed put at home to watch TV. The Secretary of State in the US declared a public holiday in order to raise the hype. European Union followed suit and requested member States to do the same. Some Asian countries declared holiday under the negotiable instrument. However, they declared holiday to all educational institutions in order to enable students to have full view and knowledge of what was happening in their life and it was bound to have a lasting impact on their future. Many schools and colleges however, decided to make it a big event. They were keen on educating all their students on the technical details of the mission to PlanetB2. Teachers and some clever students were chosen to deliver lectures on different dimensions of the mission. Some larger educational institutions organized quiz programmes for students on PlanetB2 and gave away big prizes in order to gain mileage in the media out of the event. The Indian Prime Minister declared a national holiday without consulting any official body. He was an ardent lover of the American President. It did not matter who was in that position. He declared India's love for any President of the US. Many people just came out of their homes onto the street to assemble at special places where huge TVs were set up. Pubs set up their special counters in all such places to make a brisk business. In India and Thailand all food vendors with their vehicles and pushcarts made a roaring business.

It was a virtual day of mourning in communist countries. They were not yet ready to give any credit to capitalism for what it proclaimed to be a historic achievement. They carefully went through the speech of Rustler and were severely critical of the consequences of the money he spent on such 'unnecessary' project. They declared that the mega enterprise of Rustler's was utterly scandalous for having spent thousands of billions while millions went on empty stomachs and lived on the streets in the same boastful America. They gave an ideological twist to the totally unnecessary venture that sucked the blood of the poor in order to make the rich live in glory. People were going about with empty stomachs allover the world scurrying for at least one meal a day. Here was a country that was spending tax money of citizens for projects of unreachable heights under the garb of being an epic enterprise. They also predicted that this attempt of Rustler, being the first one, should go through the test of time before any euphoria was created about it. They were very reticent about their statements of approval for any such attempt. It was yet another occasion for them to declare capitalism as the worst enemy of the world and also croak about from their rooftops that communism was the savior of the world. They were happy climbing the rooftops while Rustler managed to ascend to his throne in a distant planet that the US scientists discovered.

Rustler became the super hero of the world even before he kick started his monstrous project. He wore a wry smile on his face listening to the utter stupidity of communist countries. They would not lift a finger to do anything creative and constructive while simultaneously they would point all their fingers at those who did whatever was humanly impossible. He found the attitude of communists very amusing. He was very confident that it was too late for them to make any pronouncement. He was on the threshold of achieving what no one in the history of the world had ever achieved and was only getting ready to push the ultimate button to his everlasting glory. That button had the biggest power on earth. Only the privileged fingers of Rustler could touch it with legitimacy. If anybody else touched it he had to cool his heels in US jails all his life. Such was the power of the button. No words uttered! Machine Age! Rustler laughed away at the ideological goofing of communist countries.

A day before the launch, students in most schools and colleges assembled to hear from experts the technical and operational dimension of Project PlanetB2. They were more curious to know what actually existed in the new planet that America had discovered. Citizens all over the world were dying to know what other things existed in PlanetB2 apart from life. They were already making their plans to book their tickets to the planet and did not want to be harmed by anything in the unknown planet. Students who were considered to be cleverer than others were asked by peers to inform them adequately about mission to PlanetB2. There were also the thugs who took on themselves intellectual leadership to guide their colleagues into an enlightened world. When other students asked them difficult questions their companions would cow down such curious students and simply accept whatever their leader churned out. The Internet and Google searches were the busiest spots those days. Facebook and Whatsapp were impregnated with postings on unimaginable information that everyone imagined. With the little they found in these sites they built up a lot of their own information into what they churned out as the truth about the voyage to PlanetB2.

Finally the moment that Rustler and Plumbel waited for arrived. They had been switching on the channels every now and then and were grossly disappointed that there was no message from the one that mattered most to them and to most of the world. Every now and then Rustler reminded Plumbel with certain anxiety that the very important message had not yet come. He did not care much about opinions of world leaders. He was the most powerful among them. But even the world needed to know that his endeavor had the final approval of that one person. When Rustler had almost lost all hope of receiving the message, the Vatican channel came up with a very important announcement. "God created man so that man may take full responsibility over his creation. Man is the zenith of god's creation. Though he sinned god sent his only son to save man from eternal damnation. Today god has willed that America should lead the world in science, military power and development. It is god's plan for the world and there is no escape from this will of god for any nation, even if they do not believe in the Christian god. It is the supreme wish of the Supreme God that man should explore all corners of nature and gain maximum advantage to humanity. The Vatican is happy that the Presidents of the United States excellently execute such a task. The crowning glory of God's creation is the present President of America, Mr. Rustler. The Pope and the College of his Cardinals are very happy about the bold and moral forays that he is making in the field of science. By doing this Rustler is taking humanity a step closer to god. He is a true son of the god of Israel. We wish and pray to God and his people to stand by the United States all the time and guide President Rustler so that he may bring greater glory to God and to Christianity."

As the message of the Pope ended Rustler and Plumbel folded their hands and closed their chests in great reverence. Though both of them were not believers, belonging to the Church mattered a lot to them. Heartbeat inside them clattered a lot. That Christ belonged to history mattered very little to both of them. He was the Alpha and the Omega, the beginning and the end of everything. Both of them became light in their bodies after hearing the message of Christendom in unequivocal voice.

Now it was time for them to get ready for that great moment in history. Rustler had given clear instruction to Plumbel that he should stand by his side when he pressed the button of the new history. Plumbel nodded his head as he always did. They had a good shower in hot water. This helped them a lot to come back to themselves, as they had not slept the entire night. Though their faces tended to shrink a little with innumerable pegs of whisky they made up for it with their anticipation of the accomplishment of the unachievable point of history. Rustler had chosen a black suit and coat with white shirt and black necktie. Plumbel had decided to wear the best dress he had, an olive suit with a red tie.

Plumbel left for the venue of the launch a little earlier than Rustler in order to make sure that everything was perfectly organized without any cause even for the slightest embarrassment for the one and only President of America.

When Rustler entered the gate the official orchestra began to play the national anthem of the United States of America. The Chauffeur drove the car rather slow so that Rustler could have a good look of all the dignitaries who had assembled while simultaneously displaying his pride that he carefully wore on his face. The car went two rounds with Rustler waving his hand to all those who greeted him with great reverence and fear. When the chauffeur stopped the car near the podium specially set up for the occasion, the media rushed to position themselves as near the President as possible. However, they were effectively prevented from going too near the President. Rustler did not rush. He measured his steps and climbed up the ramp slowly looking all around. All Americans had to cherish the moment. He was just perfect. It was exactly the moment when the National Anthem ended that Rustler had perfected himself in attention. Now he could press the all-important button at any time.

The entire world celebrated just this one thing, the pressing of the button by the lion-hearted President of the United States of America. There were firecrackers all around the space station set up by scientists of all departments in fine anticipation. Rustler experienced an uneasy happiness within himself. He tried to convince himself that this time America would succeed. Only he and Plumbel knew the failures of the previous two missions and that had an over imposing clouds of doubt on his psyche. He did not want to accept it as his personal failure. Therefore, he conveniently shifted it to America. The edges of the clouds kept coming repeatedly to put out their tongues and lick at his convinced confidence. Dusk and dawn visited him one after another on a fast track mode. The success of the launch and the failure of the previous mission visited and revisited him repeatedly. Rustler was dazed by the blandishments he received from all over the world. He extended his right arm and his index finger pressed the button firmly to glory.

Bigbelly4 split through the clouds into the sky. Its tongues of flame burned down all the tongues of clouds that it touched. Seeing a studded star coming in the opposite direction they ran hither and thither letting Bigbelly4 to wade through them towards its space of glory. It was mocking at Grandmother moon for her ugly face and old age. She was full of pity for the new entrant into the world of stars. She knew the difference between age-old wisdom and impetuosity of the young. She was forbearing of the immaturity of Begbelly4 that bordered on arrogance. All the stars were flickering their diamond eyes wondering who this new addition in their world was. They were laughing among themselves when they saw Bigbelly4 farting behind endlessly. They thought it was an empty vessel making a hollow booming noise about just nothing. They were used to move about in silence without disturbing anyone. Mother Earth was happy that a dead weight on her lap had departed in great style.

Just ten more days! Plumbel kept his fingers crossed. He did not meet Rustler that often during those ten days except when they went into Cubicle11 to get news of the progress of Bigbelly4. They had both special super computers set up in their private residence to keep monitoring the movements of Bigbelly4. But Plumbel's mind and body wavered in different directions as much as he was rolling in his bed restlessly at night. He was unable to concentrate on the mission to PlanetB2. He tried his best to live with Marissa but she eluded him. Carolina however, revisited him time and again. He tried to get a little sleep after spending many sleepless nights in anticipation of the launch. As the effects of the whisky he and Rustler had began to subside Plumbel began to come to his own. It was difficult as there were two different personalities emerging in him. He could not easily wish away the learning that he picked up in the Native American community. He could not let go of his association with the ambition of his friend. Now one side of his personality stood up and tried to drown the other with its over imposing presence. In half sleep he began to live back the memories of his research that took him closer and made him fall in love with Marissa. His research among the Native people of First Nations seemed to have a lasting impact on his psyche and spirituality. Marissa was coming back to him like the relentless monsoon rains that came in waves accompanied by heavy wind. He revisited his visit to the community of Carolina just to escape from the ineluctable surge of thoughts and feeling of Marissa. He closed his eyes for a short while to take a long journey in his subconscious memory.

The research by Plumbel took unanticipated proportions and outreach. He found out that Carolina belonged to the Cheyenne tribe that was massacred at the Sand Creek. He remembered what he read in a book about Native American tribes. He thought it was cruel that the American government should have asked the Native People to surrender all their land. They descended from a matrilineal society and had worshipped Earth as their mother. There was resistance with their bow and arrow. They refused to give up their land. It was almost like dedicating their mother for prostitution. It was a terrible clash of civilization against barbarism. Americans called Natives as barbarian because they were dressed in their ancient traditional attire. Cheyenne tribe considered Americans as weak people, sexually untrustworthy, unintelligent and ugly. There was war that broke out in 1861 and lasted till 1864.

It was with a turbulent feeling all over his body that Plumbel approached the Native people. They still maintained their militant character. A casual look at the satellite houses that were constructed around the chieftain's house infused a sense of awe in him. It was not fear but admiration blended with deep respect. He was going to the home of a person who had already made history in his world, though not yet a world history. As long as it was not revealed to the rest of the world it was only anti-history. He was there making his feeble attempt to convert it into world history. It took considerable pain on the part of Plumbel to grasp the idea of anti history. After researching much in the internet he understood in simple terms that the attempts of historians to write a history of some groups of a country submerging the history of uneducated communities of people was anti history.

He had his map and did not take much effort to locate the house of Carolina. The guide to the settlement, a Native who took Plumbel to the Chieftain's house, asked him to sit. He went inside the house, came out and told Plumbel to wait for sometime. It took a while for a lady from inside to come and sit on the chair. There were many chairs and the guide was already in one of them. His friends came from inside and sat with him. They were all talking to one another even as Plumbel was wondering what they were communicating. After some time his guide asked him, "Do you not have anything to ask of the Chieftain?"

Plumbel looked at him askance. "I am waiting for the Chieftain to arrive." He said casually.

"Here is the Chieftain. She is the one. Please speak to her." Millions of worms began to crawl crisscross all of a sudden in the stomach of Plumbel's. "Oh, I am sorry. I didn't understand she is the Chief. I was waiting all the while for a man chief."

"No, we are a matrilineal community and most of our chieftains are women. Very rarely do we have men as Chieftains. She does not know English. You may tell me what you want to say and I shall translate it for her." The guide now began to make business sense.

Plumbel began slowly, measuring his words as if they were pearls of wisdom. The old colonial American attitudes had no intentions of leaving him. "Well, I know Carolina. We work together in the space station." The guide translated this to the chieftain. She asked the interpreter what it meant to be working in the space station. When Plumbel explained that Carolina had travelled to another planet in a spacecraft all hell broke loose.

Elle, the chieftain and mother of Carolina began to lament and wail. She berated and beat her breasts thinking that her daughter must have been dead. She could not understand at all how people could travel in a vehicle to another planet. It is a place where ancestors lived. How can a human being even dare to go to meet them unless they were dead? According to her limited understanding only those who were dead ancestors would go and perch themselves in another planet.

Plumbel did not need a translation for the moaning. He rushed to change his version that Carolina did not go anywhere into the space. She was very much with him. Since she had much work she asked him to meet her people. There was nothing amiss, he asserted vociferously. The guide shouted louder than her lament to convey to her that Carolina did not go to the space yet and was alive, hale and healthy. The progenitor of this truth knew well that he was telling a white lie.

Hearing the lamentations of their Chieftain many neighbors came running. When they reached the house the rubbles were already cleared and they laughed among themselves looking at the pathetic face of Plumbel and that of Carolina's mother. Some among them knew English and it was a big relief for him. He heaved a sigh of relief. Those who knew introduced themselves to Plumbel and that brought a new brightness on the face of the Chieftain. They enquired of him why he had come and found out that he wanted to know more about Carolina. They were more than willing to talk to him. Coffee was served with adequate eatables on the table in front of Plumbel.

"I see Carolina's mother here. Where is her father? What is he doing?" Plumbel kick started the conversation.

It was Gemma who took over the role of narrator. She had by then established herself as the most talkative among the assembled women. Elle was happy that there was someone to talk fluently in English.

"He is gone to one of those planets perched high in the sky to join their ancestors. He did not need the type of spacecraft that you produce to go to those stars up there. May be one-day Carolina would go there and meet him before all of us go there. We worship Earth as our Mother. But we are also deeply united to the stars who are our ancestors." Gemma took off into a world of philosophy.

"When did he die?" This was Plumbel

"As soon as Carolina was born. It is a long story with a long history. Do you have time to listen to our stories? Usually you Americans do not have much time to know about our history and struggles. But you have come in search of us. Therefore, I think you will listen to our story." This was Gemma

"Yes! Yes! I have come here to know more about Carolina. Please go ahead and tell me." Plumbel wanted to arouse the women there into talking.

"But you are such a highly educated man. I am sure you know our history more than any of us knows. I wonder what new information I can give you about our history." Gemma gave a dragging introduction to what could be a succinct story. Plumbel only smiled in return. His smile contained many meanings. Gemma understood it as a go ahead.

"The ten houses that you see here are the only remains of our Cheyenne tribe. Carolina's grandfather was a direct victim of the war that you Americans unleashed on us with a clear intention of destroying all Native Americans. He died when Elle's husband was only a small boy. About thirty families were left after the Americans waged war against us. Carolina's grandfather was a strong fighter. Not only our tribe! Many Native American tribes resisted the occupation of our land. But our arrows and bows were no match for the guns and bombs that you had. He died as a true warrior . . . .

"It was then that the Americans and Europeans together decided to systematically decimate us by perniciously spreading smallpox among Native Americans. You are now trying to build chemical and biological bombs. This is part of your earlier work when Carolina's father was affected seriously by the disease spread through systematic planting of killer virus among us. However he survived as a very weak person. By the time Carolina was born he also died. About ten of our families died of the same cause in the course of time. Now we are happy that Carolina has got one of the most prestigious jobs in the US. She was very clever from her early childhood. We hope that our tribe will revive itself through her contribution . . . ." Saying this she cried inconsolably. Seeing her cry all other women also cried.

Plumbel pulled out his handkerchief and wiped his tears. The hand that was used to pull the trigger of the gun now began to wipe off the few drops of tears that were hard to come. But they came. "I am sorry, really sorry for what has happened to you people. Though it is past I am not the one who believes in burying history. I shall tell you a few other things about your other brothers and sisters . . ."

"Before you start let me inform you what we know. Today there are about 560 tribes of Native Americans. But many of our tribes are only living in very small numbers. From the time our struggle started with Europeans in 1800s more than 90% of our people, millions of our brothers and sisters were massacred in many ways. From 1820 to 1890 alone, in that short span of time more than 3 million of our people were killed. And even today many Americans think that we are barbarians and we deserve only death. You people do not teach your children these lessons of history to remind them of their barbaric history. Our 'Trail of Tears' that started in 1838 with the introduction of 'The Removal Act of 1830' will keep flowing, as even now American rulers have only scant respect for us as human beings . . ." She was continuously sobbing while narrating this.

There was a long silence. The women expected Plumbel to break the wall of silence. He realized that he had not gone there to break anything. He began to speak slowly. "I understand that you know more history about yourselves than I know. Am happy that you are not trying to camouflage your pain with beautiful discourses of compromises.

What happened to you and is happening to you are still very bad. But tell me how did you survive? Did Carolina have any role to play in this survival of your tribe?"

"No, Carolina grew up as a very clever and studious child. Therefore, we wanted her to study, get integrated into the American society and ascend the seats of power if possible. For all our ten families, our Chieftain Elle knows sophisticated techniques of agriculture. We cultivate the little land that we have and make our living. We hope that one day Carolina will bring enough money for all of us so that our children will begin to live long a healthy life. We also hope that she will be in powerful positions to change American laws in our favor." Streams of tears now were transformed into determination for the future.

"Where did Carolina have her early education? Did she socialize with other American children? What were her hobbies?" Plumbel began to dig deep furrows into the past. It was an attempt at running away from pathos.

"She had her early education in a Catholic convent school. The sisters were very sympathetic to her flight and decided to give her good education. After seeing her seriousness about everything in life they decided that she would make a good Christian and advised her to covert, which she did without much resistance. She stayed with them in a boarding and studied there. It was 100 kilometers from here. She used to come home for holidays and some weekends and be of support to her mother. We used to assemble in this house whenever she came. She was very humble and we have not seen her haughty about being educated well. We do not know if she had many American friends. But she loved all of us unconditionally. She was fond of animals and used to complain that she could not relate to them in the convent. She did not socialize much. She always carried a photo of her father and a few of our ancestors. When she came home she would talk to her mother for sometime and then become silent. She also used to help all of us when we went for farming. All of us have to survive on our agriculture. She was very helpful to her mother and learned the techniques of sophisticated agriculture from her mother. We were surprised when we learned that she opted to go to New York to pursue higher studies. Perhaps the sisters in the convent motivated her to do so. Elle had no objection. She was very fond of her only daughter." Plumbel listened to Gemma in absolute silence.

"Are you all also Christians?" He slightly provoked them. Gemma turned to Elle and translated the question to her. Elle's face became red as soon as she heard it. Plumbel could perceive the animosity on her face. He waited for whatever was awaiting him, as Elle began to speak in her language. Gemma did the translation.

"The missionaries came. Many of our people were converted to Christianity. They did so more out of fear than out of any love for a new god. The Europeans were threatening us with many laws to cast us out of our land. They offered to spare us if we agreed to their religion and their rule over us. But most of us resisted. My husband was in the forefront of resistance. Since I was the Chieftain of our tribe it was his duty to protect our Mother Earth. For us it was a very intimate relationship with our Mother that was at serious jeopardy." Plumbel began to be disturbed deep inside, as he was a very devout Christian. He opened his mouth very spontaneously.

"If you are not Christians, do you practice any other religion? What is your faith?"

Elle understood the question without translation. She began to speak up. "We have no idea of religion. We only have our love for Mother Earth and our Ancestors. We are deeply spiritual."

At this stage Gemma intervened to say, "Elle is a Shaman and all of us follow her guidance in life. We do not believe in any god. For us Mother Earth and our Ancestors are everything. Some of our people . . ." Plumbel interrupted her at this point.

His anxiety overtook him. "Was Carolina a Shaman at any point of time?"

Elle took over. "Not when she was in the early stages of her education" But when she went to New York and was on her own she began to follow our traditional ways of worshipping Earth as Mother. She studied much about Shamanism and began to teach us that our way of living and Shamans also existed in many other indigenous communities all over the world. She is now our teacher in shamanism. During her holidays she also visited the Scandinavian countries in order to meet the Sami Shamans. Once she also went to Indonesia and Philippines to meet with some Shamans there."

"Oh, I did not know that Carolina followed shamanic religion. We always thought that she was a Christian, I mean a Catholic . . ."

Now it was Gemma who cut Plumbel short. "There is a problem with you guys. You cannot think beyond religion. Shamanism is not a religion. It is spirituality. We love Nature. We love the cosmos and everything in it. We are not the masters of the cosmos. We are just a part of it. Carolina did not have a problem in being a Christian and a Shaman simultaneously. It is you Christians who condemn shamanism as paganism and kill our shamans . . ."

It was fast eroding into a game of cutting each other short. Both did not have much patience to listen to the other's point of view. Plumbel rushed. "I am only interested to know if Carolina was or is still a Shaman. Yes, there are many issues with our faith. You know that most people of Europe and US have become agnostic though we basically maintain our Christian identity. Let us leave this aside.

Native Americans, European Americans, two worlds apart! Railway lines never meet each other.

CHAPTER EIGHT

Everybody in the rest of the world thought that Bigbelly4 had reached PlanetB2 and that was why his or her TVs and computers went blank all of a sudden. Only the scientists at the space station, Rustler and Plumbel knew that the computers in Bigbelly4 went blank much before it reached PlanetB2. The terrible possibility of the failure of the mission began to strike Rustler on his face violently. He knew that in the previous mission communication was maintained continuously till Bigbelly3 reached PlanetB2. Something was more flawed in this mission. Astronauts inside Bigbelly4 were awestruck at the sudden blackout in the computers. They tried their best to pump life into the unconscious computers that had fainted for reasons best known only to them.

All that they knew was that they were reaching the layer of waves that separated the tangible from the intangible realms of the cosmos. They had come to the conclusion that their fate was sealed. Ground Force in the US tried all knowledge and sharp acumen they had at their disposal to revive communication with Bigbelly4. They scurried all over the space station to set the malfunctioning machines right. However, the problem was that they did not and could not identify the problem. All their efforts were of no avail. Most scientists had come to the easy and safe conclusion that the mission had failed. They resigned themselves to the will of god and left the rest in his hands.

The problem was communicated to Rustler and Plumbel in all earnestness. Rustler's face had become pale like that of a dead man. No one had seen him in that state. He was hoping against hope that something would work out and had great faith in his scientists that they would ultimately pull off a scientific miracle. He called up every top scientist in the space station individually and asked him not to lose heart and do his best to reconnect with Bigbelly4. Plumbel became silent and reticent. He was not ready to talk to anyone. Deep within he began to pray to all the ancestors of Marissa. He prayed to them to save her and bring her back to the earth. He began to think intensively of both Carolina and Marissa.

Awesome7 had become totally silent reflecting the silence of graveyard in the middle of night. Death was glaring at them and was ready to devour them. Their only hope was that Bigbelly4 would somehow land in PlanetB2 even without communication with the Ground Force. It was then that Marissa decided to get back to her inner being and begin to speak with Carolina. She sent out strong and invisible waves of communication to Carolina and asked her to come near her. She was waiting for Carolina to come and touch her gently as she did on two previous occasions. She had not lost hope. She was her usual self and all others were totally shocked at the way she was composed and calm. It took a while for Bigbelly4 to cross the layer of waves that separated PlanetB2 from interaction with earthly beings.

As soon as that layer of waves was crossed computers in Bigbelly4 opened up communication.

Everyone in the space station and in the spacecraft heaved a big sigh of relief. Excitement invaded the private room of Rustler. Plumbel and he rushed to the space station immediately to shake hands with scientists. Now both of them became confident that their mission was going to be a great success. They were already in a mood of celebration. It was only a question of few hours before Bigbelly4 would land in PlanetB2.

Making use of the blackout of computers scientists decided to terminate live telecast of the trajectory of Bigbelly4. Now people started waiting in great anxiety for the news of the landing on PlanetB2.

Humanity had to compromise itself with some reversals. It was the biggest moral blow to the self-serving ego of the President of America who lived under the illusionary conviction that he was invincible. Nature has its own designs against human pride. It does not react to every step that human beings take, positive or negative. It acts. In this case it acted. PlanetB2 acted. By its very nature it does not allow any alien designed instrument into its surface. Waves that are constantly in movement and change 'destroy' any designs of humans or any other beings that contain waves of dominance, destruction and hegemony. It receives only those waves that are life giving. It engages the cosmos in communication in as much as there is openness in them to be completely life giving waves without any trace of desire for overpowering and destroying. There was no wonder then that Begbelly4 had to meet the fate of its predecessors. It melted as soon as it entered into the liquid zone that protected the cosmic beings of PlanetB2. Such was the nature of the waves that surrounded and filled the planet and its living beings. Liquid zone is the area in space that was composed of the intensity of positive waves produced in the bodies of cosmic beings. All matter and wave that emanated from negative beings in cosmos would find their liquid grave in the zone. All such matter would just melt and disappear into nothingness.

There was total cafard in the terrestrial camp of Rustler and Plumbel. All scientists in the base camp in space station envisaged Rustler to become either angry with them for shoddy job or be depressed. Neither of these happened. They did not bargain for the fact that their President was made of a totally different stuff. Angry he became. Not with their shoddy job but with the beings in PlanetB2. He surmised that it was the beings in PlanetB2 that sabotaged all his Herculean plans. Scientists of the space station were almost shocked at the way he reposed his full confidence in them. It was a bonus for them. However, he did not reveal his mind fully to them. It was a big relief to them all the same.

Plumbel and Rustler rued seriously on the fact that the landing on PlanetB2 by Bigbelly4 was almost a replica of the previous landing. Awesome7 melted without any trace. All scientists scurried for any possible survivor. They were looking keenly at the movement of bodies in PlanetB2 to make sure if there were any new arrivals that resembled even remotely human figure. They were denied even that little pleasure that they had in the previous landing.

The extra power with which scientists had packed Bigbelly4 propelled most powerfully Marissa at the very last friction of a second beyond the liquid zone. When communication was lost with computers on earth Marissa instinctively removed her space suit from her body. She was fully naked and arrived on the surface of PlanetB2 with her bare body to be welcomed by Carolina and a host of other cosmic beings. Such was her union with Carolina and cosmic beings.

Now Rustler began to imagine some connections in the survival of both women from the same community. He could see in his computer the melting of Bigbelly4. He was highly exhilarated when the vehicle almost passed through the liquid zone after recovering communication with space station. Victory smile was writ large on his face. It was only for a second. The next moment all scientists watched in sheer horror the way instant melting of the vehicle and with that all the occupants of Bigbelly4 took place. Playing the entire scene back again and again Rustler and Plumbel could see clearly Marissa removing her space suit without any instruction and landing on PlanetB2. Plumbel giggled in his heart a million times seeing the apple of his eyes enter her destiny without any difficulty. He lost her but he also knew that she would get back to him in another form, the cosmic body.

Marissa did not take a few days in human time to recover and begin to walk. It was instantaneous.

It made a huge difference. They could not identify the second being that joined Marissa as soon as she began to walk. But they could easily imagine that it could be only Carolina. There was no staggering and no dilly-dallying. Carolina embraced the entire body of Marissa and both of them began to walk around in gay abandon. Soon a few other beings joined them and they began to move faster than the computers could match. That was a big revelation to the scientists in Ground Force. They inferred that the movement of Carolina was lost to them in the previous mission because of the lower capacity of their computers to match the speed of PlanetB2. They also concluded that if they improved the capacity of their computers they could further explore the movements and lifestyle in the planet. Rustler had a strong message in this discovery.

Plumbel on the other hand was a calm man to the great surprise and to some extent shock of Rustler. He seemed to have anticipated the advent of events as they took place. In his subconscious there was a calm about what was happening with Begbelly4. He began to be more disturbed at the way things were being planned by his friends and the US scientists. An unknown feeling of discomfort began to envelop him as the time approached for Rustler to press the button. He began to be deeply disturbed at Rustler's avarice to overcome nature. He was disturbed more by what had taken place in the lives of Native Americans after the invasion of Europeans into America and less by the failures of space missions. He sensed the change that took place in him and unlike previous occasions he began to be happy about such changes. There was a comfort zone within him that such disturbance and cool headedness were his personality traits now. He began to be more in search of truth than power and achievements. Rustler realized that his bosom friend was distancing himself more and more from his designs to overpower nature and capture other planets. For him someone was either with him or was against him. Plumbel had started moving in the opposite direction of being with Rustler and that hardened the head of Rustler further. Bubbling friendship seemed to be put in the freezer. It seemed to be only a question of time.

It was almost two in the early morning in US. Many other countries were still bubbling with life and activities. Discussions in pubs, bars and in offices centered around landing of Bigbelly4 on the surface of PlanetB2. The entire world was almost sure that the mission would be a grand success, as they were able to see Bigbelly4 nearing the planet without much ado. It was on a straight trajectory for many days till their computers and TVs became blank all of a sudden. Those who were asleep in the US and neighboring countries were violently woken up.

"Bad News! The mission has failed." News flashed all over the world

"What? Is that true? What really happened?" Queries in every corner

"Unbelievable! I thought everything went on well and we were landing on PlanetB2. Any information on why we failed in the mission?" shocking suspense in people's mind

All of a sudden the mission came to be owned up by the entire world. A world that was used to many failures had qualms about accepting another failure without ever questioning the rationale of spending so much money and energy on the mission itself. Nobody's mind really functioned for a long time. The numbness of the brain seemed to have penetrated every nerve center in the body of entire humanity. It looked as if the entire world had come to a standstill.

After the initial shock for about a week the world was sharply divided into two camps. There were many further subdivisions within major divisions. Even those who appreciated Rustler for his daring enterprise and courage now began to have second thoughts about the validity of taking up such an enormous task without being fully prepared. Those who did not want to blame Rustler directly shifted the entire blame on the group of scientists in the American space research. Those who were politically opposed to Rustler found it to be their best chance to pin him down. They called it one of the worst blunders in American history. Some high school students debating on the reasons for the failure of the mission asked a pertinent question: "What were they doing before the mission took off. They were Congressmen. It was their duty to be critical of the mission in the Congress."

Their opposing group in the debate justified them by saying that Rustler, the American President was too powerful for any member of the Congress even to think of opposing his plans. He would squeeze their balls ruthlessly if only he knew someone had opposed his plans.

The Pope invited the entire Christian world to kneel down in prayer so that god might give enough strength to the President of the US to bear with one of the greatest tragedies of humanity. He also prayed openly that god gave the power to Rustler to carry the mission forwarded undaunted by any failure. Many people said that Jesus failed when he died on the cross. But it took three dull days for him to defy the belief of the entire world and rise again alive. In the same way this mission of Rustler would come back alive within a few days in another mega plan. The Pope reminded the world that as long as we remain sinners we are bound to fall. But by the power of the risen Christ we should be able to get up and walk and Rustler would soon begin his next mission to PlanetB2. Rustler got a clue from the Pope.

The Shankracharyas in India reeled out many evidences to show that Americans had not followed the principles of Vastu science. According to them this was the singular reason for the failure of the mission. They even suggested that Bigbelly4 should not have shot off in vertical direction. That was not a good omen. It should have started in a slanting position for about 500 miles and then only taken a straight upward direction. They asserted with firm conviction that the Vedas had the best knowledge on space science and the Americans failed to refer to the Vedas. They suggested that Rustler should induct an Indian Brahmin in the next mission to PlanetB2 for the mission to be successful. One of them even went to the extent of writing that perhaps the lone woman in Awesome7 had her periods during those days of journey and Bigbelly4 was polluted because of that. Since there was no one in the vessel to perform ceremonies of purification that vehicle melted as soon as it landed on the surface of PlanetB2.

The Communist part of the world was visibly happy about the failure of the mission. They revived the saying of Karl Marx that capitalism will saturate itself and will disappear from the face of the earth. Some communist leaders even organized parties for the celebration of the defeat of capitalism. "Did we not say already before the launch of the mission? Now we are proved correct." The left is always right they concluded.

Many cosmic bodies assembled in PlanetB2 to welcome the arrival of Marissa. They had been informed through the body communication of Carolina about her arrival. Since she had her human body still intensity of their communication with her body was not very high. Marissa began to feel their presence and their communication in her body cells more and more intensively gradually till she finally reached full body orgasm. Carolina facilitated this process very easily, as she had gone through it. But the process of transformation into full cosmic being in Marissa was much faster than it was with Carolina. Their cosmic bodies were getting prepared without their consciousness to receive waves of communication from such beings on earth. Carolina took her to every space in PlanetB2 so that her communication with cosmic beings would increase and all beings would begin to communicate with her body.

The arrival of Marissa in PlanetB2 had a very special effect of attracting every cosmic body in the planet to her body. There seemed to be that one special thing in her that was inexplicable. But Carolina knew that her initiation into Christianity instilled certain level of alien values while Marissa remained totally a shamanic entity while on earth and elevated herself to the highest levels through her cosmic spirituality already before arriving in PlanetB2. It was evident from the fact that Marissa did not remain within the spacesuit as soon as she realized in her body that her new world was ready to welcome her. She lost her human body much faster than Carolina did. Many cosmic bodies began to rally round the cosmic body of Marissa.

Rustler called for an emergency meeting of all scientists. His trust quotient in Plumbel had nosedived by the time he decided to call together the scientists. There were expectations of heavy tongue leashing from Rustler. Plumbel was very reflective. He began to already know intuitively what was coming from the President. There was a heavy feeling in his body and he began to become conscious of what was taking place in his body. His body went through the process of metabolism. His intuitive capacity that developed in the body was about negative energy waves that surrounded him as well as positive things that were about to happen in his surroundings. The deeper he went into his inner being he was able to identify more of Marissa there. His body perceived a negative language already much before Rustler went into the special room for the meeting. All other scientists waited in anxious anticipation of anything that might happen. They knew that Rustler was very unpredictable in his reactions to situations. What would happen remained elusive even to them, the top scientists in the world. They were not soothsayers in any case.

Rustler was very well known for his punctuality. All of them stood up looking at the clock even seconds before seeing him physically. There he was at the stroke of 10 in the morning. Rustler had deliberately decided to tie his tongue when he went into the meeting. He asked the scientists to give reasons for possible failure of Bigbelly4.

"We had done everything that was humanly possible. As you saw for yourself there was no error of any sort in the machines. There was only a mysterious blackout of our communication machines. We need to unfold that mysterious element that made our computers disconnect and go dark all of a sudden." Scientist No1.

"Since we do not have the machine with us it becomes very difficult to make a post mortem of the failure. It is possible that one of the filaments in any of the machine was temporarily disconnected and got connected again due to a later jerk in Bigbelly4." Scientist No2.

"It is possible that the belly of Bigbelly4 became overheated at the point where it entered into the liquid zone. Though we have taken all precautionary measures, it is still possible that the temperature in the liquid zone became too hot for the Bigbelly4. The temperature went much beyond the level that we had scientifically measured. That scenario is still very mysterious to me. Why did the temperature rise in the liquid zone more than its time tested level?" Scientist No3.

Rustler became a bit irritated already at this point despite the fact that he had decided not to be harsh with his group of scientists. He did not turn to Plumbel, as he knew that nothing went wrong with the preparedness of the astronauts in Bigbelly4. "Gentlemen, you are badly off the track. We are not discussing here about the blackout of our communication system. It was a minor error and it was quickly fixed well . . ."

The Indian scientist who was scientist No4 interrupted Rustler. It was unnecessary on his part. However, he could not contain himself at the way scientists were giving 'false' information to Rustler. "Sir, it was not a mistake of science that made Bigbelly4 perish. It was a human error at a different realm. If you know a little bit of astrology you will understand that you pressed the button at Rahukala, the bad time when Yama crosses the path of Sun. We should have waited for this bad time to pass in order to launch Bigbelly4." Plumbel covered his mouth with both hands in order to control his laughter at the stupidity of the scientist. Science and Vedas, the eternal conflict! He wondered to himself as to how such a person got into the gang of scientists who were bracketed as the best in the world.

Rustler was about to slap him on his face. However, he realized that it was unbecoming of the President of the US to slap a scientist in front of other scientists. It would be reported in the media and he would gain an undeserving bad name. He quickly recovered and lowered his hand from chin height to his hip level. It had the intended result. The Indian scientist innocently thought that Rustler extended his hand for a warm handshake. He rescued Rustler of a big embarrassment. Rustler grinned with his mouth wide open straining his lips. The Indian scientist's value in terms of contributing to the technical side of building Bigbelly4 to perfection was unquestionable. Therefore, America decided to put up with the farting side of his Indian personality. "Bullshit" Rustler mumbled to himself as he shook hands.

Rustler's words came from the uneven surface of his throat. It was like sliding on a very hard terrain laid with gravel. "We do analysis in order to pick up lessons for the future. Tell me what is the crux of the issue in our failed mission. Unless we identify it we cannot even imagine another voyage to PlanetB2. But I shall never give up. I shall not rest until Americans set their foot on the planet and overpower all the beings there . . ."

Rustler was interrupted once again by the Indian scientist. "Sir, one thing that is evident is that the survivor in the mission is a woman. We must see if we can send an all women team the next time." He seemed to have made up for his earlier loss of face by his total volte-face on women. There was a very difficult smile on one side of Rustler's mouth once again. He was grinding his teeth inside his mouth.

"We understand from Plumbel that the woman was Native American. The woman who survived in the previous mission was also from the Native American community. We must check if there is a connection between their survival and their culture. In order to arrive at reasonable inferences we need to know what methods were used in training her. If there is anything special that made them survive, because of the training it must be enhanced manifold." Scientist1 spoke again.

Rustler looked up to Plumbel with the same hard face that he put up with all other scientists. The look was an order to speak up. "I cannot identify anything special that can be said to be the cause of their survival. However, my guess is that it has something to do with their spirituality. Both of them are worshippers of the Elements of Cosmos and are fine tuned to communicate effectively with cosmic beings. As far as I know this is the only thing that I could identify as special in them."

Rustler passed a sarcastic smile. The sarcasm was evident to everyone with only one side of his mouth twisted to evince a hard earned smile. Encouraged by him the other scientists except the Indian also smiled derisively. "Do you believe in pagan spirits, Plumbel? You seem to have become quite weird these days. You are aware of the pagan spirituality that Native Americans practice. Can we ever accept animism as a valid principle? I cannot accept this stupidity. This is much worse than what our Indian scientist said a while ago." Rustler was not only derisive of his friend but was also angry and easily dismissive.

"You are making a serious mistake Rustler. This is not the way to look at spirituality of any people. Your arrogance on this matter is totally unwarranted. I am your friend and I wish everything good for your ambitious plans. But I differ with you on the way you are treating the spirituality of the Native people. I have seen it and experienced it and know it is a very valid discipline." Plumbel was as cool as the ice of Antarctica. Rustler was staggering in his effort not to slip and fall. For the first time in their relationship, both Rustler and Plumbel took out their pent-up anger against each other in front of others. It used to be a one-way traffic till now. Plumbel himself did not know how he gathered the courage to speak up against Rustler in front of other people. Perhaps the provocation was the audacity of Rustler. There was dead silence of the graveyard for quite sometime.

"Sirs, please be calm. This is a matter that requires our most serious consideration. Let us look at the facts one by one from the time of her recruitment to the time the spacecraft shot off into the orbit . . ." Even as scientist2 tried to restore sanity in the place Rustler interrupted him with a thud. "He is the one who trained both of them and he must be knowing all connections between their culture and survival. Ask him to come out systematically so that an appropriate analysis is made possible."

Plumbel was seeing stars. All the scientists were shaken to the core of their being. It was a first in American history. They sat up on their chairs with a big surprise writ large on their faces. No one dared to speak. Each one was looking at the other with wonder as to what was happening in that hall. Had Rustler gone mad or was he a thug?

It did not take more than five seconds for Rustler to realize the blunder he had committed in his fit of rage against Plumbel, his most trusted friend till then. He had let the cat out of the bag without anyone asking for it. He was in total embarrassment and Plumbel was the one who looked at him with all the sympathy that a haughty President of the US needed and deserved. Rustler did not fail to notice. "I am sorry gentlemen" he said in a very mild voice and looked at Plumbel in helplessness.

"Mr. President, though it was a slip of tongue on your part it makes one of the most interesting points. I request all my colleagues here to keep it as a secret and not to make any noise about it. But tell me Mr. Rustler, how many previous attempts were made to land in PlanetB2?" Scientist 2

It was Plumbel who came to Rustler's rescue this time. He explained to the scientists the three aborted attempts to reach out to PlanetB2. He also informed them that there were two survivors on the planet, both hailing from the same Native American community.

Mr. Plumbel, we understand that you have trained both of them and they have survived on PlanetB2. What were the common things that you identified in them apart from the generalization of spirituality?" Scientist1.

"He has even gone to their places and done researches on their background. He must be knowing a lot more than sheer spirituality." Rustler now began to speak in third person. It was not directly to Plumbel but to other scientists. That upset Plumbel astronomically. It was the first time that he began to see a wide chasm between him and Rustler. It caused much pain in many parts of his body. He did not know how to deal with this sudden upsurge of conflicting emotions in him. If he had to deal with issues only from a rational positioning he would have been happy. But now he was forced into an emotional situation wherein he felt his trust and friendship was totally discarded by a sheer power monger who had only deep disdain for relationships. It was only recently that he began to be in touch with his emotions in the body. He was very grateful to the indigenous peoples for this. He was just fascinated by the emotive relationship he enjoyed with Marissa. Without her physical presence near him his personality would have been disjointed from all its bolts and nuts and in her absence he found himself lay scattered in front of the scientists. He fumbled for words and in a fit of emotion he spurted out.

"When I speak about their spirituality I mean their ability to connect to each other and to the rest of the cosmos in a creative manner. They keep communicating with Cosmic Elements constantly and draw their energy from the cosmos . . ."

Scientist3 almost violently interrupted him. "How did you know that both of them live in communication with cosmos? Were they in communication with each other?"

"Yes. They are from the same Native American community and they have been trained in shamanic spirituality. Though Carolina converted herself to become a Catholic she did not give up her shamanic spirituality. For us it is difficult to understand how these two can be merged. But she did it beautifully well." Plumbel began to blabber the truths that he knew without any control over his emotions. He was still not mature enough to blend his emotive operations with his rational operations. Rustler was smiling within himself that the man was beginning to scatter precious pearls in front of his pigs. It would take ages for Plumbel to gather them all over again.

"Did he know this much about Carolina during her training? As far as I know he went for his research only after Carolina was lost in PlanetB2. How did he know so much about Carolina? He never shared any of these findings with me." Rustler began to blame Plumbel of serious breach of confidence. That upset Plumbel more.

"I came to know many truths about Carolina from Marissa. Unlike Carolina she remained a firm follower of shamanic spirituality and became a shaman herself. It was at that time that we recruited her. We became close to each other as father and daughter." Rustler was happy that Plumbel began to puke out many unknown truths in his conflicting emotional situation. He wanted to hear more from Plumbel.

Plumbel danced to the tune of Rustler, the snake charmer. In his praise of the capacities of Marissa he went a little further. "While in training Marissa had established contact with Carolina. I do not know how true this is. But I saw her communicating with Carolina one night in the thick of darkness." At this point Plumbel became aware that he was vomiting a bit of unnecessary stuff in front of those who were nowhere near consuming what he puked out. They even detested it. His rational function began to be alive and take control. He was wondering if he was doing the right thing and became silent abruptly.

Rustler was now furious with Plumbel and let go of his wild emotions. "So much has taken place between you and Marissa and you did not mention a word to me about it. Go to hell."

Rustler shouted, got up in a huff and left the meeting. No one knew what to do in these circumstances. Surprisingly there was tacit sympathy for Plumbel except from the Indian scientist. He would only toe the official line always.

It looked like a special meeting in PlanetB2. They were not used to any meeting nor did they have any need for a meeting. However, the way many cosmic bodies had come together looked as if there was a special meeting. There was no one to call for a meeting in the planet. While this was happening cosmic bodies of Carolina and Marissa began to receive tinges of waves from the earthly body of Plumbel. The communications were mild and weak. The redeeming factor was that it had started. Both of them had brought substantial increase in the communication of cosmic beings with human beings who were tuned to receive cosmic waves. The new communication from a living human body brought its own effects in the cosmic bodies of many ancestors in PlanetB2.

They began to move around the planet responding positively to the new changes that came out of the connection between earthly beings and cosmic beings. This was a follow up to the mild tremor they had experienced earlier. Added to the previous tremor was the arrival of Bigbelly4. Though it melted automatically on arrival in the liquid zone the presence of a new human body did make a difference in the communicative interactions of cosmic beings in the planet. The usual experience of full body orgasm began to be disturbed by the touch of response from Plumbel to perceived dominance of Rustler.

Cosmic beings in PlanetB2 became ever alert to the new change in the atmosphere of their planet. Ancient ancestral bodies both of human beings and of animals and plants that discharged life-giving waves had become humongous essence of entropy. They were the ones who had absolute openness to receive life-giving energy and to release the same to fill PlanetB2. Carolina's body had already become a huge mass of energy waves. She was irreversibly a life giving body. Marissa had to go through a process of cosmic change and shed her human body completely of its earlier traces.

Marissa had the innate sensation in her body that bodies of the comic beings were round in shape. She was not able to see her body being composed of legs, hands, head etc. As soon as Bigbelly4 melted she lost her consciousness of a human being. It was in that subconscious state that she removed her space suit and became absolutely naked. As soon as she shed her vests she became one with cosmic beings in terms of communication. It was only through communication in her cell that she was able to experience shape, size and movement of bodies.

Soon Rustler invited the chief of the American Intelligence Agency (AIA) and the chief of his space scientists for a closed-door discussion. He informed them of the meeting he had with scientists along with his former friend Plumbel. Now he was unable to take Carolina and Marissa and their spirituality lightly. He informed them that he found something very serious in what Plumbel shared in the meeting of the scientists. He regretted the fact that Plumbel had become a poor victim of his fancy for Marissa. "Being unmarried and not used to girls it is understandable that he behaves the way he does. But I am also a sworn bachelor and I do not become victim of any girl's sexual proclivity to me. I love my country. I love America." He made a solemn profession of his loyalty to his country and in the entire bargain also made himself a saint who could not fault on anything.

"Are you sure that the girl is still alive in PlanetB2?" the chief of American Intelligence Agency asked Rustler in all seriousness.

He switched on his personal computer and showed him pictures of the movement of many beings on PlanetB2. He pointed out to the two astronauts sent by America and said that they were the girls sent by the US. Marissa still had resemblances of a human body. But Carolina looked like all other cosmic beings, bundled out into a ball of life giving energy. "We have been continuously tracking the movement of Carolina, as she looks like all other beings there. If we lose track of her we would lose her. As you see both these figures are always together. That is another strong indication." Rustler now began to make some sense to the scientist as well as to the police.

It was expected that both of them were taken by surprise looking at the bundle of energies moving about in PlanetB2. They did not have access to such privileged pictures till now. "I want to share with you a secret that even the Congress does not know. There have been two earlier failures in our adventure into PlanetB2. Our first attempt ended in a total fiasco. In the second attempt with Bigbelly3 we succeeded to land as we did this time and only one girl survived. She is Carolina. All other members of Awesome6 disappeared without a trace. It was this particular survival that made us dare to make another grand attempt and also announce it to the entire world. We did not anticipate failure this time, as all our scientists worked to perfection and Plumbel imparted very special training to Awesome7. It is a shame on America's talent that we repeated the failure in the same fashion as the previous one. Marissa has joined Carolina in PlanetB2 but we have no communication whatever from them. Plumbel has succeeded over me through these two girls of the Native Americans. This is a big blow to American pride." Rustler avoided all possible embarrassment already at the beginning.

"Do you have any specific expectations from us?" The chief of American scientists asked him as a thorough professional.

"Yes, of course! That is why I have brought you here today. I have spent many sleepless nights thinking of the possible reasons for the failure of Bigbelly4. I do not want to repeat the same mistake again. I have thought of another approach. But before I reveal it to you I want a pledge from you that it will remain a top secret till we arrive at a way out that can be revealed to the entire world." Rustler meant serious business with his top associates.

"You have appointed us to assist you professionally and not to play with the future of our country. You please deal with your sentiments. Whatever is good for America we shall do, even if it means dying for our country. You are our President. Whatever you order us to do as the President of America we shall do. But what happens between you and Plumbel is your personal matter and please do not expect us to be involved in it." Both of them pledged professional allegiance to Rustler without eulogizing him or without becoming emotive about anything that was on the table.

Rustler pulled his head a bit down. The other two too did the same. Three heads coming together without bothering about their bodies!

They could not trust even their own bodies. Head was supreme. In a much-lowered voice Rustler revealed to them his secret plan.

When their heads became erect the two of them were looking at Rustler with awe and admiration. Mr. President, I am not the type to eulogize anyone. You know it well and that is why you have appointed me as the Chief of the AIA. But I must confess that you have floored both of us with your genius. This will be your masterstroke and we understand that we can do this only in secrecy. Their bodies became stiff with much anxiety. Rustler brought a bottle of Cognac to loosen their stiff muscles a bit. Each one took a slow sip and began let down the joy of the new information sink into their bodies slowly.

He instructed Nicky Broom, the Chief of AIA to set up a special team that would work on any possible communication and its aftermath anywhere in the world. All 'out of the way' communications and pronouncements should be traced with extreme care and reported to him directly. It should be a top class team that would not indulge in lose talk but would also talk in such a way that they would pull out from the mouths of people every small little information that would make a contribution to the discovery of the scientists. The Chief should pass on all such information directly to the President and he would in turn classify the information and pass on only relevant information to the Chief of Scientists. As they sipped their cognac in regular intervals slowly the three of them began to recollect silently what Rustler imparted to their heads a while ago.

"Plumbel informed us one day that Carolina came down from PlanetB2 to meet Marissa. A small group of scientists first laughed at him without realizing that he was indeed revealing to us an enormous truth that history had not seen till now. The truth is that there is communication between the beings in PlanetB2 and some beings on earth. We understand that communication between our planet and PlanetB2 is possible. We need to discover how it is possible. That both these girls are from Native American community and that both of them have survived in PlanetB2 and that both of them are close to each other have their necessary connections. I am not a scientist. But I have read something about entropy. I understand that waves of thoughts and emotions interact among themselves, go through a process of merger known as entropy and become new waves. I want you scientists to find out if the waves of people living on earth and the waves from the bodies of Carolina and Marissa interact among themselves. I can say only this much because I am a layman scientist and not a professional one like you. Now I leave it to you to pursue this matter and suggest to me ways and means of establishing connections with the two girls so that we may design our space strategies without any possibility for failure. Remember that there are two Americans in PlanetB2 and they are there to support us." The bodies of the Chief of AIA and the group of scientists were in mad dance of rocking joy when they heard this. Rustler's plans for overcoming nature got into their cells with an intoxicating effect. It was time for them to go home.

CHAPTER NINE

Plumbel was not a crooked man. He did not establish his relationships with ulterior motives. If he liked someone he continued his relationship. Very rarely did he develop strategic relationship. He was a friendly man unlike Rustler who supported his hard face with a stiff neck. He thought such a look was the mark of his authority. Many people in high positions liked Plumbel. Hardly did they know that they liked him as a reaction to their aversion to Rustler. There were many top ranking officers in the US military and in AIA who were dissatisfied with the functioning style of Rustler despite his enormous charisma of attracting world opinion towards him. Blaming his functioning style was the lamest excuse they used for their personal vendetta against the President. They gave vent to their vexations among themselves in the form of gossip after sending in a few pegs of military rum and the finest whisky depending on to which institution each one belonged. Rum for military and Whisky for Intelligence! They saw Plumbel as a power pole. However, they also saw him as being planted at the same spot where Rustler's power was planted. Lose talk was their only escape route.

With the disagreements between Rustler and Plumbel coming out in the open in front of them news spread like wild fire. The heat however, did not touch both of them. The moment they guessed reasonably well that Rustler rubbed off the name of Plumbel from his book of favorites they sensed their greatest opportunity. Camp positions emerged as an inevitable consequence. They carefully avoided passing on any such information to Nicky Broom about the rift.

Much before friction came into the open Plumbel had his own set of friends in all American institutions. Being a good natured and affable person he endeared himself to the sensitive among some bureaucrats. They sensed that Plumbel was in another pole in the opposite direction of their President. Two of his erstwhile friends were occupying high positions in AIA. They were the left and right hand of Nicky Broom. Since AIA worked in tandem with the top brass in US military it was normal that some of the top guys attended military meetings and not vice versa. The Army men were persona non-grata in the high-ranking meetings of AIA.

Plumbel was shocked to the core of his being at what he heard. For a long time he could not believe his ears. He pinched his thighs several times to make sure that he was in the real world. He also asked many serious questions about the intelligence system and the way it worked to make sure that both of them were not too drunk. They were not. They did not rhapsodize about him making it clear to Plumbel that they were not inebriated.

"Mr. Plumbel we did not want to communicate anything to you over phone for obvious reasons. We made it look as the most casual evening meeting. That is why we called you to this restaurant." One of their eyes was still meandering all over the restaurant to make sure that none of his former or present colleagues was there. They had selected a very popular bar for this get together. They carefully avoided any secluded place. They knew better. It was in such secluded jaunts that the agents of their own clandestine institution conducted their entire bargain.

"Have you any life-and-death information about our mission to PlanetB2? Please tell me. I shall pass on the information to Rustler." Both of them wanted to take two bottles of the Single Malt they had and knock them on their forehead. Plumbel was such a naïve and simple man.

"No, no! It is not about PlanetB2. Why should we be so worried and call you urgently if it were about our mission to the planet? It is about you Mr. Plumbel . . . ."

"About me? What is there about me that I do not know?" Plumbel was totally taken aback at this turn of the evening. He never bargained for becoming the object of gossip among the government servants.

"Sir, we have called you here with utmost seriousness. We are deeply concerned about your physical security. We have a very secret and equally serious information to give you." Plumbel's mind went haywire with imagination in a few seconds. It went all across the world and returned back to him in no time. This particular sauntering had no salvific effect on his mind. It was his mind that actually meandered. He tried to be calm and he thought of Marissa. His mind began to rest.

"Don't be joking. Who could ever think of providing me with insecurity? Yes, I thank you for the concern you have for me. But give me the information you have in full." Plumbel tried to calm down his admirers as well as himself.

"Mr. Plumbel, we don't know how you are going to take it. But it is better that we say it to you than keep it within ourselves. Rustler has given order to Nicky Broom to eliminate you physically without anybody's knowledge. Your death will pass as a sabotage by one of the Arab countries for your advise to the President to attack the Arab countries. Their actual target is someone in AIA but you will happen to travel in the vehicle that the unknown guy is supposed to travel. Thus you will become the wrong target of Muslim attack and the case will be closed." It was not a hollow boom for once. Plumbel's ears heard the actual blasting. Never did he ever think in his life that his most trusted friend would target him. His world crumbled into fragments under his feet even before any bomb blasted him. Now that the possible culprit is someone with whom he shared everything of his life shook him to the bottom. His friends became a bit jittery, as they saw him becoming pale on his face.

"Are you sure Rustler has done this? Of all the people in the world!"

"Yes, Mr. Plumbel this is all that we have to give you today. When we get more information we shall pass it on to you in one way or other." They got up to leave in a hurry. They would not spend more than a limited time in one place with anyone. It was part of their intelligence discipline. Going by the position they held in AIA Plumbel could not take even a coma or other punctuations in their statements light.

Plumbel too got up to shake hands with them. He knew their behavior. They could suddenly change their position and run away. Only they knew their ways. "Thank you gentlemen for your concern. I shall take care of myself." He shook hands with his shaky hands.

"A final word of caution! Please do not accept any letter or parcel from anyone whom you do not know. If you happen to receive any letter or parcel from any known persons please do not open them immediately. Make sure there is no bomb inside. You know all the tricks of the trade. Take care Mr. Plumbel. We are concerned about you." They did not wait for a reply from him. They vanished without leaving a trail behind. True AIA style!

It was one of the most neglected spots in America. Carolina's relatives had spoken to Plumbel about it when he visited them first. It was a hide out for the Native Americans to escape from them when they were in hot pursuit of Native Americans. But later it turned out to be the mass dumping ground for the millions of Natives who were butchered by invading Europeans. There were many such places to also pile up the carcasses of millions of buffalos and bison and set fire to them. After the end of the holocaust Native Americans started visiting these places to worship their ancestors. But the places where they burned the buffalos and bison were not visited frequently and some of them remained deserted by humans and animals alike. Relatives of Carolina showed all such places with unlimited tears flowing from their eyes. He could not bear the pain in his heart. After his association with Marissa he had learned the art of operating from his emotional zones. At times it turned out to be very ugly but on the whole he managed to be reasonably emotional. What was more important in this slow molding of his personality was that he began to be sensitive to sufferings of others. But he could not cry in front of the Native people. It would hurt his American pride.

Now things changed. Plumbel decided to take refuge in one of those deserted places when the worst came. He knew it would be only his temporary shelter. He had to take refuge permanently elsewhere. He needed to gather more concrete evidence of the designs of Rustler. He needed to verify the information that he had on his hands. He visited the community of Carolina and Marissa immediately, as any delay could possibly lead his enemies to his hideouts.

They welcomed him with open arms. But there was a big embarrassment for him in the waiting in both the places. Relatives of Carolina and Marissa enquired of their well-being. They also asked him when their children would go to visit them. Rustler and Plumbel had decided together that they would send money regularly to the family of Carolina and now also of Marissa in order not to arouse their suspicion. Plumbel continued to hide the truth as a true American military man. He informed them that both the girls were in fine mettle in a far off satellite and they would come home safe when they returned to earth. It might take two to three years. He also told them that even reaching Pluto would take nine years. They must be happy that their daughters are only in a nearby satellite. Truths and lies mixed together to make a tasty fruit salad for the innocent Native people of the First Nations.

Plumbel took some of them to his potential hide out and asked them to clean the place. He gave the lame excuse that he wanted to do a lot of meditation there without anybody noticing it. He would go there any time without informing them.

One fine evening Plumbel got another call from his AIA friends. Plumbel went to the place they invited him for a short while. They confirmed what they had informed him earlier. There was no point in giving him any stale news. "Mr. Plumbel, Nicky Broom has handed over the operation elimination to the Israelites. Even accident by any American agency can raise many eyebrows within AIA. Therefore, they find it very expedient to hand over the job to the Israelites. They are accomplished professionals in such missions. Now you see, you have to be extremely careful." They did not wait any further. They whistled past him.

Plumbel was wet all over his body. It was very cool out there. But he was hot like a burning furnace inside. It was one of those rare occasions when a wet dress could cause a burn inside his body.

Rustler alerted all members of the military to be ever alert for any emergency as a fall out of the failure of the mission to PlanetB2. Nations could begin to take the US for granted and work stealthily against the interest of America. He asked the CIA to permeate every nook and corner of the world to collect all possible data about any new activity in the world and report the same to their Chief directly. He also advised him to weed out hollow booming empty gongs from the type of information he got and take to him only the noiseless biting ones.

Nicky Broom invited Rustler to the AIA Headquarters near Washington. He made the call through his hotline. The secret meeting was called at the behest of Joshua Bucket, the Chief of the National Institute of American Scientists in the US. As was his wont Rustler reached the place exactly at the appointed time. It was a high profile meeting with also the two assistants of Nicky and some close associates of Joshua. They were all top class scientists and intelligence gatherers.

“Mr. President, we have done very serious researches on the possibility of establishing contacts with the two women astronauts in PlanetB2. It is well neigh impossible. We tried to reach out to all possible communications they have with beings on earth. This was a hypothesis on which we worked. Of course we had the lead that you gave to us in this regard. You had earlier told us that Carolina had come down once to meet Marissa. We worked on any such possibility . . ."

". . . After our path breaking endeavor we are happy to inform you that we have traced the communication sent by both of them to the earth. It is reaching the same object on earth occasionally. We are also able to track the return communication from that earthly being to our two former astronauts. But this communication gets cut off exactly at the point where Bigbelly4 had an internal blackout. It is at the periphery of the liquid zone. It is that place in space where our computers were blacked out both here and in Bigbelly4. That is the location beyond which we are unable to reach . . ."

". . . We have gone through all the intricacies of this communication. After much careful analysis of all data available with us . . ."

Rustler interrupted them at this point. "Which is that point on earth or that earthly being with whom our two astronauts are communicating? Why do they communicate only with that one person or one point?" He could not control his anxiety for long. He wanted to be the master of everything that happened around him.

"Mr. President, this something that they communicate is not merely their choice. From what we have understood from the Native Americans it becomes clear that they communicate with all those whose bodies are open to receive their communication. At the moment we have identified only one earthly being, as the communication waves have frequent velocity. However, it is very easy for us to find out the mechanism of their choices. Since they are communicating with only one earthly being it does not pose a big problem to us. We have to only identify that being and put him/her under our scientific observation."

"How long will it take for you to identify that being on earth? Is he or she in America or somewhere else?" Rustler was itching all over for quick information.

"You will be happy to know that the particular earthly being has been identified and it is your guess. However, we shall let you know of the being later. We have a few more observations to do before we come to you with conclusive evidence." Joshua Bucket had gathered enough data to convince Rustler that his department was doing its duty well. Rustler was convinced and was ready to wait.

However, he had a serious doubt from which he could not extricate himself. "You say that the communication from that being does not go beyond a certain point. Does that mean that it is a one-way communication? Am I to understand that only our two astronauts are communicating to the earthly being without receiving any communication from him? You have to explain this to me."

"Do you know the being already? You are referring to him and not to her." Nicky Broom tried to sweep under the feet of Rustler.

"Oh did I say that? I am sorry. It is a slip of tongue and my way of speaking. It can be anybody." Rustler quickly excused himself.

"We went deep into that aspect Mr. President. It is a grey area in our research. Just as there are air pockets in space there may be certain points through which communication from earthly beings may reach our astronauts in PlanetB2." Bucket poured out the information that he had scooped from his hard working colleagues.

"Tell me how they communicate to the earthly beings. If we know that probably we can break the jinx." Rustler now slowly began to manifest the genius that he was made of. It was not for no reason that he became the President of America. He was a multidimensional genius. He sparkled when it mattered most at the most unexpected moment.

"Yes, Mr. President. We have gone a few steps ahead in that. We have discovered that their communication is mainly or only through waves. Just as we have sound waves and light waves there can be also thought waves and feeling waves. Our strong surmise is that they are communicating through their emotive and thought waves. Their sound waves cannot reach the earth. We are not sure if they are able to make any sound there in PlanetB2." It was one of the colleagues of Joshua who winked eyes at him to indicate that no one else was supposed to speak. Only he was supposed to say things authoritatively.

"Well, it becomes easy then. If you are able to capture sound waves and light waves in our receivers we should also be able to capture thought waves and feeling waves. Why don't you do that?" Rustler showed signs of being impatient and impertinent.

Joshua Bucket knew that it was time to wind up the discussion lest it turned out to be disastrous. He came to the point. "Mr. Rustler, we need special equipment to capture those waves. Such equipment has not been discovered yet. But we are confident that we can make them. However, it may suck much of our budget. You need to pump in a lot of money to our scientists to create such type of machines. It will not be a loss to America. Once we discover such equipment we can fix them to the satellites and capture all the thoughts and feelings of our enemies even before they utter any word. Much of the effort that we spend for intelligence gathering can change its complexion if we succeed in fabricating a wave-capturing machine. Wow, it will be a world history Mr. Rustler. If only we can copyright such machines and not let the technology go into the open no one can assail the United States of America any more. On the positive side we can take control of the entire world and bring it under our feet."

Plumbel knew the intelligence gathering techniques of the Israelites more than most Israelites. He knew that they would travel to the nether world if they were in pursuit of anyone. The prospect of hiding in an abandoned graveyard among the Native people was not a realistic proposition. However, he dared to go there and spend quiet time with Marissa. What would be a better place to be in touch with her than the spot where most of her ancestors were either buried or burned? He ventured all alone into the spot that he had fixed even without the knowledge of the relatives of Carolina and Marissa. He took with him stacks of food and drinks that would last him at least for two weeks. He bought also enough preservatives and vitamin tablets just to keep him energetic for his long meditations. He set up his tent and began to live there. He did not want to be noticed at night. Therefore, he had taken some solar lamps that could light up his tent in darkness. He knew it was a very difficult choice, as sunlight was much less in the place he had chosen. But then he had also decided to put up with any type of difficulty.

Those two weeks were the strangest period in his life. From the second day many bears came to give him company. They also ate with him whatever he offered. Many of them seemed to meditate with him sitting there for long duration without making any noise. But they frequented him on and off thus never leaving him alone during the day. Strange as it was, he began to converse with them in his language in a few days. They seemed to understand what he said. They ate from his hand and at least two of them put their front legs over his shoulders in deep affection. He felt an electrifying permeation of feeling within his nerves and cells at the type of affection he received from them. He had the odd bison coming to pay him visits but they would move about as if he was a non-entity.

Their self-pride seemed to surpass all American pride put together. He had no need for his gun at any time. After five days he even forgot about his gun and began to eat with them during the day. One of the bears began to sip the drinks that he offered. He dared and they budged. He enjoyed the way that huge bear drank wine and began to roll all over his place in hyper excitement. He too got drunk with joy, held its hand and began to dance with it. It was a merry go round that he did not bargain for when he set out to live there.

Surprisingly wolves were attracted to him in the evening by the smell of the meat that he ate. They were initially hesitant to go near him. He was afraid of the wolves and they were more frightened of him. But as he extended pieces of meat to them they dared to go near him and eat. It was only a few moments before they became his friends. They would go for their hunting but they also made it a point to sleep all around him. It was a totally new Plumbel and he was surprised of himself.

He had spent the tenth day in long hours of meditation. He relived his entire relationship with Marissa. The more he thought of her the more blissful he was. Occasionally his thoughts went also towards Carolina whom he trained specially for the mission. But he lived the entire day with Marissa so to say. At the end of the day towards evening he saw that the bears had not yet left him. The wolves had already arrived for their quota of food. Plumbel served food for all of them. It was very little for all the beings that gathered that evening. They were ready to share the little he had. But the bears enjoyed the drinks he gave.

Wolves refused to share drinks. He enjoyed their company thoroughly. It helped to forget the physical difficulties he had in the new camp.

A wholesome transformation in the man who was once to guide the destiny of the nation to land in another planet! That day he was not sure how long he would live in his planet. He should have been weighed down with much worry. But the days that he spent in that ancestral place in the best company of his darling Marissa lightened his body immensely. All tension had taken an easy flight from his body. He was walking about like a little child unmindful of all the incredulous plans of Rustler for his elimination from the face of the earth. In the company of his new friends he completed his simple dinner. In absolute peace he went to bed and had a sound sleep.

"Plumbel, Plumbel, please wake up. We have come to visit you." He woke up in a jerk wondering how they managed to walk past his friends, the bears and the wolves.

"Do not worry about us. All of them are our friends. They knew us much before they met you. In fact we sent them here to protect you." Both Marissa and Carolina stood on both sides of his bed and talked to him. Marissa was holding his hand. Carolina was standing at his side with glowing eyes. The light from her eyes lighted up the tent in which he was sleeping.

"How are you my beloved girls? What made you come down to meet me? How is your life in PlanetB2? I understand that both of you have recognized each other there." Plumbel began to pour out words like the Niagara Falls.

"Shhhh . . . Don't talk loud. Be careful with your voice. We have known well your present unfortunate situation. You have done the right thing by leaving him." Carolina went into business straight away.

"Is it possible for Rustler to land in PlanetB2? Why is it that only both of you have survived in that planet and all others have died? Why do all the machines and space ships that we sent melt as soon as they land in PlanetB2?" The water in Niagara Falls was flowing with a heavy mix of mud and gravel. It was a fresh gush onto the earth from above.

"It is a near miracle that the spacecraft sent by you managed to reach PlanetB2. You know well that America and all other nations of the world have been indulging in production of heat waves of an uncontrollable enormity. All these warming waves have gathered in the space and formed a layer of unbearable heat. Actually the space vessels sent by you should have been subsumed in that layer of heat waves. But the US scientists have made the outer body of the spacecraft strong enough to resist the heat produced by them. That is the layer of self-destruction that the US has created. More and more heat waves are accumulating there and it will become more and more difficult for any space ship to pass the layer easily." Carolina gave a long explanation. Plumbel was happy and recollected her sharp intellectual acumen when she went through training with him.

"Even if they manage to pierce through this layer of extreme heat through their scientific machines there is another big hurdle known as the liquid zone. This zone is created by the positive energy waves that we send into the cosmos from our bodies. We are in eternal communication with beings that are open to receive positive energy waves in their body cells. These waves also form a layer in space to protect us from the entry of any negative and destructive waves or machines or beings. No one can pass through this layer with even a miniscule remnant of negative waves. Only positive and life giving energy waves can pass through this liquid zone. Since the entire mission to PlanetB2 is designed through an avaricious plan to overcome the cosmos and establish human dominance over nature nobody and no machine can pass through this liquid zone." Plumbel was equally surprised at the way Marissa explained truths rationally to him.

"Thank god that you have survived all that human folly. But tell me when you will come back to the earth? Your parents and relatives are waiting for you very eagerly. I had a lot of difficulty convincing them that you would come back soon. Have you already come back to the earth? Come let us go and meet your people. I like them very much. They are some of the finest human beings I have met in my life. They have transformed my perspectives of life in a short time." Water from the Niagara began to spread its wet wings all over the place because of the wind that blew over it.

"Give us some whisky and good food Plumbel. We are hungry. It is a long time since we had food of the earth. It is also a long time since we had food with you." Marissa took the liberty to open the fridge and take out a bottle of cold wine from there and poured three glasses for Carolina too. Plumbel smiled at the unchained liberty that both his girls enjoyed with him. He felt much privileged. All of them had wine together.

"We are not affected by limitations of planet. We have become cosmic beings. We cannot come back to the earth as earthly beings. You have to reveal the truth to our parents and they will be very happy to know that we have become part of our ancestral galaxy." Carolina started a slow explanation

"Cosmic beings? What does that mean?" He asked

"It means that we are not limited by space and time. We can move about in the entire cosmos and interact with any being. The only limitation that we have is that we cannot communicate with those whose bodies are filled with negative energy wave. It is not our limitation. It is the limitation of their bodies. All those who seek dominance and hegemony fill their body cells with unbearable level of negative energy and therefore, make it impossible for our waves to enter their bodies. Even you were like Rustler. After coming in contact with both of us and interacting with our people your body has become very open to receive positive waves from cosmic beings. That is why we have come to visit you." Once again it was Carolina who explained truths to him.

"I know that Rustler has a lot of dominant streak in him. But he is a good man. He loves America and the American people. He is concerned about the citizens of the world and their development. It may be that he makes some mistakes but he is a good fellow." Plumbel manifested the muck that still refused to leave his body cells.

"It is not that one is good or bad person. Being good or bad is very relative. What determines his personality is that his body is filled with waves of hegemony and refuses to allow any positive energy from cosmic beings. To that extent he alienates himself from harmony and peace. He lives in eternal conflict within himself and is destroying himself. Look at the way he has thrown away your friendship. It means that the new waves that have entered your body find repulsion in his body. That is why he wants to eliminate you. Both of you are poles apart. This is also because of the way cells in your body have opened up to receive positive waves from us and from partly cosmic beings living on the earth. The cells in your body that were used to negative waves are now being put to slow sleep by the resurgence of positive energy waves in your body." This time it was Marissa who spoke to him and filled his body with life giving energy waves.

"Will Rustler succeed in his efforts to land in PlanetB2?" Plumbel came back to his business queries.

'You will see it for yourself, Plumbel. But first you save yourself from his tentacles of destruction. This place is very good for you to imbibe life-giving energy from our people. Look at the way the animals are living with you with ease. But this is not safe for you any more. You must leave to another country for your own safety. You have a lot of work to do for the people of the earth. Run away Plumbel. Go to Norway. Go and stay there for sometime till your mission on earth becomes clear to you." Marissa spoke with much concern and urged him to do what they asked him to do.

The bears stood up at full alert and began to scratch the tent with their nails. Wolves began to howl uncontrollably. They ran forward and backward howling their life out. Plumbel got up from his sleep regretting that he had to let go of the beautiful presence of his lovely girls and their message. He rubbed his eyes and was disappointed that it was only a dream. The world of reality had a strong message for him. He could hear some men talking outside of the tent and shooting in the air. He knew that Rustler's men had come in search of him. But they found it difficult to approach his tent because of the wolves and bears that surrounded his tent. He could hear at a distance the painful mourning of one of the animals. He decided to keep silent and did not dare to go out. It would be a betrayal of himself to his enemies.

All the noise subsided in a few minutes. Plumbel spent the rest of the night without daring to go out. He was woken up in the morning once again by the rustling sound of human beings. One of them had dared to open the tent and peeped inside. Plumbel was ready to shoot with gun in his hand. The man smiled and stood still. Plumbel realized that it was one of the relatives of Carolina who had interpreted to him earlier in his first visit. He smiled in return and went out of the tent with him.

There was a group of Native people talking among themselves and looking at the tent. Plumbel rushed fast to see what had really happened. His pet bear the drinking companion lay in state with bullet wounds. His claws had pieces of cloth. Plumbel bent down in deep respect for the great sacrificial lamb that gave his life in lieu of his affection for him. He removed the pieces of cloth from the claws and understood immediately that they were part of the uniform of Israelite soldiers.

People stood around the bear in reverential worship. He was one of their ancestors. They rushed and brought flowers in order to give a quiet and ceremonial farewell to their much-loved ancestor. They informed Plumbel that two men in uniform had gone to their place in the evening and had left their place after learning that they did not know any strange American living in the area. Plumbel put the rest of the pieces together and understood that the men in uniform had not really left the place. They only hid themselves in the region to look for him at night. They did not see the tent in the mass of noise that his friends made and they could not shoot all of them down with the limited number of bullets they had in their guns. They took to their heels. They would return by all means.

Marissa and Caroline had come in his dream to warn him of the impending danger. He thanked both of them and all the animals that saved him from sure death. He was now packing up to leave for Norway.

CHAPTER TEN

Joshua Bucket made an unusual phone call to Rustler. It was against the usual rhythm of Rustler making a call and asking him to come for a meeting. Things had changed quite a bit after the failure of Bigbelly4. He requested Rustler to invite Nicky Broom also for the meeting. He informed him that he had very important information to share about the task that he was entrusted with. Rustler called up some of his very close associates in the US army for this closed-door meeting in the aftermath of the disastrous journey of Bigbelly4. Such a meeting was round the corner for all those who knew the nature of Rustler. However, it still remained a mystery for most of them as to whom he would invite for such a meeting. The absence of Plumbel was a surprise to many who attended the meeting. They initially thought he was unwell. But soon they came to know that he was not invited for the meeting.

News of Rustler putting Plumbel on the backburner spread like wildfire in the amazon forests. Now it had become official news among many diplomats and bureaucrats. Yet no official word was available from any government circles on the reasons for the absence of Plumbel from all top-level meetings after the failure of Bigbelly4. Lack of official word gave an easy leverage to gossip—mongers. Many admirers of Plumbel sat in the meeting quite uneasily as they always enjoyed his presence in such meetings. Both inside and outside of meetings he was always the Good Samaritan who would prod and encourage people to move on with their work in the best interest of the people of America. Knowing Rustler well, no one dared to raise an eyebrow in the meeting about his absence.

It was a leak, a sure leak. No one however, knew the little hole from which the leak originated. It reached the ears of Rustler. He was horrified of the consequences if Plumbel came to know of it. In a hurry he called up Plumbel over phone and apologized profusely for the false rumor that was spreading.

"I don't know who really spread this false rumor about both of us. Am sure it must have reached your ears already because it is so commonly spoken of. I am sorry that this is doing many rounds in our diplomatic and bureaucratic circles." Rustler was apologetic about a rumor.

"But Rustler, you did not tell me what the rumor is all about. I have not heard any rumor till now with my own ears. What is the rumor? It looks to be very serious. Don't be disturbed by rumors. They vanish as fast as they originate." Plumbel tried to assuage the ruffled feathers of Rustler.

"Oh, I forgot that you are not in your house. You may not have heard it yet. It says that we have fallen out seriously and that I have effectively put you on the back burner in American administration. It must be the work of the Russians. They are hell bent on creating eternal fissures among us at the top level. But you don't get disturbed. I shall take care of the rest." Rustler was quite fast scurrying for words.

"But Rustler how did you know that I am not at my home? You seem to be highly disturbed about a mere rumor. Be calm Rustler. Everything will be taken care of. As long as we are careful not to destroy ourselves Russians or any other nation can do precious little to us. Take care Rustler." Plumbel had changed drastically. He knew the real situation. He could have easily confronted Rustler based on the information he had on hand. But he refrained from acting as a boy.

Rustler too realized that he made a serious mistake in his over defensive mechanism by revealing that he had spied on the whereabouts of Plumbel. He also sensed that the hypothesis of Russian rumormongering did not go well with Plumbel. He was licking the wounds on his huge ego.

The glaring omission of invitation to Plumbel from this all-important meeting was a crystal clear message that he was just a peck of dust in American diplomacy under the leadership of his bosom friend Rustler. He had that gut feeling, known as intuition that his days in the US were numbered.

The meeting started with the glaring omission of one of the most important personalities in American administration. There was glee on some faces and dismay on other faces. None made a show of the latent conflicting emotions. They attended their meetings with full rationality setting aside all their emotions. At every meeting they were pumped up rationally and deflated emotionally. Rustler opened the meeting in true style though he tried hard to bring up his rational function over his emotive side. He was in conflicting emotions of having only recently ditched his most trusted friend. The trust quotient in his personality had further dipped. It crossed the yellow limit and moved to red indicators. The failure of Bigbelly4 had pulled him down. Unable to accept failure Rustler had pulled down the shutters of his emotions and started functioning fully from his intellect. He pushed all his emotions to his intellect. It was dancing all over his body in gaiety for the liberty it got to establish its control over the emotions of Rustler. Now it could dictate terms to the emotive side and put it down ruthlessly.

"Yah Joshua Bucket, please present the findings of your research and experiments in capturing the communication of waves. The floor is open to you now." Rustler sat back in a pretentious relaxed mood. He tried to smile a little to himself and looked at everyone else with the disdain that they deserved.

Joshua Bucket thanked the President unstintingly for the openhanded support accorded by Rustler for the accomplishment of the research and fabrication of machines. He said that two teams were set up for two types of research. One was to look exclusively into human communications through rational and emotive waves. The second team was to look into extraterrestrial communication with human beings through waves and entropy. The second research was the most important one in view of the mission to PlanetB2 and therefore, much of the budget allocations were spent on this dimension of the research.

"It has become very evident that our machines cannot make an outreach beyond a certain point in space. It is that geospatial spot where all the global warming energies that we emit accumulate. These are heat waves. These waves have formed a thick layer preventing our machines from capturing waves that take their origin from PlanetB2. It is our own making. If only we did not have such thick layer of warm energy waves it may be possible for us to capture waves that emerge from beings in PlanetB2." Joshua Bucket poured out all the information that he had gathered in his research bucket.

"But then how did our machines reach PlanetB2? We landed there and have observed beings moving about. We are still seeing Marissa moving about without fully losing her human shape. I have also heard from Plumbel that Carolina came to meet Marissa when she was in her period of training. How was this possible? Your research seems to be a mere bullshit." Rustler was in his devastating worst. He could have shot down Bucket if he were a little angrier.

"We studied this particular dimension of our machines reaching PlanetB2 and getting burned out there on arrival. The velocity of our propelling machines in Bigbelly4 was quite high and therefore, it was able to penetrate that spot without being burned out completely. However, the heat waves had a telling effect on Bigbelly4 in its journey through the layer of heat waves. Just when it was about to be burned down it landed in PlanetB2. If we had not aimed the spacecraft at landing in PlanetB2 it would have evaporated in space without a trace." Joshua tried to legitimize his researchers with certain amount of pride restoration. He could not sell all this arguments with Rustler.

"Alright. I can accept your researchers' point of view on this. But convince me as to why only one person was still alive and why Carolina was able to come down to earth." Rustler would not let go the bucket of information. He wanted to scoop everything that was possibly in it.

"Mr. President, I think you are handing out to us the biggest joke of this millennium by saying that Carolina came down to the earth. Do you, as a rationalist believe in this? May be it is your Christian faith that urges you to believe in such miracles. But then there is no god in your design of things. We are speaking of science. Someone must be fooling you wholesale." Rustler was becoming furious at the scoop of Joshua Bucket. With so much of ego surrounding his self-image Rustler could not but personalize all such statements. However, he controlled himself lest others projected him as a dictator under the sheath of democracy.

"As far as the survival of the two women in our Bigbelly3 and 4 is concerned our scientific surmise is that there was something extraordinary in their body that had the capacity to withstand the heat. Our scientific inference is that the heat waves that our world has generated have killing effect. They destroy. There must be something in their body that acts as a powerful antidote to the gargantuan level of global warming that we have generated. We cannot measure the power of this antidote unless we have the bodies of Carolina and Marissa with us." Rustler did not speak much now as he had already a terrible plan in his mind after getting this information from Joshua. Rustler's bucket was full to the brim. Fortunately for him another scientist opened his mouth before his bucket could overflow.

"Tell us now something about your research on thought waves and feeling waves of humans living on the face of the earth. Were you able to capture them?"

Joshua did not even look at the guy who asked this question. However, since the question was relevant he looked at Rustler and gave his reply. "Mr. President, we have done extensive research on the possibility of capturing the thought and feeling waves emitted from human bodies. I must confess that as soon as these waves are emitted they merge with other existing waves in the space and enter into a process of entropy. They become new waves. There is a spiraling of these waves. More and more waves begin to merge among themselves and it is well neigh impossible to capture any wave in its original source. Our machines cannot emit thought and feeling waves. They can only emit heat waves. But the entropy of waves from human beings and animals is impossible to be captured by any machine. In order to capture such waves we need to create cells that can receive waves emitted from living bodies. We have to wait for many millennia before we are able to create cells of living bodies."

The same scientist came back again to pin down Joshua Bucket. "But we are cable to capture sound and light waves in our machines from thousands of miles away. Why does it become impossible to capture thought and feeling waves? Have you done your research properly?"

Joshua was literally angry with the scientist who did make sense in his questions. However, he did not want to get into the bad books of Rustler whose face had already hardened quite a bit. Therefore, he became calm and replied. "Unlike waves emitted from bodies of living beings, sound and light waves have a straight trajectory. As you will know well these waves are captured in receivers exactly as they are produced at the source. That is not the case with thought and feeling waves. They immediately merge with other waves generated in living beings and become new waves. They are received only by other waves from living beings or by cells in other bodies of living beings. Only living organism act like receivers of such waves."

Rustler was grossly disappointed at the end of the meeting. 'Is it for this that America had to spend billions of dollars?' He thought to himself and left the meeting stone faced.

Rustler was even more furious with all of America when he was authoritatively informed that his long trusted companion and friend, Plumbel had escaped the spy net of the Israelites and made good his way out of the US. No one knew where he fled. Most of Plumbel's friends in the US were happy for him when they heard the news of his fleeing to an unknown country. They wished that he did not go to Russia or China, as he could be a potential informer of highly classified information. Nicky Broom and Joshua Bucket were highly disappointed that a man as important as Plumbel was let out of the US so easily. They suspected that the US administration had a hand in his escape. Rustler suspected some of his subordinates. It was a time of growing suspicion in the US. Gossip had it that it was Rustler who made Plumbel escape because of their deep friendship. There was also the gossip that Rustler had an ultimate plan for sending out Plumbel. It was a plot hatched by both of them and that Plumbel did not actually flee. Their falling out with each other was a highly guarded secret plan for some unknown purpose.

Rustler telephoned the Prime Minister of Israel and blasted him left and right about the casual attitude of his intelligence staff. The Israeli Prime Minister on his part shifted the blame to the doorstep of Rustler and asserted that Plumbel could not have fled from the US unless insiders helped him. He asked him to find out where Plumbel was in hiding.

There was no need for Israel and US to make strenuous efforts to find out the whereabouts of Plumbel. News Channels in Norway announced in the open that Plumbel had sought political asylum in their country and was given a safe haven in Norway. He had entered the country with a diplomatic passport that he had. Rustler did not expect Plumbel to move his cards that fast. He thought the Israelites would accomplish their job quickly without anyone noticing. He knew that this mercenary task was what they did for him in the past meticulously. On his part Plumbel knew that death was in hot pursuit of him, like thunder that follows lightning without fail, after the midnight event in his American hide out and the unfortunate sacrifice of his pet bear. Holding the bear in his hands that night he cried like a little child lamenting that he would have been ready to die in the place of the bear had he known that his enemies were coming.

Crowning the chain of misfortunes was the high level meeting that Rustler had convened without inviting Plumbel. It was evident then that Rustler's hand was behind the midnight foray of the Israelite agents. He slipped out of New York quietly with active assistance from some of his associates in the AIA and slipped into Norway on a valid passport. A global red alert was rather too late in his case. However, it was issued. Many insiders were still in dark as to what really had taken place between both the stalwarts for that type of an unsavory escalation of differences.

The Secretary of State went on news asking Norway to hand over Plumbel to the US as he was now a proclaimed offender who breached the trust of the American President and who could potentially act against American interests. The

Norwegian Ambassador retorted immediately saying Norway was within its legal and moral rights to have granted asylum to Plumbel. According to the document that he possessed he was still a diplomat in service and was not dismissed at any time. Proclaiming him an offender when he had already reached the shores of Norway did not validate the proclamation, as he was already in Norway and was governed by the laws of the land where he was. It was a question of human rights and that Norway would protect the individual rights of all global citizens. There was no question of extraditing him from the Norwegian soil, as the US had not yet charged him with any grave offence. Norway also made the fastest arrangement to provide Plumbel with a Norwegian citizenship in order to legitimize its protective claims.

That type of strength was only one side of Norberta, the Prime Minister of Norway. She also invited Plumbel for a personal interview. She gathered all possible information on the circumstances that led to his flight from the US. It was a sad story. The whims of a dictator could wreak havoc in the lives of many diplomats in the name of democracy. It could also spell doom for the rest of the world. She took a personal interest in providing the best treatment to Plumbel after listening to his story. Plumbel liked the way she respected and treated him.

"Oh we have also the Sami people in Norway who are like the Native Americans. There are many shamans among them. It is tragic that when Europeans occupied and settled down in Norway they targeted the Sami people for conversion. In order to make our colonization much easier our forefathers also set out to destroy their culture and language. They derecognized the Sami language and began to impose Norwegian as the official language of the Sami people. Much worse was what was done in the name of religion. Sami people had their sacred drums, which they worshiped and used in worship. European Christians branded these drums as profane and asked the Sami people to destroy their drums. Being simple and naïve they did what the Europeans asked them to do . . ." Plumbel was wondering on which side of the boat the Prime Minister of Norway was standing. Was she genuinely regretting the mistakes of her forefathers or was she just sympathizing with the Sami people. If it were a genuine regret of what was done to the Indigenous people the solution was much simpler. The Norwegians had to simply offer an apology and offer the reins of governance to the people of the country that they unjustly occupied.

"Yes, you are right. This is what we should have done. But you know human nature. Once we get power and wealth it is very difficult to let go of them. Moreover, the art of governance also requires that we make compromises for the sake of citizens and for the sake of retaining power. Where will the present Norwegians go in order to make amendments for the mistakes that their forefathers committed. They can only resolve not to walk in the same path. No other country will be ready to accept them." She spoke as if she could see through the mind of Plumbel's. She also knew his embarrassment at her reading of his mind correctly.

"Don't worry I am the daughter of a Norwegian father and a Sami mother. I know what it meant to be a shaman woman for my mother in the house of a Norwegian husband. Many of her friends who did the same thing had to divorce their husbands as they could not live with their Sami identity, leave alone shaman identity as my mother had. I cannot read the minds of all people. But sometime I can read the minds of those who are tuned to live in harmony with nature. I liked you from the time we met. There seems to be a recent transformation in your life towards shamanic values." Norberta was like torrential rain that came in waves, wave after wave. Fortunately he was not blown away by the power with which the torrent came.

"I am totally surprised that the Prime Minister of Norway is half shaman. How come that even we in the US did not know this? Perhaps we are happy to live in the darkness we have created around us. Such light may disturb our vision badly. Was your mother treated badly?" Instead of stopping the torrent he actually instigated it.

"Leave alone the horrible situation of half shamans. When Europeans converted our people they branded them as pagan converts. Everything that belonged to Sami culture was branded as paganism. Our dress, our language, our education and our worship were all ascribed as products of Satan and that we would go to hell and burn in eternal fire if we did not give them up totally. But the worst thing was that the Europeans openly advocated the killing of our shamanic gurus branding them as agents of devil. Many of them were simply burned alive. Many of them fled to

Oslo and other cities and hid themselves. They began to live as any Norwegian citizen giving up all their cherished values. The bolder ones among them continued their shamanic practices stealthily in their private residence." Norberta wiped the few drops of tears that popped up in her eyelids. Plumbel controlled himself with much difficulty.

"I am much ashamed to have descended from such a cruel race that boasts of its superiority. We are never taught in our schools and colleges these truths. Even in our history classes such things are never revealed to us. When we come out of schools we come out with a pride that smacks of racial arrogance. I am very thankful to Carolina and to Marissa for having shown me the other side of human life and spirituality." It was now becoming common that Plumbel became emotional every now and then. He was not ashamed of being emotional after he realized that every human life is a bundle of emotions and rationality. If only humanity learned to blend both proportionately, there won't be this much of dominance and violence in the world.

Norberta clarified with him about the identity of Carolina. She only knew about Marissa from the media. Now Plumbel revealed to her all the clandestine plans of Rustler's and the ambition he nurtured to be the absolute leader of the world some day. There was much more to Rustler than sheer planning to land on PlanetB2. She was shocked to the core hearing about the ambitions of Rustler's.

"But he always speaks of democracy and goes about attacking many sovereignties for not being democratic enough." She thought aloud.

"I am sure you have read the New Testament. Jesus calls the 'holy' Pharisees as wolves in sheep's clothing and as white washed sepulcher. The only difference is that Pharisees did not have the power to strike at the rest of the world with their arms and weapons of mass destruction." Plumbel began to slowly melt in front of Norberta.

Their interview ended with Norberta inviting Plumbel for a private dinner that evening in her official residence. He gladly accepted the invitation. He understood that she still continued with shamanic spirituality privately and did not make big news of it to the rest of the world. She had also married a pious Christian diplomat who thought that her spirituality was nothing but animism and hated it. She explained to him that animism's axis was worshipping the spirits and the Christians were right about it. However, animism was not just a set of rituals invoking the spirits for destruction. It was the worship of spirits for absolute love, peace and harmony. It is worship of the spirit of our ancestors, of all the cosmic elements and what we understand as the cosmic spirit. Christians hate animism only because there is no belief in god in shamanism and there is no centrality of Jesus Christ. 'This is what our ancestors desired for their children and this is what all of us desire for the world.' There was a soothing of the heart in Plumbel after a few glasses of wine gulping. His spirit was high and he was much closer to cosmic spirituality than ever before.

After many days of restlessness and anxiety Plumbel had a good night's sleep. He in fact overslept. As he got up late in the morning he could feel the gentle touch of Marissa and Carolina on both sides.

Norberta kept herself bright-eyed and bushy-tailed after what she heard about Rustler. He could send his AIA agents or Israelites into Norway to spy on the whereabouts of Plumbel. She chose some of her most trusted lieutenants to take personal care of him and provide necessary security to him. Together with her they drew out a blueprint for keeping his stay in Norway in dyed-in-the-wool secrecy. It was decided to shovel him out of Oslo and other main cities of Norway where his presence would make news. Simultaneously Norberta also wanted him to have first hand knowledge of Sami culture and history as she found him getting fine-tuned towards cosmic spirituality.

Grandmother Moon in the horizon! Mother Alta on the earth. Both of them joined hands and were dancing in gay abandon on a full moon night. Dancing ground of these two personalities in the cosmos was the waters of river Alta. Like all mothers her movements were measured but in excitement of being caressed by Grandmother moon she giggled and nibbled wherever she flowed. It was a white carpet all the way splattered with silver petals of flowers from the sky. Mother Alta was bubbling with laughter, as she was moving forward up and down in regular rhythm.

Father sky was generous with both of them and did not want to interfere in their play. He hid himself from the sight of Plumbel. Stars on his face, the ancestors of yore of all human race blinkered their horns and were constantly pushing Father sky to join the play of the two ladies. Young clouds came to his rescue by playing hide and seek with the three of them. Brother Sun went to sleep early as he was almost in hibernation. He woke up very late and went to bed too early. But his absence did not deter Mother Alta and grandmother moon from their fun-games. Their path on the white carpet was fanned out with golden petals of shining flowers.

Plumbel walked along. He was unable to keep pace neither with Mother Alta nor with Grandmother Moon. Both of them were playful totally unmindful of the stalker on the sidewalk of their path. Occasionally Mother Alta touched his feet with affection but soon withdrew herself as if she was a shy teenager meeting a stranger for the first time. He felt an electrifying effect passing in all his nerves. It was cold. Very cold to bear! Mother Alta was well protected by tall and stout guards all around her. Lush green on the mountains added no fear to those who visited her. They were in fact most inviting security guards. Her flow of life impeded neither by casual visitors nor by those who drew regular life from her. As Plumbel walked along in unison with this great mother he saw her being pregnant with many varieties of life. They provided the much-needed nourishment to the Sami people. Varieties of fish worshipped as ancestors by some tribes of the Sami people were hilarious at the way the new visitor was only watching them swim. They wagged their tails in hilarious mocking of the stranger on the fringes of their dwelling. They were used to giving a run for the lives of the Sami people who chased them in their boats. When they escaped they wished better luck for the Samis the next time. When they were caught they were happy to become part of the life essence of the Sami people, their people. At some places Mother Alta was an emaciated personality running thin in her lifeline. Weakness of nature, man's pride! Plumbel got into the weak spots of Mother Alta. She trapped him in a playful mood. She pushed him down into her hidden spots that only she knew. He was drenched to the full, got up and tried to wipe off his shame. But it was too late. He conceded that Mother Alta was after all a Mother and bowed to her in deep reverence. He ran for cover in her banks. She welcomed him and gently caressed his feet. He washed himself in her love.

Plumbel was replenished with energy that he never knew of. The more he touched Mother Alta the more he became energetic. He forgot all his worries. He felt totally light in his body and his cells became open to receive waves from the cosmos like never before. He sat in the comfort of the refuge he had taken in the banks of river Alta. Now he began to speak to his beloved Marissa. She started replying to him for every sentence that he spoke to her. For a moment he thought that he was imagining and was creating an illusion of Marissa. But it did not take long for him to realize that Marissa was walking by his side and was comforting him. He could see her in the waters of Mother Alta. She told him to take courage and not to be let down by reversals in his life. Everything had a design in his life. He had to be part of the flow of life just as he did with Mother Alta. If he did that he would be filled with a new life that he never bargained for. That new life would make him stand to any type of challenge Rustler and his cronies would pose.

"Plumbel, your body cells are becoming more and more open to receive different types of waves from cosmic beings. It is a big advantage. You will soon realize that true freedom is that of the body. Your mind resides in your body and without your body nothing can be done. It is through your body that you think and act. Without body cells there can be no communication with other beings. Without communication existence has no possibility. Think and feel more and more for the welfare of the world, of other beings, of animals and plants. You will realize that animals and plants have much better life than human beings. They do not desire to dominate. They move with the cosmic order. You will be happy in as much as you are part of the cosmic movement." As he looked deep into the flowing waters to touch her and have an embrace from his beloved she was gone with the flow of her Mother Alta.

"Marissa, please do not leave me alone. I am struggling a lot in this transition from dominance to harmony with cosmos. This is totally new to me. Am glad that I have begun to understand your type of cosmic spirituality. Am very happy that I begin to interact with animals and plants. I am enjoying it to the full. But as you probably know, I am completely lost to the designs of dominance planned and executed by human beings who assume that they are indomitable. I do not know how to react to people like Rustler who were my close friends for a long time. I almost lived for him. But now everything is changed all of a sudden. Please be with me always Marissa. I love you always. I feel lost without you. Please guide me from wherever you are." This prayer of Plumbel was completely different from the way he used to pray in church when he was young. It was not a prayer. It was just a recital of printed words. This was different. He enjoyed it. Mother Alta added to the glory of his interaction with his new fascination in life.

It was part of the plan that he should not stay in one place for long and should keep moving from place to place under different identities. Norberta had taken his predicament very seriously and wanted to ensure his security. In Alta his security guards changed without ever knowing who he was but only with the general understanding that he was a guy who was very close to their Prime Minister. They took him from Alta to Kuatokeino by bus. This was a special place as it had the biggest Sami University, the Center of learning of Sami language and culture. Finmark region, a history in remaking! The Norwegian Government had decided to part with this vast stretch of land. They transferred the title to the Sami people. A colorful people who survived on reindeer herding! Those big and sober animals needed grazing land, a lot of them. It was a special type of grass that they ate. The region was chillingly cold, sometimes going down to minus 50 degrees. The Sami Parliament had full ownership over this vast stretch of land. A remarkable achievement by the Sami people who numbered only about 16,000 in Norway! Their extended arms went into Finland, Russia, Sweden and Denmark. Their struggles were known all over the indigenous world as determined and strong. The Norwegian Government manifested its hypersensitivity to issues of human rights by easily granting the rights of the Sami people.

As he travelled by bus along the land, grazing reindeers went rushing to the wire mesh that covered the entire stretch to protect the animals from human cruelty. Some of them showed unknown familiarity with Plumbel. They rushed as if to have a peep at him through the windows of the bus. He opened the window glasses a bit wider despite the cold wind and had a good look at them. When he ultimately reached Kuatokeino he realized that he had travelled for more than four hours along the Finmark region. All that land belonged to the reindeers. It belonged to all those who lived in the Finmark regions, both Sami people and Norwegians.

The bus stopped in front of the huge university complex. It was surrounded by snow all over and was situated in jaw-dropping landscape. Plumbel was quickly whisked away by the Principal to his room.

"I am very happy that you have a University of your own. I believe you teach here the indigenous science." Plumbel was a bit provocative in order to draw out some information.

"Yes, we teach our science. But the University is open for all. It is not exclusively for Sami students though we teach Sami language, history and culture here. We have actually at least nine languages in our community. But there is a common language that we want our people to learn. This was lost to us because of large scale conversion to Christianity." The Rector of the University began to yield to Plumbel's provocation.

"But if you teach your Sami language to your people and revive your culture, will they not be isolated? Yes, it will give them some sense of pride. However, how will they get integrated to the Norwegian society or to the world outside of Norway? Are you not afraid of isolationism of your people?" The tempo of provocation increased. Plumbel felt quite lighthearted in the University. The tension of being on the run had disappeared after the acceptance he received from Norberta.

"Who is isolating whom is the big question for us. So, if we have to be integrated we have to learn Norwegian. This is the assumption in your question. Let me reverse the question to you. Why does not the Norwegian society learn our language in order to integrate itself into our country? After all, this is our country and the Europeans have inserted themselves here and occupied our land. It is they who should learn our language and get integrated. What you suggest is a sort of subjugation of the Sami people to the aggressors." The Rector was a no nonsense man. He did not mince words on what he wanted to say. There was a collective thinking in the University on this, as most non-Sami people who visited the University invariably asked this question. Stereotypes, the questions and the replies!

"Yes, you are very right. Even I belonged to a school of thought that believed that the mainstream is the dominant group in any society and that others should toe the line of the dominant group. But because of my close association with some indigenous people I have now changed my perspective and I believe that it is the dominant society that has to learn to provide the legitimate space and resources that belong to them. As long as this is not done there will not be any cosmic harmony and there will be no peace on earth." Plumbel gave voice to the feelings that welled up in his body. He also placed on the table unwittingly an important element of advocacy.

"If there are at least 10% of the global population that thinks like you then those of us who languish in the periphery of development will not have to struggle so much for survival and dignity. We are doing a lot of work with the UN on this and have a few strong advocates of indigenous rights in the UN from our University. In this context we appreciate our Norwegian government much. They are very sensitive and understanding about our culture, history and our right to be a people of our own. They also have set up a Sami Parliament in Karasjok and allocate regular budget for the development of the Sami people." The Rector was becoming more and more vivid and vibrant as he spoke.

"Yes, Yes. I am going to Karasjok from here. Hope I shall have a good time visiting your Parliament.

None of us is informed anything about this in the US. Well, we Americans are like the proverbial frog in the well. We know only our world and care a damn about the plight of people elsewhere. For us ignorance is bliss. For you cosmos is bliss. We think of reindeer only in terms of many kilos of meat whereas you consider reindeer as your ancestor. These are two diametrically opposed world." The Rector realized that the dialogue with Plumbel assumed very serious dimension and wanted to lighten up the air in the University. He invited Plumbel to be introduced to all his staff. But he declined the offer. Only he knew the risk he was running in exposing himself to the world unnecessarily.

Hills on both sides brimming with radiant life and light even in those dark days of the Northern region! The car that carried the mystery man from US took turns in the curves majestically with a cool that belonged to all of Sami people. Even in their rocky formations the hills on both sides of the road were resplendent with life giving trees and water all the way. What looked like a hill became a valley as the car moved triumphantly after crossing every curve. It had that magic power for transforming the complexion of the terrain in no time. Chill, chill, chill . . . close the window. Shouted the driver without knowing who the occupant of the car was. The Rector had arranged a beautiful Benz car to take Plumbel alone to Karasjok where the statuesque Sami Parliament was situated. But that was still only a distant expectation. He had to travel some way before reaching the Sami Parliament.

Both his bodyguards were disposed off at Alluska, the Sami University College.

Sapmi, the Sami Land had a compulsively transmogrifying effect on the man who once was in the company to overcome the cosmos. Now in Sapmi the cosmos was hemming in his body in a gentle and soothing manner in contrast to the 'Rustler brand' of weapons and destruction. It was a mesmerizing journey all the way with different aroma emanating from the hills and the occasional reindeer that raised the branches of its horn to put up a grand show of an antique piece that it treasured on top of its head. Plumbel wanted to run and grab that horn like a little boy. But the big man in the driver's seat had no such inclination even to notice the boyish mollycoddle sitting behind his seat.

And finally the magic moment arrived. Samediggi, the Sami Parliament was indescribably magnificent. It was any artist's envy without any doubt. From outside he had no wonder that he was gazing at an architectural marvel. The mouth of a fish on top flowing into a sprawling building! There were the two reindeers to welcome him and old replicas of Sami tents. He got down from the car, stretched out his hands and looked up. "Why was I not born here, o god!' the words did not come through his mouth. They went back into his body.

As he was still enjoying the fresh air and cold wind that surrounded the Samediggi the driver saluted him good-bye and left. Plumbel spread his eagle eyes all over and turned back to go into the Parliament building. No big motorway to build up a tempo. There were no exotic trees on both sides of the road. No colorful flowers adorning the way to the Sami Parliament. No art pieces on the way! Not even a welcome board for the guests and visitors! It was a simple welcome. Plumbel alighted from the car and walked into the door of the Samediggi.

"Welcome to the Sami Parliament. Do you like to come into the Parliament first or go to your room? We have a hotel just next to the Parliament where we have booked a room for you. If you like to refresh yourself I shall take you there and then you can go with me into the Parliament. My name is Barbara. I work in the Sami Parliament and they have assigned me to look after you as long as you stay with us." She extended her hand and he shook hands with her. It did not go beyond a mere ceremony.

Plumbel was still very fresh drawing much energy from the hills and the concomitant fresh air. He could go energetic for another month or so. Such was the replenishment of young energy in his body. "We shall go into the Parliament and when we are finished I shall go to my room and relax."

Barbara seemed to have expected that looking at the way he bubbled with young energy in his old body. "Okay then, come with me." She opened the huge door of the Parliament building. For a minute Plumbel had to close his eyes. It was all lights everywhere, small little lights glittering and brightening up the entire space. He wondered if he was inside a building or in the open air on a clear sky night.

"It is just breathtaking." Plumbel could not resist the temptation of giving superlatives to his feelings. There was a big smile on the face of Barbara. "Why are there so many lights filling the entire building?" He asked without thinking for a second for himself.

"They represent the stars in the sky and the stars represent our ancestors who keep constantly replenishing us with their life giving energy. As a symbol of the presence of our ancestors amidst us always we keep these lights on. Even at night when we close the building we do not put off these lights." Barbara explained the significance of lights and walked him slowly into the room of the Director of Samediggi.

He seemed to have anticipated the arrival of a VIP without knowing his real identity. He stood up to welcome his special guest. They sat together and had coffee. The Director himself walked Plumbel all around the Sami Parliament. The Hall of the Parliament was just awesome with a blue artwork as the backdrop. It represented the sky and all the stars in it. He explained to him the seriousness with which Sami community worked. There was a global competition for the backdrop and a panel of judges chose the best. Plumbel was almost frozen in front of the blue circle. He stood still without talking anything to the Director who wondered if something was wrong with Plumbel's health. The blue sky and the deep blue sea enraptured his senses all at the same time. In those few minutes that he was captured by an unknown something he became totally empty within himself. He had tried to empty himself totally several times in the past but could not succeed even for a few seconds. Now he was totally empty inside and was in full body orgasm during those moments of intensity. He felt that Carolina and Marissa had descended together to be with him in that all-important place. He felt that his body energy was squeezed into a drop and merged with the energy concentration of Carolina and Marissa's.

"Are you alright? Anything wrong with you? Are you tired?" The Director asked with genuine anxiety.

"I am sorry. I am okay. There is nothing wrong. I just forgot myself for those few minutes. Cannot explain that to you. It is that one moment in your life that you always want to have but it will come only once in a lifetime." Plumbel fumbled in explaining the inexplicable. Yours is truly a breathtaking place.

"You mean full body orgasm?" The Director was casual in asking about it. His question put Plumbel flat on the floor.

'You know about it? It is such a precious moment in life. How do you know it?" asked Plumbel

"Well. I have had it a few times in this hall and in Mother Alta. From the way you stood still as a pillar on the floor, I could guess that you were going through a deep experience of bliss in your body. Yes, this is the heritage that we have imbibed from our shamanic ancestors. I am glad to know that an American like you have had such a deep experience." Plumbel was a plumb of surprise unable to believe all that was happening to him and around him.

"All because of my two darlings out there." Plumbel swallowed his words lest the Director heard them. They slowly moved back into the Director's room. Barbara was there in the waiting. She took charge of Plumbel from there and took him to his hotel room.

"I shall meet you tomorrow at 10 in the morning. Be ready to go with me to visit a few places of interest in Karasjok." The Director shook hands with him and sent him away.

After a good night's sleep in the company of the two reindeers that kept silently ruminating the grass they grazed during the day, Plumbel had a fresh shower and was ready to walk out with Barbara. She would not walk out of the hotel with him until he had his breakfast with her. He took out his purse faithfully to pay but she held his hands and pushed it down to the table.

"You are the guest of the Sami Parliament. I have been instructed to take full care of you." She took the bill and made the payment.

Their next station was the beautiful Sami Theatre that was situated a few meters away from the Parliament. Barbara had made arrangements for a special documentary show for him. Within 20 minutes he was able to get a full grasp of Sami history and culture. Such was the high quality of the Video with an acoustic that mesmerized the visitor.

Plumbel was startled literally with the start of the video with that heavy booming sound. It was qualitatively different from the hollow booms that he used to hear in the scientists theatre in New York. The words followed immediately after the totally unexpected explosion of music.

"Reindeer is our Ancestor." When the video started with these words Plumbel just forgot himself and his history. He forgot America. The Video then went on to narrate one by one the history of invasion of Sapmi by Europeans and the heavy loss of culture that they suffered. Plumbel just shook his head in disbelief. 'Have we done so much of harm to innocent people all over the world?' he thought to himself and was gnawing his teeth.

"What happened Mr. Plumbel? Are you okay? Do you need any medical assistance?" Barbara was deeply concerned that no harm should come to her guest.

"Nothing, nothing! Am all right! I just can't digest the fact that innocent people have paid so much for the welfare of the rest of the world. It disturbs me much. I feel helpless." He said and began to listen to the rest of the documentary.

The documentary further laid bare the facts on how a people, a culture and a history was almost lost first due to colonization by the West and later by Hitler during the World War. At the end of the show the technical man went to him to get an opinion of the show. Plumbel was very generous in his comments. "Superb! Highly professional production! I am amazed at the way you have used technology. It is just equal to any Hollywood movie."

For the rest of the day Plumbel was somber in his movements. Barbara understood that the man was disturbed much. Immediately after the show she took him back to the hotel and asked him to take rest. He agreed to her suggestion.

He took the book 'Yoikana' that was kept in the room. It was a novel of a romantic revolution. He opened the pages that he remembered about the World War and what happened to the Sami people. He read all over again the page from the novel. It was the following:

'It was World War II. The year was 1944. Hitler is the giant of a man whom you saw in the dream. His forces entered Norway and destroyed our land. It is still considered today as a national disaster in Norway. Come I will take you into our museum where you can see all this in the paintings.' She put both her hands under his arms and lifted him. He was too heavy for her. But he made her life lighter by getting up and acknowledging the warmth that was readily forthcoming.

'But how did I get a dream like this? I have no idea at all that this had happened.'

Veeran was snooping as they were walking towards the museum.

'You do not have to know something to have a dream Veeran. The pains and sorrows, the celebration of destruction by evil forces, the aspirations to have better life after destruction remain in the universe as thought waves and feeling waves. If the cells in your body are open to receive these waves in the universe they enter your body without you being conscious of them. When you begin to sleep, not all cells in your body go to sleep. Some cells in your body begin to wake up when most other cells go to sleep and their working comes out in the form of dreams. I am not at all surprised that you had this dream in this part of the world.'

'From where did this angel descend? She seems to have a convincing argument on any issue that I raise. She seems to be the total embodiment of knowledge and wisdom.' Veeran hid his secret admiration from Ramona.

It was all too philosophical for him at that moment when his body was still slumbering with the weight of the dream that he had. He decided to ruminate over her philosophical interpretation at night.

It was a series of paintings by the famous Sami artist not only about war but also about the cultural destruction that was wrought by people coming and settling down in Norway as Norwegians. There were paintings that depicted the pre-Christian Sami life and glimpses of the rebellion that brewed as part of the reconstruction of the Sami people. Too heavy to digest!

'How did you manage to become what you people are today? No one can even imagine that in such a short period of time you have become a people of this stature. We see only happiness on your faces and not any scar of the destruction that was caused not only to your lives but also to your psyche.'

'That is the beauty of all of us, the indigenous people. When you were describing yourself as an untouchable, discriminated wholesomely I was trying to identify some scars of that experience on your face. But what I saw was enthusiasm, burning energy glowing all over your body.'

'Nice to hear you like my body.'

'Correction please! I said I like your face.'

'Don't you like my body?'

'Who will not? Most of our Sami girls will fall for you. But I shall not allow them.'

He liked this exclusive ownership immensely.

'What our artist had painted is what happened to Norway in 1944. It is still imprinted on us as a national disaster. But it was in this national disaster that a new history was being written in golden letters. It was from these burning ashes that the Sami people were rising as a people of their own.'

'That woman you saw in your dream is the symbol of the women of the Sami community who took leadership in the reconstruction of the Sami history and culture. It is our women who are the modern architects of the Sami community.'

Fatigue and sadness began to play a game of Ping-Pong and Plumbel went to sleep without deciding to do the same. He kept the novel down and slept.

CHAPTER ELEVEN

It was a routine meeting. Rustler was quite serious whenever he had meeting with Nicky Broom. They had a cup of strong coffee. Both of them liked strong coffee.

"Yes, tell me. Do you have any new information about Plumbel? Have you found out his whereabouts?" Rustler started business straightaway. He never had the habit of beating round the bush.

"I have both positive and negative news for you. The positive is that we have got some clue to what Plumbel is set to do. But before I go to that I shall tell you in short the negative." Nicky started with an introduction, as was his habit. Rustler generally disliked his intros but this time he liked it as the subject was close to his heart and head.

"Yes, go ahead. But don't tell me that Plumbel is dead somewhere." Rustler provoked Broom.

"That is positive for you. I said I should start with the negative. We have not been able to identify the hide out of Plumbel's. Even all our panopticons set up in satellites are unable to trace him. It means that he is not on the run. He is hiding himself safe in a building or in a cave." Nicky lowered his voice considerably in revealing the truth about Plumbel. He knew that Rustler did not have a nose for truth.

His own position would be at stake if he said too much of unpalatable truth.

Rustler only nodded his head without saying anything positive or negative. Nicky got the meaning of the look and the nod. He shifted gears as if by an instinct to save his skin.

"But Mr. President we have come to know where he spent his first days of departure from the Department. The Jewish guards whom we had commissioned to assassinate him missed him. But before they went in search of him to the desolate place where he was perhaps staying they met the Native American community of Carolina and Marissa's. They found out that already during the training period he was very close to Carolina and much closer to Marissa . . ." Though Rustler knew that Nicky was in a mood to share more information he could not help interfering.

"Oh bloody shit! I took that motherfucker lightly. I should have woken up much earlier. He pretended to be a simple guy and I entrusted the very important responsibility of preparing the astronauts for the journey to PlanetB2. What a mistake . . . what a terrible mistake . . ." Rustler was lamenting.

Nicky continued his recitation. He somehow wanted to complete his narration and escape from the presence of Rustler. "It seems he had a long conversation with both the communities and shared with them that Carolina and Marissa were together in one of the planets to which we sent them. They are safe and sound there. The most vital information that we have is this. He told them that they are in constant communication with him."

Rustler did not show any sign of disturbance. Nicky expected it for sure. He was grossly disappointed. "What do you infer from this information?" Now Rustler became serious.

"One of the inferences we have drawn is that both Carolina and Marissa are truly in communication with him. There is the terrible possibility that the beings in PlanetB2 can choose to communicate with human beings." He was shivering mildly while communicating this to Rustler.

"If your inference is to be taken seriously why is it that both the girls are not communicating with anyone else? I cannot accept your inference. I shall not accept anything unless you have adequate proof to convince me that your inference is substantial. You may leave now. Come back with enough proof on this." Rustler's face became frighteningly hard and his voice became coarse. Being the Chief of AIA he knew that Rustler could break out into an uncontrollable beast anytime. He grabbed his papers, excused himself and took a flight.

After his departure Rustler went into a silence all by himself. It took a long time for him to come back to himself. It was a pity that he behaved like a tortoise. Whenever it was convenient to him he would withdraw his head with an apparent feeling that the world was not watching him and that his hard shell would protect him from potential danger. There was a point in what a tortoise did.

But Rustler did not have the luxury of a hard cover over himself. He created an illusion that he had a strong shell all around his body. He imagined that the power of his authority was unbreakable. But all those who knew him also knew well that only small pinprick was needed to provoke Rustler into a fit of rage. Though Nicky rushed out in fear he laughed within himself at the utter fragility of the President of the US.

Rustler was becoming more and more obsessive. He played and replayed the computer pictures of Carolina and Marissa in PlanetB2 to watch their movements. It was evident that they were constantly surrounded by many other beings in PlanetB2 and not left alone. There were many other beings that just kept to themselves but the two figures that scientists had identified for him, as Carolina and Marissa were never left alone. Rustler's obsession was not whether they were alone or together with others. He was more obsessed with their movements in order to see if they would venture out to the earth to meet Plumbel. He had instructed Nicky Broom that whenever the two Native American girls in PlanetB2 came to meet Plumbel, the secret service of the US should rush immediately and capture all the three of them.

The failure of the AIA to locate Plumbel further screwed up Rustler no ends. He had believed in the invincibility of the AIA in unison with the Israeli intelligence agencies. They often operated together except in times of spying on each other.

They had penetrated every nook and corner of the world with their hi-tech surveillance on every country and noted individuals. They had also invented adequate mechanism to pervade all means of communications and sieve out all the information that they needed. They knew that it was daylight robbery and intrusion into the privacy of individual freedom on which the living principles of the US were constructed. But American interest could never be put to risk. Rustler ordered Nicky to intensify all mechanisms of spying in order to locate Plumbel.

Hardly did he know that Carolina and Marissa were watching every movement of his along with many other beings in PlanetB2. It was not on purpose that they did it. But they knew in their cosmic bodies everything that was happening on earth as it was the only other planet where beings lived with communicable bodies. They did not have to create machines to spy on human beings. They knew everything that happened on earth with earthly beings instantly. Rustler, being one of the most arrogant and dominant beings on earth with considerable ability to wield oppressive power had been affecting the entropy of life giving energy waves. Though the cosmic beings did not allow any such negative waves to enter PlanetB2 by the very structure of their bodies, they did feel the impact of the astronomical level of negative vibes that was created on earth.

This phenomenon created an unprecedented intensity of communication among the cosmic beings as well as among all those who were tuned to receive life giving energy waves in their bodies. Earthly beings were being influenced by the intensive emission of waves from PlanetB2. Such communication defied the theory of Rustler's scientists that waves from PlanetB2 were not passing through the layer of heat waves in the cosmic space. They did pass but human scientists simply did not have the knowhow of deciphering them and capturing them in their machines. Rustler remained blissfully unaware of the ways of cosmic beings. It was their huge advantage.

Human beings on earth who came into the orbit of communicative waves from cosmic beings began to think differently and more and more positively about realities. Their positive thinking created waves from their bodies that reached the bodies of other human beings who had the receptivity in their body cells to receive such waves. More and more people began to think alike. They also began to think in terms of many common values.

There were a lot of other human beings that were operational at the emotive level more than their cognitive and rational levels. They too derived emotive waves from the cosmos that had their origin in the cosmic beings of PlanetB2. These waves began to capture the bodies of human beings much faster than thought waves and a lot of people in the world began to develop love for new values in their lives.

Quite a few magazines and newspapers began to write in favor of global equality and peace. They began to write books against the use of arms and weapons of mass destruction against innocent citizens in any part of the world. Some of them even decried the way Rustler's army went about destroying liberty of sovereign nations in the name of establishing democracy. Those beings who were able to receive waves that had gone through entropy of rationality and emotions became powerful speakers and leaders for dignity and rights.

Occasionally such news reached Rustler and they began to rattle him a bit. He convinced himself that he was a cunning fox living in a palm grove and such a fox does not get disturbed at the rustling of palm leaves. He could feel the pinch of tightening screws in different corners of the world. But he was ready to screw the entire world.

With Rustler's permission all the space scientists had a meeting without him. It was one of the biggest challenges that they faced in their career. They had to find a solution to the problems posed by Rustler on what could be the device that could capture the waves of communication from PlanetB2. They were aware that this was the next biggest American agenda. All of them put their heads together to look into many possible ways of finding a solution to this voodoo. They were all in a mood of despondency.

McDowell, the Chief of the group of space scientists tried to boost up the morale of the group. "Friends and colleagues, there is nothing that we scientists cannot overcome. We can make an illusion a scientific truth and a truth scientific illusion. Some years ago no one ever imagined that we would one day land in the moon. Even now we have done good. We have sent out Bigbelly3 and 4 to PlanetB2. It is unfortunate that they melted into nothingness as soon as they entered the liquid zone. That need not deter our determination to go ahead. We have one of the best Presidents that America has ever seen. You are aware that he has got approved the entire budget that we asked him for. Such is his generosity to the scientific community. Such also is his obstinacy to plant the American flag on the surface of PlanetB2. I can assure you that our President is not going to rest until we reach the goal. Take heart. This is a monumental mission that we have taken up. There will be certain ups and downs. We should dust them off our feet and move forward . . ."

"How to move forward is the big question sir. We are all resolved on the achievement of the mission. But how to break the mojo? That is where our challenge lies." A young voice interrupted the chief.

"Have patience young man. I am coming to that. I have done extensive research on this issue with the help of some seniors among you and this is the conclusion that we have arrived at. If there is a consensus among us we can present it to our President as a potential wizardry breaker." McDowell continued with patience.

"I want to know what has happened to our gr.. great leader Plum . . . ha what is his name . . . yah, Plumbel? He has disappeared all of a sudden. There are many of us who have been trained by him. It is very difficult for me to accept the fact that we even do not know where he is. Please . . . let . . . mee . . ." One of the scientists was a bit inebriated already after lunch and came into the meeting drunk. Since he knew that Rustler would not be present in the meeting he took it easy and attended the meeting. Some of his friends helped him to sit down also simultaneously asking him not to speak. He obliged.

"We are not here to discuss politics. We are here to deliberate as a scientific community and allow me to present our findings." McDowell continued to present his case without caring a damn for what others had to say. His patience started running out.

"What has flummoxed all of us is that Carolina and Marissa have survived in PlanetB2 albeit with transformed bodies. We had high hopes that they would send us vital information about PlanetB2. Unfortunately they have become completely taciturn. Yet we have news from our AIA that they remain in communication with Plumbel. The President asked us to invent machines that would capture this communication and decode their conversation. You know that we could not produce such a machine . . . .'"

"You can decode any complex comm . . . communication if you have two more pegs of whisky . . . The inebriated scientist made fun of McDowell. He continued unmindful of the ridicule.

". . . We have now discovered that decoding of the communication among cosmic beings, as they are known, can be done only through cells of bodies. These bodies can be either animal bodies or human bodies. Without these cells it is going to be neigh impossible for us to decode any communication from PlanetB2. If you noticed the recent phenomenon of increasing writings and other crescendo raised about alternative values and anti-American sentiments expressed publicly it becomes evident for us that cosmic beings of PlanetB2, especially Carolina and Marissa have increased their communication to human beings manifold. We are also sure that they are doing it through the body cells primarily of Plumbel who has turned against American interest ever since our President cast him out of the scientific community . . ." McDowell was in a mood to continue his devastating best. But another young scientist interrupted him.

"Sir, do we have scientific evidence that the increase in the clamor for alternative values springs from the Cosmic being of PlanetB2 and that Carolina and Marissa are in any way involved in it?" Many turned to him and smiled appreciating the courage and vigor of his young blood.

"What more evidence do you want, young man? You are reading and seeing such developments ever since our mission to PlanetB2 failed. You know well that Plumbel is the one who trained both of them. We have credible information that he went to the living areas of the Native Americans to communicate with both Carolina and Marissa. Now that Plumbel has turned anti-American it is evident to us most scientifically that he is instigating Carolina and Marissa against the interests of the United States of America and they in turn are heavily influencing other cosmic beings on PlanetB2. This may spell an eventual doom not only for us as Americans but also to the entire human race." McDowell solemnized his scientific findings in the group of top scientists in the US.

"Hahahahaha, what a stupid conclusion you have arrived at and you call this scientific? Mr. McDowell, what do you think of the strength and power of the US. We have an arsenal of arms that no power on earth can match. Have you found any one nation that can be our rival on equal footing? Do you think that all other countries in the world put together can match the Herculean power of America? We are the only Superpower in the world and we have managed to undercut all our potential rivals through our multiple strategies. And here you are threatening us with the destruction of our big country by one scientist who has defected and by two women astronauts who have been lost in another planet. Who are these two astronauts? Just two women who do not know the ABC of American history." One of the senior scientists in the group was both sarcastic and impassioned in his pronouncements.

"I think you are badly mistaken. If it were only Plumbel and the two Native Americans, perhaps I would have said the same things that you said and in the same tone. Our scientific researches clearly point out to this one stark reality that America may have to face the mighty power of the cosmic beings in PlanetB2. If we know their technology, we can definitely develop a counter technology that can be superior to theirs. This is the struggle that we do not know how they communicate to earthly beings. We have no means of knowing whether they are with us or against us. It is too early to pronounce anything at the moment. But all findings till now point out to something clandestine evolving in PlanetB2." Another senior scientist on the side of McDowell came to the rescue of his boss.

"That is very true. But that is not all the truth. We have discovered through our technology that they communicate with earthly beings through waves. Where we are still lacking in equal strength is developing a machine that can capture their waves. We need human cells in order to do this. But I am sure that with our scientific advancement and the type of funds that we are allocated we shall be able even to create human cells. If it comes to that we shall even go to the extent of creating a human body of our own. When we do that the history of human race itself will be completely rewritten. We Americans will be able to create a new human race of our own making. Then we shall destroy the present human race and there will be only one race. That will be the American race on earth." McDowell spoke a bit more emotionally but clearly than it was warranted. His old companion pinched him a little to remind him that he was revealing too many secret plans of Rustler. He realized his mistake and shut his mouth.

His friend took over the proceedings and asked for consensus to give the findings and conclusions of the scientific community to Rustler as the unanimous opinion of the entire group. Those who agreed raised their hands in brimming emotions. Those who did not agree opted to keep silent without realizing that silence in such situations was more dangerous than open dissent.

News about the scientists meeting was taken faithfully to Rustler by staff of AIA who sat among the scientists as one of them. No one knew how the news reached Rustler's ears. As soon as he heard the news he went ballistic in a fit of rage. His anger was not against the scientists. In fact he was very happy about them. His anger was directly against the beings in PlanetB2, against Carolina and Marissa and horribly against Plumbel. His did not know much about beings in the planet. He only saw them moving about there but knew nothing about their characteristics. But he knew Carolina and Marissa. Like most of his colleagues in the American government he had a natural dislike for Native Americans. He did not consider them worthy of even being talked to. The prospect of both of them influencing the cosmic beings of PlanetB2 just took the shit out of him. He could not resist believing the natural connection between the two and Plumbel. He had seen it himself and he had heard many times Plumbel speaking about Marissa in emotional superlatives. All that he had heard from the horse's mouth now started replaying in his mind.

Rustler made a formal announcement that Plumbel was the first and foremost dissident in America and announced a reward of 50 million dollars to anyone who either gave clue about his place of stay or brought him dead. He called Nicky Broom frequently for meetings and asked to be updated about the progress in finding out the whereabouts of Plumbel. He wanted to change Nicky as the

Chief of AIA, as he always kept saying the same thing about the progress vis-à-vis Plumbel. In Rustler's point of view the news that Nicky brought every time was a grand step towards goofing. The entire America now knew that Plumbel was the archenemy of Rustler's. Newspapers reeled out page after page about the retrogression of Plumbel to disgrace. However, there were many newspapers, supported by the Left and encouraged by conscientious Americans that wrote boldly that Plumbel still continued to be the hero of hearts among most Americans. They blamed Rustler for ditching a trusted friend who stood by his side without even marrying for the sake of Rustler.

Norberta telephoned the Director of the Sami Parliament and asked to talk to Plumbel. She wanted to assure him of her and Norway's full support to him after verifying that he was in the know how of the biggest news in the world that day. Plumbel thanked her profusely for her unstinted support and solidarity. She assured him that Norway was ready to face any consequence for the sake of safeguarding him and protecting the integrity of truth and that of the cosmos.

The Native Americans gathered together to worship Mother Earth and their ancestors as soon as they heard the sad news of the break up between Rustler and Plumbel. There was a huge mourning for the departure of Carolina and Marissa from the earth, perhaps permanently. But reading the newspapers they also became proud owners of a new legacy that their beloved daughters had left behind and were still generating from another planet. They were proud that their daughters were the most talked about entities in the entire earth. Elderly people among them delivered big lectures that the two had left the earth to become living part of the galaxy of their ancestors in the sky. They knew intuitively that in such breakups it was the more powerful one who usually emerged winner. When truth finally won it was always too late for the one who was the victim of untruth. They had a very serious discussion among them and decided to invoke the support of all people of the Four Nations. They stressed on the need for one united voice in support of Plumbel. The two communities that he visited earlier were in tears for most of the time of the meeting. There was a groundswell of support and good vibes for Plumbel from all the indigenous peoples of America.

Opinions and emotions within the US was more on the side of Rustler and less on the side of Plumbel. No one was able to be neutral. One had to take sides one-way or other if one had to be accepted.

The resurgence of positive thoughts and feelings favoring Plumbel had an unanticipated effect in the world and in the cosmos. These waves emanating from the cells of human beings and some animals that knew Plumbel began to enter into a process of entropy with other waves in the cosmos and had a spiraling generation of new waves. The movement of entropy was much faster than usual. This fast movement and change in the cosmos led to the springing of many cosmic beings reaching PlanetB2. It had a twin effect in turn. In PlanetB2 there was a resurgent movement among the cosmic beings and their communication among them was much faster than usual.

Rustler, Nicky Broom and Joshua Bucket were watching together their giant computer and were horrified at the fast increase of movement and the number of cosmic beings that came together briskly. They were unable to make out if the cosmic beings existing in PlanetB2 were coming together in large numbers or if there was an increase of cosmic beings because of the sudden spurt in entropy process in the cosmos. Whatever might be the reason the trinity of secret maneuvering became twitchy about the unexpected development in PlanetB2. They were collectively at a loss to understand what they should be doing next. This seemed to be an insurmountable moment of truth that flew in the face of all their designs and calculations.

In their utter helplessness they decided to bring together top scientists and intelligence officers to elicit their opinions and suggestions to tide over the watershed. It was a top-level meeting. Everyone who was invited for the meeting assumed that it was all about the crisis in US management because of the serious rift between Rustler and Plumbel. The air in the US was already overflowing with gossip on why this happened in the history of a great country. Many went as far as to roll out statistics after statistic to prove their point that this was not the first time that US had to face such monumental difficulty in its governance. The saner ones among them commented that Rustler would find the going tough without Plumbel at his side.

The type of information that Rustler dished out to them took them aback. It was not any more Plumbel who was centric to the future trajectory of American strategies. It was a multiple axis. There was Plumbel no doubt. But there were also Carolina and Marissa. And above all there were the cosmic beings that seemed to pose the biggest threat to the security of America. And Imagine the three joining together to form a united axis to turn the settings of America's future. Rustler sounded Don Quixotic. Simultaneously he would turn an Oliver Twist. Shallow abyss of America's false security!

"We must get hold of Plumbel at all costs. Please employ all the resources that we have in terms of spying technology and hound him out. We were able to bomb entire mountains and raze them to the ground without a trace. Cave men had to run for their life. Why not Plumbel? We must also identity the person or the country that has given him asylum and annihilate them from the face of the earth. You should do it in the best interest of the citizens of America". One tried to be more patriotic than Rustler himself.

"I just can't believe that two girls from the Native Americans can pose such a big danger to the security of the most powerful nation in the world. There is something amiss here, Mr. President. Let us begin to destroy the rest of the Native Americans one by one and it will bring back the two to earth. I am sure they are in communication with their relatives if what you said about Plumbel and Marissa is to be believed. In as much as we are able to see their movements in PlanetB2 they should also be watching our movements and the fate of their own people." Another one dared Rustler.

"The previous suggestion is just ridiculous, Mr. President, to say the least. If we threaten them we are only going to increase the risk of security to the people of America, as we are not yet sure of the type of strength the cosmic beings in PlanetB2 have. There is a big spurt of movement already just by a mere churning of thoughts among us. We have not yet done anything to them. If this is the case we do not know how they are going to react when we try to harm their people. To me, that seems to be a path strewn with thorns and nails. We should somehow attract them to come back to the earth and pull out all the information about PlanetB2 from their mouth and design our future path." An elderly woman among them gave a weighty advice.

"The best option available to us, according to me is to create artificial beings with human cells and make them communicate with cosmic beings in PlanetB2. America should be ready to spend any amount of money for such an enterprise. Mr. President himself should take personal charge of such a mission. Once communication with cosmic beings is established it will become easy for us to draw out all information about PlanetB2 and about cosmic beings and design our counter strategies to defeat them and take over PlanetB2." There was a spontaneous clap of hands from some as soon as a young scientist said this.

"Thank you Ladies and Gentlemen . . .", Rustler got up slowly speaking at the same time. ". . . You have given very valuable suggestions. Each one of you has said something that is very valid by itself but makes no sense if only what you have said is taken out. There is a need to put all your reflections together and find out what comes out. It is evident. What comes out is that we should get hold of Plumbel, Carolina, Marissa and all the cosmic beings in PlanetB2. Today I promise you solemnly that I shall do everything possible to get into the core of PlanetB2 and draw out the essence of its life. However, we shall try our level best to make sure that the cosmic beings, Carolina and Marissa are not working against us. If there is any trace of them being together against American security and democracy, then I promise you that they will surely have the taste of American power. When they realize what we truly are on earth it will be too late. They will not live to see how we Americans have made the earth a prosperous place for all individuals to live in freedom. We shall not hesitate to decimate anyone or any force that stands against the integrity of American freedom. We Americans are the masters of the Universe. Now it seems to be a war, a holy war, a war to the finish for democracy and peace in the world against the infidels living in PlanetB2. It is going to be a war between Planet Earth and PlanetB2."

There was a big clap of appreciation for Rustler's determination to fight to the finish.

Newspapers and TV channels all over the world flashed the news that Rustler was determined to wage a war against PlanetB2 if America would not succeed to discover the secret of cosmic beings in PlanetB2. There seemed to be secret machinations in the center of the planet against human beings. The entire world had another chaff to grind endlessly on the pros and cons of a war against an unknown PlanetB2.

CHAPTER TWELVE

Plumbel read about the news of his friend's decision to wage a war against cosmic beings in PlanetB2. On the one hand he had a hearty laughter at the monstrous stupidity of Rustler's and on the other hand he was trembling a bit. More than that he could not help laughing at the ludicrousness of the top scientists and agents of 'intelligence' that surrounded him. "Is there no one to infuse some intelligence into the empty pockets of Rustler's brain.' He was speaking to himself as he was smiling and laughing. On the other hand he was sad that his bosom friends Carolina and Marissa had become the bête-noirs of Rustler's and the prospect of them becoming so also for most of America in the near future. He sat in silence for a long time as if he wanted to meditate. His thoughts and intense feelings were naturally directed towards Marissa who had by then become part of his being enveloping his personality. Was she an octopus that wanted to cling to its prey and empty its life giving fluids? Was she a parasite that grew on the strength of the parent body whose lifeline it would suck to the death of the parent body? Was she like the baby monkey to cling to its mother as long as it felt secure under her care?

All such questions mattered very little to Plumbel. He was enjoying a sort of bliss, a full body orgasm the moment he entered into communication with her. He did not have to consciously bring her down into his body. It happened almost without his consent. He did not have to make an effort to even think of her. She seemed to think of him and descend on him wholesale. Without his consciousness his body waited for the advent of Marissa's permeation into his body cells. She would choose the time. Nay, there was no time for her. He could not choose his time because she was always there. That bliss of being in total union with her transcended all limitations of time. The more he was filled with her the lighter his body became. He forgot his body. His being became as light as a feather. He felt like being a butterfly.

Plumbel remembered his early boyhood. His house had a small little garden on the backyard. There were many plants that his mother grew there. Gardening was her fascination. Plumbel used to be with his mother often more out of curiosity than out of a desire to be of any help to her. One evening he noticed a beautiful butterfly. He wanted to catch it. But it escaped from his cruel hands at least three times. Just when he gave up hope of catching it in his bare hands it sat on a leaf in a particular plant. It would sit on the leaf and fly away. It repeated this action a few times. Even as his mother was talking to him he kept watching the butterfly. Finally it sat on the leaf for sometime and lowered its bottom. It extended its bottom to the bottom of the leaf and quickly flew away.

As it stayed for a few seconds in that position Plumbel showed the butterfly to his mother. She delightfully informed him that the butterfly laid an egg under the leaf. She also explained to him that in a few days the egg would hatch and become a larva. After about eight days the larva would weave a cocoon for itself and would go into hibernation within the cocoon. After a few days there would be a beautiful butterfly coming out. Saying all this she kept watering the other plants.

Plumbel plucked that particular leaf with the egg of the butterfly. He found at least three eggs in the same leaf. "Oh why did you pluck that leaf?" his mother chided him when he showed the leaf in excitement. But then she asked him to find a good box for it so that the larva might break out of the egg at the right time. He lifted the cover of the box everyday to see if the egg had already hatched. His excitement knew no bounds when he saw the first tiny larva that had come out of the egg. His mother instructed him to spread some tender leaves from the same plant for the larva to eat. The next day another of the eggs hatched and the next day the third one too hatched. After a few days he took the box of larvae to the school to show to his friends. Some of them ridiculed him. But there were some of the girls who liked what he did. Rustler scorned at all such love for insects.

Disappointed at the reaction of some of his friends he did not dare to take the box again to the school. But as soon as the school was over he would rush home to have a look at the way the larvae were eating non-stop and were growing fast. Unfortunately he could not see the weaving of the cocoon by his friends. When he returned home one-day one larva was missing and there was sadness in his body. He thought something bad had happened to the larva. He opened the box to search for his pet larva. To his great surprise he found a new cocoon fixed to the top of the lid. It was stuck well. The cocoon was very beautiful with green shining dots in a circle on top of the cocoon. There were some golden spots all around the cocoon. He wondered where the beautiful colors came from.

It was a Sunday. He kept the box open and while working on his computer he also kept a careful watch on the cocoon that had already changed colors. His mother told him that the butterfly might come out any time. He could see one part of the cocoon breaking slowly and the movement of some insect inside. His mother had instructed him strictly not to touch the butterfly till it came out fully on its own. It did not take long for the fully developed butterfly to come out. He stretched out his palm to the new butterfly. It climbed on to his hand with its legs walking as if it was a model walking the ramp. It had no fear. It moved on his hand for a while and slowly began to fly. He did not want to catch the butterfly. Instead he let it fly to its land of freedom. On two subsequent days the other two cocoons also became butterflies and flew to their freedom.

Later in life he wanted to be a butterfly himself. It symbolized the freedom that he cherished most. He compromised to the way of Rustler when he saw that it was this freedom of the people at large that was at stake in the name of democracy. Rustler had mastered the art of playing on words that would sell the product that was contrary to the one that they wanted. He was a master craftsman in convincing the people that what he sold to them was what they wanted. Plumbel, being timid by nature did not want to antagonize his boyhood friend. He kept mum on several occasions when he wanted to cry out loud in protest against Rustler's ways. But somehow his throat did not allow his cry to come out.

It was his relationship first with Carolina and later with Marissa that slowly began to bring his inside out. It was not the effect of the many words that he spoke to them or they spoke to him. It was the consequence of being with them, especially with Marissa, that had an unexpected ramification on him. He was slowly becoming what he truly was inside. Rustler was a personality that shadowed him always. Even if he was not present physically at a particular moment Plumbel was always conditioned by what he thought as the expectation of Rustler. This was a heavy weight on his personality. It was like the heavy anchor of a ship that made mobility impossible. A butterfly enjoyed the freedom of mobility. It was always in the process of becoming in a cyclic movement of life.

Three butterflies had now started fluttering their lightweight wings without conditioning anyone's freedom in the world. He realized now in his consciousness that the freedom of the world was in serious peril. He knew the consequences of the deprivation of freedom from what he saw and experienced among the Native people and to some extent even saw it among the Sami people. Many in the world had become filthy rich at the cost of the life, dignity and freedom of many others. It had started digging deep burrows in his personality. He did not know why but he was pained deep inside when he saw people suffering for lack of freedom and dignity. He sat alone and shared this sadness deep in him with Marissa who also lived deep within him. Rustler was looking out for Marissa in PlanetB2 and wanted to bring her back into the world in order to gain the maximum information from her. Plumbel was enjoying the presence of Marissa within himself taking all the strength that he needed to live and work for the freedom of the people to whom it was systematically denied. He was aware that for Rustler all those who did not stand with him were against him. Plumbel was always aware that Rustler wanted to keep even air and water in fetters that he fabricated. Now he was out to chain the sky.

Marissa and Carolina had by now become almost one personality existing in two cosmic bodies. It was only a question of time before they became one personality with one cosmic body. Many other cosmic beings were attracted to them. They were the cumulative essence of the entropy of waves that desired freedom and dignity. The type of changes in the thinking of people in different parts of the world began to attract the two towards further entropy with cosmic waves, especially with strong waves that emanated from the Earth. Both of them came down to meet Plumbel in their form of waves. They entered into his body cells and permeated his entire being. He was in full body orgasm that is possible only for transcendental beings on earth. Karasjok provided the much-needed ambience for such bliss.

However, they could not remain in another's body for long and they came out and began to communicate to him. It started with invisible conversation with both of them and began to be shadows of both of them. Gradually Plumbel began to see both of them with his naked eyes. He squeezed his eyes to make sure that he was not dreaming. He pinched himself also to make sure that he was still living in a real world. The bliss effect in his body increased manifold and he liked to remain in that state forever. But Marissa touched him gently on his left shoulder. He submerged himself into an ocean of love. He liked to remain under that ocean and wished that the waters of the ocean would never dry up.

At that intense moment Carolina touched him with the same gentleness on his right shoulder. It was a double ocean. For Plumbel who was never given to be emotional till he came in touch with these two women it was an enthralling world that encompassed him. He was drowned to have a new life.

"It is a difficult time for you. But both of us are happy in our body that you have gathered all necessary courage to face difficulties with magnanimity. We keep receiving communications from you unceasingly. For both of us it is nice to be with you." Carolina started the conversation

"Whenever I have serious difficulty I remember both of you, especially Marissa with whom I have had a very special bonding. I am highly energized when I have problems. I think both of you step in with your energy waves when you see my tribulations." Plumbel went straight into his rational functioning. He was totally unaware that

Carolina's waves entered his body very powerfully even though he was more aware of Marissa in his human consciousness.

"It is not only both of us any more. There are many other cosmic beings that have stepped into this communication. You will not always understand it at your conscious level. It is like the slow permeation of fragrance. You can only smell it and you may not always know where it comes from. In our planet we cannot remain in isolation. We live in communication. In as much as you also live in communication with all cosmic elements you become a cosmic being already on earth. This is the slow transformation that is taking place in you and this is the reason why we are drawn to you. We do not take a conscious decision to come and meet you." Carolina explained further.

Plumbel looked at Marissa in perplexity and amazement. She moved towards him and embraced him. He was completely silent and enjoyed the moment of bliss. She began to inspire him with her verbal communication. "The full body orgasm that we all have as cosmic beings is not our selfishness. It urges us to further action to resist all waves of dominance that weave a web of enslavement of the poor and the innocent. At different phases in history such dominant waves begin to fill the universe and the entire world begins to tacitly agree that dominance is an accepted way of life. They are callously indifferent to exploitation and violence that take place in their own courtyard. There are intermittent wars by powerful nations. They invent one or other legitimizing reason for waging war against poor nations. They enjoy violence, war and killing. Where there is no war they make life impossible for the poor by closing all doors of survival and decent living. This is anti-cosmos." Plumbel began to listen in deep silence and reverence to the great wisdom of his two disciples. A total transformation of the teacher into a student in the presence of his students!

"Our being in cosmic communication will invariably urge us to action of resistance. The resistance that we put up spring from a very natural urge to translate our full body orgasm into a spreading of creative energy to the rest of the cosmos. It is a natural extension of full body orgasm. You are in bliss and this spreads into other beings in the world. When most such beings begin to receive waves of cosmic harmony and begin to live it in fullness it comes out in the form of resistance. You cannot sit in solitude for long enjoying full body orgasm that is cosmic harmony. You will be urged to get up and dance, a dance that will symbolize the slow dissipation of the energy that resists integrity of earthly beings into cosmic elements." It was Carolina who took turn to communicate precious waves of cosmic wisdom.

"But how will individuals like me begin to resist? Now you are with me and I am filled with confidence that I can take on the rest of the world. But when I am alone I get frightened." Plumbel once again got into this shell of rationality even in that moment of galvanizing emotional living.

"You will soon liberate yourself from your exclusive rational functioning. Very soon you will become a beautiful bundle of flesh that is simultaneously rational and emotional. Then you will not be calculating your strength and weakness. Nothing in the world will look insurmountable. It is not a military strategy that you will be working on. You are the military. You body is the armory. There will be no conscious decision on your part to fight anything. Your being in eternal bliss will take you into an ineluctable state of being of resistance." Carolina took him on quite rationally. She stooped into his plane of communication.

"We are always with you. Your body has already become cosmic to a large extent. All the beings in PlanetB2 are in steadfast communication with you. You are a powerhouse on earth in human body. You do not have to be conscious of the full potency of your body." Both of them now began to assume a form that filled the entire space with irresistible energy. They embraced him without a body. They filled his body. He lost weight of his human body. He was in total bliss forgetting his human existence. When he came into his own Carolina and Marissa had left him. Plumbel was no more the same.

Rustler commanded that all the Chiefs of the US Air Force, Navy and Ground Force assembled in a secret place for an emergency meeting. He also invited Nicky Broom and Joshua Bucket. He felt a bit weak now without the active presence of Plumbel. But he rationalized that no one was indispensable in the ethos of US governance and girdled himself with a false sense of security and comfort. All the five of them were used to such emergency calls and were hyper alert for any action at any time.

"Gentlemen, our country is in one of the most critical periods in history. According to all the information that we have at our disposal there are inimical forces that are gathering storm against the US. They aim to destroy the unquestionable authority of the US over the economy and governance of the world. That we have not yet been able to locate Plumbel clearly reveals the chinks in our armory. This is a real challenge to US power. We cannot let this continue for long. There is an immediate need to relocate ourselves as the supreme force on earth, not only on earth but in the entire universe." Rustler kick started a discussion with all seriousness that it deserved.

"First let us plug the loopholes in our intelligence and satellite surveillance system so that there is no individual on earth who does not come under our intelligence scanner. This is a serious business for American prestige in the world. On my part I want to assure you, Mr. President that our Air Force is on high alert as always to strike at any target that you specify in any part of the Universe." The Chief of Air Force kicked the ball moving.

"It is not a question of loophole in our intelligence system Mr. President. I can assure you that our system is flawless and I vouch for it. But there seems to be that extra helpless edge that goes beyond human comprehension and the surveillance of our machines. You know that our space scientists have discovered the existence of communication through waves. My assumption is that Plumbel has got into one of such orbits that our machines are not yet capable of discovering. As mentioned to you earlier this may not be possible unless we create a human body with cells that can receive and emit waves in abundance. According to me this is the crux of the problem." Joshua Bucket half emptied his bucket of data collection.

"Plumbel is not the only serious issue on hand for the US. There are those two women astronauts who have landed on PlanetB2 but have not returned. We are tracking their movement in that planet. They are very active. Carolina has changed her body into the shape of a ball and Marissa is in the process of such a change. There are fast movements among the beings there every now and then. They assemble together. Though we are unable to capture what they communicate among themselves I can reasonably assume that they are discussing about waging a war against the United States of America." The Chief of Scientists discovered a hitherto unknown scientific truth.

"Your assumption has to be verified Chief before we get into any action." The Chief of the American Navy interjected.

"Gentlemen, the art of governing a nation such as America that wants to keep its unquestionable unique status on earth is incessant creation of alibis. An alibi, as you all know, does not have to be scientific in the way the world understands science. But the presentation of the alibi as scientific and letting the world discuss it threadbare without really understanding it is the art of military action. People across the globe will create their own science based on our alibi and that is the success of our strategies." Rustler made a mild strategic intervention in the discussion.

"You are a genius Mr. President. The alibi is very much alive. The strange beings in PlanetB2 are very powerful and they visit the earth every now and then. Now that the US is growing more and more powerful and has a plan to take over PlanetB2 in order to make citizens of the world to inhabit it they want to wage a war against the US. They are making use of Plumbel in order to execute their secret war plans. If they wage war against the US, it is going to damage not only the integrity of the US but also of the entire Planet Earth. This will be a war between two planets. It will endanger the existence of human race itself. From all that we have seen it is evident that they have a huge stockpile of weapons of mass destruction. We do not know the true power of these weapons in another planet. But we know that it will have devastating levels of destruction. Planet earth may not exist at all if PlanetB2 manages to have its way. The American scientists have discovered huge piles of arms and ammunition in PlanetB2 and we are presenting some pictures that Bigbelly3 and 4 captured before they just vanished as soon as they landed on PlanetB2. That is the indication of the potent weapons in PlanetB2. It is unfortunate that three Americans have joined hands with our enemy planet in order to destroy humanity. We wanted them to work peacefully for the promotion of American science and democracy. But this 'trinity' has decided to betray our trust for reasons best known only to them. This is treason of the worst kind in human history. Even after this America tried its level best to set its feet on PlanetB2 with peaceful means. We never imagined that there would so much of acrimony against our peaceful endeavors in PlanetB2. Now we are left with no other option but to face the might of PlanetB2 and we shall face it." There was a huge clap of hands and a standing ovation as soon as Nicky Broom laid out his alibi in unquestionably clear terms. Rustler stood up helplessly at the quality of genius among his 'boys' that was much superior to that of his.

Rustler signaled to the boys to sit down. He took over from there. "Actually our next war is not against any nation but against PlanetB2. America will be the first nation in the history of human race to have won a war with another planet. We shall place all our resources at your disposal to jointly strategize this war. We have overcome resistance from every country on earth against American pride by militarily defeating them whenever they went beyond certain tolerable level of democracy. Now it is time that we show to the earth how great is American power and determination. What can Plumbel and two Native American dames do against the might of America? It will be a shame on humanity if that happens. We should never allow that to happen. We shall convince the entire human race that it has to stand as one against the hegemony of PlanetB2. On our part let us prepare deadliest weapons to simply annihilate all beings in PlanetB2 and take over the entire planet in our possession. Such violation of democracy on their part can never be tolerated at any cost by America. If we are able to capture our two women astronauts alive, it will be good for us to gather more information about the terrain of PlanetB2. But if that is not possible let us destroy them. Nicky Broom will make all possible efforts to trace Plumbel and eliminate him with a ruthlessness that humanity might not have witnessed till now . . . Also keep a keen watch on all those who are inimical to our plans in different countries. Depending on their position deal with them appropriately. Whoever has to be eliminated in the best interest of our mission, do eliminate them without even asking me. You need to take my personal approval only for the elimination of Heads of States. You know well that our close ally Israel is the best technology for such elimination." Once again there was a ceremonial ovation for the indefatigable genius of the President of America.

". . . On your part all of you, put your forces on high alert. Choose the best among you and with them let us form a special elite team 'Planet Strike Force'. Equipment, weapons and training for them must be planned carefully. Our scientists in the US Institute of Health have discovered a new neuro-technology for brain control. You are aware that we developed the technology of bio control and have succeeded well in controlling the bodies of humanity. Human bodies in the entire world have been ordained and conditioned to behave in the way we have designed them. We have again and again redesigned our education system so that this bio control becomes easy for us. We know by now that through our multiple strategies of medicines, media, and social engineering human beings have behaved exactly according to our strategic plans. Our biggest success has been the control over the sexual behavior of humans . . ."

". . . Now we are all geared towards neurocontrol by which we decide how people across the globe should think. For this we systematically manipulate the brain circuit through production and distribution of new drugs. Our Health Institute has already developed a new stimulant that can mildly be mixed with simple medicines that people normally take so that there will be a general condition of neuro problems all over the world. People will begin to flood mental hospitals and experts in neuro sciences. That is when we begin our brain circuit manipulation. It has been discovered by our scientists that through the new technology of optogenetics it is possible to exercise very good control of brain circuits. Many will begin to believe that their neuro-system is badly in imbalance. The medicines that we produce for rectifying what people generally believe as neuro-imbalance will be the one that will engineer and control people's thinking in our way. They will not only rationally believe that whatever we do are the right steps for the progress of humanity but also will begin to speak and write about it all over the world. This neuro-weapon will be one of our biggest tools against PlanetB2. We shall make the human race to believe that this planet is the biggest threat to Planet Earth and to the existence of human beings." Rustler stood in front of them like a wax statue that deserved to be touched and admired. It was a master plan that he made. By all standards it was a deadly plan. There were many murmurs in the meeting. For a minute Rustler mistook it to be a dissension among his wards. Soon Joshua Bucket clarified that it was a bursting forth of admiration for the genius of the American President. They were all happy to have such a genius President.

It was a day of standing ovations. This one for Rustler was the best by all standards. It lasted almost for about ten minutes without any interruption.

"Mr. President, this mega project should not be linked to any of us. We are the executioners. This is a project that needs slow transfusion. It will be good to leave it completely to the US Health Control Institute under your direct supervision." The Chief of the Ground Force in the US army looked with legitimate pride in his eyes for the magnificent truth that he presumed to have revealed. He looked around to see the types of looks that his words evinced on the faces of the assembly.

Rustler treated him less than a shit, as he could do hardly anything in the war against PlanetB2. "Joshua Bucket however will be the supervisor for all operations related to implementation of our technology of optogenetics. We do not want to leave any of our major operations in the hands of minions."

Rustler addressed the nation once again on this very historic moment of the world. As usual the media, both visual and verbal, were farting in the best way that they usually do. Farting, one of the best resources available to human race! Rustler made a public announcement of America's intent to wage war against PlanetB2. It was supposed to be a pre-emptive strike to safeguard humanity against the attack of an alien force from an alien planet. He asserted the need for the world to stand together as one, as it was an attack against the very existence of humanity. He also made it manifest that this was his ultimate mission in life to save humanity from sure destruction. He would be the first one to lay down his life in order to save humanity and to establish American power on earth as the most unquestionable and formidable. His genius was the proportional mix of arrogance and intelligence that could easily be taken as humility by his listeners.

It was with a certain amount of surprise and shock that Plumbel read the news of the announcement of war by Rustler. His call for a war on PlanetB2 was totally unwarranted and Plumbel was deeply disturbed at the news. The prospect of war, death and destruction loomed large on his horizon. He knew that America was stepping into an era of Don Quixotism. But who could prevent it? War was inherently written on its forehead from the time it invaded America under the guise of discovering India. The news came in waves creating uncontrollable ripples all the way. The news had its ripple effect all over the world. The optogenetics did not yet have its impact on peoples of the earth.

For the first time the relatives of Carolina and Marissa came to know that their own country was planning a military attack against the dwelling of their daughters. It was a mixed feeling. They were brainwashed to believe that they were Americans but deep down in their being they knew that the America they owned was completely different from the America that the Europeans discovered and built. But they were awestruck at the fact that their daughters were being discussed all over America both in negative, degrading way and in a positive way in some circles. They were shivering at the bottom of their being thinking what would befall them when the war actually broke out between planet earth and PlanetB2.

The American Health Department unleashed its neuro-technology all over the world without the knowledge of the peoples of the world. It had its salvific effect sooner than expected. The opinions in the world were getting slowly but sharply divided. Polarization was inevitable. Those who came under the influence of neuro-technology on the one side supported the war and those who escaped the tentacles of it were on the other side opposed to the idea of war. European consumers were one of the first ones, along with citizens of USA to legitimize and support the idea of a war against PlanetB2. Loyalties to nationhood understood as patriotism, more than consideration of what was right and wrong, appropriate and inappropriate played a crucial role in such polarization of support and opposition to Rustler. Both ways, Rustler became the center of concentrated attraction and hatred in the world and he enjoyed it thoroughly. Intense discussions all over the world also made people to keep shifting sides every now and then. It was not easy for anyone to remain neutral in such hotbed of polarized opinions. Neuro-technology aimed at oscillation of human beings.

There was obvious antipathy to the proposal that came from the US. In the forefront of their opinion amalgamation was the fact that America had not yet succeeded to land its astronauts successfully on PlanetB2. It was only creating an illusion that two indigenous women set their feet on the surface of the planet, but no one actually knew what really happened to the two Native American astronauts. America was only morphing the images of beings in PlanetB2. Actually they were some sort of footballs and there were no living beings in PlanetB2. Some even went to the extent of doubting the very existence of the planet. Sharper analysis and scathing attack on the proposed military forays of Rustler came from Russia and China who were openly opposed to any such move. They even predicted that such steps would ultimately spell the doom of the USA and the end of capitalism. Simultaneously they also rang the alarm bell that innocent masses of people would be destroyed if the beings in PlanetB2 also decided to retaliate the war efforts of the USA.

Surprisingly enough, Vietnam took the leadership in taking a stance against the US and the surprised West and East were taken aback by this development. The fact that Vietnam once defeated the US in war weighed heavily on the psyche of the cheerleaders of Rustler.

There was an unadulterated rebellion in the entire body of Plumbel. The soft and now emerging mystic that he was, every cell in his body stood up as strong metal to face the challenge to the people, animals and trees of the world. Any war with other planets would bring a special imbalance that the earth would not be able to balance. Human race was endearing a cause that would spell self-destruction. The leader of the bunch was none other than his one time friend Rustler. He pitied him. The full body orgasm or bliss that he experienced in his body now propelled him as a missile in action. He decided that he would oppose the war against PlanetB2 tooth and nail with all his might. He would leave no stone unturned in his efforts to bring sanity in the thinking and feelings of humans.

He discovered to his great surprise that his body was filled with anger and yet he was light. It did not weigh him down. It was this anger that led to his determination that he would never allow Rustler to succeed in his evil designs of war and violence. The enormity of his just anger touched the bodies of Carolina, Marissa and a few other cosmic beings in PlanetB2. He hardly knew that his waves of just anger also entered into the body cells of many human beings, animals and plants on earth. It was a mild festival of anger that was developing in the world. Cosmic bodies of Carolina and Marissa had that tumbling effect. They rushed to Plumbel.

"Yes, now the situation is turning to be serious and you need to act in accordance with what your body feels and says. Do not mix your learning in school that anger is bad. You only need to see if your anger is against injustice, violence and all the values that you cherish. You also need to check if your body becomes lighter when you are angry. If there is heaviness in your body and it results in unnecessary tension you can understand that there is compulsion in your anger. Whatever does not come from freedom will not resonate with cosmic order and movement. This anger in you has to develop and spread. We shall do all that we can to spread this anger. Not only both of us, there are also many among us in PlanetB2 who have been affected by the intensity of anger that is generated in many bodies on earth. It is a very creative insinuation that you need to indulge in. We are all with you." Their intervention with Plumbel was very short but he was happy that he experienced that bliss even for a short while. The assurance from both of them transformed him to a man of steel in his determination to fight against all forms of injustice and violence.

Plumbel informed Barbara that he wanted to be left alone that day and that he would not go for food at any time. However, he made a secret visit to the office of the Director of Samediggi, the Sami Parliament. He knew that the Director knew much more than he did about the developments in the world. Both of them discussed the issue first and gradually began to be angry together against the designs of war by Rustler. Plumbel explained to the Director of Sami Parliament that he knew all of the secrets of satellite surveillance and intelligence network of AIA and the type of arms that US possessed. They decided to communicate their concerns to Norberta through the Director's hotline.

CHAPTER THIRTEEN

Preparations for the war were done in right earnest and in high speed. Joshua Bucket realized that besides optogenetics there was a need to link all the satellites to the brain waves of human beings in order to measure the proportion of support and resistance to the declaration of war on PlanetB2. Rustler became hyper active moving every institution and individual towards working vigorously for the start of the war. Scientists and engineers were put on ever-alert mode. There were series of boardroom meetings to fine-tune all equipment and armory. Industries started working overtime to produce all kinds of weapon necessary for the strike.

The most significant in the stockpile was the arsenal of nuclear, biological and chemical weapons. The American space scientists had developed Bigbelly5 with far superior technology with more than enough propelling technology. One of the biggest concerns among them was the way Bigbelly5 would handle the heat at that particular spot in space though this was taken care of in Bigbelly3&4. Now the biggest question was landing on PlanetB2 and not melting, as did the previous two spacecraft. Many non-melting substance were mixed with the body building of Bigbelly5.

Landing on PlanetB2 was not however, the highest priority for Rustler. They fixed many machines in Bigbelly5 to forewarn the astronauts of possible melting. In the event of Bigbelly5 being caught in the liquid zone where it could possibly begin to melt it had to be saved by some extraordinary measure. In order to do this, scientists had integrated compressed escape velocity. This was of a high velocity so that in a fraction of a second Bigbelly5 would just shoot out of that zone and land on PlanetB2. If the warning were of a serious nature the astronauts would propel another space vehicle that would shoot into the belly of PlanetB2 and cause deep gashes in its structures. Bigbelly5 would then travel a few thousand miles and return to repeat the same action by turning back and the plan was to keep repeating such action till all the cosmic beings in the planet would be destroyed without a trace.

Rustler's rancor was unmatched. He had decided that he would give direct command to destroy the entire planetB2 in case of the bombs not being able to destroy the cosmic beings. In this case the astronauts would make use of the deadliest weapons at their possession. After exhausting the bombs at their disposal the astronauts would take back Bigbelly5 to the earth in order to repeat the attack. As usual the vehicle would be camouflaged with chemicals so that it did not come under any attack from earthly enemies. People could only see the fire and brimstone produced by the farting ass of Bigbelly5. It would fart and shit simultaneously with a heavy roar. It would indeed be a bloody shit that would emanate from its ass.

Another of the dastardliest weapons in the armory of Rustler was the chemical weapon. It was purported to spread into the entire PlanetB2 with a corroding effect on all that existed on the surface of the planet. Any leakage of this chemical substance in the belly of the space vehicle would spell a doom for all the astronauts and the vehicle. The compression level of the vehicle was carefully researched at all possible conditions so that there would be no rupture of the containers in any way. The idea was that if the bombs were unable to destroy cosmic beings on the planet the chemical bomb would do its work. Nothing could escape from its toxic effect. Scientists used more than 200 different chemicals in the form of liquid, gas and solid. They integrated high vapor pressure and had different types of liquid agents that could evaporate quickly. These volatile chemicals were capable of spreading fast beyond human comprehension. Among the stockpiles of chemical weapons there were the lethal ones and the incapacitating ones. They had also stored quite a few chemical combinations that would spread and become clouds of chemical dust. These chemical clouds would destroy all beings that came beneath it. To be sure of total destruction of cosmic beings Bigbelly5 also had provisions for the use of mustard gas. All the scientists who worked on this destruction force in Bigbelly5 remembered gratefully Richard Kuhn, the Austro-German scientist who was given Nobel Prize for his discovery of Soman, the nerve agent that was part of a series of chemical weapons of mass destruction.

At the end of such heavy preparation Rustler was extremely happy that the best or the worst destructive power was loaded into the underbelly of Bigbelly5. He made a personal survey of the inside of the vehicle and satisfied himself that his scientists would not fail him this time. He satisfied himself about the proportional mix of NBC that is Nuclear, Biological and Chemical weapons. The belly of Bigbelly5 was filled with enough nutrients and it was ready to make the biggest burp in human history.

Rustler designed the chemical warfare against PlanetB2 with twin intent. The most lethal one was to serve a deathblow to the cosmic beings in the planet if it were ultimately warranted. But his primary intent was to cause gaping holes in that liquid zone in space that prevented the capturing of their waves coming into the earth. He had a lingering suspicion that they had a channel of communication with select human beings and that escaped the capability of American machines. The next best option open to him was to cause serious ruptures in the special layer that formed a thick guard in protection of the cosmic beings.

It was a serious call. It came from the Prime Minister Norberta to the President of the Sami Parliament in his hotline. Unable to bear the heat for long the President buzzed the button specially set up between him and Plumbel's room as an extra security measure. He took the call of Norberta from his room itself. The gravity of the global situation after the announcement of an all out war on PlanetB2 disturbed Norberta no end. Public opinion in Norway against the war was on an upswing. Norberta and her predecessors had carefully nurtured the entire region of Scandinavia in human sensitivity to issues of people's rights. Unlike the US they went all over the world to set up strong walls of defense of people's human rights according to certain basic human standards as well as according to the Universal Declaration of Human Rights by the United Nations.

Ruling parties in many countries resented the intervention of Norway especially as it took a firm stand on behalf of the underdogs. They often accused Norway of violating their sovereign status while simultaneously indulging in serious violation of rights of common and ordinary citizens within the boundaries of their countries. Rustler's government was always fidgety to countries that genuinely stood for human rights questions. Now that the war was declared US agencies were put on extra alert to watch over countries that were human rights sensitive. The war was planned on more than two fronts. One was the direct attack on PlanetB2. The other was to destroy somehow the trinity of Carolina, Marissa and Plumbel.

Norberta had to take care of herself. She was made not of ordinary mettle. She discussed frank and plain about this unusual development in global politics and asked for Plumbel's advise on what Norway should do in such vicious circumstances. Plumbel insisted on the inevitability of polarization of the world on the question of war and violence. But Norberta was more interested in knowing why the man was behaving the way he did. What was wrong with him? Was it in his genes or was it a question of his growing up in a milieu that he wanted to overcome not only the world but also even the cosmos. Norberta laughed at the thought that Rustler could be so stupid as to even imagine that someone could hegemonize the cosmos.

"Only the most stupid person on earth could think and behave the way Rustler wants to do. I could perhaps not see another such congenital idiot," She said in jest.

"Oh Norberta, we were almost childhood friends. I really do not know the building up of genes in his genealogy. But I know for sure that he comes from a very rich family in our city. Later he used to boast to me that he had royal blood in his family tree. I did not go deep into this question, as I thought that Rustler was only an empty gong. However, his family enjoyed much political clout in our municipality. We could see Rustler showcasing the political power derived from his family. He would behave in the worst possible manner with his peers. Already at that young age every other student had to respect him as a far superior being. He and his cronies would thrash anyone who refused to do it mercilessly. Whenever I reproved him for doing this he would go to my parents and tell them many cock and bull stories about me. The next day he would be my friend as usual. They were six brothers in the family and Rustler was the fourth one. He was not a pet child in any way. His elder brothers would often clobber him for his mischiefs until his father or mother intervened to save him. It was a way of getting his parents attention. He would indulge in all sorts of mischief making behind his parents against his brothers. When they began to rain blows on him he would become the 'poor victim' in the sight of his parents.

Later he would tease his brothers for being such fools as to be scolded by his parents . . ."

". . . As if to compensate what he lost out in the family because of his brothers he began to take part in all sorts of competitions in the school and began to gain a lot of attention and recognition from many students and teachers. My reasonable guess is that this chain of success got into his head. He began to convince himself that no one in the school would be able to overcome him in any of the competition. He took this glory in the school to his brothers and showcased his success against their failure to recognize his true worth. Often his brothers were put to shame for their inability to achieve as much as Rustler did. He always compared himself with all his elder brothers and boasted that none of them could stand up to his standards of achievement . . ."

". . . One of the fears that Rustler developed was that of possible failures in his competitions. He would single out potential rivals and gather his friends to 'fix' them. Sometimes this fixing of potential rivals would turn out to be violent and Rustler would not care a hoot for what happened to his companions. What was very important for him was his success and nothing else mattered. In all these violent forays he always needed me at his side to fall back upon as if to wash off his guilt. There was no remorse in him, however. I was like the catholic priest who would sit in the confessional and listen to the sins 'confessed' as a routine. Even without seeing who was in the confessional the priest would absolve the sinner with nominal punishment that meant nothing. I had to often do similar tasks for my friend Rustler. I could already see ominous signs in the development of his personality. He began to splash it with streaks of racial superiority. However, whenever he took up the question of the inferiority of the Blacks against the Whites I stood as a solid rock of defense of humanism against his racism. He knew that on this one issue I would not legitimize his thinking and action and therefore, he was very cautious of making any serious pronouncements on this. I knew all the same that inside him lay a sleeping volcano that was churning and it could spit fire anytime in future . . ."

". . . When I contained his abnormal tendency towards racial prejudice he skillfully diverted it to American pride that later transformed into American supremacy. He took recourse to this so that no one would blame him for anything. Instead he got a lot of adulation for the wrong tendencies that he developed. It is good that he did not turn to be a racial purist. But the consequence of this was much worse that he camouflaged his individual and insatiable thirst for power by his patriotism. He has become a single minded American and that is very dangerous to the rest of the world. He is not in any pursuit of Americanism, as we all understand it. He is in hot pursuit of himself, his ego, and his castle of power. This pursuit is horribly deprived of the values that one normally associates with being American. For him the crux of the issue is not being an American. Instead it is being himself. It is this self of Rustler, mistaken as the self of all Americans that could spell the ultimate doom to all Americans and perhaps to the rest of the world . . ."

Norberta listened to him with a lot of patience. She was a learner and sat on her chair as a bundle of flesh smeared with discipleship. She forgot her sense of time. She submerged herself in the intricacies of personality traits.

"The one thing I do not understand is, why did you stick to him for this long despite knowing that he had so many negative qualities that had great potential to harm others?" Norberta let go of her one doubt that lingered in her mind, as Plumbel was talking almost non-stop.

He had a legitimization for his past relationship with Rustler. "He was a fourth boy in the family and was dominated over by all his brothers. Once in a way his eldest brother would manifest some signs of love and concern for the little one. Otherwise Rustler always grew up with the feeling that he was the underdog and the most neglected one in the family. This psyche of neglect infused an insurmountable sense of insecurity in him. This is part of the psyche of all dominant nations that build military strength as their security. They suffer from a basic sense of insecurity. Just look at what Lyndon Johnson said, "If you let a bully come into your garden, the next day he'll be in your porch and the day after he'll rape your wife." Such is the sickness they suffer in their inadequate psyche. Rustler had to take a lot of pain to prove himself to his parents and teachers that he was much better than his brothers. When he ultimately succeeded in proving himself and had the power in his hands he imitated his brothers very subconsciously to prove himself superior to his brothers. He wanted to be the dominant one in every situation just as his brothers were in every situation of his life. Arrogance, aggression and violence had their value in this design of his. You will say that this was an evil design. But I saw him only as a poor victim of his own subconscious that was dictating terms to his personal relationships. I empathized with him. I genuinely loved him. He was my friend. I opted to ignore many of his inadequacies. You call them evil designs. But for me evil and good are very relative. It was important that he saw his actions as evil for others and ultimately for himself. I decided to part company with him only when I realized that he was no more a victim but a master of what grew in his subconscious. Such incorrigible personalities are usually sent to jails. It was Rustler's genius that he became the President of the most powerful country in the world. As years passed, he managed to bring what lived in his subconscious to his conscious levels of functioning and began to enjoy them. That became dangerous to the world."

Norberta woke up with a jerk. She realized that her call to Plumbel had a totally different reason. "Plumbel, I enjoyed the way you have analyzed the personality formation of Rustler and what this horrible personality has done to the world and is now leading to unsettling the cosmic balance. But the reason I called you is to warn you of the impending danger that AIA may be very near your door. It is not difficult for them to identify your presence in Norway. We do not have a watertight security proof. Our systems are quite open to surveillance by the American machines. You have been safe till now because of the hideout in the Samediggi, the Sami Parliament that is generally not under the radars of the US. It is an insignificant place for the Americans in terms of security threat. But now that they are pursuing you with a single-minded determination they may gear up their radars in all possible directions and it may not be too long before your presence in Karasjok is discovered. Therefore, my advice is that you shift to another country where you will not be easily detected and where the government will take care of your personal security just in case your presence is discovered in their soil." Norberta let it go in one go.

"I see your point clearly. As long as I was with Rustler I did not care much about death. It had become an essential part of my mindset and I was prepared to lay down my life anytime. But now it is a different story. I have now a relationship and a mission in life. I want to live for my two girls, Marissa and Carolina. I want to live for the mission of saving Planet Earth from the evil machinations of my one time friend Rustler. I have a mission to prevent any American entry into PlanetB2. It is important that I lived till Rustler was defeated fully. Am wondering if I could escape into Russia or China." Plumbel sounded a bit emotional.

"These are the two countries where Rustler would expect you to escape into. Therefore, the Americans would be on high alert to pick you up en route Russia or China. I would suggest that you flee to Vietnam. Though it defeated the US once, it is still a poor country. The government will be very happy to have you in its soil. They will not only protect you but also will be happy to proactively plan your operations across the world. I know the President of Vietnam personally well. He is a very sensitive human being and symbolizes the pains and pangs of his people at the hands of the American government. The scars of Vietnam War are still fresh in many places. They may take a few centuries to obliterate the scars. The entire world knows that it was a horrible decision to wage war against Vietnam and many of us are happy that this tiny nation brought the might of the US to its knees. I shall speak to the President and apprise him of your presence and situation here. I have made necessary arrangements for your departure from Karasjok tomorrow. The President of the Sami Parliament will inform you of the details. All the best! I shall find a way of communicating with you through different channels besides our communications through waves." She cut off the phone, as she began to become more and more emotional.

"Where is Mr. Plumbel who stayed in this room?" The President of the Sami Parliament was almost shitting in his pants seeing the man inside the room of Plumbel. He thought no one knew his whereabouts. While looking at the man the President's eyes made a flashing search of the room to see if Plumbel was laying down dead in any corner of the room. The uncontrollable anxiety was writ large on his face.

"Don't worry too much President. I am Plumbel with a silicone mask on my face. I had a stock of them with me. All of us in our status in the US government were supposed to have these always with us as we could face life threat at any time in life. We had to camouflage our appearance and escape. They have come in handy now to escape from the very same forces that developed these very special masks." Even in that hurried situation Plumbel could not be stopped from his talkative explanations.

Tension was overflowing on the face of the President of the Sami Parliament. He wanted to get rid of Plumbel at the earliest from Sapmi, the Sami land. Whatever might happen to the planet wars initiated by Rustler he did not want the Samediggi to be involved in any broiling controversy. A special car would take him to Alta and from there a helicopter would take him to Oslo International Airport. He was whisked away at the airport without the usual procedures of immigration. Norberta had made all necessary arrangements to prevent public viewing, even in disguise, of the most important man in history, as she perceived events.

Norberta had timed the escape of Plumbel well. It was Plumbel who used to educate his minions that any success in governance and military operation much depended on timing. A loss of a few minutes or an unnecessary hurry by a few seconds could spell disaster in military operations. The Minister of Foreign Affairs in the Norwegian government had an official trip to Hanoi, the Capital city of Vietnam. She realized that it was her opportunity to smuggle Plumbel out of Norway to a safer destination. She personally spoke to the President of Vietnam through a second hotline that both countries had set up, as they suspected that the Americans had not much difficulty in bugging their regular hotline.

A Norwegian diplomatic passport was made for Plumbel with his new appearance so that he could go through the regular immigration without arousing the slightest suspicion. Norberta also calculated that such a passport would be handy for him at any time of need to escape. The Foreign Affairs Minister of Vietnam received them at the Hanoi Airport and took the most important diplomats in a special car. Plumbel participated in all the formalities that followed. When all dignitaries from Norway were introduced to the President of Vietnam he did have a wry smile on his face while shaking hands with Plumbel.

That evening just before going to bed Plumbel took time off to spend close moments with his blue-eyed girls. Things had changed a lot between him and them. As soon as he thought of them he could feel their presence within his body as well as near him. Within his body it was full body orgasm which spiritualists of yore called 'mysticism'. Outside his body he felt their physical presence without really seeing them and touching them. That experience of living with someone special without physically touching and seeing was one of the most sensational experiences of his life. He never bargained for it as long as he was an official partner of a dominant empire. This time around the bliss was much more than usual. Plumbel could feel the presence of a throng of cosmic beings. The full body orgasm in his body reached a different horizon altogether. He was lost in an immeasurable ocean of love. His being became the embodiment of love and in that lost ocean he was becoming love. That was the mystery of love. It was being and becoming at the same time. The essence of cosmos! The inside of Plumbel's broke into an amateurish poem.

I wander in the yonder
Inundated in your fragrance
Draped in your breath
That venture out in waves

The silky touch, the Milky Way
The messengers of stars in the sky
Envelop me uninhibited
Butterfly inside a cocoon

Love deep within me
Living in the inner being
The 'be' of the beings
Interior walls most flexible

Being is love, full body orgasm
Inexplicable state of being
The essence of all beings
Bedrock of all existence

Dynamic in being
Dynamite in becoming
Complacency no refuge
Internal stirring ever eternal

Being is cosmos
All beings are cosmic
Cosmos is matter
Indestructible into eternity

Love, being of the beautiful
Being of the 'ugly'
Essence of the 'cruel'
Goodness embodied

Being is the becoming
Two-in-one being and becoming
Boiling cup of coffee
Inseparable aroma

Without you I am nothing
Without me you are nothing
We are two in one being
Being and becoming

The conjoint twins of cosmos
Bliss eternal, full body orgasm
Words inexplicable, paucity supreme
One moment of bliss, eternal orgasm

Becoming angry, Bliss
Being calm, Bliss
Becoming resistant, Bliss
Being mystic, bliss

Life eternal, Bliss eternal
Being eternal, becoming eternal

In that submergence in love he could see his ladies love eternally plunging him into action. Their mystic communication was much more real for him than all the verbal communication he had in all of his life. Plumbel was in total comfort and freedom about his new association with Vietnam. The very idea filled him with an unfathomable liberty of body cells. He felt quite light about it.

Marissa and Carolina with a host of other cosmic beings surrounding them told him that his decision to take refuge in Vietnam was the best at the moment in time. He also realized that there was a certain amount of urging in his body from the cosmic waves while taking decisions. He was in incessant communication with the cosmic beings both in PlanetB2 and with other human beings who were evolving into cosmic beings. The entropy of life giving energy had now begun to assume an intensity that was unanticipated. More and more beings in the world whose bodies were tuned to love and life began to come under intensive communication through waves. A different world seemed to be evolving in different parts of the world that could not be deciphered with scientific tools and with human rationality. It felt that Plumbel had a major responsibility in the evolution of intensive communication of waves leading to the evolution of a new world of resilience and resistance.

Both of them also urged him to speed up his conscious endeavor to gather forces of the world that would stand for equality, justice and value based human living. The essence of human life was in living as a community, in communitarianism and not in extreme individualism. Individuals constituted the community but without being in communicative interaction with communities the individual would be doomed to perdition.

"You have taken on yourself an impossible mission. You were not cut out for such a mission by your upbringing. You grew up in an extremely dominant world. But your inner being always loved what you are today. It was dormant within you as other dominant cells in your body took over the reins of determining your personality building. You inner being was helpless in many ways. Often your intellect and rationality would take over control of your girdles and crush you inner being under their weight. The conflict that you see in the world between the rich and poor, the powerful and the powerless, the ruling class and the ethnic communities, capitalism and communism, all these are very much alive within your body. In fact what you see in the world is only a resurgence of what aspires to live within you. It is only in some beings and at some times that the inner being begins to come alive. Once you begin to live by your inner being fully you begin to experience full body orgasm, bliss. You become a mystic among human beings to mystify mysticism as an unreachable aspiration."

Plumbel was awestruck at what he heard from Marissa. He took a few minutes to be in that state of full body orgasm. They too allowed him to enjoy bliss to the full.

"This full body orgasm that you are enjoying is your being. It is what you are in your inner being. But you have already realized that the more you are in full body orgasm the more you are also urged to get out and act. That is what I call the becoming. This comes from a basic aspiration to excel in your being what you are. There is an inevitable urge always in you to become something in accordance with your being. This movement of being and becoming is in consonance with the cosmic movement of change. The changes that you see in dominant world arise from intellect and rational decisions. These are good as long as there is a coherent resonance for these intellectual decisions with the inner being. Unfortunately the dominant world cares a damn about inner being and what aspires to live at that level." Plumbel was in full admiration of Carolina. Between both his wards he found Carolina to be more rational in her personality traits and Marissa to be more emotional in her trajectories. Both of them seemed to him to be an unassailable fusion of being and becoming.

"Your becoming from the depth of your being is the hope of the world at the moment. Give full vent to your emotional being and your rational being. Their coalescing will influence all those good-hearted human beings in the world towards the evolution of a new world. When this coalescing becomes effective it will manifest itself as strategies against the hegemony that Rustler is planning to plant. You will be surprised to know that animals and plants play a very important role in this evolution. The indigenous peoples of the world have an innate knowledge about this inseparability of animals and plants from their world and from cosmos. You will symbolize the synthesis of all cosmic energy on earth with a human body. To that extent you will also represent all those who stand against Rustler and his blind approach to hegemony. Rustler is the embodiment of evil though there are many positive dimensions that are dormant in him. He has to either let the positive dimensions in him wake up and come to life or face the consequences of the over imposing confluence of positive energy in the world. Such confluence will spell the final doom of Rustler. You, Plumbel will be our symbol. We shall be constantly communicating with you from PlanetB2. It is in this communication that cosmic energy flows into you and us. We shall be mutually strengthened and our strength will dissipate all evil energy in this world. We are always with you Plumbel. Be strong."

Both of them embraced him, or rather they engulfed him with their ever-flowing energy. The three of them enjoyed full body orgasm of the mystic order. The battle line was drawn clearly in two different ways.

The President of Vietnam sat with Plumbel for an initial appraisal. After listening to Plumbel he recollected to him how five subsequent Presidents of the US had waged a non-stop war against a tiny nation of Vietnam only because it subscribed to Left ideology and was supported by China and Russia. They formally recognized the Democratic Republic of Vietnam under the leadership of Ho Chi Minh. The five Musketeer Presidents who could not tolerate this recognition were Truman, Eisenhower, John F Kennedy, Lyndon Johnson and Richard Nixon. They in turn supported Bao Dai installed by the French in South Vietnam. This was the American ball game of dividing countries to reap a rich harvest of capitalism. It was a sad story that Lyndon Johnson snowballed Operation Rolling Thunder against Northern Vietnam to bomb it to total annihilation. He also raised the number of US troops in Vietnam to 520,000. They had to pay a heavy price for such foolhardy endeavor. In their 302,380 sorties they lost 922 warplanes.

Ultimately Vietnam stood tall in the left side of the world as the one country that could stand against the arrogant might of the US that had to swallow the bitter pill of military defeat. He was a proud man that such a tiny nation could defeat the might of the most powerful nation in the world.

"This is not a conflict between capitalism and communism. In fact there is no conflict. The cosmic beings simply live their lives. They do not live in reference to others. Nothing, no other being affects their being. They simply are and their becoming is based on their being and not on other beings. Rustler and most human beings live always in reference to others and want to be superior to other beings. Rustler unfortunately thinks that he is invincible. He believes that he is the superman. He lives under the illusion that there should be no one, nothing that can be superior to him. He wants to have the last laugh in everything." Plumbel began to get into the depths of realities that governed the world.

"Yes, I understand that it is because of our living in reference to others that we have divided ourselves into different nations and fight among ourselves. But is there a way to make people live in reference to themselves? It seems to be an impossible proposition." The President began to slowly open up.

"It has started taking place in the world. All those who live their lives in simplicity without ever desiring to dominate over others will find their unity through the interaction of their waves. This convergence of all those who desire peace and justice will be inevitable in the cyclic development of the world. This is the hope of this world." Plumbel highlighted the future with a calmness that was admirable in the eyes of the President.

"I am glad at the underlying message of peace that you are espousing, Mr. Plumbel. I can see that you are not speaking of religion but it is evident that you have stuffed your discourse with deep spiritual essence. I like the absence of any heavenly being in your vision for the world. That is wonderful. I am with you and Vietnam will stand with you till the end of the road wherever it leads us to. Let us meet again to get into the nitty-gritties of strategic planning."

The President had arranged Plumbel's residence in a high security zone within Vietnam without even confiding to his close associates who the man really was. Everyone knew that he was a top diplomat and could not move an inch closer than that.

CHAPTER FOURTEEN

"Gentlemen, we are at a critical period in human history. As you are aware, the development model of the US and the British is the only abiding hope for humanity. It is here for all to see how human beings experience prosperity and full freedom. Both countries have made great strides in taking the world to different planes of development. It is in that trajectory that we have launched our mission to land in PlanetB2. However, we have had an enemy inside who is out to thwart our mission. We shall be missing a big scope of developing ourselves if we lose this chance. We need to hole out this man Plumbel if we have to succeed well in setting our feet on PlanetB2. I request all of you to put your intelligence gathering systems on high alert and capture this infidel live or dead . . ."

"Before we go into nitty-gritties Mr. Prime Minister please let us know how far you have progressed in your preparations to land in PlanetB2 and how your confidante Plumbel turned a foe all of a sudden." Claudia, the German Chancellor made an intrusion into the smooth speech of Blaringtone, the British Prime Minister who spoke as if he was the President of the US. Rustler and Blaringtone had hatched the plot well in preparation of the meeting. Besides member states of the Commonwealth, both of them had handpicked a few Heads of States as special invitees for the meeting.

Blaringtone had to explain all the finer details of the mission to PlanetB2 that was almost now ready to be launched. There were some serious but mild rumblings at the news that Rustler was planning a NBC attack on PlanetB2 if landing and capturing the planet was not possible. Plumbel paled into the background at this surprising news from the British Prime Minister.

"I stand by the President of the US in his decision not only to land on PlanetB2 that is very crucial for the progress of human race as a whole but also to wage a war against the same planet if the beings in the planet are hostile to human race. This cannot be tolerated at any cost. We must show them the power of human race. I know for sure that Plumbel is a pain in the ass of Americans. The sooner we get rid of him the better it will be for the success of our mission to PlanetB2." Blaringtone made his stand clear on behalf of all the British people. It was a fashion among all rulers to speak on behalf of their citizens without having a legitimate mandate from them. Since all of them did the same thing no one bothered about propriety.

"It is too early on my part to say anything definite about this issue, especially the question of war against beings in another planet. It disturbs me greatly to even think of such a possibility though Mr. Blaringtone, you may have your legitimate reasons for taking up both the mission and the war. I shall have to actually make an assessment of public opinion in my country before I come out with a firm stand on this. Please give me some time." Claudia was more than clear and was louder in her assertions on behalf of Germany. This was a huge disappointment for Rustler who was watching the proceedings of the Commonwealth meeting through a very private channel that was set up between him and Blaringtone. Much-depended on Germany not only to legitimize his stand on war but also to provide him financial support. It was a clear setback to the President of the US. For Blaringtone the stand of Germany was sort of on expected lines.

"The people of India love Mr. President Rustler. On behalf of the people of India I endorse the stand of the Presidents of the US and of England. (Leave alone the fact that the Prime Minister of India was unable to distinguish between the President and the Prime Minister and therefore, clubbed them together conveniently.) The Queen of England is like a mother to all the people of India. My country has benefited much from the goodwill of the British Queen and subsequent Prime Ministers. Though we were a colonized nation we have only benefited more from the British rule than suffered. I promise India's unstinted support to this major project for the progress of humanity and India will make ten billion dollars available for the mission to PlanetB2 and for the war if it became inevitable in the course of time." The Prime Minister of India declared his support even before he was called to speak. He was in obvious hurry to manifest his loyalty.

Pakistan followed suit. Between both of them one wanted to outdo the other in reference to the US. If India was loyal Pakistan had to prove that it was more loyal. The President of Pakistan traced the very cordial relationship between the US and

Pakistan even at a time when India had blatantly tilted towards the USSR. It pledged its blind support to Rustler. The Pakistani Prime Minister promised 15 billion dollars. He knew well that he would get back more than the money he promised through development aid and other grants from the US. He was also aware that the Indian Prime Minister was quite naïve on this count of getting back through the backdoor more than what he promised.

It was expected that the Australian and the Canadian Prime Ministers would stand by the President of America in whatever he did. They did not belie the hopes. They were ardent adherents of the views of Rustler without ever trying to look at the validity of his pronouncements and actions.

Members of the European Union were sharply divided among themselves. Some of them supported Rustler strongly and some others opposed his war plans as vehemently as they could. They thought that there was an ego that was at work and not a cause in the best interest of humanity. It was a foregone conclusion that the Scandinavian countries stood together firmly in their opposition to the question of a mission to PlanetB2 spending much of the tax money of American citizens. They found a natural ally in Germany. History was being tinkered with in the revisiting of the same history by both the countries. Germany was not any more the country of detestable Hitler. Gone were days when Hitler used to be a hit. Now there was a Rustler.

Kenya refused to toe the line of the British and America because India supported the proposed project to overpower PlanetB2. India was not an economic collaborator in their perspective. It was more of an exploiter of the wealth of Nigeria. The colonized chasing the ways of the colonizer! Rulers in Kenya simply followed the general feelings of resentment of Kenyan citizens against India's colonizing enterprises. A funny path of development of the Third World! Most African nations however, faithfully toed the line of their former master, Britain. They supported Rustler without even knowing who he was and why he actually wanted to wage a war against PlanetB2.

Rustler cared a hoot for what the African and Latin American countries said and did. He did not count on their support for his historic mission. He knew that India and Pakistan were playing their silly games of gaining fringe benefits from the US even in such a climacteric global situation. What shocked him most in his pants was the attitude of Claudia the German Chancellor. She was almost the European Union, the most powerful nation in Europe and he found it hard to digest the fact that she did not agree with him at the first instance itself. However, his diplomats assured him of hard negotiations with Germany and promised to bring Claudia around in a very short time. They reassured him of the magnificent support he received from Britain, Canada, Australia, and India etc. Rustler was quite skeptic of their assurances. He wanted nothing short of open support to his stand. He could not tolerate fence sitters.

❧ ❧ ❧

That evening Norberta, the Prime Minister of Norway had a long private meeting with Claudia. Both of them were already good friends. But this meeting was a very special one. Norberta explained all the complicated developments vis-à-vis the war against PlanetB2. It was more than a sheer shock to Claudia who was generally a very sensitive woman. Both the women shared many things in common. They had a very healthy family with two children each. Both of them came from well-placed families in their respective countries. They managed their husbands and children very well. It was a clear strength for both of them to govern their respective countries. It was Norberta who used to ring up Claudia occasionally to get her inputs on issues of governance and human rights. Claudia used to call her over phone whenever she was alone and was bored to death. They used to chat for long hours about books, reading, music, dance, drama, and movies and above all about the way their children were taking paths that were not designed by them. Both were happy that their children were able to set the trajectory of their life in a healthy manner.

This was a different cup of tea for Claudia to digest all that Norberta began to share. At times things became rather too much for her even to hear. Could a human being be so self-centric or eccentric that he was ready to jeopardize the entire human race only to satiate the needs of his ego? But Claudia knew everything about such people at her own courtyard and therefore, was able to rationalize the malicious developments in the US around the President. Claudia felt sad for Plumbel and was surprised that there could be such a person at the top-level administration in the US. It was hard for her to grasp the mystery of Carolina and Marissa communicating with Plumbel directly. She rubbed her eyes when she heard that they came down to enter the body cells of Plumbel and provide him with all the mystic strength necessary for him to withstand all pressures from human world. Norberta was able to understand that it would take some more time for Claudia to perceive the mysteries of cosmic communicative interaction.

Claudia was eager to know the exact location of Plumbel and the type of security risks that he was going through. She agreed with Norberta that Vietnam was a good choice. However, she also knew the American-Israelite intelligence system and their penetrating power. They could pierce through any hard cover and peep into the secret chambers of any national secret. She wondered if Vietnam could provide the type of security cover needed in such extreme situations. She was sure that the Americans would catch up with Plumbel very soon through the Israelites and that would be end of Plumbel. She was concerned about him and wanted to put him in a watertight security. She knew much better than Norberta who was ready to do anything that Claudia suggested only for protecting the most important man in the world.

It was Norberta's turn to take to task Blaringtone in the next day's meeting. "Mr. Prime Minister, both you and the President of the US are on a destructive path. You do not understand that there is another world that aspires to live a life in harmony with nature and in peace. Your idea of peace and approach to peace is terribly jinxed. Peace is not what you gift to the world. You demand subservience of nations as a price for the peace that you offer them. This is not the essence of peace. Please understand that peace is something internal to human nature and human beings. Such a peace cannot be gifted from outside. It is a gift that one draws from deep within oneself and offers to the world. You seem to propagate a peace that borders on subservient acceptance of the precepts that are given by dominant societies. When sovereign nations begin to question your ways, you wage a war of attrition on them till you finally decimate their sovereignty. This is the price that many nations have to pay for their aspiration for peace."

Blaringtone was in jitters and wanted to avoid such a huge embarrassment to him and to Rustler. It was a bolt from the blue. "We have assembled here to discuss on the agenda that we have set for the Commonwealth and I request you to refrain from digressing." Blaringtone blared his tone to numb the voice of Norberta.

"Yes Mr. Blaringtone. I am very much within the scope of the agenda of this meeting. World peace is what is at stake because of the decision to wage war against PlanetB2. I have no problem with your landing on PlanetB2. But your weird decision of capturing, overpowering and even destroying the beings in PlanetB2 is atrocious. You will also be killing two American citizens. The world has a right to peace on its own terms and not on the terms of Britain and America. You must give world peace a chance by not hegemonizing other planets and destroying life of other planets. Norway will do all it can to resist such a war." Norberta was very emotional, angry and vituperative in her assertions of peace.

"You are such a tiny nation. You do not have the knowhow of even sending a satellite to the orbit and you are daring to challenge the special might of America. Please know your limits, Norberta." Blaringtone challenged Norway.

Norberta did not retort. She had already looked at Claudia who winked eyes at her to indicate that she should not reveal all her plans to Blaringtone. Not revealing the truth does not amount to telling a lie. This was the principle that Claudia followed. Prudence required holding back of truth for sometime. Norberta bent her head down and looked at Blaringtone through the frame of her spectacles. There was a wry smile on her face. Blaringtone did not like it a bit.

"The space for negotiated peace must be made sacrosanct. It should be a non-negotiable proposition for all countries of the world. I have a lingering doubt that the mission you have taken up to capture PlanetB2 will lead to a total disruption of peace in the cosmos. It will violate the normal rights of beings in the other planet. We do not have any right to disrupt the order of living of beings in another planet. There must be a limit to the level of arrogance that we exercise as human beings." The Kenyan President picked up necessary courage in the model of Norberta. Claudia produced yet another wry smile on her face.

The Commonwealth meeting of States ended nearly in a fiasco. Rustler was greatly disturbed at the fact that tiny nations dared to speak against such hugely charismatic person as he was and against the might of America. Rustler personalized all issues and saw them only through the prism of his ego.

After the meeting Claudia and Norberta met again to make a final strategy for the security and safety of Plumbel. Claudia was very confident that with the type of technology that Germany had developed post world war it could stand the pressures of US and Israelite intelligence network and provide protection to Plumbel. Norberta concurred with her friend. They decided that Norberta would take another chartered plane to Germany to have discussions with the Vietnamese President in Claudia's hotline. The alibi was that Norberta would take a holiday trip to an unknown destination after the Commonwealth meeting.

The President of Vietnam had already alerted Russia and China on the secret developments from the bottom. The official line of news and information from their intelligence services focused only on the mission and Rustler's plans for a NBC war against PlanetB2. But they were grossly inadequate to understand the lifeline of the cosmic beings in the planet. Even the Premiers of China and Russia were unable to understand the cosmic dimension of life and resistance and what a NBC war would cost the world. They were always tuned to understand realities only from the perspectives of power equations between capitalism and communism. It took sometime for them to accept that they were inadequate to understand the complicated web in which Plumbel was caught up with. They were however, fully prepared to protect him and make the best use of his position to defeat capitalism. The President of Vietnam understood that Russian and Chinese perception of realities was grossly inadequate for the task on hand. He also realized that nothing much more than that could be expected of the two giants of power in the world. He was hopeful of convincing them of the need for being in the forefront of the battle at all costs.

It took sometime for Claudia and Norberta to convince the President of Vietnam of the need for entrusting Plumbel into safe hands for protecting his life. The issue for him was not any more security of Plumbel's but the distancing of a close friend. In the meantime both the great men had become great friends. The President was often engrossed in the thought waves and feeling waves of Plumbel. He not only understood the nuances of cosmic communication but also became part of the cosmic movement and change. The process was like a trap. Once caught into it no one would like to come out of it. It was not a compulsion to which one became a victim. It was an enchanting enticer. It was not that one could not extricate himself/ herself from the fabrication of multiple webs around his being. It was simply that one did not want to leave the web. It was such bliss to be caught in that web. It happened to the President of Vietnam. He did not want to leave the company of his friend Plumbel.

However, Claudia and Norberta succeeded finally. The President agreed to part with Plumbel on one condition that he would always have an access to Plumbel whenever he wanted within the given limitations of security arrangements. Plumbel was instructed to use the same silicon mask that he used when he left Karasjok and Oslo.

Norberta received Plumbel at the Frankfurt airport disguising herself as an ordinary citizen. She had to use a mask and a veil to hide her true self. She was the only one who could identify Plumbel as Plumbel in that huge airport. He was soon whisked away to a huge Benz car that took him to Ulm. Claudia had made arrangements for Plumbel to be the guest of the Rector of the Ulm Cathedral. It was an irresistible sight for Plumbel. He requested the driver to stop for a minute. Caring the least about his security and willing to take the worst security risk he alighted from the car and stood as dwarfed dwarf in front of the tall Cathedral admiring the architecture of the marvel that stood in front of him. The driver showcased his knowledge of Germany. With a legitimate pride on his face he informed Plumbel that in fact it was not actually a Cathedral with a bishop. It was just a Lutheran church. At 530 feet it was the tallest Church in the world. Architect Ulrich Ensingen took charge of the construction of the Cathedral in 1377 when the construction was started. It took a long time for the construction to be completed in the year 1890. The Rector had no idea who his guest was and why he was entrusted with him. He only knew that the Cardinal of the Catholic Church had sought his help to keep his friend for a few days in the Cathedral.

Plumbel was a recluse amidst a moving mass of people and tourists who visited the Cathedral every day. He sneaked into the chapel occasionally without anybody noticing him and was lost in the mass of tourists. At night he was with himself and did not need to take refuge in an unknown god.

It was the private villa of the German Chancellor. The setting was just fine to talk about all that Plumbel wanted to communicate. The villa was full of the rustling sound of the trees rhythmically intermingled with the chirping of birds. He liked the ambience for the sharing. Claudia was casually dressed. Sipping hot coffee Claudia started raising question after question about PlanetB2. Plumbel had to confess in all humility that he had never been to the planet and all that he knew was what he picked up from the information available when he was in the space mission of the US.

"That is not what I am looking for. Our friend Norberta has told me all about your relationship with the two American astronauts who are in communication with you from PlanetB2. Plumbel looked at Norberta reprovingly. She told him that Claudia was more interested to know the way beings in another planet communicated to human beings. He explained to Claudia all the minute details of communication through waves, entropy, body cells etc. He could not explain any of these without romantically describing his relationship with Marissa and Carolina. A natural setting for all this was also the life and struggles of Native Americans.

Claudia reached out to Plumbel without any hesitation. He was likeable. She liked him immensely. There was a bonding that was developing between both of them. "Yes, there have been several occasions in my life when I regretted the way Germans, both the ruling class and the public treated the Jews only because they were Jews. In many Germans there was no racism but they were more interested in looting the wealth of the persecuted Jews. In many towns the Jews either fled Germany or were caught and put in the gas chambers. The local Germans who knew these discussed among themselves and appropriated the houses and belongings of the Jews and became rich."

"Please do not cry Claudia. I know what levels of difficulty your mother had to go through in those difficult times. I hope soon you will be able to recover completely from the trauma." Norberta tried to console a sobbing Claudia.

"Was your mother a Jew?" enquired Plumbel.

"Yes, Claudia is a half Jew. Her mother was married to a rebellious German who belonged to the nobility in Germany. They were very happy and rich. But during the holocaust Hitler's forces did not care to check the antecedents of her father and killed him mistaking him to be a Jew. It was the best chance for the waiting eagles and sharks. They plundered their wealth. After the war Claudia and her German husband were able to recover part of the property and in sheer anger and frustration Claudia entered German politics. Like an avalanche she stormed the citadels of political power till the Germans recognized her worth as a woman with a heady mixture of German nobility, Jewish blood and an unassailable determination to restore the legitimate pride of Germany. She became the Chancellor of Germany." It was Norberta who narrated the partly known history of Claudia.

"How was it possible to recover the property after the war?" Plumbel's naïve personality put up a magnificent show of itself.

By then Claudia had recovered a bit and took over from Norberta. "It was not that all Germans subscribed to the Swastik of Hitler. There were many Germans who were highly sensitive and were angry with Hitler. However, they were unable to show their anger for fear of losing their lives. Followers of Hitler had permeated every sphere of German life in all nooks and corners of Germany. It was then that some conscientious Germans did a very beautiful thing. They printed the names of owners of properties in particular streets in a metal plate and planted them in front of the houses of the Jews who fled or who were caught to become gas in the chambers. Some of them planted these on the streets or in public parks near such properties. Some others even carved out the names of Jews on the pavements. After the war when Germany became saner many Jews dared to return from Israel in order to recover their homes and settle down in Germany."

Norberta intruded in the narration. "Claudia was a very strong personality partly also because of the just anger that she had. In your words, I must say that she was filled with life giving anger that began to create many new avenues for Germany instead of being blindly destructive just as your friend Rustler is." There was a big smile on the face of Plumbel and Claudia. Norberta was happy that she was able to lighten up the atmosphere.

She continued. "Claudia's husband was one of the finest human beings I have ever seen. He was filled with remorse of what his countrymen did to the Germans. When Claudia took up rebuilding the international image of Germany as an open place for all races he lent his full support from behind and stood with her as a pillar of support. It is unfortunate that he died early of cancer."

Now it was Claudia's turn to interrupt Norberta. "I am glad that Germany has come back with full life to set a true model of development opening up its national space to all peoples of all countries. Am happy that I have been able to contribute what I could in this process of rebuilding Germany as a robust nation. But what you have said just now about the madness of overpowering PlanetB2 will pose a very serious challenge to the people of Germany and to the German nation. It is not an issue that Germany can ignore easily." The intellectual bonding was also very strong among the three of them. All of them agreed to resist the evil designs of Rustler. Plumbel explained to Claudia the enormous significance of Marissa and Carolina. Claudia nurtured a secret liking for Plumbel. She was not yet able to identify the churning inside her. She decided not to blurt out anything prematurely till she was very clear of what was happening deep inside.

The frequency of her secret visits to Ulm under the pretext of devotion to Jesus Christ began to increase. The Rector understood that there was some special reason for the new happenings around the Cathedral. But then he thought that Claudia had a special relationship with Plumbel and that she did not want the world to know of it. As a mark of loyalty to the Chancellor of Germany he desisted from speaking to anyone about the new guest in his Cathedral.

For the first time in life Plumbel yielded to the desires of his flesh. His experience of bliss now began to assume an added dimension of intensity in his sexual organs. He began to imagine Claudia in all her nakedness often and wanted to embrace her and rest his head in her laps. He wanted to possess her fully as his own. He realized that he had been living in denial for a long time. He started waiting for Claudia's visit almost everyday. But he also knew the risks. Whenever they met the inhibitions were giving way to more freedom and closeness. He felt to have come to a new form of life that was unavailable to him till then. He remembered all the dreams that he had in his sleep when he was still a young boy. Now it was real. A two in one life! When he was alone thinking of Claudia he joined the great philosopher Augustine and said, "Late have I known thee".

Claudia called for a meeting of the European Union to specifically discuss the issue of Rustler's planned attack on PlanetB2. Rustler had given a call to the European nations to join the US in its historic effort to take possession of the planet and expand the human horizon of life to other planets with visible signs of life. Britain and other supporting nations had singed a Memorandum of Understanding to provide moral and legal support, to provide necessary finances and also make their aircrafts, weapons and manpower available in abundance. Rustler had sent a copy of this MoU to all nations and asked them to follow suit. He sought the unstinted support of the entire world to his mega plans. The meeting of the European Union was convened precisely to discuss the MoU that Rustler had sent. Many other nations in African and Latin American continents endorsed the stand and the request of Rustler's without even winking an eyelid over it. Rustler was becoming happier by the day receiving solid and substantial assurance of holistic support in his historic endeavor.

It was a shock that Scotland and Ireland had issued negative statements against Rustler's inexplicable ambitions to overcome nature. It seemed to upset the applecart of Rustler's. But he dismissed it easily as these two nations were only tiny entities in the world. Nations like Sri Lanka, Nepal and Bangladesh waited in the fringes to see the positions of their economic allies other than India before taking a firm stand. In any case they could never take a firm stand on anything, as their survival as nations was more important than the principles on which their nation had to be built. It was a compulsive living that they seemed to enjoy.

At the very beginning itself Claudia presented the entire issue of the MoU that she received from the President of the US. But she carefully added her personal view to make it look like the view that all of them should subscribe. It was very evident for member States that Germany under the leadership of Claudia stood firmly against any human dominance over cosmic beings and other planets whatever be the nature of life they contained. Expansion as planned by Rustler was untenable. Any attack on PlanetB2 would be totally unacceptable to Europe under her leadership. Claudia engineered necessary confusion already in the beginning of the meeting and then let the member states to discuss the issue. Most of them were naturally inclined to take the line of Claudia's argumentation and present the position of their respective nation.

There was an impasse in the European Union meeting. Some were still much guided by their old loyalty to the US without realizing the gravity of the new proposition that Rustler made. Claudia and Norberta did not press their issue too hard on the nations. They focused on the issues pertaining to true democratic decisions. That led to the consensus that there should be a referendum in the entire European Union to elicit the views of the citizens and then take a firm stand either for or against the attack on PlanetB2. European nations decided to go by professional standards rather than what could be possibly interpreted as whims and fancies of any individual leaders. This was exactly what Claudia wanted to happen. She wanted the people to speak out instead of their leaders presuming their views on such a serious matter as this one. Claudia took parallel measures through her government machinery to educate the citizens through the media. It became a hot topic of discussion all over Germany and all other European countries. Claudia also encouraged the media to give their impartial views and elicit as many public opinions as possible. She stood firmly against Rustler's promotion of paid media.

Plumbel had prepared many reading materials for different levels of people. There was one for the common people, another one for academicians, another one for writers, authors and intellectuals and yet another one for political leaders. The topic of cosmic communication of waves began to enthrall many citizens of the world. "Yes, I know this is very true. It has happened to me many times. I did not realize that there is a knowledge system like this." This was one common talk. "Yes, when my girlfriend was 8000 miles away I could still feel her communicating to me. I never realized that there was something like cosmic communication through waves. This is just wonderful." Many bars and restaurant reverberated with men and women pouring out this new thing in their lives. More and more people began to rally round the new idea of wavial communication. New communication theories started emerging. Habermas was analyzed threadbare. Many professors and writers started writing in newspapers and magazines their understanding of the new global phenomenon.

Lovers began to write new songs of love to their beloveds trying to live the new truths they discovered about communication through cosmic waves. Many parts of the world were in full excitement of the new discovery of communication. Many even forgot about the enormity of the prospective danger that was dangling like the sword of Damocles over the entire world. Plumbel read these writings and was amused how peripheral the world became in understanding truths of life. Most people were like those goats that grazed only the top edge of grass in times of prosperity and did not care to take time to have a taste of the entire grass. But there was an unknown happiness in him that the world was slowly beginning to wake up to new realities of the cosmic order.

There was hyper excitement across borders in indigenous communities. A new hope was born in the world. Many of them began to organize small conferences here and there to discuss about a truth that they knew for ages but the world refused to accept only because it was largely 'their' truth. Some members of the Sami Parliament even raised the issue in their official discussions and said that the Sami University in Kautokeino should intensify its teachings on cosmic waves to non-Sami students. Native Americans were the happiest people as news had spread among them that the man behind the new churning in the world had picked up his lessons from their communities and that he was a sort of 'disciple' of their two girls, Carolina and Marissa. They gave many interviews in small community radios in New York and Washington on the need for the entire world to recognize the knowledge system of the indigenous people, which could provide a genuine alternative to a world that was in eternal search. People in Alaska and Hawaii joined their kin and kith in the US and in Canada to take pride in their system of knowledge. It became a hot topic of discussion as far as New Zealand and Australia. The Maori people and the aboriginals of Australia organized joint conferences to identify their common knowledge system based on cosmic communication.

This information from the intelligence agencies created flutter in the circles close to Rustler. His anger against Plumbel intensified manifold and he was more determined to hunt him down. He was not much perturbed by all the discussions and conferences that took place in different parts of the world. He was very confident that his weapons would see him through in his epic battle. Strategists of US government went full swing on an information spree from their point of view. They paid all possible media all over the world to inform that Rustler's decision and action were the best available option for the world. Their basic argumentation was that the world was expanding in all realms of life and it needed to make forays into the universe to make its self-realization possible. If people all over the world had to be prosperous and rich they had to move into other planets and exploit resources wherever they were available. Many graduates, past and present from Harvard University were in the forefront of this propaganda on behalf of Rustler.

Harvard had a name, a big name and it was enough for many people to accept anything as gospel truth if it had emanated from Harvard. From the part of Rustler it was an all out three-pronged war. The first and foremost one was with weapons shortly known as NBC war, the Nuclear, Biological and Chemical war on PlanetB2. The second one was a war of words between the world that evolved a new philosophical paradigm of cosmic communication and peace and Rustler's United States of America that believed that American power is the ultimate in determining the daily affairs of the world. The third one was only in the offing and no one surmised on what it would be.

CHAPTER FIFTEEN

Vrrrroooom! Vroooom! Vroom! Boom! Boom!! Boom!!!

Cars crisscrossing! Fire crackers emptying themselves of their hollow booming blasting up in the air and on the ground. Everyone who heard the sound wondered what was happening around Rustler. Was it one of his space rockets that had already landed successfully in PlanetB2? Some wondered if Rustler had already initiated the planet war in order to take the world by surprise.

The news spread like wildfire in the Government circles in America. There was a special news bulletin in all the news channels. Just received . . . and there was the news that Plumbel had been done away with. He was assassinated within the premises of the Ulm Cathedral. The sun was just then getting ready to retire for the night. Clouds had descended to the pinnacle of the Cathedral. They were still playing their chase game. The first cloud would touch the top of the Church and run away. The second one would come and do the same chasing the first set of clouds. The third one went deeper and got pierced in its womb by the sharp end of the tower with a cross. It was blood all over splashed across the floor of the belly of the church. Three consecutive bullets entered one after another into the chest and head of Plumbel felling his gigantic figure to the ground. He slumped first, went flat then and was no more. Everything happened according to some hidden meticulous planning. The execution seemed to be highly professional. Americans could not have done it. Only Israelites were known for such precision in killing.

Plumbel had returned from a few days of outing with Claudia. It was their first ever outing together. It was quite an unusual outing. She herself was unable to figure out why she liked this man so much to the extent of going out of her professional way. She liked everything in him. The positions he held in the US government, the inside knowledge he possessed of the government as well as its unquestioned head, Mr. Rustler, the complete transformation of the man at the helm of affairs to the journey to PlanetB2 into the one who loved not to disturb any planet in the cosmos, his ardent love for Marissa and Carolina, his deep respect for the cultures of the indigenous peoples, his commitment to peace of the world and above all his admiration for her, everything in him fascinated her. She was almost blind with love for him. After the death of her dear husband, Claudia began to light a candle in the life of someone who had never ever experienced what a woman's carnal love meant for him. But the strong wind from outside blew her candle out. She was desolate.

Norberta was the first one to arrive to be at the side of Claudia. The loss of Plumbel in her life was very significant. The Prime Minister of Vietnam sent his Economic Affairs minister under a false pretext to be present at the funeral of Plumbel. Rustler sent out a strong public message of protest and condemnation of Claudia for the clandestine help that she accorded to a proclaimed offender. He also highlighted the secret love she had for Plumbel. According to him it was unbecoming of the Head of a State to have fallen in love with a criminal in the US. The people of Germany retorted in one voice that their Chancellor had every right to ordain her personal life according to her liking and did not need the approval of the President of the US to fall in love with a man of her choice. They also pointed out that falling in love was not a rational choice nor was it a national choice. It was her individual choice. It belonged to an emotional order. If Rustler did not have such emotions, as he remained a staunch bachelor he should perhaps consult a medical doctor. The message was strong and clear about Rustler as well as a message of strong solidarity of the German people with their beloved Chancellor.

Irrespective of public opinion in Germany Rustler sent out a serious warning to Claudia and Germany that at that critical juncture in the history of the world the attitude of the German government would be a severe setback to cordial relationships and economic cooperation between the two countries. The Germans became angrier still at the outright arrogance of the President of the US at the time when their Chancellor needed more emotional support. They were totally angry with Rustler for having thrown to the winds the traditional cooperation between the two countries.

A similar message went out also to Norberta in Norway that the country should know its limitations and should not carry its concern for human rights too far. It was not the time to speak of rights of the people, said the message of Rustler loud and clear. It was a time when all nations of the world should stand united to face the attack from PlanetB2 on the Earth. The people of Norway did not fail to notice the change of equations in the message of Rustler that it was he who wanted to attack the planet and now he was saying just the contrary. The tradition of victim blaming in war situations was becoming more and more evident in the pronouncements of Rustler. Strange were the ways of politicians all over the world. It was widely discussed all over the Scandinavian countries. They saw Rustler's strongly worded message as a serious infringement of the rights of the people of Scandinavia.

The United States of America sent a formal request to hand over the body of Plumbel to its embassy in Berlin. The US Ambassador in Berlin sent also a terse message to the Government of Germany that Plumbel being an American citizen should be buried in the US and that his body should be handed over to it. The German Parliament assembled in an emergency session first as a mark of solidarity with Claudia in her time of emotional turmoil and secondly also to give a fitting reply to Rustler and his cronies. Bundestag took a very serious view of the violation of the sovereign right of Claudia as the Chancellor of their country and formulated an official reply. It said that Plumbel was an ordinary citizen of the US and was not indicted in any court of law in the US. He was assassinated in Germany and therefore, his body had to be in Germany for future investigations into the murder. There was no request from any of Plumbel's kith and kin to take back his body to the

US. Therefore, the German government was within its legitimate rights to refuse the handing over of his body to the US embassy in Berlin. This was a major embarrassment to Rustler personally as well as to the US government. Tension mounted. A strong Germany with him was always an asset to him. A strong Germany not being with him would always be a liability to him. Rustler needed more assets and less liability in his design of things. But his ego always deluded him.

Claudia gave a quiet burial to Plumbel. Norberta supported her friend in her emotional trauma of losing such a close friend whom she admired for many impossible qualities. The Economic Affairs Minister of Vietnam discussed everything but economy with Claudia. He was commissioned to speak to her about the impending danger to the world at the hands of the egotistic Rustler. Plumbel came on the scene as a beacon of hope. Now that he was no more with them they had to change the complexion of their strategies for peace and justice in the world. He promised to Claudia that Vietnam would stand with her on whatever Germany did towards world peace.

The celebrations in the US reverberated in PlanetB2. It caused tremors in the bodies of cosmic beings. They knew instantaneously that there was something seriously wrong in the world. All of them were naturally attracted towards Carolina and Marissa who knew that their trusted ally and friend, their mentor on earth had been brutally assassinated. It disturbed the cosmic order. Any violence on earth, any abnormal dominance on earth had it immediate ramification on PlanetB2. But the death of Plumbel was a cause of joy and celebration in the planet. Their full body orgasm increased manifold. They seemed to be happier about the death of Plumbel than Rustler and all the others who subscribed to his hegemonic ways. The beings on PlanetB2 were rushing hither and thither in a very happy mood.

Already during his lifetime Plumbel had started emitting life-giving energy intermittently that merged with other similar waves in the cosmos in a process of entropy. The spiraling effect of entropy in the cosmos through the waves emanating from his body cells was just waiting to assume the form of a cosmic being. But for the death of Plumbel the waves would have taken another form of a cosmic being and would have reached PlanetB2 to add to the galaxy of beings there. The dead body of Plumbel stopped all communication with other beings in the cosmos. Now he existed only in his waves. He filled many beings on earth with his life-giving waves already when he was alive. His wavial existence after death intensified the entropy process of all the waves that emanated from his body. The intensity of entropy of his waves spiraled into yet another cosmic being and Plumbel was welcomed as another cosmic being in PlanetB2. It was not the way his girls Carolina and Marissa became cosmic beings. But they were all together in one planet now.

The waves that Plumbel left on earth through all his newfound friends and admirers, especially through Norberta and Claudia had their salvific effect in the entire gamut of cosmos. These waves spread fast all over the world immediately after his death, as they were now free of a body. The communication with beings in PlanetB2 intensified and the deep desires for peace and justice began to affect the beings in the planet simply because of their intensity. The perception of serious danger to world peace had its impact on the beings and their communication among themselves on this particular dimension intensified. There was an urge in all of them to stand as walls with their waves against any intrusion into PlanetB2 by forces that wanted to dominate and overpower. The waves that emanated from their bodies deeply desirous of peace and harmony developed as a thick wall that reached that level in space which had already formed a sort of protective layer of PlanetB2. There was an intermittent assault of negative and dominant waves in that layer and the beings of PlanetB2 could perceive this assault though nothing of these negative waves could enter their being. Their bodies began to generate waves that gathered at the liquid zone as a layer of protection to PlanetB2.

The intensity increased in whopping proportion because of the intensity of discussions and preparations for NBC bombing by Rustler. It had its impact on their bodies and they became extra alert to any such intrusion of dominant waves into their planet. The merger of Plumbel as an inseparable part of PlanetB2 increased the intensity of the beings there for a total preparedness to repulse all negative onslaught on the planet. Carolina, Marissa and Plumbel were in the forefront of this creative resistance to negativism. Anything that destroyed peace and cosmic harmony would have no way to reach even the peripheries of PlanetB2 because of this high intensity of preparedness.

While this is only one part of the defense that life-giving energy centers created there was a vacuum on earth in their communication. There was no Plumbel on earth. He was on the other side of the universe. The focal point of the convergence of life giving energy waves on earth now had to be shifted to preserve a semblance of peace on earth. It would also mean active resistance to all endeavors of dominance and violence on earth. This implied that the intensity of wave generation in human bodies had to shift from a few key beings such as Plumbel, to many ordinary beings on earth. His presence in PlanetB2 increased the full body orgasm of the cosmic beings manifold. He himself was in a different orgasmic world. No memories of the past, no concern for the future, no botheration about the present, the being lived, just lived its life! Plumbel's life giving waves began to envelop all those who desired peace and were open in their body cells to such waves.

A serious concern was what would happen to good beings on earth. This was almost a strategic shift on the part of the beings in PlanetB2. Their waves began to spread all over the world, especially into the bodies of all those who desired peace, justice and harmony. The world began to witness a seesaw change in its thinking and feeling patterns. More and more people began to think and feel like the indigenous peoples of the world who were till then actively neglected. The worldview and cultures of the native people became the center of discourses in many universities and intellectual centers. The face of the world was gradually changing thus posing a serious threat to the strategic plans of Rustler.

Carolina and Marissa were happy that Plumbel and Claudia made that fatal mistake in their love life. It was necessary that he were in PlanetB2 more than being in the world to defeat the nefarious designs of Rustler. Claudia invited Plumbel to a three days holiday for her first physical intimacy with the man she loved after the death of her husband. She had asked Norberta to make arrangements for her secret holiday in the shores of the Antarctic Ocean. She threw away all the paraphernalia that were attached to her position as the Chancellor of Germany. She was just a woman. There she was standing as a woman in front of Plumbel. She invited him to hold her in his arms, something that she badly missed for many years. "You do not know how difficult it is for a married woman to be deprived of the touch of a man." She whispered into Plumbel's ears as she gave her all to him.

It was a serious mistake that she committed to have taken Plumbel back through Norway. She underestimated the skills of the Israelites in their intelligence network. The same person traveling twice to the same place began to make their hyper inquisitive minds walk that extra mile. They worked on all angles including the silicon mask. They guessed that it could be Plumbel. They worked on every suspicion that arose in their heads.

Back in his room in Ulm the first thing Plumbel did was to remove his mask. His face was very precious to him. He went again and again to the mirror in his room to have a good look at his face. Claudia had told him repeatedly that he was not only beautiful in his personality but also was handsome to look at. In fact the first thing that attracted her to him was his face. He took it light. But in that intense moment when he was thrusting himself into her she remarked about his face once again and began to kiss him all over his face. That made those words of hers indelible. He came to Ulm filled with that experience of a different type of bliss and orgasm. Full body orgasm of the cosmic order added another very interesting and exciting dimension to his life.

"Hey who is it?" Plumbel was shocked to the core of the being at the face that he saw in the mirror. He saw himself, no doubt. But he also saw another face behind his face in the yonder. He turned back to see who it was. There was none. He opened the door to see if there was anyone around. There was none. He convinced himself that what he saw was only an illusion. If there were anyone outside he could not have run away that fast from his sight. Plumbel had quick reflexes. After a good wash and shower with singing all the way, he wore his mask again and went into the Church to have a look at all the glass paintings in the Church. One could spend one's lifetime just looking at those paintings. They were immortal and so was Plumbel. He became an easy prey to the bullets of the agents of Rustler. Even as he was falling he had a last thought for Rustler. 'Finally, you my friend, you caught up with me.' He thought and departed from his body. His joining the beings in PlanetB2 coincided with the announcement of the undeclared war against all those forces on earth and in the cosmos that constantly kept working against cosmic movement and change. Rustler, the most powerful and brutal man that the earth had ever seen, effectively represented them.

It was on expected lines. The people of Germany and Scandinavia celebrated the result of the referendum. It was an overwhelming mandate to their respective governments to go ahead in search of world peace and preserve the integrity of the cosmos. It directly meant that Germany should take the lead on behalf of the European Union to offset the negative forays of the USA into the cosmic order. Norberta and Claudia were extremely happy at the result of the referendum in both countries. They waited for the declaration of the results from other countries of the EU on similar lines. There was only a minor hiccup. It was from the Netherlands where the verdict was slightly tilted towards the US by a thin margin. In all other countries it was a firm no to Rustler's madness to destroy PlanetB2. But the observations in European Union were very interesting. One of the best ones was that Rustler was not only trying to capture PlanetB2 but in the process he was out to destroy the earth. They also opined strongly that there was an inexplicable madness that was at work behind the entire strategy to capture PlanetB2. The madness was attributed to spending so much of money of the taxpayers for a project that was euphoric just for the ego of one man on earth.

The European Union met together in their Parliament to discuss a collective strategy. The question before it was whether the EU Parliament endorsed the stand of the US for the occupation of PlaneB2 and if that failed to wage a NBC attack on the planet and destroy all the beings living there. All nations took the results of referendum conducted in their respective countries. Public opinion in Europe swelled against any such Don Quixotic endeavor. The citizens generally felt that there was no problem if the US astronauts landed on PlanetB2. But they were terribly against any attack on the beings in the planet. They had their right to live as living beings of another planet. The Netherland was the only dissenting voice and it was needless to say the EU Parliament voted overwhelmingly against the designs of war on PlanetB2. It also decided against any financial and military assistance to the US on this particular mission.

The Heads of Russia, China, Vietnam, Norway and Germany had many secret meetings to work out a strategy to somehow prevent Rustler from going ahead with his mega plans of attacking PlanetB2 with NBC weapons. They feared that it would shower destructive elements on earth and possibly destroy humanity and other forms of life on earth to a large extent. The only option that was left open to them was to educate the peoples of the world on the possible havocs of the NBC attack in order to prevent it. Norberta and Claudia were of the opinion that such thought and feeling waves against the machinations of Rustler would form a strong shield against all destructive forces on earth. The other men in the group concurred.

Cosmic beings on PlanetB2 were very happy that the cells in the bodies of the Heads of States were becoming more and more open to waves of justice and peace instead of working on cruel machines of war. They also started working on sending out powerful life giving waves to all plants, animals and humans on earth in order to from a resistance force against all forms of dominance.

The Prime Minister of Vietnam was much emboldened when he heard of the decision of the European Union Parliament. This was the first time that EU had decided decisively against a major decision of the US. He saw Claudia and Norberta as solid centers of support. He travelled first to North Korea to meet the President there. He knew the tension between the US and North Korea. However, his decision to meet the President of North Korea was to enhance the economic cooperation between both countries. They signed an agreement for cooperation for the development of both countries. What they did not sign was the agreement to oppose tooth and nail the 'evil' designs of America to disturb the cosmic order and consequently jeopardize the life of human beings on earth. They also agreed that North Korea should organize a global conference on impending dangers to global climate and the responsibility of the world to preserve the integrity of the earth.

Rustler did all he could to sabotage this conference. He called up personally some Prime Ministers and Presidents not to attend the Conference. He assured all of them that the US would do all it could to respond to all their demands. Simultaneously he also accused

North Korea of possessing weapons of mass destruction and of subverting democratic values. He threatened North Korea with nuclear war if democracy was not restored in its soil. He assured the world that he would do all he could in order to root out dictatorship in North Korea. He instigated South Korea to issue inimical statements against North Korea and promised all support to the South if they decided to wage war against the North and capture their territories. But South Korea was heavily weighed down with the defeat of the US in the hands of Vietnam and did not want to take a serious risk. Rustler was grossly disappointed with the dilly-dallying of South Korea but had no other option to save its face except to project that South Korea was its very friendly country.

Russia and China were in the forefront of supporting the endeavor towards a meaningful global conference on global warming mitigation. The Kyoto Protocol came in handy for them to give a lame excuse for attending such a blatant conference to defeat the 'diabolical' designs of Rustler. Both the Premiers of Russia and China made scathing attack on the ways of the US to disturb and subvert global peace and justice by intruding into the spaces of peoples of the world. Rustler's plans came in for vituperative attack by both of them as the worst decision in human history and they promised that both Russia and China would join hands to oppose every move of Rustler's in the direction of disrupting cosmic order.

"Ladies and Gentlemen! All of you are aware, I am sure, of the ways of the US in projecting itself as the champion of the peoples of the world. The

US itself was limping on borrowed legs. It was the country of the Native Americans and not of people who forced them into that region through Christopher Columbus. All of us are aware that Native Americans discovered Columbus as the major culprit in their history in the year 1495, which took 1600 Arawak as slaves, 500 as slaves to Spain and caused the death of 200 on way to Spain. From then on America has indulged in slave trade and has harped on democracy as the biggest camouflage of its guilt over all the harm it did to innocent humans. The US has kept alive this twin trajectory of enslaving people and simultaneously preaching democracy from its rooftops in a shameless manner. The zenith of the double standard of the US is now manifested in the designs of Rustler to go and establish democracy in PlanetB2. While we appreciate the US scientists for having discovered this planet with life we also condemn equally the desire of the US to somehow capture the PlanetB2 or to kill all the inhabitants of the planet if they fail to capture it. This is simply odious and stands against all human values on which the world has somehow managed to position itself for survival. It is high time that we gave a quiet burial to our ideological differences and stood united as one human race against such hegemonic screwballs. We shall not allow this to happen." The Russian President made a speech mixed with emotions and rationality proportionally. It was a humdinger of sorts. The speech enticed the entire world towards a serious polarization. More and more small nations were emboldened to take a firm stand against the iniquitous designs of humans to overcome cosmic order.

At the end of the meeting it was formally decided that Germany should take up the leadership for leading the world into an unknown future. They were quite apprehensive that all their people might have to face unsurpassable difficulties if Rustler decided to inflict hardship on the citizens. He could possibly do it, as he could be quite blind. It was a strategy that they evolved so that Rustler would not be able to use the communist card against his enemies. Russia and China along with other countries pledged their full support to the finish in their battle against Rustler. They saw no reason to thwart the forays of Rustler into the orbit and beyond to PlanetB2. For the time being they only decided not to lend any support to Rustler. They also decided to actively campaign against him in his battle against the planet. Claudia promised that she and Germany would stand by the alliance of global friends for peace and harmony.

Rustler would normally take such things in his stride. But he developed jitters at the fact that the European Parliament took a firm stand against him under the leadership of Claudia. He was fully aware of the ubiquitous role that Norberta played in bringing Claudia around. He was uncontrollably angry with the two women. He felt particularly humiliated because they were 'only' women and wanted to take revenge. He swore to himself that he would destroy both of them and if need be also their countries. He would spare no one who dared to oppose his plans to take over PlanetB2, especially if they were women. In sheer jittery he convened a meeting of all friendly nations to garner more support for him and his designs to overcome the hurdles that he faced.

He placed before them the serious threat to the world that was looming large because of the union of all communist countries headed by Russia and China. He argued that communism posed the biggest danger to the world at any time of the day. He vowed to fight communism tooth and nail till his last breath lasted in his body. All Americans with the exception of a miniscule minority concurred with Rustler on his opposition to communism. Their problem was Russia whom they saw as a 'godless' country and as the only rival on earth to the 'unique' position of the US in the globe. They pledged their full support to the decisions of Rustler though there were some scarcely attended street protests against his plans. Rustler himself engineered some of these protests and gave wide publicity to such street demonstrations to create an illusion that he was an upholder of democracy. Many intellectuals in Asia, especially Harvard educated Indians pointed out to these protests as role models for the rest of the world for democracy that was alive and kicking. Many African countries that were former colonies of the British also supported Rustler's plans of attack on PlanetB2. South Africa was an exception to this mad rush of formerly colonized nations. It took a firm stand against any military attack on any other planet.

Rustler took stock of the global responses to his announced war on PlanetB2. His AIA agents, his media managers, his diplomats in many countries who were also spying for America brought in their stock of information gathered assiduously from all over the world. It was a clear verdict in favor of Rustler's strategic acumen and an assertion of faith in his leadership. Many countries of the world were still euphoric about the discovery of PlanetB2 and Rustler's aborted endeavor to land on the planet. They cared a damn about attacking an unknown planet. Human life itself was not a matter of great concern for many and they had no time to bother about unknown life in an unknown planet. Rustler was greatly encouraged by the enormous feeding into his ego. He deeply desired the rest of the world to recognize him as the unquestioned leader of the world. It meant that no one had any right to question the wisdom of his decisions. The chanting of 'Rustler, Rustler, and Rustler' filled his heart to the brim with happiness. All Americans who mattered in America fed him with the truth of overwhelming support to America's plans to assault PlanerB2.

Beings in PlanetB2 had no recourse to weapons of any sort to counter the endeavor of America. They were beings who depended on the goodness generated in their cosmic bodies and did not have instruments of destruction. They could never have waves that enjoyed any negative destruction of anything. They belonged to the cosmic order where 'destruction' was anathema. They lived in blissful love that saw clearly that anything or anyone who was against love would naturally be destroyed. It was the inevitable process of the cosmic movement and change that showed an apparent destruction. The cosmic beings knew it in their bodies that every creation had to go through the process of transformation that was seen as destruction by the limited intelligence of humans. The beauty of cosmic beings was that they never were disturbed by such perceptions of humans. They knew in their being that nothing could assail the cosmic order. They lived in the bliss that cosmos is eternal and that cosmos would live even without human beings. When human bodies became less, cosmic balance would still be maintained with more plants and animals. When animal bodies and plants became less because of human greed and brutality, human bodies would increase uncontrollably to maintain cosmic balance. Cosmos recycled its energy level always without necessarily depending on the fluctuations of human nature.

Their assemblies were not called for nor were they convened by figureheads. There was no authority exercised in PlanetB2. When communications in their body cells increased on a particular dimension they would naturally be attracted to one another and come together without anyone making a conscious decision. It was thus that most of them came together to welcome the arrival of the entropy waves of Plumbel. He was a new arrival and the cumulative essence of his entropy was fast and powerful. So also was the arrival of Marissa and Carolina. These arrivals increased the full body orgasm of the cosmic beings manifold. It was a long time since Marissa lost her human body in PlanetB2. It was this full body orgasm that became thick layers of waves in the special orbit and formed a protective layer. Rustler had a very hard task on hand.

CHAPTER SIXTEEN

Rustler's camp was hyper active. They gathered information on all fronts. Putting all they had together it became evident that Claudia was the epicenter of all political mobilization in the entire world. She went stealthily to all possible countries in order to mobilize as many countries as possible against possible attacks on PlanetB2. It was still a big mystery why Claudia had such deep love for PlanetB2. Rustler tried to break his head to solve this puzzle. It belonged to a realm that AIA could not enter. He thought that with Plumbel's removal from the scene he would be totally free to do whatever he wanted with his war on PlanetB2. But his tribulations seemed to have increased on multiple fronts. Claudia supported substantially by Norberta seemed to be shadowing him wherever he went. In whatever he did she seemed to weigh heavily on his mind as to what would happen to his action if Claudia came to know of it. He allowed her personality to shadow all his decisions. It was a sort of paranoia, a compulsion in him. He always lived under one or other compulsion. When there was no need for any compulsion he would create one. Plumbel disappeared and now Claudia seemed to have replaced him. Paranoia, an incurable disease of the timid and insecure!

On their part Claudia and Norberta travelled secretly all over the world not necessarily speaking against Rustler. They spoke more on the need for the entire world to stand together to preserve its integrity and unity with nature. Claudia took on the world of politics convincing rulers of nations and all who mattered in diplomacy about the need for preserving the world as one unit. The Earth had already been raped enough and the wound caused to Mother Earth was too much to bear for her children. It was time that those who considered themselves as inseparable part of the Universe tried their best to preserve her integrity.

Rustler was completely unsettled when he learned from his intelligence agencies that youth all over Europe were rallying round the idea of a united universe. They wanted diversity in all aspects of life. Simultaneously they also did not want any disintegration. If conflict had to be avoided man had to give up his proclivity to dominate over nature. The message from Norberta was loud and clear. The youth were enamored at the idea of communication through waves when Norberta explained it to them. Most of them in the universities were giggling at what she said. It was already happening among them in their romantic love and friendship with peers. They happily recollected the many times when they said the same thing together without any plans. Living hundreds of miles away they were still able to communicate to each other when they were in love. Norberta made it sound romantic in order to make it attractive to the young people. They found it a bit hard to understand when she explained about the beings in PlanetB2. She underplayed it when she found it out. The politics of communication through waves was the prospective battle against PlanetB2. She mixed diligently the rational and emotional well enough so that it made great sense to the young people all over Europe.

This unanticipated information angered Rustler no ends. He shook his head violently in disbelief. He could not accept the fact that some people were actively campaigning against his plans. He was out to prove that human beings had the greatest capacity in the universe and that America possessed more such power. He had an uncontainable desire to run and catch hold of Norberta and teach a lesson or two to her in his military style.

More and more students rallied round the idea of a unified universe where people in other planets had a right to live on their own rhythm of life without being determined by human power. It soon spread like wildfire. Students and youth all over the world began to get a fever that began to accelerate their communication through their body waves. A new vision of life was slowly evolving on earth. Russia and China who were in the forefront of leading the resistance against Rustler's mad rush only saw a political advantage out of this global movement of youth. Claudia did not mind that. She knew well that not all countries would get on well with their perception and living through the cosmic waves.

The generation of youth energy on the earth had its natural impact on the beings in PlanetB2, especially in the bodies of Carolina, Marissa and Plumbel. However, since Plumbel died on earth and went into PlanetB2 through an entropy process his identity was not any more that of a being on earth. He became just another being in the planet though his communicative interaction with Carolina and Marissa was of a much higher velocity than all other beings. Carolina and Marissa were not even able to recognize his as the same Plumbel whom they loved on earth. The waves on earth reaching PlanetB2 through that special outlet beyond the liquid zone in cosmos had a natural attraction in the bodies of the two women. As positive energy waves among youth began to intensify, Carolina and Marissa also began to indulge in communication with such waves and finally they landed up on earth moving about freely without anyone seeing them. American scientists had not yet succeeded to invent a device that would identify waves from PlanetB2.

The movement of the two earthlings from PlanetB2 had a tremendous positive impact on human beings who were disposed to receiving positive energy on earth. Sadly though such human beings on earth were numerically a miniscule minority. There were many who spoke of such phenomenon and wrote about it without actually allowing their bodies to go through that particular process of cosmic communication. Most of them understood the phenomenon in their intellect but were unable to lend their emotive side of personality to take over communication. One needed a healthy blend of cognition and emotions to activate such cells in his/her body. Carolina and Marissa were all over the world at the same time. They entered into the bodies of humans who had the receptivity for life giving positive waves. Not believing in dominance and not being dominant was a pre-condition for their free rendezvous with earthly beings. It was their being and becoming.

They were communication in their essence and this communication brought about changes in individuals, in communities and in the world at large. They were what they were in their being. However, it naturally looked like polarization of the world, as there was another part of the world that was constantly in movement without necessarily communicating. This world sought dominance as the essence of life. It enjoyed dominance and destruction. It cherished violence and war. It had removed itself far from its inner being and there was no becoming from that inner being. Their actions and communications depended much on greed that they gained through a compulsive desire to accumulate and amass, a deep desire for self-aggrandizement and an illusion that they would live in the world forever. Polarization was inevitable from the other side of Carolina and Marissa, Claudia and Norberta.

Rustler could not understand what was happening in the world. It was still a mystery shrouded in magic that many people could so vehemently oppose his plans for capturing PlanetB2. After all he was trying to do something good to the world, he legitimized. He was determined to go to the logical end of his desires. He intensified his intelligence network all over the world, especially in Scandinavia and in Germany. In the meantime Germany and Scandinavian countries too sharpened their intelligence network suspecting Rustler's cronies to become overambitious. Germany was the first country to cry foul over the interference of the US even on the personal phones of Claudia and her hotline with Heads of States. The German government called the

Ambassador of the US in Berlin and reproved him for this silly interference. Newspapers in Germany condemned unequivocally the intrusion into the sovereignty of their Head of State. This was unbecoming of a super power on earth. It was undemocratic.

The final verdict on America being undemocratic jostled the self-pride of Rustler. He immediately flashed a counter message saying that the US never interfered with the communication network of Heads of States. The next day US ambassador in Berlin issued a press statement that the US government would guarantee that AIA did not intrude into the secret communications of the German government. Rustler fired him in two days for having said that without authorization from him. He said that the US Ambassador in Germany should have positively denied any such mechanism instead of eating his humble pie. Being humble was never in the governance ethos of the United States of America.

The Stirring Five, namely Russia, China, Germany, Vietnam and Norway met more often to work out their political strategy to offset the evil designs of Rustler. Their gelling was a heady mixture of the rational and the emotional, sometimes proportional and at other times disproportional. Claudia and Norberta brought in the emotive, communicative and the cosmic dimension rather powerfully into the Stirring Five. The Prime Minister of Vietnam was a milder blending of both in his personality. Russia and China were the more rational and strongly speculative among them. But all of them had a collective value binding among themselves.

Claudia dropped the biggest bombshell right on the head of the Stirring Five in their meeting. It was a total shock but the group was well prepared for any sort of eventuality. "One of the first things my country did as soon as we learnt of the mega plans of Rustler was to sharpen the intelligence network of Germany. Our agents have proved their mettle beyond most of the American AIA agents. Now it is clear that Rustler would strike at all those nations that take an open stand against his project of attacking PlanetB2. He would not tolerate even the slightest opposition to his pet project, as succeeding in it meant his life. This is his final assault and he thirsts for sure success in this mission. He is just mad after success in this final assault. Now he sees that we are planning to thwart his efforts. He is a very brittle personality. He takes everything personally and becomes jittery easily. He fears that we may succeed in scuttling his efforts to overcome PlanetB2. He cannot accept a failure on that front. Therefore, he has made a fatal decision. It is fatal not for him but for our citizens."

All the other four were looking at her in great anticipation. They thought that Claudia was just speaking of the ordinary. They looked at each other with a big question mark on their faces. Claudia understood their anxiety and did not want to prolong their pain. She ignited the bomb. It blasted instantaneously. "Rustler has decided to wage a war against our countries. He thinks that we are his common enemies and therefore, is prepared for any eventuality. It is now for us to decide how we are going to face a mad man like Rustler."

It was a grave situation without anyone being dead. Russia and China were stoic. Claudia was still smiling. The Prime Minister of Vietnam was stone faced. He seemed to be determined for another war against the US. It was Norberta who could not accept the idea of a war. However, she was resigned to the fact that Rustler might thrust a war on the otherwise peaceful Scandinavian region. The inevitability of a war was laughing loud at them. They decided to laugh back whatever might be the cost. The Stirring Five wanted to have more details of the plans of Rustler on a possible war on them. But Claudia could only tell them that she had definite information on a war plan on the part of Rustler but not yet all the details. She promised them to get back to them. They decided collectively to further activate their respective intelligence networks and intrude the AIA and other US installations not only for further information about a possible war but also to strategize counter attacks if the madness of Rustler could not be prevented from getting into action. The gravity of the situation saddened them. However, they did not want to be mere spectators in such situation where the madness of one man could determine the future course of the world.

That evening Russia, China and Vietnam met together without the company of others and made secret plans to face the situation. They were surprised to a great extent at the attitude of

Claudia and Germany under her leadership. It bordered on a shock that the people of Germany were so different from the era of Hitler. Among them they discussed on how expedient it was to put Germany in the forefront of an alliance that would take on the might of America. The Russian President gave the following logical reasons for his choice of Claudia's Germany.

Half of Germany is still Left and social in its ideological positions. Therefore, it would make greater sense to bring about a convergence on this.

Germany had suffered heavily in the hands of England during the war and most Germans were still not well disposed towards the Brits on this count. Since UK was an ardent and almost blind supporter of the US it would be much easier to mobilize public opinion and support for any war against Rustler. This was also evidenced by the strong opinion of the German public against Rustler's proposed war on PlanetB2.

The third strong reason was that the German people wanted to wash away the scars burrowed in their collective psyche as Germans by the many true and false ascriptions arising out of the legacy of Hitler. Taking a stand against hegemony and dominance of Rustler and his alliance would be a huge psychological advantage for citizens of Germany.

The fourth reason was that according to the information gathered by Russian secret services it was evident that Germany possessed much more strike power than generally imagined by the world. Germany was keeping it as a secret only out of the inhibition of the legacy of Hitler. It would come out with all its force when it mattered most.

The fifth and perhaps the most important reason was that for reasons unfathomable for all others, Claudia seemed to be in communication with beings in PlanetB2 along with her friend Norberta. Though they were not conscious of this communication many of their decisions and actions did not seem to come totally from them alone. These two women leaders were exceptionally determined and strong with the type of messages and inspiration they got from cosmic beings in PlanetB2.

Now they had to see how the entire European Union would react to the prospect of a war in case Germany was attacked. Would they stand with Germany militarily or would they only lend their ideological support to Germany and refrain from a war against the US. Worse still was the thought for them that some of them might even shift their loyalty to the US only because Rustler was more powerful than all of Europe put together. But they were greatly enthused by the seriousness and determination of Claudia and Norberta to face any consequence arising out of their support to the beings in PlanetB2.

Norberta and Claudia had their usual tete-a-tete in the evening. Norberta was a much-worried woman as to what would happen to her friend if there were a real war. Claudia on the other hand was flamboyant, smiling and laughing over the drink that both of them had. Claudia had ordered a few glasses of Weissenbier and she was enjoying it fully. She did not seem to have any botheration about a possible war.

"Are you worried Norberta about a war? We are not itching for a war. We are fully for world peace. Unlike Rustler we do not believe in waging war against countries in order to establish either democracy or peace. We are just being peaceful people. But if someone who believes in war and violence takes the first step we shall not simply sit and watch. Our being peaceful also urges us to act against violence and war. Our resistance of a war will definitely look as a war on our part. But we are only resisting war and would not be waging war." The roles seemed to have been swapped. It used to be Norberta who educated Claudia much on communication through waves. But Claudia seemed to have mastered the art of this communication.

"No, I was wondering what Plumbel would have said to us if he were alive and had to face the situation that we are facing now." Norberta was a very simple woman President of Norway.

"I have no heaviness in my body when I think of resisting the madness of Rustler. It is our collective responsibility to resist such uncontrolled madness. I have no second thought about it Norberta. If my body were heavy I would have thought twice about a possible resistance. But I feel so light in my body when I think of taking on the might of Rustler. I may be killed in a possible war. But death is not the reason for my living. What I am in my inner being is the reason for my living. As you know well by now death will be only my transition into a different way of living. May be I shall go to PlanetB2 and continue the war in a different way and not through bloodshed." Claudia was in her philosophical best. Norberta was wondering if Claudia was the Chancellor of Germany or if she was a shaman. The Chancellor of Germany could very easily pass as a shaman.

After a drink and discussions among themselves the Heads of Russia, China and Vietnam invited Claudia and Norberta to join them for dinner. The three men informed the two women that there was nothing much to worry about the hollow booming threats of Rustler. They knew the type of weapons he possessed. But they also knew that Rustler had knowledge of the type of armory that they possessed. They hoped that he would not dare to start a war of weapons, neither on PlanetB2 nor on their countries. They hoped that good sense would prevail on Rustler. But they were also prepared for the worst if Rustler for one or other reason decided to trigger the war button.

"You people are so confident of taking on a mad man like Rustler. But did you calculate the gargantuan damage that a war would cause to innocent masses of people. If Rustler has to really fight against our combined might he would not hesitate to use his Nuclear, Biological and Chemical (NBC) weapons on our people. That would spell a major disaster to the entire world and human race. Can we afford to go for a war like this that can be absolutely destructive? Please let this disaster be averted. Let the innocent people be saved from disaster." Norberta was almost in tears while saying this.

"We do not want any war in the first place and we are fully aware of the consequences of NBC war on the world and its innocent masses. But what other options do we have if Rustler, in his madness decides to attack our countries? We shall be in a catch22 situation. If we do not fight our people will be destroyed. If we fight also there is going to be unimaginable disaster to our people. If we fight we can prevent total destruction to some extent. It is okay if he manages to land Americans on the surface of PlanetB2. By now we know that he has failed in his many attempts to land on the planet. He is already quite frustrated with his failures. If he does not manage to land the Bigbelly5 on PlanetB2 his frustration would increase multifariously and we do not know what would be his next decision after his failure. We also do not know the nature of the beings in that planet. He is already very angry at Norway and Germany and many European nations. It was a reversal that he did not expect. Now when he comes to know that we have joined hands together in the best interest of the world and of PlanetB2 we cannot even surmise on how he would react. It could turn out to be a mad rush into anything. It will be in the best interest of the rest of humanity that we remain alert and stand prepared for any eventuality." The Russian President took the lead in assuaging the rather well founded ruffled feathers of Norberta.

Claudia put her hands around the broad shoulders of Norberta and comforted her gently. She assured her that there was no reason to be too anxious about the consequences of a possible war on earth. Destruction and resurgence were part of the cycle of nature and a war against America need not scare the living daylights out of all of us. Her assurance surprised Norberta. 'How could this woman be so naïve?' She thought to herself.

"I am not naïve Norberta. I am fully confident. It is from this conviction that I speak. I know that we can take on any power on earth because we have our goodness and truth as our strong fort. We also have our weapons that can take on any power on earth. As long as we remain together and are tenacious no force on earth can cow us down." Asserted Claudia

Norberta was gaping at the invisible stars. "But how did you read my thought?" She asked openly.

"Did I read your thought? I thought I heard you say that." Claudia retorted.

All of them bade farewell to one another in a high spirit. Back in their respective countries they called together all the chiefs of different armed forces in their country and alerted them of impending war. The Army Generals were taken aback at what they heard. They were simultaneously happy that they got some job to do at last. The Heads of States informed them that it was stale news. They had known these long back through their intelligent networks. But they did not want to press the panic buttons, as there was a sort of madness at work at the other end. But with the assassination of Plumbel things began to heat up and now it could be any time that a war might break out. Army Generals in Russia, China and Vietnam were elated to hear the story of the turn around of almost all of Europe as possible allies because of the efforts of Claudia and Norberta. They immediately took stock of possible alliances that might take place on the other side. They did not learn to under estimate the enemy, especially the ones like Rustler. They were all the same itching to take on the mightiest fellow on earth in a war of weapons.

In terms of number of countries the Cosmic Alliance, as they codenamed themselves, had more numerical strength. But the Comic Alliance, as they codenamed Rustler's forces with derision, had many potent killer weapons that Cosmic Alliance did not possess. The Russian and Chinese Generals assured the Cosmic Alliance that there was only a marginal difference in terms of firepower tilting the balance in favor of the Comic Alliance. But that marginal imbalance could be made up in the interim period even before the start of the war, if at all there would be any war.

One of the huge advantages that the Comic Alliance had was the American stealth weapon. Their radars, attack planes and missiles could not be easily detected. Though countries of the Cosmic Alliance also had developed the technology of stealth weapons the Americans exceeded them in this arena. This was a felt lacuna in their technological forays. The Heads of States of the Stirring Five talked this over through their hotlines and decided that all the Army General of the five countries should meet together with the Heads of States of Stirring Five to chalk out an actual war strategy ahead of Rustler as a defense preparedness and not as an aggressive strategy.

Claudia once again sprang the biggest surprise of the century on all the members of the Stirring Five and their respective Army Generals. Norberta was just a bundle of fleshy admiration for her bosom friend. To the delight of all assembled, she announced the happy news that German scientists had developed much superior technology of stealth warfare. The Americans would not be able to match the technological superiority of the Germans on this one count. The Americans spy network was unable to locate the huge stockpile of German stealth war machines. Their radars, missiles, war planes and other weapons could strike at America at any time without even the best American detective machines noticing them anywhere. German scientists were just unmatched on this. America was living under the illusion that Germany did not have the military potential to attack any country. 'Germany is indeed a super power.' All members of Stirring Five said this to themselves together without letting the word into the ears of others.

Claudia was laughing loud at the illusion of the rest of the world. "Yes, many say that Hitler was a mistake of history. But the same world that wants to bury history has not cared to restore the legitimate rights of Germany. We do not have Hitler any more but the restrictions imposed on us because of Hitler still remain. They are the biggest stigma that we Germans have to live with. The moment we say something strong we are accused of inheriting Hitler's legacy. We do not know how long it is going to last." Claudia let out a huge sigh. No one knew if it was a sigh of relief. But everyone knew that she let out some hard truths. The assembled Generals clapped their hands in a standing ovation to the woman who could determine the future course of history of the world.

The war had already started in the media. They started creating hype about a possible but imminent war between the powers on earth and the powers in PlanetB2. The media war bordered on the ideological and national positions that both the alliances took. However, not many knew that there were already formations of alliances on two sides. It still remained a much elusive issue. The alliances remained largely informal and there was no declaration of alliance from respective countries. However, the media started indulging in wild slings at countries, grouping them into one or other alliance of countries. Unmindful of what the media was busy with key countries that supported Rustler met in the US to consolidate their strategies for the war.

The USA, UK, Canada, Australia and Israel were the countries that met together on the other side. They called themselves 'The Earth Alliance'. Unlike the Cosmic Alliance they followed everything that Rustler laid out for them. They agreed to whatever Rustler said and demanded of them. He was their big brother. Rustler made it clear that the Earth

Alliance would first launch a peaceful landing on PlanetB2. Rustler was extremely confident that the US space scientists would succeed this time by all means as they had vastly improved their technology and their Bigbelly5 without any flaw. Only a miracle could fail them. He thanked all other countries in the Alliance for their solid support and financial contribution towards the success of the mission.

"What if we faced resistance from the beings in PlanetB2? I am sure you have given a serious thought to this and have prepared necessary counter strategies. Please let us know what your plans are on this score." The Prime Minister of Australia wanted to have more details, as he was the one who was far away from the inner circle of the Earth Alliance.

"We show no mercy to anyone Mr. Prime Minister. Anyone who resists our attempts will be dealt with ruthlessly and be eliminated without much delay. We have no patience to forgive any force either on earth or in space to indulge in inimical strategies. We shall not allow any other consideration to fail us. There is only one unquestionable purpose for our Alliance and that is not only to land on PlanetB2 but also to make it a property of our Alliance. Unlike the previous missions we are sending the flags of all our Alliance partners to be planted on PlanetB2. Does this make things clear to you?" Rustler spoke from his deep throat. It was a coarse voice.

Just then there was Nicky Broom who knocked at the door and entered the room without waiting for a formal approval from Rustler.

"Excuse me Gentlemen" Rustler apologized as a formality and turned to his Intelligence Chief in AIA. Nicky did not speak. He only handed over a note to Rustler. As he read the note Rustler's face became red with anger and started turning pale slowly. The others became anxious. Nicky maintained a stony face without giving any expression and without betraying his emotions. "Don't worry. We shall take care of this. Thank you for the information." Rustler looked up to Joshua Bucket who was standing tall at the side the chair of his boss.

"Gentlemen, now things are becoming clearer and catchy. The opponents to our mission to PlanetB2 have formed a formal alliance under the name Cosmic Alliance and have decided to sabotage all endeavor of ours for the progress of humanity. They are preparing even for a war against the US if we go ahead with our mission. It is now open game. There are no more behind the scene action." Rustler did not want to elaborate as his voice became even coarser. He asked for a glass of water and then a cup of coffee. The gathering became silent for sometime and was numbed at the news of a prospective war even before America could launch on the much-hyped mission to PlanetB2. They were aghast and dumbfounded without knowing what to say in the given circumstance.

"Who on earth can oppose such a mission as ours? We have no bad intentions. We only want to land on PlanetB2 for the progress of the world. What the fuck is going on Rustler? Who are these mad caps that want to oppose us? I am sure Russia and China would do this. But China of late has been quite friendly with you. It will be against their projected interests to oppose our plans. Why the hell do they want to oppose us? Do you have their names? We shall teach them a fucking lesson to the mother fuckers." Blaringtone was blaring in full throttle. He had taken only coffee.

Rustler obliged him knowing well that others were also eager to know the names. "You may even be shocked to know that Germany has taken up the leadership for what they call the Cosmic Alliance." He carefully avoided mentioning the derisive name given to his alliance. "This is unfathomable that two European nations are taking the lead in the war against us. We know that Russia and China are in the forefront of any battle against us. It is an age-old ideological fight that we have. Vietnam is the fiddler, the acolyte of all these in the Cosmic Alliance. The name sounds good." Rustler sounded obviously scornful and did not want to elaborate further.

"It is the subversion of history that Germany has taken the lead. I cannot accept this turn of events." The Prime Minister of Canada shook his head in sheer disgust.

"Do not be much worried about this bloody Cosmic Alliance. As you know they cannot go too far. There is no way. They cannot match our strength in any department of war. They are out to chase a mirage. We shall plunge them into a quagmire of war from which they cannot get out at all. This is our best chance to turn the world towards us. Do not hesitate to invest on the media in our favor. Throw millions of dollars in front of them. They will run after us like mad dogs. Get hold of all the media empire to our side. We should win the media war first and only then we shall win the military war." Rustler gave a rousing talk though it was only of few words.

After closing the meeting of Earth Alliance Rustler called for an emergency meeting of his Generals along with Joshua Bucket and Nicky Broom and apprised them of the seriousness of the situation. He also told them that there was no time left to start the journey to the PlanetB2. It was not just one space shuttle that was going to the planet this time. Besides the group of leading astronauts in Bigbelly5 there were many similar vessels that would carry attack forces to PlanetB2 in order to numb all possible resistance from the beings in the planet. There were also exclusively attack vehicles that carried NBC weapons. There were many similar space vehicles on ground to take off just in case there was any emergency need in space. He asked all the Generals to be ready to launch the space vehicles and attack vessels as soon as they got a clear command from him. It would be the pressing of a button specially designed to signal the start of the launch simultaneously to all the Generals. From then on it was a war. They had to only wait for the telecast of Rustler's speech to the world. He would press the button any time after the conclusion of his speech.

What he kept close to his chest was the information that the top strategist of the planet war had already set up many attack vehicles as space shuttles and satellites at different distances. In times of emergency these satellites would function as attack vehicles on PlanetB2 as they were already loaded with NBC weapons. This would avoid support vehicles taking off from earth stations every time there was an emergency need. They would also be ready to attack any nation on earth if there were any such need to attack partners of Cosmic Alliance.

He discussed with his Generals the issue of potential war with Cosmic Alliance just in case their resistance to America's plans grew in velocity. American Generals informed him that no force on earth would be able to stand up to the firepower of the combined strength of the Earth Alliance. "We shall crush them in no time Mr. President. You have nothing to worry. Please carry on your plans with overpowering PlanetB2. We shall take care of any type of resistance on earth. Cosmic alliance has word power. Earth Alliance has world power." The Generals said it aloud together. Rustler's heart cooled a bit after hearing this. Rustler liked the suggestion of one of the generals that a new legislation must be enacted to empower all American citizens with a gun each. He wanted to remove the license regime for carrying guns. All American citizens should have the liberty to protect themselves against any enemy aggression by freely carrying weapons with them. All other Generals looked at him askance. But Rustler put them to rest and comfort saying it was not a bad idea and that he would discuss it with

Congressmen and if they agreed his party would move a bill.

Rustler asked Nicky Broom to leak out the news of the plans of Earth Alliance for an imminent attack on PlanetB2. He had also given special instructions to the astronauts in Bigbelly5 to particularly look for Carolina and Marissa and pull them out of the PlanetB2 or if it was not possible to assassinate them without any hesitation. The media followed exactly the tract that American government had set out for them. They praised to the sky the great military power of the US and that no opposition could even imagine taking it on. They also announced to the world the emergence of a Cosmic Alliance in opposition to the allied forces of the US. While this publicity gained them a lot of money they also were keen on promoting the name of their print and visual media by sensationalizing the opposition to the mission to PlanetB2. They began to analyze the combined strength of Cosmic Alliance and the possibility of many hurdles to Rustler in his single-minded cruise towards American control of the Universe. They almost created a model war in the media in which some media giants predicted the victory of Rustler's forces and some others predicted the victory of Cosmic Alliance. They proposed the reason that Germany's shifting loyalty would have that final edge over the allied force and that Cosmic Alliance would emerge victorious in the ultimate analysis. Deep down in their mind they knew that bringing in Germany in the news would arouse the anger of Rustler and that would further bulge their coffers. Others wrote against the treachery of Germany to have deserted

America in favor of the communists with the fond hope that this would gladden the heart of Rustler and would in turn fill their coffers. Both the media camps knew why they were doing what they did. They hallucinated on the tremendous stockpile and power of the weapons in the possession of Cosmic Alliance. They also brought out secret research documents that had discovered the existence of NBC weapons in large quantity in the storage facilities of Germany, Russia and China. The war was already won and lost in the media by both the warring groups over many pegs of whisky. Little did they know that they even were not informed till then of the existence of the Earth Alliance and that more and more countries were joining this Alliance on a daily basis.

The Global Council of the Indigenous Peoples issued a statement in the media while all their publicity war was in full swing. They said in unequivocal terms that they stood against any war. They firmly opposed the war against PlanetB2. They made it clear that it did not fit into the ethos of indigenous peoples to wage war against another planet. They considered the Cosmos as one unit and all that existed in the cosmos had a right of its own. Cosmos itself was a unit that had its movement and change and no human being had any right to violate the cosmic movement and change that was unfathomable. They said that Earth is their Pachamama, their mother. The sky was their father. The moon was their grandmother. The Sun was their brother and all the starts in the sky were their ancestors. The plants and trees were their sisters, big and small. All the animals were their ancestors along with the stars. Could any part of the body try to be superior to another or destroy another part because it wanted to be more powerful? Earthly beings had their serious limitations. They were only one insignificant part of the cosmos. They could not survive except within the cosmic order whereas cosmos could live without human beings on earth. It had many other variety of living beings that could keep the cosmic energy level in fine balance. Human beings must be humble enough to realize that their life lasts only once and within this one lifetime they should not imagine that they are above the cosmos and its order. It would be preposterous and absolutely dimwitted on their part to conjure up that nothing else mattered in the cosmos except themselves.

They also decried all attempts to violently overpower other people on the earth. Dominance of any kind is against the value system of the indigenous peoples. The decried vehemently the proposed war either by the US or against the US by other nations. War of any kind was anathema in their moral order. Therefore, the Global Council of the Indigenous Peoples would not take a stand in favor of any Alliance that was at loggerheads in pursuit of war.

The very well balanced statement of the Global Council fell on deaf ears in the din of the high-pitched war cry in all corners of the world. The global media had no time even to have a look at the statement that the Global Council issued only because such a statement came from the Indigenous World and the rest of the world cared a hoot for them. For the media it was not a salable material and no one was ready to pay them for giving publicity to such an important value based statement.

PlanetB2 however had a lot of incessant churning at the discussions and statement of the Global Council. The waves of positive energy reached its beings and their full body orgasm increased. Many of them descended in all directions of the world wherever indigenous peoples lived without getting co-opted by dominant worlds of thinking and feeling. They permeated the indigenous world in their wavial forms and increased the energy level of the indigenous peoples across the globe. Many of the beings of PlanetB2 that descended were previously members of the indigenous communities who lived in harmony with the cosmic order as individuals. They spread their waves into all the bodies of indigenous peoples that were open to receive the waves. There were also many among the non-indigenous peoples who were very cosmic and whose body cells were fully disposed to welcome cosmic waves. The Cosmic beings had no other criterion except that of cells in bodies being open to receive their waves. It was a global movement. Nay, it was a cosmic movement of life giving energies triggered by the heavy discourses of violence and war.

The indigenous peoples across nations decided to live their life as usual without heeding to war cries and the opposition to it by dominant countries. The world at large could not spare any time to give a dime to the value systems of indigenous peoples.

CHAPTER SEVENTEEN

The world never waited for any day with its stomach in knots as that day. On the day of the launch of the final mission to PlanetB2 Rustler addressed the entire world in the company of most partners of Earth Alliance. The faces of the Heads of States were already filled with euphoria as much as they were decorated with artificially produced facial cream. It was the Cosmic Alliance that was on tenterhooks. They too had assembled in an unknown place to watch the event of the day. They did not need the specially designed and produced glasses by a US scientist and producer to see clearly on TV the launch event. In fact there were two glasses, one for the hundreds of thousands of people who went to the launch venue to have a good look at Bigbelly5 as it shot off into the orbit. The other one was for those who watched the event in the TV. Someone made good money. Germany and Russia equaled if not outwitted the US in producing such glasses much in advance. The Russian and German spies spent overtime in discovering the special chemical that was used in the outer body of Bigbelly5. Much before America produced the glasses Russia and Germany produced them. The AIA came to know of it only in the last minute when it was too late and their top guys decided to hide the truth from Rustler.

Rustler exuded extravagant confidence. He might have had genuine confidence or he could have camouflaged the lack of it. No one could make out what he actually was. That was the charisma of the man, the elusive hermit of a man who dictated terms to the world. People all over the world had made a beeline in the streets to watch the greatest speech of the American President live on giant screens. The old and the aged decided to stay put at home and watch his speech over a drink. Pub goers had no liking either for home or for streets. Their pub was their world on important occasions like this one. The air was filled with whistling and screaming as soon as Rustler ascended the specially erected and protected podium and appeared on the screen. He had a special make up by specialists for the grand occasion. The victor, the one who was born to overpower the universe, was decorated well to mesmerize the world even by his looks. He could pass as a Hollywood actor easily. But he was in any case an actor par excellence. Those who came without the specially designed glasses for the occasion could not see Bigbelly5. There were innumerable vendors at the venue that made a quick buck.

"Ladies and Gentlemen . . ." His initial words were lost in the din. Hundreds of thousands of whispers made a huge noise. The crowd became silent. It was trained from childhood to behave on such occasions. Rustler knew Americans and for a moment he thought there were hosts of non-Americans. He was right. Soon he realized that Americans were not the only disciplined people. It was pin-drop silence. "Ladies and Gentlemen . . ." Rustler started all over again to make an exception for the exceptional occasion. "We are here to make peace with the cosmos. Today we are reaching out to PlanetB2 with a clear message that we want to co-exist with them as fellow beings. When our astronauts land on the planet the beings there will realize that we are the most peace loving people on earth. The mission of Earth Alliance is to extend our grand efforts for world peace into cosmic peace. When our men and women land on PlanetB2 the world will know that peace has arrived not only on the earth but also on the cosmos. This is the strong message that Bigbelly5 is carrying."

Rustler's starting of the speech was changed in the last minute after Rustler and others watched the beings in PlanetB2 in their computers. All of a sudden, as the 'great moment' was approaching fast the cosmic beings stopped all their movements in the planet. They became still wherever they were. It looked as if they had gone into mystic silence, into meditation. It was intensive. The computer communicated clearly that they were all more alive in that meditation than in their movement. It was total peace that prevailed in PlanetB2 and Rustler wanted to rise to the occasion in his speech.

"Long live, peace! Long live, global peace! Long live, Rustler!" The crowd chanted repeatedly.

Egged on by the crowd Rustler continued his speech with invigorated energy.

"I appeal to all people of the earth and to all countries who have blindly opposed our peace mission to mend their ways and come to negotiating table. I appeal especially to Germany who was our ally till recently and has shifted sides for unknown reasons. It is a European country and cannot afford to break our natural alliance. Germany is on a path of self-destruction by joining hand with the unholy alliance of Left parties and godless infidels. We are not against any nation. We are ready to forgive all those who opposed us and move together towards building one world, a world that would courageously walk in the path of progress. As Earth Alliance we have clearly shown the path of progress to the entire world. It is now left to each country to decide whether they want to tread the path of freedom, peace and prosperity or to move towards sure perdition. I feel sorry for the innocent people of such countries. It is not too late now to turn back and come and join us. Let us build one world and one path."

"We are for peace, we are for prosperity. Let America triumph." The crowd chanted along with respective leaders of their countries.

"You have chanted right my people. With firm faith in god we know for sure that America will triumph bracing all hurdles that it faces. With that firm faith that America will triumph I declare the final mission to PlanetB2 open." Saying this Rustler pressed the button for the shooting off of Bigbelly5 exactly at the time that it was programmed for shoot off from its base into the orbit. Only then it became visible to the millions of people who watched the roaring giant swirling its way into space. Bigbelly5 had already filled its belly with millions hope. The biggest of them was that of Rustler's. Hope had no color and no price. All those who waited for that moment in world history and in their history were filled with a new hope that their world would be different for their children and for all future generations. They live in that particular phase in world history wherein something that was never dreamt of was being achieved. They thanked Rustler profusely for making it happen in their lifetime. They thanked god for creating a person like Rustler for the world. He was the miracle man of history for them. They saw Bigbelly5 move into space majestically but in higher speed than they imagined. It was much faster than their imagination. Faith in god had taught them that they had to believe in the unknown, the unseen, the unfelt and the impossible. Bigbelly5 carried all their faith into the future. The take off was a grand success.

Rustler was a worried man that night. The thought of Plumbel haunted him throughout the night. The thought of Carolina and Marissa being in PlanetB2 came round him many times like the wasp that went away only when he chased it but came back in no time to deafen his ears with its buzzing sound. Rustler struggled to get the wasp out of his way. But he could not succeed.

The greatest man on earth could not keep a little wasp away from disturbing him. The mystery of the cosmos! The buzzing of the wasp! Rustler missed Plumbel at the most pivotal moment in his life. He knew he was succeeding and the contribution made by Plumbel towards a possible success could never be undermined. For the first time in his life after a long time Rustler felt lonely without his friend Plumbel. He was no more. Even if he wished he could never bring back to life someone whom he eliminated in the most brutal manner. It was the call of his duty. He legitimized his past. He was the President of America. The friend of Plumbel lay shattered into many brittle pieces of dry clay and live worms. He tried to wish away the history to which he belonged. The more he tried to cast it out of his memory the more powerfully it came back to him. He could not shirk off his legacy. He had all the power in the world. But deep within he was still powerless against a thought. He needed to depend on the strength of many external factors.

The man Rustler, the President Rustler! The chasm between the two was huge. It was a deep valley. When he looked down he was frightened. The external on which Rustler depended could not come to the rescue of the President. Bigbelly5 was going up in the sky into the unknown space. Rustler was looking down the valley from which he could not rescue himself. The valley was full of emptiness. He did not dare to take a plunge into that emptiness. He thought he would commit suicide if he dared.

Plumbel had told him often over a glass of sober whisky that he should draw his strength from deep inside. Rustler would ridicule him no ends. Power is in the world. It is what I show and prove to the world. We have to gain power from the external. What is the point of having power inside which no one can see. You need to have the power to control. You need the power to overcome. You need the power to succeed. You have to gain the power to govern. You cannot control the world with the power inside of you. You need the military to exercise your power. You need the media to show your power. You need weapons to showcase all your power. Rustler would argue vehemently with Plumbel. Two different worlds! Two different perceptions! Two different equations! Now Rustler began to feel slowly powerless. The valley was gazing at him from its vacant depth. It was empty all the way. Would he win over PlanetB2? Would he win over the cosmos? Would he win over the world? Would he win over his mortal enemies, the Cosmic Alliance? Everything stared at him with suspense and suspicion. Rustler began to feel the brittleness deep within ready to give way at any time, at the most unexpected time. He drowned himself in countess numbers of pegs, his only refuge when he felt lonely.

Many shamans of the indigenous communities felt totally helpless at the way things were moving fast in the world. They could not even reckon with the fast pace in which the world was moving towards destroying itself. They wished that people in the world realized that life is lived just once and that no one is even going to turn back to see that he/she was dead. But then they were no one in the world to educate the rest on their fine realizations. In sheer helplessness they sat in silence. It was a sort of trance. They began to converse with all their ancestors, the animals, the plants, the stars, the wind, the fire and all cosmic elements. Energy of an unmitigated level emerged from their bodies in that meditative state and entered into a process of entropy with similar waves in the cosmos.

Plumbel, Carolina and Marissa and millions of others in PlanetB2 were in deep mystical meditation. They were in their full body orgasm. They were not even aware of themselves. They were producing energy from their innermost power. There was no Plumbel, no Carolina and no Marissa in reality. They had become cosmic beings in their innermost strength. They did not need the external any more to realize their power. In fact there was no power. Only they were.

It was a full week of excruciating wait for all the member states of Earth Alliance. They were glued to their computers all the time tracing the movement of Bigbelly5 in its journey towards PlanetB2. Rustler was constantly moving right to left and left to right on his bed. Sleep was hard to come in all those days. It was not very different with member states of Cosmic Alliance. They were also equally anxious about the outcome of the great undertaking of Rustler and his crony nations, the Comic Alliance. There was no disturbance on the path of Bigbelly5. Everything worked towards perfection according to their plans. Their computers and other technology could not fail them all the time. The Catholic Church organized formal prayers in its churches all over the world for the success of this mighty journey. It was a time of blessing from above. The Pope and the Bishop of Canterbury made it a point to telephone to Rustler every now and then and assure him of God's unmistakable promise of man's success if only he had faith as small as a mustard seed. But the Pope and Rustler had faith as big as a walnut. They must succeed by all standards of faith.

Rustler and his team of scientists had greatly improved the speed of Bigbelly5 from the previous ones and they had programmed it to reach PlanetB2 in five days instead of the previous seven days. It was cruising to its destination at the speed that was prefixed. On the fifth day a few hours before reaching its destination there was information from the computers in Bigbelly5 that the heat level in that particular zone in space was much higher than the levels during the previous journeys of Bigbelly3, 4 and 5. It caused great consternation among the Ground Force scientists. They tried to increase the speed of Bigbelly5 further as this was anticipated already before the take off of the spacecraft. Close on the heels of Bigbelly5, there were five attack vehicles with Nuclear, Biological and Chemical weapons. Missiles were fitted into these vehicles with high speed and velocity so that they might traverse the heat zone just in case Bigbelly5 failed to cross the Rubicon. The Ground Force instructed the astronauts to accelerate the speed of Bigbelly5 to the maximum so that it would cross the danger zone, called the liquid zone because it was feared that the vehicle would become a liquid if it did not cross the zone in any time. The astronauts in the belly of the craft beamed a message of hope that at the speed that they were cruising they should be able to cross any hurdle. The machineries in the vehicle were in fine mettle and there was no technical problem with any of them.

The Ground Force communicated this message to Rustler that it was only a question of time before Bigbelly5 finally landed on PlanetB2. 'What a moment it would be' thought Rustler. He would become the epoch-making hero of world history. He paced his steps to and fro in his office. He could not sit quiet in any place. He called up all the leaders of Earth Alliance and informed them of the impending success.

The pot broke when the milk was boiling. All communication from Bigbelly5 became blank when there was just one more hour to land on PlanetB2. This was a remarkable success for the scientists in Ground Force who had put in all their energy, imagination and creativity together to make the mission a grand success. Rustler mumbled a prayer with his lips. This was something that he had not done at all in his life. But the success of Bigbelly5 was more than his life. He did not intend to say the prayer. It automatically came on his lips. He pleaded with god that for once he should not fail him in this mission and looked at the computer. He could not close his eyes. It was the darkest screen that he had seen in all of his life. His most sophisticated computer had gone blind at the most crucial time when success was written large all over the US. It was a let down, a big let down. The space vehicles following Bigbelly5 sent out messages seeking Rustler's command to shoot their missiles with NBC bombs, as Bigbelly5 had just disappeared in the way of the previous Bigbellies. Rustler had no choice. He was uncontrollably angry at PlanetB2, at Carolina and Marissa. He let out a wild cry asking them to help America from where they were stationed in PlanetB2. There was no reply for him. The astronauts in the five other space vehicles were waiting for his reply. In a mad rush of frustration he gave orders to shoot down all the beings in

PlanetB2. He asked them to destroy the planet itself, as there was no other choice before them.

It was a mission. They were born and trained to shoot. They were commissioned to shoot the missiles without thinking anything else for a second. The computers showed the missiles traversing the special space at much greater speed than Bigbelly5. All those earth scientists who were watching their movement carefully with elation began to clap hands as they had gone a little beyond Bigbelly5. It was now sure that the warheads with NBC weapons would strike successfully at PlanetB2. They seemed to have crossed the 'danger zone'. An erect cock drooping at the most crucial moment! That is how the earth scientists felt when suddenly all the cruise missiles disappeared from their computers. No man-made machine seemed to be able to trespass into the special boundaries of PlanetB2, the liquid zone. It seemed to be much thicker and stronger this time. One by one all the missiles began to disappear at the liquid zone. Rustler and with him all the scientists in Ground Force looked at their computers. Glasses with liquid on their tables disappeared as fast as the missiles in space.

To their greatest exasperation the beings in PlanetB2 were in the same position unmindful of what the US and all its allies were trying to do to them. They were totally unperturbed and were fully plunged in their mystic meditation that gave them full body orgasm. It made Rustler even angrier beyond his control. He ordered all the space vehicles following Bigbelly5 to exhaust their entire arsenal they had in their respective vehicles. The pilots and astronauts in those vehicles knew that it was suicidal to exhaust all the weapons at their disposal, as there was no hope of reaching the target. But they could not retort sense to Rustler in that moment of historic senselessness.

It was a mad rush of anger and frustration making a tasteless pudding or rather it tasted very badly in the palates of Ground Force. But Rustler cared a damn about anybody's taste. In his palate only he knew the taste that he enjoyed. He ordered all other space vessels to be kept ready to take off without counting the cost. He knew that success was missed only by a whisker and he did not want to let go the momentum of attack. Minor setbacks in a war had to be taken in their strides without allowing emotions to have a free play. Rustler had kept in readiness five sets of space vehicles with huge stockpiles of NBC weapons. The first set with Bigbelly5 was a total disaster. Rustler did not anticipate by any stretch of imagination that Bigbelly5 would be lost with all the astronauts inside. It vanished in the space without any trace. Now there were only limited options for him. The second wave of attack on PlanetB2 seemed to follow a slightly different trajectory from the first. This was done on purpose by the Ground Force that guided the missiles from the stealthily stationed satellites at different points in space. To their great dismay the second set of weapons too disappeared in thin space.

Rustler faced a very embarrassing situation among his scientists and officers. He had to either take the bold decision of continuing with the attack or eat his humble pie and ask the forces in space to return to ground. One of his advisors went near him and whispered something in his ears. Rustler pretended as if he did not hear. It was too serious a matter even to pretend not to hear. Rustler knew it much better than anyone on earth. But eating his humble pie was the most difficult thing in his life. As a last attempt he ordered the third set of missiles to go on attack. They did with as much force as they could gather. It was a do or die game for them. And die they did. Do, they did not. The third set of attack force also vanished without a trace. Rustler looked at the computers in front of him with rage. The cosmic beings were still in their meditative posture with Carolina and Marissa very visible among them. He tried to locate Plumbel to punch him on his face. But he was just lost among the millions of cosmic beings in Planet B2. In sheer desperation Rustler took his precious whisky glass that gave him company all through his life and threw it on the computer screen that went into many pieces and fell at his feet.

The whisper in his ears was ringing with rage. Rustler woke up with a jerk. His advisor had informed him that the Stirring Five was together in Germany watching the proceedings of the war against PlanetB2 and that they were making a mockery of Rustler. They were celebrating his failure to reach out physically to the cosmic beings or anywhere near them. They were happy that PlanetB2 was intact and was well protected from the folly of a mad President. They were also carefully listening to all the information that secret forces of their respective counties were sending to them uninterrupted. Rustler had kept all his military forces on high alert for reasons best known only to himself. At the failure of the third attempt he did not want to face any of his scientists in the space station. It looked that he left the place in a huff. There was an unmistaken call to all Generals to assemble immediately. His discussed with them the major failures of the US forces on this mission. He blamed his scientists for having betrayed him and told them in unmistakable terms that the Generals were his only hopes left now. They asked him what he expected of them to do.

He then turned his terrible ire towards his enemy force that was the Cosmic Alliance that was making a mockery of the 'Comic Alliance'. Rustler was foaming at the mouth to the core of his being. He wondered how they saw the Bigbelly5 shooting off into space with their eyes. His scientists had used all possible chemicals and technology to make the Vehicle invisible in space, especially from their sight. What happened was exactly the contrary. He could not imagine that they had developed a technology that was more superior to the American technology. He wanted to teach them an immediate lesson and recover some of his lost glory.

Rustler ordered the remaining sets of missiles and attack vessels to return to the earth. It was this return that made the Cosmic Alliance laugh their life out. However, they appreciated the wisdom of Rustler's to have ordered the return of the NBC weapons along with their carriers.

Vrooom . . . . Boom . . . . Vroooom . . . . Booooom . . . . All the Premiers of the Stirring Five instructed their Deputies to take charge of operations and they rushed back to their countries to face the attack. It was the follow up of the provocation by Germany issuing a public statement on behalf of Cosmic Alliance that the failure of Rustler was very welcome in the best interest of humanity. It was unprovoked and unwarranted on their part. It was a full-scale attack on Germany. Simultaneously the American warplanes and missiles launched their attacks on Germany. That was totally unanticipated. It took the entire world by surprise.

"Germany is our soft target. They do not have the weapons to face our attack. We shall not use our full might against Germany but this first attack should neutralize the sting power of many countries that want to test fire their armory on our forces. We should spring the worst surprise on this Alliance at the most unexpected time. We should launch a pre-emptive strike. 'Neutralize and Pre-empt' should be our regular strategy against the infidel forces of the Cosmic Alliance." The Air Marshal of the US Army thundered in his uncontainable anger against Germany.

Rustler's decision was controversial. An unprovoked attack on Germany was the least that Europe and most Americans expected. They were prepared for the worst for Germany in the light of its joining hands with Russia and China. But they did not think that things would go to the extent of a military strike by America on a long time friend. Before the world could wake up from its slumber and recover from its initial shock the first ever TV tower of the world set up in Stuttgart was demolished without an inkling of where it was. Such was the precision of the American missiles. While everyone was expressing total shock and Germans were mourning the demise of their TV tower and the people of Stuttgart were shedding tears another strike on Germany devastated the Cathedral of Ulm. Rustler had set his vengeful eyes on this Cathedral, as it was the one that sheltered his archenemy Plumbel. It was a sweet revenge for him that the Cathedral was itself no more in existence after the brutal assassination of Plumbel. Cologne was getting ready to be attacked with its longest constructed Cathedral.

Before running away to their respective countries, all the Premiers embraced Claudia and assured her that they would always stand by her come what might. Before, they could reach their respective Capitals they heard the news from their Intelligence Chiefs that Germany stood missile for missile against America. What Rustler started off as a warning shot was now blowing into a full time war as Claudia's Germany unleashed a firepower that even the alliance partners did not anticipate in their wildest imaginations. No one in the world could imagine that Claudia possessed such powerful missiles that could destroy targets in America surpassing their radars. Bomb for bomb! Missile for Missile! That was the response of the German military that seemed to be in dormant existence till then. Rustler and all his American Generals were shaken to the bottom of their pants at the power that the German weapons produced from their long-range missiles targeting American space installations with precision. It was a shock to the world and a pleasant surprise to partners in Cosmic Alliance.

Rustler did not anticipate even in his wildest dreams that Germany would target Cubicle 11 that the world did not know anything about and all of America did not know its existence. Germany seemed to know more secrets of his military base than many American army chiefs knew. Many were shivering in their pants at the amazing capacity of Germans in intelligence gathering and in their strike power. The world waited with bated breath on the streams of weapons and missiles that proceeded from the stockpiles of Germany. Germans came on to the streets risking their lives to celebrate the re-birth of Germany as a military giant whose power had to be reckoned with by the mighty forces on earth.

Claudia went on air calling for unity of all Germans all over the world and all Europeans at this critical period in history. Nothing was new to Germany. "We have faced many threats to our existence and lives. Many of our fathers and mothers have courageously sacrificed their lives for Germany. We live at the time when we have obliterated the stigma of Hitler from our land. Just then America is rising like a giant of a Hitler against us. Do not worry my people. Germany is not what you all thought it to be. Germany is a mighty power on earth, as indomitable as any other super power. We have nothing to fear. We shall overcome all the combined might of this so-called Earth Alliance. This attack on us is a manifestation of Rustler's total frustration at the failure of the space mission to overpower PlanetB2. I want to announce to you that America has failed in its iniquitous design of planet war against a very peaceful planet in the cosmos. Even before Rustler knew about its failure we in Germany knew it. That is the power of our Intelligence technology. Stand together my people. We have nothing to fear anything or anyone on this earth. We shall overcome." There were a few drops of tears in the cheeks of Claudia followed by a flood of tears in the cheeks of citizens all over Germany. With their right hand on their left chest all Germans vowed that they would fight to the finish to see the end of Earth Alliance. All Germans in their moment of helpless pride began to sing and the entire Germany was singing the song of victory.

Germany retaliated the American attack weapon for weapon. The American army found it hard to face the stream of attack from Germany. Many American military installations were the main target of German attack. Quite unprovoked Britain joined the American forces in attacking Germany as the Americans found it impossible to withstand the multiple pressure of German attack. Every country in the Earth Alliance was totally taken aback by the firepower of Germany. Russia retaliated by joining the attack against Britain. Russia issued a strong warning to the Earth Alliance that it would not wait as a mute witness to the attack on its alliance partners and increased its attack on Britain allowing German Army to intensify its attack on American installations. Britain found it difficult to withstand the pressures from within and without in this murky situation. Many English citizens advocated that Britain should refrain from military attack on Germany in order not to revive the historic wounds inflicted on Germany during the previous war. Besides the missile attack Russia also made simultaneous foray into the waters and caused severe damage to British navy. At the very first strike it destroyed two very important nuclear submarines of the British. England retaliated by destroying one nuclear submarine of the Russian forces.

Surprisingly Israel did not lend support to Earth Alliance in any military attack on Germany. It feared another big holocaust of its citizens who had returned to Germany and made reconciliation. It meant also a loss of wealth and money for the Jews. In the meantime China caused the biggest embarrassment to American army by destroying three American storehouses of weapons. That was a huge loss to America, as it had already lost quite a bit of big weapons in its attack on PlanetB2.

In a big festive meal, all that happened till now was only like soup. Starters had to follow and then the main course would come. Rustler had a new computer and was aghast to see heavy movement of cosmic beings in PlanetB2 and he did not have a clue as to why they started moving in their abode. He and his army Generals were closeted to constantly monitor the developments in the war front and to reinforce weapons and manpower to their strike forces. Hotline calls to the Alliance partners intensified on both sides. Russia and Germany gave a break to the soup session before they could resume their starters.

It was however Britain that started the fireworks after a short lull. It sent an array of bombers towards the office of the Chancellor of Germany that was a soft target. The German Parliament building was adjacent to the Chancellor's office. "What a shame!" The German newspapers and visual media cried loud the next day. All the bombers were surrounded by Chinese air force and they were both attacked and threatened to get back to their base. Unable to proceed further many warplanes of the British Air Force returned without fulfilling their mission. In the bargain Britain lost more than half of the planes that they sent to the Chinese warplanes. This angered Rustler immensely and he decided to send his long distant missiles to China to attack Chinese communication network and heritage buildings especially of the Communist Party.

In order to deviate the firepower of Earth Alliance, North Korea and Vietnam joined hands to attack South Korea. It was not able to withstand the unexpected combined attack. An attack by North Korea was on the cards any time. But a combined attack was a surprise. Canada and Australia joined hands with the Earth Alliance on all fronts of war. So did many other countries and the Netherlands in Europe. Norway intensified its support to the Cosmic Alliance. Missiles flew in all directions mainly targeting the military installations and communication networks of enemy countries. Reinforcement missions were hyperactive to restore communication networks and supply of weapons. The arms produces of all countries were producing weapons on a war footing.

At this point Russia sent its emissaries on a secret mission to Arab countries seeking not only their financial support but also asking for their active involvement in the war. Russia was careful enough not to give out the secrets of it secret emissaries and therefore, avoided Saudi Arabia that was always on the side of the US. It was a hard negotiation. Finally Iran, Egypt, Syria, Palestine and other Arab neighbors issued public statements in the media condemning America for its blind mission to PlanetB2 wasting the money of tax payers on the idiotic pursuit of unreachable goals and asking the US to stop attack on countries of Cosmic Alliance. They directly threatened the US that in the event of America not stopping its attack on Germany immediately, the Arab alliance would be forced to join hands with the Cosmic Alliance. Russia destroyed three nuclear submarines of the US with much ease. It shocked the sensitivity of Rustler. He retaliated by submerging one of the biggest submarines of Russia.

It was then that Germany did something that the world did not anticipate at all. It took recourse to cluster bombing of certain places that were supposed to be the American base for producing the space vehicles known as Bigbelly. Germany now went on the media to announce that it had succeeded to destroy Cubicle11 that was the most cherished center of Rustler and American scientists. The biggest surprise in this cracking of a war was that Americans could not see the German missiles. The media was taken aback by total surprise at what Germany announced. Many in American media ridiculed Germany for indulging in a cheap propaganda war to demoralize American forces. The Cosmic alliance was euphoric at the emerging power of Germany that it could target such a secret place with precision.

Germany announced to the world that it would be well neigh impossible for America to produce another Bigbelly series, as all necessary infrastructures to produce the huge space vehicle was dismantled with precise strikes by the German and Russian forces. Germany had the spy network and technology needed for identifying such invisible production centers of Americans. The Chinese people took to streets with firecrackers to celebrate such huge achievement. Skepticism turned into total disbelief. The American media was mournfully acknowledging the receipt of official news from American Government that indeed such a production center was ingeniously set up by American scientists. Only a few in the US knew of it. Not even the Senate knew of its existence. Rustler apologized profusely for keeping the American people and Senate in dark about such a huge enterprise. He acknowledged that such cherished heritage of America was now in rubbles. 'Plumbel must be turning in his grave.' Rustler thought several times after the demise of Cubicle11. His anger was then directed to Germany and he vowed to destroy Germany in no time and teach Russia a fitting lesson in a short time.

Norberta spoke to Claudia and expressed her fear that she might lose her precious friend. She asked Claudia to go slow and shun too much of violence. Claudia legitimized her military action in order to teach Rustler a lesson in history and if possible also to eliminate him from the face of the earth. She said that she was not targeting citizens but only military and communication establishments. One of the Heads of States of Cosmic Alliance, namely Norberta congratulated Claudia for her extraordinary courage in intruding into the impossible arenas of American secret establishments.

The American media, paid and unpaid, was in total disbelief. It was in a state of stupor. It was then that Rustler let loose the firepower of America. He asked his military Generals to destroy all the nuclear installations of all the countries of Cosmic Alliance. Germany did not resist much. The Germans were surprised. Norberta thought that her advise to Claudia began to bear some fruit. Claudia ridiculed Rustler the next day in the media. She said that Rustler was capable of removing the teeth of a poisonous snake that was dead ten days back. She explained that Germany had already decided to dismantle all its nuclear installations because of their very bad impact in global warming. Germany had taken recourse to solar and wind energy instead. The American attack only made the task of the German government much easier. Rustler felt humiliated by a woman. He could not bear it. He was angry to the core of his being. The combined attack of Earth Alliance on the well-fortified nuclear installations of Russia and China could not intrude easily. However, provoked by the series of missile attack on the nuclear installations of allies, North Korea did something that was not collectively decided by the Cosmic Alliance. It dropped the first nuclear bomb on South Korea. Though the allies reproved the Premier of North Korea for this very stupid and egotistic measure it was too late. It caused havoc to the people of South Korea. It killed millions of people and destroyed most buildings and military installations of South Korea. The nation was not only paralyzed but was also maimed and motionless. Heedless of the rebuke, North Korea followed up the first attack with subsequent nuclear bombs to devastate and decimate the people and the country of South Korea almost totally. For the first time in the war one country became extinct. A just reward for making many animal species extinct! Many thought of the world.

The world was in a state of shock. The least the world expected was a nuclear war. That a partner of Cosmic Alliance started it shook the conscience of the world. It was numbed in its senses unable to predict what would be the outcome of the mindless war of violence and destruction. Rustler rushed his media personnel to take the risk of their lives and shoot pictures of the devastating scene of the wreckages. Some of them took the risk seriously and went to South Korea, others just borrowed their pictures for a price and published. Limbs scattered on the roads and streets all over South Korea. Dismembered body parts lying scattered and shattered. Headless torsos making a horrible site. Dilapidated skyscrapers, though symbols of human pride and achievement bowed out quietly into the land of oblivion. Roads were corroded like burned human bodies splattered with blood all over. Unbearable sight for the human eyes! For Rustler it made one of the best commodities to be sold in the war market.

War strategists on both sides met at their ends and discussed very seriously on how to proceed. The room where they assembled resembled the silence of the graveyard. No one was willing to let the first word out of his mouth. It was necessary to stop the war if human sensibilities had to be respected. It was necessary to consider the foolishness of the North Korean Premier as an aberration and cry halt to any further nuclear attack. That is what many crusaders of peace cried for. Feeble cries for peace rose from the quarters where indigenous communities lived. Such cries were too feeble to be heard in the din of bombings. But a war is a war. It is more emotional and less rational. The strategy of war was ruthlessly rational or irrational as one might call it. The consequence of war was highly irrational on all counts. Both irrationality and hyper emotions had a field day in the first phase of the war. Cosmic Alliance wanted to cry halt to the war on human beings. They were upset that one of their own alliance partners had triggered a totally unexpected trajectory to the war. They set out to stop the madness of Rustler imposed belligerently on an unsuspecting world. But now they placed themselves in the most awkward position of defending their people and their self-pride with the additional burden of avoiding a nuclear holocaust.

CHAPTER EIGHTEEN

Japan was evasive till then. They did not take any position either on behalf of Rustler or on behalf of Claudia. They cherished the value of neutrality. But now it was no more possible to remain a silent spectator when so much was at stake for the entire world. They had gone through all traumas that were associated with nuclear war. Many people in Japan were slowly wiping the scars and the plasma that was still oozing out of the wounds of war. Japan taught a true lesson to America by building itself up as an economic giant through its hard work and scientific excellence. It could not imagine a military coup against the US. But now was an opportunity offered to Japan on a golden platter. Japan and America never saw each other eye to eye. It was not easy for Japan. The Premier of Japan sent a secret messenger to Claudia and asked her to consider Japan as an ally.

Claudia took up her hotline and spoke directly to the Japanese Prime Minister. "Why did you have to send a secret messenger? This is our war, the war of all good thinking people on earth. Though it is unfortunate that it has assumed nuclear angle and we regret it, all nations of the world have to unite against this unholy Earth Alliance. You are most welcome to join us. We shall see to it that your people will not have to suffer the same loss of lives and damages once again. You can give an open statement against the war mongering of Rustler and his cronies."

"No Madam. We do not want to come out in the open. As you are aware we do not have a strong strike power against the US though we do want to teach them a lesson. But we cannot allow our people to suffer once again in the hands of America. We shudder to think of the abominable consequences that a nuclear war can cause. Therefore, we shall be happy to provide you our tacit support by supplying you with all emergency needs such as high-tech communication equipment that are essential in this war preparedness. We shall put all our work force to get involved in the production of all your needs in the war front."

"Well, Mr. Prime Minister. That is an excellent idea. We do not want to inflict much hardship on your people once again. But this is very generous of you. You need not give any public statement. Instead you can give us all logical support for war secretly. I shall speak to our alliance partners and ask them to keep your contribution in this war as a secret as much as humanly possible in a war situation."

Both of them further discussed on how Claudia would ask her Military experts to get in touch with him directly and work out the warehouse needs from Japan. He bowed his head to Claudia as a habit without realizing that it mattered very little to her. She could not see him doing his venerable action. It did not take too long for the news of tacit support of Japan to reach the ears of Rustler. He was enraged like a fireball of a burning inferno. 'Small people are acting big', he thought to himself.

Seething with anger Rustler called his Generals to sing requiem to Cubicle11. He considered it as one of the biggest humiliations in his life after the total failure of Bigbelly5. A twin disaster! America on the downhill! Russian and Chinese media blared their horns in hyper elation. Blaringtone made a dashing visit to New York to be at the side of his friend. He flew in a special plane fully surrounded by British warplanes. When his plane reached the skies of America the American warplanes took over security and the British warplanes retuned to their base. Both of them made necessary strategies for the future of the war. Germany had to be taught a fitting lesson for its exhibition of groundbreaking strike power. Blaringtone only incensed the already burning anger of Rustler instead of trying to douse it. He left for the UK leaving everyone behind in serious suspense as to what transpired between both of them.

It did not take long for the world to grasp the secret plans hatched by the two bosom friends. The rest of the world saw the consequences. Before they could witness the full consequence Russia got wind of the impending nuclear attack on Germany. Three powerful missiles carrying three nuclear bombs zoomed towards Germany. It was only a question of time before more than half of Germany would be destroyed. Russia spared the blush for Germany. It destroyed two missiles with nuclear warhead over the sea. However, one nuclear bomb was dropped in Cologne destroying the cultural and economic centers of Germany along the twin cities of Cologne and Bonn. Young and old wanted to be very sad that the lover's locks that they put up in a bridge over the Rhine near the Cathedral was obliterated totally without a trace. But they could not be sad as none was spared to see the destruction of their twin cities. Young and old lovers would go to the Lover's Lock Bridge and put a lock on the wire mesh along the bridge to lock their love. It was a sight for all the tourists who had the twin pleasure of seeing the Cathedral that was still in construction from 14 Century till the 21st Century and invariably all visitors to the Cathedral in search of divine love had a taste of human love over the Rhine. All that romantic memory became a part of dilapidated history. No one remained to see the debris.

It was a shock, a huge one for the Germans that their cities of pride and their people, friends and relatives were no more alive. They could not imagine Germany puncturing the pride of Rustler's by bombing and destroying Cubicle11. The image of the Cubicle was only an imagination. The death of their near and dear ones was a reality. Russia and China entered the fray without much inhibition. There was not much time to think. Russia and China together sent five nuclear bombs to attack NASA. They lost three but two of their very powerful bombs fell on the space station and destroyed all the technical centers of the US in its space stations. It was a success that Cosmic Alliance croaked about from their rooftops. The attack had a tellingly crippling effect on the space technology and missions of America. It would take more than two centuries for the US to rebuild their space centers. More than that Rustler and his cronies felt horribly the devastating impact of the loss of all their top scientists at one stroke from Russia and China.

America, Britain, Canada and Australia now took recourse to a combined attack on Russia and China with their missiles and nuclear warheads. There was a vehemence of unpredictable proportion against these two countries. But they were not licking their ice creams. They were fully prepared. There was no calculations any more of human and material casualties. All countries were prepared for any eventuality. It was a full-scale world war without a number necessarily attached to it. All nations had to take sides with one or other Alliance for fear of being totally annihilated from the face of the earth if they did not take sides. The World Council of Indigenous Peoples was the only global outfit that refused to take any side with a clear statement that Indigenous peoples stood against any type of violence and they condemned both the Alliances for their blind pursuit of a sure self-destructive war.

There was a strange sadness that permeated the cosmic beings with so much violence and destruction in the world. The loud cry of pain and death from the dying people reached a crescendo that could not make the becoming of cosmic beings as neutral beings. But what permeated all of them was the firm stand of the World Council of Indigenous Peoples against any type of violence and war. This loud cry for a war free world was totally lost in the din of bombings and nuclear blasts. Just as the indigenous peoples the cosmic beings also felt inside their cosmic bodies a helplessness at the way the war was developing into total destruction. There was no way that they could arrest the onslaught of destructive forces except that their positive and life giving energies were constantly empowering all those whose body cells were open to receive their waves.

Russian and Chinese warplanes destroyed the nuclear warheads of the combined assault of Earth Alliance. Both countries chose big oceans for their counter attacks to avoid havoc among human beings. The nuclear bombs fell into the ocean. However, American forces did manage to drop nuclear bombs on Kremlin and on Tiananmen Square with unmistakable precision. They numbed the sting power of Russia and China. It was suffocating for the powers that be in Russia and China. The Cosmic Alliance was a disillusioned lot with their lead counties receiving heavy blows. Japan came to the quick rescue of Cosmic Alliance by supplying all necessary spare parts for the assembling of many more nuclear bombs in quick time.

The Vatican in Rome issued a stern warning to Russia and China that many more tragedies would afflict their people and their countries if they did not mend their ways and turn to god. They attributed the disaster to their atheism thus further deepening the wounds of a people who stood ravaged by the blind fury of Earth Alliance on the streets and public squares. As if to challenge the faith side of the Pope, China bombed and destroyed the Vatican almost immediately after the Papal statement. The Pope disappeared without a trace of his faith without any god coming to his rescue. Strangely enough animals and birds escaped into forests and hills where the bombers had no inclination to attack. Forest and Hill dwellers took care of these animals and birds by providing them food and water. They were blissfully unaware of the goings on in the world. The nuclear attacks diverted the flow of rivers and inundated the dwelling places of human beings. Governments had no time to give relief to citizens on these 'natural calamities' and left their people to the mercy of nature that was in fury at human folly.

Norberta spoke several times to Claudia to cry halt to the ravaging fury of Cosmic Alliance. She could not put up with the crazy pace with which the world was being destroyed by its own folly and blind pursuit of power. Claudia told her repeatedly that her hands were tied by the Alliance and by the foolhardiness of Rustler. It was a war between the madness of one person and the sanity of the rest of the world, she insisted. Norberta became furious.

"No Claudia. All of you people are equally mad. Look at the way you are destroying innocent lives because of your egotistic pursuits. Please halt the war. This is an all round madness that you should take the initiative to stop. Please instill some sense in the partners of your alliance to ask for a ceasefire without giving free vent to your ego pursuits. This is just destruction Claudia. You are just destroying the people of the world. Does this not disturb your conscience? . . ."

Claudia interrupted Norberta her bosom friend. "There is no way Norberta. The war cannot be stopped at this stage. Yes I agree that there is an all round destruction all over the world. But as a woman I cannot give an impression that I am weak. I am the strongest woman on earth just as

Rustler claims to be the strongest man on earth. Germany cannot withdraw at this stage. The world has been grossly unjust to Germany and now it is high time that we prove to the world that Germany is a global power to reckon with. I cannot let down womanhood as a weakling in the chain of power."

"But Claudia, to whom do you want to prove your womanhood and in what way. I am ashamed of your thinking dear. This is the least that I expected of a close friend of mine like you. I hate war. It is against the order of nature to wage war and kill people. This is just unjust and unacceptable. What are you people doing to the world and to the cosmos? You have called yourselves the "Cosmic Alliance". That is ridiculous my dear. You are neither an alliance nor cosmic. I am very disappointed at the way you have changed in this time of war. You want to be equal to men in warfare. That is not womanhood. We, as women have to prove that we are the ultimate lovers of peace and harmony. You are not woman in your essence. You are a man in the body of a woman. Unfortunately we have many such women in this world who think that they have to be blind imitators of men to give a competition to men. I am sorry Claudia." Norberta gave many pieces of her mind to her bosom friend.

Claudia retorted in typical style. "I have no time to listen to your lamentations Norberta. Yes, we have been good friends for a long time. But this is something that I cannot rescind from. This is a war and not a goody, goody wish. I have been mandated to carry Germany to its destiny that is to be a force on earth to be reckoned with. I cannot sacrifice this. Please tell Rustler to stop the war. Ask him to stop his mad mission to PlanetB2. Ask Britain to stop its traditional hatred to us Germans. Ask the Netherlands to stand with one of its European allies instead of joining hands with America. I hoped that Norway and other Scandinavian countries would stand me in good stead. It does not seem to be the case. This is a war. Allies will turn enemies and enemies will turn into allies. I am prepared for everything. If you ask me I am prepared to lose you and all of Scandinavia. The war cry is constantly ringing in my ears and I shall fight till the end on behalf of my German people. I too want peace on earth. But peace on earth is not possible as long as Rustler lives with his hegemonic pursuits . . ."

". . . You are a shaman. I am not. Therefore, it may be time that we depart from each other. I cannot agree to your shamanic ways. Yes, Cosmos is very important for me, as I understood from Plumbel. But remember he was not a shaman nor was he a Native American. I loved him. But it was Rustler who brutally assassinated my man love. I shall take revenge on him come what may. I shall not rest till I hear the good news that Rustler has met the same fate as Plumbel. I wish all your cosmic beings understand the meaning of love and the longing that I have had for the one I love. I shall fight to the finish. Goodbye my friend Norberta. I do not know where we shall meet next." Claudia spoke a little more than what the situation demanded.

By the time Claudia completed her talk with Norberta, the American forces had already destroyed more than half of Germany. German forces were not lagging far behind. They launched a combined attack with Russia, China, Vietnam, Iran, Egypt and North Korea and brought important cities like Washington, Chicago, Los Angeles, Philadelphia, and Detroit that was claimed to be the ultimate dream of all Americans, Houston and Boston/Miami to mere wreckages of war.

Rustler immediately appealed for a ceasefire. There was euphoria all over the world that the American President had become a humble human being. There was elation in the US that good sense started prevailing in the leaders. Remaining Americans took to streets appealing to world leaders to stop forthwith this holocaust of innocent masses of people. "It was not for this that we elected you. Change your behavior lest we decide to teach yall a lesson. This is not the time to insist on your personality conflicts and your egos." Said a People's Statement from the remaining Americans who were desperately wishing to live.

This was immediately countered by another set of Americans who wanted to draw blood for blood and life for life without realizing that 'an eye for an eye will only make the entire world blind.' Internal conflicts as unresolvable as the war all over the world!

War cry from Americans rented the air all over the country on the dead corpses of innocent Americans. Rustler heeded more to such sordid cries than to the sober appeals for peace and co-existence. It suited him well. He was not loner in America. There were many others all over America who wanted the war to continue with more intensity and bring the rest of the world to an abrupt end at the earliest with American might. They were still wondering why America was not manifesting its full might to the rest of the world.

What the Cosmic Alliance suspected became true. The truce proposed by Rustler was only a ruse to buy time. He needed time to reinforce his forces and to produce more horrific weapons. They suspected him to be buying time. But they also had a compulsion. They also needed time to recharge their batteries on all fronts. Therefore, the truce was easily agreed upon. It took a lot of time even for rulers to recover from the huge loss of human beings and materials in their respective countries.

Egged on by internal protests clamoring for war, endless war Rustler unleashed the second set of his armory. It contained abominable array of biological weapons. It was directly aiming at killing citizens of enemy countries through viruses, diseases of unknown origin and magnitude. They were not targeting so many material centers any more. Germany was much more adept at biological weapons than the US. It informed the alliance partners of its capacity to destroy all Americans and British and if needed also all of Canada and Australia in a few days through viral infection. America would have to struggle hard to find appropriate medical remedies for the viruses that Germany and Cosmic Alliance partners would unleash. By the time a remedy was discovered more than three fourth of the people in these countries would be killed stealthily. It was only a small provocation on the part of the Americans to have dropped a few biological bombs on Munich. People in that region were afflicted with unknown viral diseases. Their skins started eroding for no reason at all. Doctors were at a loss to know what were the causes of these diseases. Even Japan struggled hard to find appropriate remedies for the American diseases in Germany. Human beings were disfigured very badly that one person did not want to look at another. Some became so ugly to look at that passersby started throwing up just at the very sight of such afflicted persons. All the important cities of Germany starting from Bonn to Hannover, Hamburg, Munster and Berlin were attacked with Biological weapons. People going to offices just dropped dead for no reason at all.

Other countries of Cosmic Alliance followed suit in retaliation. They dropped biological bombs on all the major cities of America, Britain and other countries of the Earth alliance. The people who were most afflicted by such dastardly attacks were the African countries who had no idea to defend themselves against such attacks. When the attacks took place actually the alliance partners could not provide remedies to all the countries, especially the traditionally poor countries and former colonies of the British. Innocent people in African countries just died along with their children only because their rulers decided to support their former colonizers blindly.

Men and women lost their libido because of the viral attacks and they lost all their interest in sex. They became incapable of producing any more children. Resistance power in their bodies began to decrease gradually making most people immobile from their homes. Many people had to be taken to their homes often by ambulances from their work places, as they fell down without the strength to walk. Human psyche fell flat as much as the skyscrapers in the cities. Domestic animals were not spared of the havoc that the biological weapons caused. Trees and plants were not spared. Animals and plants played no part in the enormous stupidity of the human to have started this war.

The combined and intermittent essays of the Cosmic Alliance had many twists and turns that the Earth Alliance did not anticipate. Their strike power was huge and was wrought with precision. Their intelligence network was something that the Earth Alliance did not anticipate. Rustler lived under the illusion that he and his country were indomitable. He tried to find out what was that edge that cosmic alliance had over Earth Alliance. Nicky Broom informed Rustler that the two close associates of Plumbel's in the American Intelligence Agency had defected to Germany some time ago even when Plumbel was alive. It was a lapse on the part of AIA not to have informed Rustler about it. It was not required as the top officers in the AIA took stock of the situation and closed the matter at that. But that was disastrous. Already when Plumbel was alive Claudia had inducted them into the secret services of the German Intelligence network and they were sure landmines of information on the American defense systems. They had knowledge about every nook and corner of the American space bases, military bases and civil bases. They also had the know-how of intelligence gathering at a very sophisticated level. Both of them had been trained earlier in Israel. Germany made the best use of them by also rewarding them with huge monetary benefits and security coverage.

Plumbel further motivated and educated them on the need for resisting effectively the onward march of Rustler in his mad rush towards global destruction. They became easy collaborators with Claudia. Earlier Rustler was surprised that Norberta and other Scandinavian countries had become rather silent and were not actively participating in the war front. He did not have a clue as to what transpired between the two close friends. Norberta was a bundle of nerves after the way Claudia treated her as shit. She went into her shell and did not interact with anyone outside of her country. She just did the routine duties of the Head of State in her country. The Scandinavian countries praised the low profile that Norberta kept. They did not wish and did not expect the war to assume such disastrous proportions to the detriment of human race. It was at the brink of sure destruction. The Sami Parliament even passed a resolution in deep appreciation of the Norwegian Prime Minister who infused some sense among her people not to participate actively in the war. It was at this time that Rustler's evil designs played havoc with Norberta and Scandinavia. At one stroke of a nuclear bomb he obliterated the memory of Scandinavia. Only the far off North and reindeer were spared.

A shell it was. Most leaders of the countries actively engaged in the war had to get back into their shell in order to save their skin. Their military Generals also rescinded into their highly protected underground buildings in order not to be affected and afflicted by the attack by biological weapons. The situation in the United States was much worse as it was the prime target of all the countries involved in the war. While this biological war was going on Britain went into a state of stupor and mourning as the German forces efficiently targeted the Buckingham palace and all other royal establishments for their sporadic missile attack. One of the missiles found its target while Britain was defending itself against the nuclear attack of Russia and China.

For the first time during the war Blaringtone appeared rattled on the TV wearing the saddest possible face to announce to the world that Germans assassinated the Queen of England in the attack. She was a soft victim. But cosmic alliance croaked about it saying that she was the one who signed the British resolution for war and had to pay a heavy price and perhaps the second major human price for approving the war. There was a big mourning all over Britain, Asia, Africa and Latin America in the former colonies of the British. There were only a few people in those countries to mourn the death of the Queen. They had no one to mourn the death of their own near and dear ones.

The death of the Queen of England was an unbearable disaster for the Earth Alliance. That was the least expected casualty in the war. No one ever imagined that the Queen would be targeted so early in the war. But then they did not assume that the war had already assumed uncontrollable proportions moving into nuclear and biological warfare. There was only one more left in the armory of both Alliances.

Earth Alliance could not take the loss of their Queen Mother easily. Rustler got into another secret cubicle with all his Generals. He had a few of them for the sake of security reasons. They discussed for a long time while their warplanes and missiles were pounding many bases in Europe, Russia, China and other countries of cosmic alliance. Vietnam knew the knowhow of resisting American war strategies more than any other country in the alliance. However, even it could not prevent the fall of two powerful biological bombs falling on its soil. Rustler and American Generals were particularly elated at this success, as they considered it to be a 'sweet' revenge for their earlier defeat at the hands of Vietnam. It was repaying with human casualties for its earlier military victory. The war scene of a young girl running naked on the streets was revived in the memories of the Vietnamese people. But then, there was no time to dwell on such memories as the reality of war now was much more devastating now than before. Destruction and devastation had entered into the doorsteps of every home in Vietnam. China did its best not to allow too much of attack on its alliance partner.

Angered by the death of the Queen of England the military Generals of the Earth Alliance took the final step to end the war. They imagined that they had to put an end to the war by totally destroying countries of cosmic alliance. There was no other option left to them. The onward march of cosmic alliance in the warfront was intolerable in the dominant psyche of Earth Alliance to presume that they were indestructible.

Cosmic Alliance, on its part also had similar secret meetings at places that were impenetrable and worked out their strategies. Now there was no more room for counter strategies. Every Alliance worked out its strategy without bothering much about the power of the other alliance. It was an all out war now with no holds barred. Each alliance found it necessary to go on full-scale attack with all types of weapons in their armory only to protect themselves and their people with their establishments.

The first weapon in this escalated war was sent by the United States. It was the third one in the array of weapons that the US and its alliance partners possessed. Rustler gave personal order to the Generals of the Earth Alliance to have an all out attack on all countries of cosmic alliance with their NBC weapons. He had spared them after losing quite a bit of them in the war on PlanetB2. They came in good stead. The first of these chemical bombs was dropped on Russia and not on Germany. There was still a soft corner for Europe in the thinking of Earth Alliance. They did not want to destroy Europe entirely, as they were their own people. Russia and China were the worst enemies with their communist principles of socialism and equality of all peoples. Germany was more socialistic and deserved to be decimated. "Now the time has come to exterminate all those who wanted to wipe America off the face of the earth.

Everyone who likes to see the end of America should see his own Waterloo." Rustler spoke to his Generals with a vehemence that they had not witnessed in him before.

Rustler pressed the final button of ultimate liquidation of all his enemies on planet earth. Having been checkmated on all fronts in his assault on PlanetB2 he turned his full ire towards his earthly enemies only to prove to himself that he was the ultimate of human existence. Nothing on earth should exist beyond the realm of his hegemonic control. He was the master of the universe and no one else had a right to rob him of this unique position on Planet Earth. Having been turned back from getting the better of PlanetB2 it was now imperative to feed his ego by taking over all the reins of rule over the earth. Before the final strike on his enemies Rustler wanted to have the full satisfaction of having eliminated his ultimate betrayers. These were the two officers of the AIA who defected to Germany through Plumbel. It was because of them that most secrets of American firepower were known to Germany and as such this crime was intolerable in the dictionary of Rustler. The other penultimate target was Claudia herself. He could understand the enmity manifested by the Premiers of Russia and China. But he would never endure with the deviatory path of any nation in Europe against the absolute power of the American President.

He set up a special team of Intelligence and army experts to hunt down the three infidels and finish them off on sight. He knew the glitches. But he could not imagine that such worst enemies were still active on the warfront against the Earth Alliance. Claudia and her colleagues in the alliance were preoccupied with the implementation of war strategies. The two former associates of Plumbel were not in the striking range of American firepower. They were not always in the nick of action in the war front. One fine morning both of them knocked at the door of the very fortified room of Claudia. The security guards refused permission even to knock at the door. One of them took his mobile and rang up Claudia in her private phone that was accessible only to the most important people in the war front. That precious evening Claudia had sent them to have a serious discussions with the army officers in one of the camps that were set up to make a few sorties on the British targets. She expected some good news from them and spoke to the security guards to let them in.

Just as the security guard opened the door there was Claudia wishing the two former AIA men and asked them to step in anxiously asking them what information they had. It was then that she noticed that there was another man behind both of them. What she did not notice was that he had guns in his hand that were touching the back of their chest region. She panicked and became numb in all her nerves and cells in the body. She was immobilized by her own freight. It was the best moment. The man behind pumped in a few bullets on her soft body without making the slightest noise. The two men turned back to see the German security guard completely flat on the floor. They did not have to think that he was dead. Just by their intelligence reflexes their hands went into their hips to get hold of their guns. That was the last they knew of themselves. They too slumped like the Chancellor of Germany. Three in one for the American executioner of the AIA!

Rustler was very happy that Claudia was done away with along with his spies who shifted sides with Plumbel. Just as the killer informed Rustler over phone of the professional execution of the German Chancellor, one of the German Generals noticed the stranger talking over phone. It was the most unusual thing to happen. Generals were supposed to have better reflexes than soldiers and intelligence personnel. It was a flash in the pan. The man licked his own blood on the floor before he breathed his last. Two bullets from the General found their way straight into his temple! The second one was a waste.

Mourning bells rang all over Germany. There were only a few more people left to mourn their most loved Chancellor in German history. She endeared all German citizens by her sharp acumen on governance, her high level of sensitivity to the needs of German citizens. Even when the entire world went through a fiscal crisis she braved the storm through her economic sense borrowed from socialistic principles. She distributed the resources of her country among all the laboring classes of Germany and among the citizens. Germans were highly motivated to stand with their Chancellor in the hour of Global crisis and their hopes were not belied. They withstood the crisis well unlike most other countries in the world including the US. She was no more. The woman whom all of Germany loved without even one person standing against her! She loved her people like no other ruler ever did before. All of Germany knew this, that they had one of the more unique Chancellors in their history. She fell a prey to the bullets and to the machination of a man whom they considered as the most evil in the world. He was the most powerful in the world.

Hearing the sad news of losing one of their leaders Russia and China unleashed missiles after missiles and sent a few of the nuclear bombs that Claudia had stored with a high level of advanced technology. No one knew, including Rustler that Germany's NBC weapons had a special technology to hide them from the sight of pilots in enemy aircrafts. America had not yet discovered the much-needed technology for their pilots to locate them. This was a sure military edge that she had developed. Only Russian and Chinese Generals knew of this. Now they decided to unleash such invisible weapons on American and British forces and civil targets. It had a devastating effect. They sent only the nuclear and the biological weapons that struck with telling effect. More than half of America was destroyed. Rustler was a psychological wreck seeing the devastation of his people right in front of his eyes, through his computer of course. He vowed revenge. He celebrated the death of Claudia and the two associates of Plumbel's with more pegs of whisky capped with a few rounds of cognac.

Russian and Chinese Premiers along with their counterparts in Vietnam and North Korea went into a state of mourning. However it could not last long as the attacks on their countries continued unabated. They took immediate revenge on the demise of Claudia. Blaringtone attended the funeral of the Queen Mother under heavy security. No one could approach him. The funeral procession was royal and slow. All army personnel took their positions to give a fitting send off to the Queen. The procession progressed slowly from the Church to the burial ground of the royals. It was a fortress that did not allow any intrusion of any unknown persons. British guards in mufti surrounded the entire stretch of the procession. The body of the Queen Mother was kept at the burial ground for prayers before being buried. The Archbishop of Canterbury performed meticulously the funeral rites. The body was taken again near the grave. People rushed to the grave to have a last look at the face of their beloved Queen. Four people lifted the coffin of the Queen and pushed it into the special slot that was meant for the queen. After sending the body into the slot some masons started cementing the grave of the Queen. Just when Blaringtone thought that everything was over for the royal family of the United Kingdom and slowly took the returning step a few bullets pierced his head and chest before he could turn fully to walk back. One of those who pushed the body of the Queen into the burial slot stood there with a gun in his hand. He did not try to run away. The guards of Blaringtone took a potshot at the culprit and finished him off instantly. Three funerals on the same day in Britain!

He was the secret spy of Russia smuggled into England through the Russian Navy. Earlier in their strategic discussions the Cosmic Alliance had clearly decided that Russia should be the leader in sea battle as it had the best knowhow. Germany was weak in sea warfare. Through their submarines of supra terrestrial capacity the Russian army managed to smuggle out a few of their agents and spread them out into Britain. Many of them owned coffee shops in London and moved in the evening in the open alluring susceptible British army personnel with money and an assured future. One of them was the smartest of all. He managed to first drug a British soldier. After drugging him he poisoned him at his own home over dinner. He took hold of his British uniform, weapons and identity card. He made a silicon mask that looked exactly as the face of the killed British soldier and managed to penetrate into the top echelons of the British forces. While in London in the coffee shops they managed to acclimatize themselves with the mannerisms of the British and familiarized the British accent. When he got into the British armed forces he passed off easily as the murdered soldier.

The whole of Britain was shocked to the core of its being. There was no whole indeed. Britain had become a maimed part of its entire being and was ready to be reduced to fine dust of its old resemblance. Its ground forces had also been transported to the US and were largely annihilated in the bombings.

The killing of Blaringtone was a huge blow to the moral strength of Rustler. Chilling waves of death passed through his spine without any interruption. But he put up a courageous mask. He pretended to be totally unperturbed among his Generals. He never anticipated such close alliance between Germany and Russia. But then even he could not predict the intricacies of war. No war in human history ever followed a stereotyped strategic pattern. Victory belonged to the one who was ready to break the jinx of stereotypes through diplomatic maneuvers. Claudia proved till her death that she was the best in making bold forays into all the stereotyped bastions of male designed wars. Russia liked her boldness and her highly intelligent perceptions of realities. It liked her human values. Norberta too liked Claudia for all this and many more human qualities that others did not know about her. But she was totally flabbergasted at the German pride of Claudia that would not accept anything lying down. Claudia died as a very proud German woman leaving behind a legacy.

All the Heads of State in both alliances had exhausted much of the money that they were entrusted with by the people of their respective countries. They had to make a lot of special dresses, helmets and medical kits that would protect them from viruses and possible chemical attacks by enemy forces. This war was very different from the previous wars in the sense that it did not require much fighting on ground though it was not minimized in any event. This was mostly a defensive war, as it was just one man who started it against PlanetB2 and not against any particular country. His expansionist ambitions were directed to the other planet and he triggered off a war of values. But how long could a war remain value centric? It turned out to be as murky as any war was.

Rustler bellowed like a wild elephant with vengeance after the assassination of Blaringtone in the most humiliating manner. His voice could not reach the ears of the world this time as he had hidden himself in his underground bunker. The way Russians executed Blaringtone sent high voltage shock waves in his raw nerves. He began to suspect even his own security guards and began to live in fear that one of them could be his murderer. In a country where sunshine was rare he even feared his own shadow sometimes. That some other country could excel in such techniques much better than AIA disturbed him no ends. He rang up the Prime Minister of Israel and requested him to take care of his personal security. The government of Israel was only too happy to get involved in protecting the President of America, especially after the brutal assassination of the German Chancellor. Israel now was out in the open in support of their traditional friend America. They were holding on to their self-imposed restriction with uncontrollable uneasiness. Now that their tethers were untied by the death of Claudia they were let loose on the warpath. Advantage America!

This was what they waited for. Rustler had already become a toothless tiger because of the intensive and intermittent attacks by Cosmic Alliance forces. Israel had waited for this chance from time immemorial. However, it was Iran that twisted the war script. As soon as Israel announced its allegiance to America and its decision to join the war Iran directed its nuclear and biological bombs on Israel without much hesitation and discussion with alliance partners. More than half of Israel was demolished in no time. Israel did not need this provocation. They had kept their forces ready to invade and take over Palestine and subsequently also many other Islamic countries. It only needed the press of a button by the Prime Minister of Israel to destroy the entire Iran in no time. Israel marked the start of a full-fledged NBC war. For the first time in the war Israel unleashed Chemical weapons with a lot of exhilaration. Before being devastated Iran too guided its missile power with chemical warhead on Israel making the entire region the most amenable region for biological death due to chemical outflow. There was a rain of destructive chemicals all over the region and began to eat the bodies of all beings with skins. Biology and Chemistry stood against each other and wreaked havoc of unimaginable proportion on human race. Abraham's children indulged in mindless killing of one another in the name of their state identity and did not rest till they finally decimated themselves totally. The secret bunkers constructed for the Presidents and Prime Ministers of countries in the region were invaded easily not by human soldiers but by viruses and gas mixed with abominable chemicals. They made no difference between the body of a poor man and that of a President.

News of the chemical attack by and on Israel made a sad reading for Rustler. He had invaded many countries and killed millions of people in different countries by creating false ascriptions that Heads of State in those sovereignties possessed chemical and biological weapons. Now he was faced with the stark naked challenge of one of his close associates having used the same to destroy an entire region including its own people.

But the toothless tigers had to assume false teeth. Falsehood was not anything new to Rustler. It was the cementing factor in his life. The death of the Premier of Israel who was a close friend of his began to corrode his self-confidence little by little. He had to act fast before he completely lost confidence in himself.

Rustler ordered chemical bombs to be sprayed all over Russia and China. The news was flashed across to the Premiers of both countries through their secret spying channels. By then Russia had already identified the secret bunker in the US where Rustler was hiding along with his Generals. They were surrounded with all types of communication equipment. It was one of the most fortified places in America. AIA knew that Russia was targeting Rustler and passed on the information to their Chief. Immediately Rustler was shifted to a different underground zone by AIA and the Generals commanded their forces with all their communication equipment. Assuming that Rustler was in his usual underground zone in Washington DC, Russia managed to drop a nuclear bomb spot on the place. All the American Generals had to meet their Waterloo simultaneously. Their spirits were safely confined to the nether world in which they lived for sometime. What AIA did not bargain for was simultaneous attacks by Cosmic Alliance forces on the hideout of the Generals of Canada and Australia. The smell of war was now stinking in high places. It was only a question of time before the Russian and Chinese forces found their way into the privacy of the Premiers of these countries and beheaded them with their bombs.

Dismembered torsos of these Premiers were taken to Russia as war relic.

Russia and China tried their best to thwart the onrush of chemical bombs on their respective countries. But the US almost exhausted all their biological and chemical weapons on these two countries sparing mostly the nuclear bombs for the smaller countries of the Cosmic Alliance. Strategically Rustler had already stationed many of these bombs in Britain and in Israel in peace times. Now the British Generals took their own decision to also utilize them against these two countries. Both the US and Britain took multiple simultaneous attacks with biological and chemical weapons and Russia and China could not totally resist the combined attack of Earth Alliance. Citizens of these two countries began to drop dead without their own choices, at homes, at work places and in public spaces. Children were the worst casualties in this obnoxious war.

Surrounded by fireworks all around the remaining world mutely witnessed two funeral processions at the same time. Television channels were under repair all over the world. With the sporadic pictures that appeared on the TV screens the surviving members of the human world were able to make out that two great and very important leaders had become victims of the war that they engineered. Rustler had no time to celebrate. He was almost a fugitive in his own country, as he had lost all his Generals at one go. He had trusted too much in his egotistic power and therefore, only made his sycophants as his Generals. They were busier with pleasing Rustler like faithful dogs and forgot to prepare a force that would take the reins of war in crisis period. The heavy weight of being left alone began to haunt Rustler endlessly. Nothing needed to chase him. His own fear of being defeated was constantly chasing him to all corners of America. He knew the two leaders of Russia and China whose funeral procession was taking place elsewhere. But he was more worried that the next procession could be with his corpse. He shuddered to think of that. He remembered the two leaders in good times. Forgetting all their differences he mingled with them in diplomatic meetings and dinner parties for the Heads of State organized by his Government and by their respective governments. Now they were lying in state. War had a devastating effect on his fragile psyche. These were not minions. They were great leaders of the world who assiduously built up their countries as world powers. Rustler could not digest the truth that the Premiers of Russia and China fell victims of his chemical and biological bombs. Despite all sorts of fortifications the viruses and the poisonous gases pervaded through the highly fortified underground world of theirs and made them seriously ill. Doctors in Russia and China could not even understand the true nature of the poison and virus and struggled hard till their venerable leaders kicked the bucket.

Though Britain lost its queen and Blaringtone, they had set their system in place firmly. The Generals took over the entire war regime without their official head of war. They increased their Navy power multifold and gained a distinctive striking edge over some nations of the Cosmic Alliance. With the death of the Premier of Russia it became easy for them to increase their attacks through navy. Rustler had earlier alerted the British secret services chief of the nefarious technical support that Japan was providing to Cosmic Alliance. Britain made a bold NBC attack on Japan all at once and that small island nation was no more. The Chinese Generals wanted to teach the British an unforgettable lesson for the future. They also wanted to prove that China could not be wished away by Earth Alliance. They launched simultaneous NBC attack on Delhi, Kolkata, Mumbai, Chennai and Bangalore and did not leave any semblance of the existence of what Indians claimed to be a great country. Simultaneous attacks also took place on Pakistan and it could not resist the onslaught of Cosmic Alliance till it caved in. Both the countries with all their tiny neighbors vanished with their caste legacy.

The coffee shop owners of Cosmic Alliance now spread their tentacles all over the small remains of London and Birmingham. They managed to gather together and discussed their own future in the light of the death of their Premiers. There were not many option left for them in the given situations. Together they decided to surrender, as they were sure that they would be caught on their escape route to Russia. They also wondered if they would be recognized at all by the remaining key people in the Russian army. They sent word to the British Generals of their intent to surrender and live the rest of their lives in Britain. They were also ready to give out all the secrets that they possessed about the Russian, German and Chinese military strategy. They knew the technical knowhow of the making of the bombs of partners of Cosmic Alliance.

The British Generals liked the idea and were badly in need of vital information. The situation also warranted them to believe the coffee shop owners from Russia. However, they were extra cautious and therefore, asked the messenger to make Russians to meet them in one of the restaurants that still remained intact. They had gone with all their weapons hidden under the vests that protected them from viruses and chemicals. The Russians however went to meet them only with their blazers. They excused themselves for not having such vests as the Generals were wearing after the initial exchange of pleasantries. It was ironic that even in such a disastrous situation the British did not give up their customary way of wishing. They sat together for dinner and ordered for some good food. The Russians were very happy that their request for a meeting was accepted by the Generals and thanked them profusely. They took out a few maps to show to the Generals and began to explain to them the secrets of Russian military strategy. The British Generals were rigid in their looks though they were happy inside that they were getting genuine vital leads to counter the prospective Russian attacks. They wanted more information on vital installations in Russia that they could attack. One of the coffee shop owners took out another set of papers and spread them out on the table. The Russians gave away almost all the military truths that they knew. All Generals were curiously looking at the maps. Their over enthusiasm did them in. The coffee shop owners pressed the hidden triggers in their vests. All of them together with all the British Generals were blasted into hundreds of pieces of human flesh that went into millions of pieces. The entire restaurant was razed to earth by the power of the blast. With the blast the Russian Generals knew instantaneously that the execution of their project elimination was accomplished to perfection and sent a series of NBC weapons to obliterate the entire England. A monarchical legacy went into oblivion.

All other smaller partners of both the Alliances became easy victims of NBC attacks on both sides. The remaining generals of Russia, China and other major countries fell easy prey to the chemicals and viruses that penetrated every nook and corner of the world.

CHAPTER NINETEEN

Rustler was the only leader of sorts that still survived. It looked that finally he was the winner. He himself was surprised, shocked and cursed himself for being alive. Finally some remorse seeped into his system. He watched in his computers with inexplicable awe the total devastation of the entire world including his own country. What lay shattered in front of him and under his feet was his dream of capturing and overpowering PlanetB2. He did not even know what he would do with his own world and his own country. Only some computers were still working in his underground hide out. His computers showed him still some places in the US that still remained intact. There was an unwelcome smile on his face. He did not know why he was smiling. Soon his smile gave way to laughter. Rustler was laughing unendingly without knowing why he was laughing in the first place. Loud laughter gave way slowly to the resurgence of his dream of overcoming the world. He still had some hope that he could succeed. Accepting defeat was the most difficult thing in his life. He was born to succeed and was ready to fight all over again and bring the remaining world to his knees. He could still see similar scenes in Germany. He could also see movement of human beings in some remote areas of the world. That Germany showed still signs of life was a very difficult proposition to accept in his design of things. He scurried for ways and means of wiping out all traces of life in Germany and looked for the storehouses of the left over weapons in the US. He himself wanted to take command over the mechanical operations of his weapons.

Little did Rustler realize that Claudia had outsmarted his and America's technological superiority much before the start of the war. She had programmed her machineries in such a way that they would remain invisible in any situation and would start functioning automatically in case of human casualty. The mechanism that she had devised was that any rattling of the building in which the computers were kept would automatically trigger the computers to give commands for bombing. Rustler made the fatal mistake of shooting his bombs near the building in which these computers were kept and the building was rattled rather badly. Claudia had kept a stockpile of invisible weapons programmed to attack the nerve centers of American military in Washington and New York. Her computers started automatically firing them and there was no resistance from America. Some of the bombs fell right at the place where Rustler was in the underground earlier and had moved out two days before. He could see that he was being attacked and realized that staying within the bunker was one of the most dangerous things for him, as the next bomb could fall on his bunker. He was at a total loss to understand how bombs could still attack him.

He came out of the bunker and began to run for his life. It was instinct, the reflexes of the man who wanted to capture PlanetB2 and take pride as the only person in the history of the universe who could do that. He had earlier seen the maps of the places where human movement was visible in his computers. He began to run in that direction. It was difficult to run with all the protective vests that he was wearing. 'Run, run, run Rustler! Run towards your final destination that may be your destiny. Do not stop. You will be the winner. No one can defeat you. Success will be finally yours.' He heard a host of spirits whispering in his ears. He wished that his eardrums were torn to thousands of pieces. He ran and ran till he was faced with a small hill in front of him. He ran up the hill thinking no harm could come his way over the top of the hill. He stood there looking at the surroundings. He was fatigued and wanted to stand still without any movement of the body. Finally he would be the most unchallenged human being on earth. He heaved a big sigh of relief. He stood still, then sat down and looked around to see that he was in the midst of trees that almost looked like forests. He was used to such sights in Washington and New York that were built in the midst of trees that looked like dense forests. It was not new to him. He began to relax and closed his eyes for sometime unable to think and feel anything in total fatigue. When he opened his eyes he found himself surrounded. A host of bears had surrounded him. Among them there was no wild and domestic. They were just bears. They came round him for sometime. They seemed to be laughing at his lunacy of trying to be the uniquely indomitable being on earth. They were indomitable now. They ridiculed him for his helplessness. He was at their mercy now. He began to laugh. His laugher insulted the bears. They pounced on him and began to lacerate his body. All the negative waves emanating from his body made them angry with him.

Rustler the 'greatest', the most powerful, the unquestionable and the ultimate human being on earth pleaded with them for mercy. He had no weapons. Nor did they have any. They had only their bodies. He had a body but it was of no use to him any more. His body was of no use to the rest of the world either. They tore his body into many bits and pieces, each of them taking out the cells in his body containing negative energies. They could not stand the sight of any unified cumulative essence of negative energy.

Rustler lay dead without anyone attending on him. The vultures in the sky soon smelt his raw flesh and assembled to claim a share of the pieces of his body. As they flew down to pick a piece they felt repulsive and flew back without even touching his raw flesh. Rustler disappeared in thin air as a decayed body untouched by anything in nature. It was unfortunate that the President of the most powerful nation in the world who wanted to overpower the entire universe did not find any one and had no time to explain why he codenamed his Kabbalistic project as PlanetB2.

America was totally destroyed by the programmed war of Germany. There were only a few Germans left and they had no inkling of the total destruction of America by Claudia even when she was dead and gone. There were only machines left in the whole of Germany. After their batteries exhausted all machines were faced with inconsequent death. The chemicals that were left over in the world corroded those machines without leaving a trace of the technological superiority of human beings.

When the final stocktaking was done by Carolina and Marissa not everything was destroyed on earth. There was a remnant community of human beings who were completely open to receive life giving energy waves from cosmic beings in PlanetB2. The cosmic beings began to communicate freely with the remnant community of human beings that were left behind after the war. It took sometime for the world to get the stink of war from its face. None of the living beings on earth cared a hoot about the debris of war. They lived their lives as usual. Those who were not involved in the war at all and were in constant communication with all that communicated positive energy from their bodies were left untouched by the weapons, viruses and chemicals of war. The cosmic beings got into intensive communication with such human beings on earth already before, during and after the war. These were mostly from the indigenous communities of people. However, there were quite a few others from all communities who remained in uninterrupted communication with cosmic beings in PlanetB2. In the previous world they belonged to different nations, different races, different communities. But now the borders of nation states did not any more exist. There was no nation, no ethnicity, no caste and no race. There was only one community living in absolute peace and harmony with the cosmos. The only thing common to them was their communicative interaction through life giving waves.

When the intensity of war started on earth cosmic beings went into a state of being still. It looked as if they were in meditation. They were in a state of mysticism. The intensity that was generated in their bodies emitted enormous waves that went into forming the liquid zone beyond which human machines and bombs could not penetrate. Their state of being in mysticism opened up a special outlet for their communication with cosmic beings on earth. The intensity of this communication with cosmic beings formed a wave around such people that viruses and gas that were generated from the bombs did not touch them. They lived their lives unaffected by all that the dominant, arrogant and negative beings in the world were doing. When the entire world was in violent turmoil they were in a mystic state of being, in full body orgasm.

With the destruction of all that human pride had constructed and the death of all negative and dominant beings the world began to transform itself into a cosmic entity. When there was no more possibility of violence and war, when only the remnant human community remained, the communication between their bodies and the bodies of the cosmic beings in PlanetB2 began to intensify. The positive energy began to dissipate the liquid zone, as there was no more need for this protective cover for the beings in PlanetB2. Interaction between the remnant community and the cosmic beings began to intensify without any layer that prevented the waves from human beings reaching PlanetB2 without any inhibition. It was cosmic freedom all the way.

The remnant community on earth continued to live its normal life in intensive communication with beings in PlanetB2 thus restoring cosmic movement and change. There was no authority to rule over them and guide them. They were their best guides, as they lived by the urges of their inner being and total freedom. That was bliss, the full body orgasm. It was uninterrupted bliss to all beings on earth and in PlanetB2.

There was a difference. The full body orgasm of human beings had also a lot to do with sex. The full body orgasm of beings in PlanetB2 had nothing to do with sex. Free sex for all! Freedom of the butterfly! A free world!